TALONED HEART

ALSO BY EMMA HAMM

The Otherworld

Heart of the Fae

Veins of Magic

The Faceless Woman

The Raven's Ballad

Bride of the Sea

Curse of the Troll

Of Goblin Kings

Of Goblins and Gold

Of Shadows and Elves

Of Pixies and Spells

Of Werewolves and Curses

Of Fairytales and Magic

Once Upon a Monster

Bleeding Hearts

Binding Moon

Ragged Lungs

and many more...

TALONED
HEART

Visit author online at www.emmahamm.com

Cover Design by Trif Book Designs

Just because it's over, doesn't mean it has ended.

You are the fiery, bright, brave, torn, and taloned creature.

Never forget who you really are.

Hall of
Dracomaquia
Castle of the Lost
Umbral
The
Solis

Kingdom of Umbra
alis
Stygian Peaks
Field of Somber
City of Tenebrous

CHAPTER 1

The salt air tangled in her hair as the clouds parted and a dragon soared overhead. Lore sucked in a deep lungful of salt, brine, and the scent of an open horizon before them. One last time.

Soon they would reach the ports of Umbra. Soon, they would face the reality of their decisions and that they were not yet finished with their quests.

But right now, she wanted to pretend that she stared out at the open ocean with nothing but her own adventurous nature to slake. Maybe they would sail until they hit a new land. They didn't need to worry overly much about food, because Abraxas had proven to be very helpful on their journey. He'd dove into the oceans more times than she could count, only to return with a massive tuna in his mouth. He could feed the entire ship if he wanted to.

They had no fear of food or clean water. They could continue on until they all found a new source of discovery and excitement.

Except they couldn't. If she'd been so capable of giving up their world, then she would have stayed on the dragon isle with her beloved and her children and never cast another thought toward Umbra.

"Are you ready?" The song-like voice interrupted her musing.

Allura stood behind her on the deck, her legs spread wide for balance as the ship moved with the waves. The siren never looked like a single hair was out of place or that the salt had abraded her skin. She was, as ever, beautiful.

Lore felt rather grubby in comparison. Her entire body was slick with salt, and no matter how hard she tried to keep her hair washed, it was always slightly stiff. She'd tried a hundred different ways to clean it, but the sea always won. Apparently, Allura knew something she did not.

"I'm ready for a bath," she grumbled, refusing to turn and look at what was behind her. "I'm not ready to see my homeland again and the people within it. I fear what is waiting for us."

Allura eyed the skyline behind her, and the siren nodded firmly. "As am I. I usually get some sort of reports from the sailors that stayed behind. They send me hawks to let me know what to expect when I get back. I am used to already having a list of other jobs waiting for us the moment we hit the shore."

"And this time?"

The siren's mouth twisted. "Nothing. Not a single hawk has found me. And they would send at least one out every day, no matter how long I've been gone. The hawks find the ship when we're close enough to shore."

That was troubling indeed. Lore's brows furrowed and finally she turned. Her eyes found the skyline beyond and the shambles of the port that she could just barely see. Just a dark smudge where she knew people lived.

What waited for them there? Just how far had Margaret gone in all this madness?

Allura's eyes narrowed upon her, and Lore could almost feel the other woman's stare like a physical touch. "You're afraid," the siren whispered. "I don't think I've ever seen you afraid."

It wasn't that she feared Margaret, but Lore was desperately afraid of what she'd find waiting for her in Umbra. Her gut twisted at the thought, knowing without a doubt that some of it would horrify her.

Margaret had been left to her own devices for far too long. And that was Lore's fault.

Opening her mouth, she turned toward Allura to explain herself. Thankfully, she was saved from having to voice her fears. A blast of wind struck both of them, sending them to their knees on the deck as they tried to stop themselves from being tossed overboard. More than one sailor had been thrust into the sea when Abraxas landed.

They'd had quite the argument convincing him that he wasn't allowed to land on the deck any longer. He'd left a dent in Allura's ship the first time and the siren had almost pulled his wings off in her anger.

Now, Abraxas had to land in the water beside the ship. He changed mid air. The blast of magic was the wind that they'd felt as he fell into the water nearby. The sailors all laughed, shoving at each other as they decided who would be the person to fish the dragon out of the sea.

She watched them with a small smile on her face. They were all so much more comfortable than they had been even a few weeks ago. Though they'd had to travel with each other for months, it had taken the mortals a very long time to be truly comfortable with her dragon.

Abraxas tried. Hard. He spent hours on end working beside them, each day making sure that he was pulling on ropes, forcing the boat to move as he wanted, sometimes even fully changing into his dragon form in the water and pushing the boat when the winds died down.

And finally, the others had cracked. They'd given up the fear of the dragon and saw him as a man.

Her heart thudded hard in her chest as a few sailors flung a ladder over the side of the ship. She knew what he'd look like long before his dark hair appeared over the side of the ship, but she never got tired of this part. He hauled himself up, water dripping down his sides and the white conjured shirt that he always wore. Hair slicked back, a knowing grin on his face, his eyes sought her out as his muscles flexed and he brought himself back onto the ship.

Abraxas shook out his hair, water spraying all over the sailors who surrounded him. They all groaned, shaking their heads at the "animal" in their midst. But he had eyes only for her. As always.

Allura let out a little tsking noise before shaking her head. "You two. You need to get yourselves together before you get to Umbra."

"Why's that?"

"Because you're going to make people sick if they see you acting like this."

Perhaps. And maybe their obsession with each other would wane as there were more things to do, people to fight, a kingdom to save. It had before. But she finally had him to herself, for the first time in what felt like ages. Lore intended to use that to her advantage for as long as possible.

She left the siren's side and walked down the ship. Closer and closer to him, where he stood still and watched her as a predator watches prey. A few of the sailors walked away, muttering with jealousy under their breath as they realized what was about to happen.

No one ever interrupted them, though. Almost as though it was rude to interrupt gods when they greeted each other, even if it had only been an afternoon.

She was the moon, finding herself in the sky with the sun once a month. She wouldn't let him go for any moment of their time together.

Lore stopped a few feet from him, drinking in the sight of him. His wide shoulders, sharp features, the way his eyes heated when he realized what she was doing.

"Come here," he growled, his voice sending a slow shudder through her whole body.

That tone of voice always danced through her entire body. She wanted to drop onto her knees before him and do whatever he asked. Or maybe she wanted to grab a fistful of his hair and send him down onto his knees before her. They never figured out which one of them wanted to be more dominant, and she supposed that was their life. The push, the pull, and the inevitable giving.

"Good hunt?" she asked, not taking a step closer to him at all. In fact, she made him stand there and wait, wondering what she was going to do next.

"Always." Somehow his voice had deepened even further until it scratched at the inner part of her brain that screamed for his arms around her. "Lore."

She knew what he wanted. But she was having so much fun denying them both. "Umbra is almost upon us."

"I am aware."

"You know neither of us can guess what waits for us there."

"I do." His hands clenched at his sides, then forcibly loosened as he restrained himself. "Do you really want to talk about this right now?"

Breathless now, she shook her head and bit her lip. "Not particularly."

"Then come here."

She jolted forward as though prodded with a hot iron. Lore flew into his arms, her own wrapping around his neck as he caught her against him. A low growl rumbled through his chest and he kissed her, his teeth biting at her bottom lip.

"I don't like to wait for you to be in my arms," he said against her lips, and she couldn't help but grin.

"I know."

"Then why do you insist on making me?"

"Because I like your reaction when I don't."

He gave another sharp nip to her lips. "You wouldn't know how to behave if you were held at knifepoint, now would you?"

She tried her best not to smile. If she could stare at him very seriously, perhaps he would understand how important her words were. But Lore grinned all the same, knowing that he'd see her smile and roll his eyes. "No, I do not. Especially when you are involved."

And there it was. The eye roll that always made her laugh because she already knew what he was thinking. She was ridiculous, his woman, and he was the only one who got this side of her. Their children weren't here, so she had to always be the strong, powerful woman who could take out the world with a blink of her eye. Other than with him.

With her dragon, Lore knew that she could say or be anyone she wanted to be and he would love her all the same for it. No matter who she became or how powerful she was.

To him, she was just Lore. The girl in the forest who had convinced him to find a blue butterfly but who stole his heart instead.

All those months ago, they were both so different. She sighed into his lips, pressing a kiss firmly there one more time before she leaned back in his arms.

"But we do have to talk about what we're expecting," she mumbled. "I don't know if Margaret knows we're returning, or if she sensed that I'd been in the room with Zephyr."

"We cannot plan for what we do not know."

But she wanted to. Lore would spend the rest of the few days she had left trying to think of every possible outcome and how they were going to face them. Even the smallest detail needed to be considered for her mind to rest.

Abraxas drew their foreheads together, winding her tighter in the comfort of his arms. "Lore, listen to me. If you run yourself ragged thinking of everything that woman might have planned, then you will not see what is right in front of you. There is nothing we can plan for. Nothing we can fix. Not until we stand in the center of Umbra and find out for ourselves what she has done."

He was right. Of course, he was right.

Blowing out a long breath, she nodded. "I understand."

"Do you?"

A feathery laugh erupted from her chest while she shook her head against him. "No, I don't. I'll probably be up all night and then I'll be as bad as the wights when we first picked up Zephyr."

His gaze softened as he leaned away from her, holding onto her arms so she still at least felt like he was there. "Lady of Starlight, are you being emotional about when we first found Zephyr?"

"Of course I am. He was just a child. Don't you remember the look on his face when we all walked into that crypt? He'd grown up underground, and we brought him out into this world. Showed him what else there could be and... And now they put him back in a crypt."

Tears pricked behind her eyes at the thought, as they always did when she remembered the horrible conditions he was in.

"Lore." Abraxas swiped his fingers underneath her eyes. "We will find him."

She just hoped they would get there in time.

CHAPTER 2

Abraxas shouldn't be disappointed that their ship docked without incident. No one stood at the edges of the planks, ready to get their wares off the ship. But Allura claimed that was fairly normal, considering no one had known they were coming.

But the siren's eyes had darkened as she stared around the quiet docks, even in the middle of the day. They were, clearly, much more empty than they had been when they'd left.

That unsettled feeling in Abraxas's stomach never left. He'd picked it up from Lore. He was quite certain of that. She had fed anxiety into his body as he took it away from her, like he could make it better just by... what? Absorbing it himself?

Foolish. He shouldn't have tried to feed off her anxiety, as though that would make it better. He knew by now that her feelings spread like a plague. If she didn't want to feel them, she wouldn't. But giving them to him would only succeed in just that. He'd suddenly be anxious as well, and he couldn't afford to be so when he had a job to do.

Protect her. Protect the people that he cared about and make sure that this mission didn't fail. He needed to be certain that Lore never stepped too far out of his sight.

Perhaps he was being a little overprotective. But these few months on the ship had opened his eyes to something he desperately wanted. No, needed.

Her.

He could never survive the feelings of losing her again, and now they were marching toward a future—again—where that could happen.

Tilting his head back to the sky, he took a deep breath and told himself to calm down. Dracomaquia was the one place where he could feel uncertainty. He didn't know his homeland as well as this place. He'd lived in Umbra for hundreds of years, and he had followed in the footsteps of kings. This was his home just as much as it was hers.

Together, they would stop whatever was thrown at them. They would change the very fabric of the world, just as her prophecy had claimed they would.

Still, the quiet docks made him uncomfortable.

Lore shouldered her bag beside him, her eyes skating over the empty docks. Only a few people trailed toward a much smaller ship, one of the few that was still in the harbor.

"What do you think?" he asked.

"I think it's very quiet," she replied, and her eyes followed the same track his had taken. "I don't like it. There were hundreds of people the last time we stood on these docks."

"We?" He arched a brow. "You were here without me last time."

"Oh." She shook her head, the fog clearing in her gaze as she turned to him. "I forget that I was looking for you. I think I've... tried to forget that."

With a soft snort, he reeled her into his arms one last time. Tucking her underneath his chin, he took a deep breath and felt her take it with him. In and out. Slowly, quietly tucking away both of their fears. "I was here with the King. He frequently enjoyed pleasure rides on ships when he was younger, like his father before him. And we both know that man was long lived."

"Indeed." She pressed a kiss to his bare skin where his shirt parted just underneath his collarbone.

Heat flared through him, but now was not the time for that. He knew there were very few things they could do now that they had arrived. After all, they had a kingdom to save.

Their own pleasure ride through the seas between the continents had been wonderful. They were memories he now needed to keep close to his chest as they meandered through the docks.

"Ready?" Allura's melodic voice interrupted them. "We have a long way to go."

Abraxas frowned. "Go? I thought we were parting ways here."

The two women looked at each other and then back at him. Clearly, they had been talking while he had packed their things in the cabin.

He hated it when they did this.

Again, he rolled his eyes to the skies and counted to ten before he looked back at them. "What plan have you two cooked up, then?"

Lore eyed him as though he were going to argue. "I think we should look around the docks first. I'm not sure what is the best way to tackle this kingdom, nor do either of us know what has changed. Margaret clearly has her claws in everything and I want to know what that means, and just how much she's affected before we make any more plans."

Why would he argue with that? Hadn't he been telling her the same thing?

His woman was the most annoying person he'd ever met, and yet, he was madly in love with her.

Abraxas gave them both a nod and then reached for the bag that Lore held. "Lead the way, ladies. I won't get in the way while the two of you plot."

"I can carry that," Lore said with a little grumble.

But he didn't give it back. He gave her a very unimpressed stare before he jerked his chin to the plank that would bring them down onto the docks. Let her try to take it from him. He was nothing if he wasn't a gentleman, and his woman would not carry all her own bags.

He was no fool. Nor was he anyone's whipping boy. He just wanted to make sure she was happy and comfortable. It wasn't too much to ask.

Lore shook her head at him, but he saw the glittering pleasure in her eyes. She loved it when he did things like this. It reminded her that she wasn't alone.

Meanwhile, Allura gagged. "The two of you are disgusting, you know that?"

"Ah, you're just jealous."

"A bit," she grumbled as she started down onto the docks. "You can come to my house to get settled if you want. I can't host you for long, though. I don't intend on staying here."

He tilted his head to the side as he watched Lore balance down the gangplank without any issue. "Itching to get back to the sea already, siren?"

As he joined them, his booted feet heavy on the plank that groaned underneath his weight, he felt the air still around him. Abraxas looked at the siren, only to see her staring off into the shambles of buildings with a troubled expression on her face.

"No, it just feels like something is wrong. I don't want to be here when it all boils to the surface." She shook her head, and then gestured for them to follow her. "Come on."

Abraxas remembered many of the times he'd been here. The docks were a mixture of mortals and magical creatures. They moved as one. The sea brought everyone here, and many of them had learned how to get along with each other. A very different place than the rest of the kingdom.

Zander had hated it. As had his father. Both devious kings thought that the magical creatures shouldn't be near humans.

The first time he'd come here, Abraxas had been shocked to see them all. Together. Working as one and teasing each other as they went about their day in whatever safe manner they could manage. The docks weren't safe. They were a place where the rough and the dangerous ended up to survive.

And yet, it was always still full of life. He'd always known that there was a place here, in this kingdom, where magic and non-magic could live with camaraderie.

Until now.

As they walked through the streets, he scented the air and listened for whatever he could find. There were no humans left. Only magical creatures darted from the shadows and moved along to get their labor done for the day. And none of those creatures looked well.

He noticed a small pixie who ran across their path. The woman's face was gaunt and dark hollows underneath her eyes suggested an exhaustion that only came from being overworked. She looked terrified that she'd even seen them, and then raced away into the shadows.

None of this was normal. None of it was right.

He stepped closer to the women ahead of him and muttered underneath his breath, "What is going on?"

"Not sure." Allura peered down a dark alley before making a low sound in her throat. "There should be a lot more people here. At least a hundred more, if not two hundred."

"That's what I thought." Abraxas made to look down another one of the streets, but again, it seemed... "Abandoned?"

"No reason for it. This is the only place any of them can go. They don't hide from the crown anywhere else in the kingdom, that's for certain. Besides, sailors are sailors for life." Allura's troubled expression deepened, furrows carving through her face. "I know nothing that would have made them leave."

Lore interrupted their conversation, her voice low and full of dark omens. "Unless they were forced."

The thought had crossed his mind. Margaret truly hated humans. She'd stop at nothing to get them away from what she thought might be a sanctuary for humankind.

They turned down a street, following Allura as he leaned low to whisper in Lore's ear, "You think she targeted the docks?"

"I do."

"It would be a good plan to attack where the most people were living in harmony."

Lore shook her head. "It's the first place people would go if they wanted to leave. She'd want to make sure they couldn't escape."

He had hoped it wasn't that, but the certainty in Lore's voice gave him no other way to think. Of course Margaret would want that.

He said nothing else until they reached Allura's home. The small shack had seen better days. Salt and wind had battered upon the outside edges, tearing the wood and rotting parts of it until it looked almost abandoned. The thatch roof was rotted, but he assumed she needed to replace that yearly.

Grumbling under her breath, Allura slammed the door open that was no longer locked.

"Bastards," the siren hissed as she stomped through the piles of her clothing on the floor. "They just couldn't wait a few more days to rob me, could they?"

Abraxas filled his lungs with the scents of the room. Old scents. Very old. "No one has been in here for months, Allura."

She froze in the middle of the small room. "What... How do you know that?"

He tapped his nose. "I can smell them."

As the siren swore about thieves who couldn't wait even a few days to steal from her, he eyed the small room. He'd thought it might have a secret area below the cabin, but this was it. Just a single room with a miniature stove in the corner, now covered in dust and grime. A cot on one side of the wall, jammed up against a small table and a single chair. A wardrobe on one side had been placed haphazardly, although maybe the thieves had yanked it out. The floor was covered in layers of clothing and picture frames. But other than that, there wasn't much in the siren's house.

He had no intention of staying the night here. There was no room to move with the three of them crammed inside these small walls. If anyone tried to attack them, and he had to assume that it was already known that they'd arrived in the kingdom, then they could not protect themselves.

Allura gestured. "Sit down friends, I'll see if they left anything to eat. Probably not, the backstabbing bottom feeders."

As the siren grumbled and rifled through her things, Abraxas took the chair in front of the bed and turned it around. Lore sat in front of him, and together, they leaned in close.

"What do you think?" he asked.

"I couldn't feel any of them, Abraxas. They're all gone."

"We thought she might do something like this. If she's trapped Zephyr, then it's likely she's gone after all the mortals. Just keeping the next in the bloodline in a dungeon won't make the humans follow her. Not in the slightest."

"Then we need to figure out who else she's trapped." The heartbeat in Lore's neck fluttered. "I haven't checked in on Beauty. Or her father. There are others we need to have with us before we do... anything."

"We should know more about what's going on in the kingdom, yes." He tucked a strand of her hair behind her ear. "But we cannot stay here."

"There is nothing for us on the docks. And I think we both agree, there is nothing left without gathering up those who are still here." She watched his features, her eyes flicking back and forth between his. "Do you understand what I'm saying?"

He knew she was worried about who might listen through the walls. Margaret's shadows were all around them, and though she could cast a spell to keep them all silent enough that even Margaret's magic would not hear them, he also knew the waves of that magic would also give her away. Lore needed to tread carefully. Just as carefully as he did.

"Home," he whispered, knowing that if he said it, whoever might be listening would assume they were going to the castle. "We go home."

Lore nodded, and he had to mentally prepare himself for Tenebrous.

It would take days to get there, and days for him to trudge through the swamp and the muck that surrounded her home.

They'd survive it. They would find Beauty and perhaps then they would discover what was really happening in this place. But until then, they had to keep their ears open and their wits about them.

"Fuck," Allura hissed. "We're going to the pub, I suppose. Not a single bite of food left in this place that isn't moldy or turned to dust."

Lore eyed him, the question in her eyes about how smart it would be for them to go anywhere right now.

He didn't care. They needed food for their journey, and he needed to get those shadows out of her eyes. He stood and pulled their cloaks out of their bag, carefully wrapping one around her shoulders and drawing it over her blonde hair.

"To the pub, then," he said with a soft smile. "Let's fill our bellies while we still have the chance."

He tried to convey that he wasn't worried about anyone seeing them. After all, he was made to protect her. And protect her, he would.

CHAPTER 3

Lore hated to take anything from Allura when it was so clear the siren had very little left. Though her friend waved off her concerns with a laugh.

"I don't need any of it," Allura had claimed. "The sea is all I need, and I have my ship back because of you. I'll steal a few items before I go and no one will ever know I was here. Leave the rest to rot and keep the seas on my horizon."

She'd heard the quote from Allura before the few times she'd seen her off, but this time seemed different. Allura seemed different. The siren was on edge and kept glancing into the shadows like she was waiting for someone to attack them.

And considering the company the siren kept? It was entirely likely.

So Lore didn't argue much. She took what Allura offered after that, slid new boots on her feet, wrapped a moth-eaten shirt around her torso, and kept on her own leather pants that would offer her much better protection against the elements.

They couldn't steal horses. Though it would make travel much faster, it wouldn't get them very far before they were noticed. And they certainly could not travel on the back of a dragon. Abraxas would make the entire world tremble again. The magical creatures knew him as a symbol of what the mortals could do. They'd enslaved the most powerful of all their kind and forced him to kill others for their own enjoyment.

The longer they could keep it secret that either one of them had returned, the better.

So they would walk. Again. All the way from the docks, past the castle, through the swamp, and into Tenebrous. It would be yet another long journey and it would take them longer than she feared they had.

Still, it was the only plan they could think of. Otherwise, they might be looking at a dead Zephyr and the rest of the mortals as well.

Lore cared very little for the rest of the humans. She didn't care what Margaret was doing with the kingdom either, but she would not lose her friend. Not another one.

"Ready?" Abraxas handed her a bag, although he looked like he wanted to grab it right back the moment she shouldered it.

"We talked about this, remember?"

"Yes, I realize if you weren't carrying any bags that someone might think you were important. You don't need to remind me again, Lore." But he muttered underneath his breath, "It doesn't mean I need to like it."

Her dragon. Always the gentleman.

She cupped his cheek in her hand and smiled up at him. "I love you."

The anger lines around his eyes and mouth softened. "I love you, too."

They started off their day and set a good pace. Allura hadn't wanted to see them off. The siren needed to get back to the ship, figure out where the rest of her human sailors had gotten off to, and make sure they weren't stolen. There weren't a lot of them, half her crew maybe, but enough for Allura to be worried.

Lore couldn't think about those men who had gotten them here safely. She couldn't think about the fear that burned through her at the thought they might be dead because they had returned. She could have offered them another life. Another way to live in the dragon isles where they could still sail and adventure but have a safe place to rest their heads. She could have...

A warm hand landed on her lower back, the heat spreading through her skin. "Easy," Abraxas said quietly. "You're letting your thoughts get away from you."

And she was. Again.

Lore took a deep breath and focused on every step they had to take. "Right. Stop thinking about the madness of the past few days and focus on the now."

"You got it."

So she did.

They passed through multiple hamlets on the way. And the closer they got to the castle, the more magic she saw in the land. At first, she almost didn't notice the tiny changes.

A scarecrow moved in the corner of her eye. Its head turned to watch the crows that circled the crops before settling back to staring straight ahead when they moved on. Laundry floated up from a basket that a woman had set on the ground, twining itself around the line without her having to lift a finger. Wood chopped itself with an enchanted axe that had made a very good pile beside it.

Little things that her mind seemed to remember and said, "this is normal," but then she realized how not normal it was. These were homes of people who had lived in fear of ever showing a single ounce of magic. Now? They showed it without care at all.

The very earth seemed seeped in it as well. Ancient roots had stretched from deep within the earth, seeking out sunlight as they pulsed with green magic that would help them grow. They wriggled underneath her feet, sensing that an elf was among them. They seemed pleased that she'd returned, but she was afraid of what they'd do to her.

And the grass... Oh, it was greener, wasn't it? Everything here seemed to be so much more than what it was when they had left.

When they stopped to eat lunch, settling on Abraxas's cloak while pulling out a small block of cheese and bread, she eyed the ground that was dotted with flowers she'd never seen in her life.

"Do things seem... different?" she asked as she sat down on the cloak.

"How so?"

"Just... more." She didn't know how to voice her concerns or what she was seeing. This wasn't the world she had come to expect. There was more happening here, more growth and development than she'd left behind, and she didn't know what to do with that.

Abraxas grunted and handed her the center portion of the small loaf. "Magic, yes. That's what you're seeing. There's a lot more of it than when we left."

"That's what I thought." She bit off a large mouthful and then said through the food, "Seems a bit odd."

"More magic, more creatures, fewer humans. Maybe the earth is coming alive again after a very long wait." He shrugged, and it seemed to be that easy for him to cast it aside.

She couldn't.

Lore could feel the earth changing underneath them. Her magic stretched out, testing the boundaries of this new power that flowed. She could feel where it came from, and that was each individual who had finally been allowed to show who they were and what they could do. That didn't make her feel strange. She enjoyed knowing that the land was feeding off the magical creatures. But where was everyone else?

Creatures could live like this while the humans were still there. They could all agree that there was magic in the world. It wasn't scary. Humans could live beside them without feeling like they needed to destroy those who were different. That should be enough.

And yet, this had been taken too far. Now there were only magical creatures, and the earth was feeding off it. The trees, the ground, the land itself was changing, and she didn't know if that was a good thing.

Lore took another bite of her bread, chewing and pondering her thoughts. She didn't want to be left in the dark like this. She had to know at least what had happened already.

"I want to talk with someone," she said, the words coming out of her mouth before she'd really thought them through. "A villager or someone in the next hamlet we come across."

Her dragon shook his head. "We're too close to the castle, and I doubt they've forgotten you that quickly."

She hummed underneath her breath. He was right. She couldn't afford to have Margaret find out she was here this early in their game, but there had to be a way for her to hide herself while still talking with someone about the changes here.

"I have an idea," she said. "But it would require that I talk with someone on my own."

"Absolutely not."

"I can't hide both of our identities at the same time without Margaret feeling the spell."

He shrugged. "You probably could. But if it was too distracting, no one knows what I look like, anyway. If you want to wander over and talk with someone, that's fine. But I'm not going anywhere."

A woman only had to die once, and he suddenly felt the need to be attached to her like a leech. Narrowing her eyes, she muttered, "Fine. But you will say nothing."

"I'll pretend to be a mute."

"They're still going to be very suspicious of why I have a giant walking with me when I could very well be someone important. The only people with bodyguards are the rich."

Abraxas shrugged. "Then say I'm your husband."

"Little on the nose, don't you think? A giant man and a small woman, wandering through the woods on their own?"

His eyes flashed with a bright heat. "I will not bend on this, Lore."

She finished her food quickly after that. She hadn't expected him to change his mind, but she had wanted to distract him from her talking with anyone. Threatening to do so without him had made sure he'd argued that he could accompany her, not that she shouldn't talk with anyone at all.

The next hamlet they came upon, she let her power flex through her. It was a small bit of magic, sleight of hand really, but enough that she worried Margaret might feel it. Anyone who was sensitive to magic might feel the ripple. Hopefully, there were no enchanters in the hamlet or there would be questions she couldn't answer.

Thankfully, it appeared to be a small cluster of satyrs. Most of the people in the village had tiny horns on their heads and cloven hooves that clopped along the stone streets that were hand built and gleamed in the sunlight.

Lore went to the farthest house. The one that stood a little aside from the others and was a bit more rundown. A single woman inhabited it, and she stood outside with her laundry in her hands. She wasn't as powerful as some, so she had a wand in her hand to guide the clothing up the line.

"Who are you?" Abraxas asked under his breath. "So I know what name to call you."

"I don't know who I am." That was part of the fun. Lore grinned up at him. "I'm who she's been missing, but who won't be coming back."

"Excuse me?"

The satyr looked up and a little shriek erupted from her mouth. "Alyss? Is that really you?"

Lore opened her arms wide and nodded.

The satyr dropped her wand onto the ground and launched at her. Perhaps it was a little cruel to be the person that this woman had missed the most, but she had to make sure it was someone that wouldn't come back. Just like she'd said. She could only assume that Alyss was long dead, or worse, that she would soon be.

Clasping her arms tightly around the satyr in a hug, she hoped that this would give the woman closure she very much deserved. "I'm back, but not for long."

"What are you doing here?" The satyr leaned back, holding onto her biceps and holding her still. "You were supposed to be across the seas by now! Is it Devlin? Did he not make it onto the ship?"

Lore could piece the story together in her head. Young Alyss was in love with a human. He'd fled to the ships with her, likely the last ones leaving, and they had sailed across the seas. Hopefully that was where the story began, and didn't end.

"He's safe," she said with a bright grin on her face. "I didn't make it onto that ship, but I'll make the next one. I wanted to come say goodbye."

"Well, and what a goodbye it will be! I'll get the others. They'll be so pleased to see you!"

"Wait—" Lore grabbed the other woman's arm before she could leave. "I just wanted to see you."

A shadow crossed over the satyr's eyes, and then the woman looked behind her to see Abraxas looming there. The woman swallowed hard. "And who's this?"

Damn. Not her husband, clearly.

"A friend," Lore tried. "Do you mind if we go somewhere private?"

"A friend? He looks like he's in the Rebellion." The satyr swallowed. "You were never involved in that, darling."

Oh, but she was. She was very much involved in that and if she didn't get the woman inside where she could at least pry into her mind in peace, then all of this could fall apart around her ears.

Lore glanced over her shoulder at Abraxas, her eyes wide. He misinterpreted what she needed. Her dragon took a heavy step forward, malice in his eyes and strength dancing down his strong shoulders.

"Heavens," the satyr woman whispered. "What have you gotten yourself into, Alyss?"

"Nothing all too dangerous."

"It seems as though that might not be correct." The satyr swallowed, her eyes flicking over her shoulders, and Lore knew she was about to run. "Why don't I get your father?"

No, no more family. No more hugs. No more people who would never see their dear Alyss again. This was a mistake. She should have thought up a plan that was less dangerous... and less cruel.

"Can we come inside?" She tried one more time. "Please?"

The satyr looked her over and something inside her died. Lore saw it. She saw the hope and the pleasure of seeing her drift away until there was nothing left but exhaustion and sadness. "You're not my Alyss, are you?"

Lore bit her lip and then slowly shook her head. "No, I am not."

"Why are you here?"

"To ask questions and get answers."

"From me?" The woman pressed her hand to her chest, the fingers blunt and short. "I don't know anything. We just moved here only a few months ago, and we were hoping for a quieter life away from the city. Surely you need the village elder, someone with more power than me."

Lore shook her head, sadness stretching through her entire body until her limbs felt heavy with it. "No," she whispered. "I need you. I need someone who will tell me what happened, honestly, without the filter of responsibility. I need to know from someone who lived it, and I believe you are that person."

The satyr licked her lips. "What is your name?"

"Alyss."

The satyr's eyes filled with tears. "What's your real name?"

Lore shook her head. "I cannot tell you that. The magic I conjured only shows you what you want to see. I do not know who you are looking at. Only that you see a beloved."

"What kind of awful magic is this?" The satyr pressed those blunt fingers to her mouth. "What kind of creature can cast such a spell?"

Lore looked on helplessly as the thought came to life in the other woman's mind. The thought that likely none of the creatures had even hoped to dream as their world shifted and changed.

"Goddess Divine," the woman whispered as though the two words were only to be spoken with reverence. "Could it be you?"

She didn't like the title, but if it got her answers... Lore nodded. "Now, will you let us inside?"

The woman's eyes flicked from hers to Abraxas behind her. "And that means you're..."

Her dragon was never subtle. Lore didn't need to glance back for her to know that his eyes had flashed red and gold, like coins mounded in his cave. The satyr lost all the blood in her face, but then she nodded.

"Yes," she whispered. "Come inside, and I will tell you all that you have missed."

CHAPTER 4

Abraxas walked into the satyr's house before Lore. Though the other woman was clearly uncomfortable with him being there, he wasn't here to make her life easier. Lore forgot that she was known throughout the kingdom. People looked at her as some otherworldly being, and they needed to remember that she wasn't theirs to keep.

His gaze swept over all the details in the small home. One wall had been built with what looked like a window seat that the satyr clearly used for a bed. The pillows and blankets were still mussed from when she'd risen this morning. A small fireplace on the back wall served also as the woman's kitchen, and a small pot still bubbled above the cheery flames.

The floors were covered with carpet, and he figured out why as the satyr walked away from him. Her cloven hooves made no sound as she meandered through her home. Carefully, the satyr set her basket down next to the door and gestured for them both to come in.

"You're safe here for now," the woman said. "My name is Myrna."

Abraxas only grunted. Lore could make the small talk with the woman if she wanted, but he would waste no time on such things. All he cared about was their next step. And this woman could apparently give them such information.

His elf gave him a glare as she walked into the room, clearly unimpressed by his rudeness to their host.

"Thank you for your time, Myrna," Lore said. "I'm going to drop the spell now, if you don't mind? I know this must be all rather uncomfortable for you."

Myrna cleared her throat. "Alyss was a dear friend of mine. I was very sad to see her go, and I'll admit, it is rather nice to see her face again."

"Would you prefer I continued the spell?"

The satyr shook her head. "No. I think it would be best if I talked with you."

Abraxas narrowed his gaze at both women. He didn't think it best if Lore revealed herself. At least right now, no one could say they'd actually seen her. The story would remain muddy. This woman had only seen an old friend, one who shouldn't be here, but who claimed to be their Goddess Divine.

As Lore lifted her hand, he caught her gaze and slowly shook his head.

"You disagree?" Lore asked, her voice low.

The other woman caught her tone and looked over at the dragon standing in her living room. Tension built in the room until he could cut it with a knife if he wanted.

"Leave the spell," he grumbled. "No one can know you were actually here if you do."

"I would never tell anyone—" Myrna tried, though he interrupted her almost immediately.

"Right now, you never saw her. You could be spreading rumors and lies, for all that anyone would know. If you see her, then there are more details you could use to make this story seem plausible. Not to mention if any magical user went through your memory, they would not see her face." He glared, his eyes burning with flames. "I would find you and kill you if I found out you were the one to give us up, but hunting a single woman takes a very long time. I'd rather avoid such a hunt entirely."

The woman paled again, and Lore glared even harder. But the spell remained.

His woman stepped in front of him as though her slight form could hide him as she gently guided the satyr to sit on her bed. "We just want to know what happened. Obviously, I have not been here for a very long time."

"You died."

"I did." Lore never hesitated from the truth. "But I did not stay that way for very long."

"Obviously." The satyr waved her hand up and down, gesturing to Lore's body. "You look healthier than I am."

He watched the pain twist Lore's expression, and he knew the reasoning why. She didn't want someone like herself, a woman who had spent months on a ship traveling here, to look more healthy than the people who were farming. He agreed with her. These people should be prosperous and live a quiet, happy life. Not wondering why a woman like Lore looked so good when they were struggling.

Still wincing with her thoughts, Lore asked, "Can you tell us where everyone went?"

"Oh." Myrna looked down at her blunt fingers and curled them into fists in her lap. "They all went away. We don't know what happened to them, only that once you were gone, and the castle turned over to the elves, humans started getting rounded up. They were good folk here. We moved knowing that there was enough space near the sea, and my neighbors weren't like the guards. Those people in the city deserved what they got, but I quite liked everyone here. They were welcoming. My neighbor used to cook me dinner when she saw me working hard in my garden. Good people. They lived off the land and respected it."

"How long ago?"

"Not long. A few weeks, maybe? One day they were here and the next... They weren't." Myrna's big eyes filled with tears. "I thought maybe I'd see if she was sick, you know? So I went into her house and everything was upended. She put up a fight before they dragged her out of that house. I'll tell you that. But no one was left. Not her. Her husband. Not even their two children."

Lore glanced over her shoulder at Abraxas and he knew what she wanted to do next. She wanted to save them.

Of course she did. She wanted to rush out of here like an avenging goddess and bring everyone home. But they couldn't. Not unless she had a plan to do that, remain hidden, get Zephyr, and then high tail it out of here.

Deep in his gut, he knew this would no longer be a quick trip to save their friends. She'd never been able to deny someone help if they needed it.

And the entire kingdom needed her now.

He cracked his neck to the side and nodded. "Where are they taking the humans?"

Myrna's gaze flicked to him, her eyes widening at the question. "Well, I don't know."

"There are no rumors?"

"Some say they might be brought to the castle, but there are thousands of people who have disappeared. They can't all be in that castle."

They could be if magic was involved. He met Lore's gaze, trying to see if she could piece together what Margaret had done with the humans. Magic was hard to come by that could hide thousands of people, but portals were much easier. His first guess was that Margaret was bringing them all to the castle and then throwing them into a portal to keep them locked away somewhere no one would find. Of course, elven magic was strange. If she'd found a spell that could shrink them, that might be possible as well.

He didn't really know what was possible with elven magic, if he was being honest. There seemed to be no limits to their power sometimes.

Lore hummed low underneath her breath, and then nodded. "I'd like to give you a gift, Myrna. You have been more forthcoming with us than I expected."

"I can take no gift from a goddess."

"You can, and you will." Lore smiled at her. "What do you need?"

The satyr's mouth gaped open, trying her best to say something before she shrugged. "I have everything I need here. My family is well, my friends are happy, there is food and safety. I have nothing that I wish for."

He knew that wouldn't satisfy his elf, and Abraxas crossed his arms over his chest as he watched her dip into the satyr's mind. Myrna froze, apparently able to feel the cool sensation of Lore pawing through her thoughts. He knew what it felt like.

Then Lore sighed and flicked her fingers to the side. At her gesture, a spell threw itself out of her body and twined into the floor. The house shifted, rolling beneath their feet as though it had come alive. The floor unfurled, the wall stretched back, and then there was another room with a round door that opened on its own.

Lore had built the satyr a bathroom, it looked like. The tiled floor dipped into a recessed round circle, where warm water bubbled already. A hot spring? He didn't think there were any this close to the ocean, but he wouldn't put it past his powerful love to have summoned one to life.

"A place for you to relax," Lore said, her gaze softening at the tears that glistened in Myrna's eyes. "It looks very similar to your homeland, I presume? That is what it looked like in your memories, at least."

"It's exactly what they looked like. We haven't been able to... that is, the land didn't want to give us..." Myrna shook her head. "I have no words to give you in thanks."

"You already gave them to me." Lore touched underneath the woman's chin, forcing Myrna to look up at her. "You told me where to find them."

He watched as Lore's hand slid away from the other woman's face and then followed her out of the house without a word. Lore drew her hood up over her head.

"We need to see what's happening at the castle."

He struggled to keep up with her as she darted away from the hamlet. "Do you think that's the best idea right now? I thought we were going to find Beauty first. That way, we would have some kind of backup when we go to get Zephyr?"

Apparently, she had forgotten how to use her ears. Grumbling under his breath, Abraxas picked up his pace so he could catch her. "Lore?"

Still no response. Her face had darkened with that angry expression he knew too well. The one that suggested she was going to make a massive mistake.

"Lore!" Abraxas grabbed her arm as they reached the edge of the forest, spinning her around into him. "Would you listen to me?"

She looked up at him then and he saw the tears in her eyes. He felt the frustration pouring off of her in waves and how she was struggling to hold herself together when all she wanted to do was fall apart.

"Starlight," he whispered, drawing her against his heart and squeezing. "Why are you crying, love?"

"I could have been here," she said, her voice catching on a sob. "I could have prevented all of this from happening. What if I hadn't gone to find you? What if I hadn't been so selfish and stayed for them?"

His heart broke for her. And not only because of the pain, but because he would never feel guilty that she had chosen him over this kingdom. Where she could wallow in this guilt and feel it crashing over her head, all he could feel was the happiness that she'd chosen him. The same as the first moment he'd seen her.

Kissing the top of her head, he rocked her back and forth. "You are not responsible for the world, Lore."

"Then why do I have this power? This never-ending gift that could change the very fabric of the world. That's what the prophecy said. That's what everyone expected of me, and instead, I left to go find you." She tilted her head back, eyes already rimmed with red. "And I would do it again. Does that make me a horrible person? I would always choose you over everyone else in this kingdom."

He cupped her jaw, trailing his fingers up her cheeks to gently smooth away the tears there. "No, it does not make you a bad person. It makes you a woman in love. You are mine and I am yours, Lore. We will never choose another over each other. It is who we are and there is no shame in that."

She swallowed hard and nodded. "I cannot save them all."

"No, you can't." He ghosted his lips over hers. "But we will save the ones we can. If you want to see the castle, then we can. We have to walk right by it. But we will not charge into that building and tear it to the ground without knowing what is actually going on here."

"You're right." She pressed her forehead to his and sighed. "You're always right."

"Now that's what I like to hear."

He tucked her hood around her hair a little better, making sure no strands would fall out, and then took the lead. He knew these woods like the back of his hand. Abraxas had spent many evenings wandering through them, wishing he wasn't in the position that he was. Every tree, every rock, every animal had known exactly who he was and what he could do. Now, they all rejoiced that the dragon had returned.

It was strange to be here after all that had happened. The death of the king. The hatching of dragon eggs he'd been so certain would never see the light of day. Falling in love with an elf. Seeing his homeland. All of these memories played through his mind as he brought them to a ridge that overlooked the castle.

By the time they reached the rocky precipice, the sun had disappeared from the horizon. But he'd planned it that way. He wanted Lore to see through those castle walls while the moon could fill her magical reserves.

It was the only way he could care for her. Making certain that she was glutted with power.

Lore crouched beside him, her eyes narrowing on the castle. "Where is everyone?"

"I do not know."

There should be guards on the castle ramparts at the very least, but the monolithic building appeared empty. No movement. No sound. Nothing but empty stones and the racing sound of wind.

His eyes cast over the castle, wondering what went on in the walls, when he noticed a movement across the field nearest the castle. He pointed silently, lifting his brow as a line of humans marched across the plain.

Then there was sound. The wailing efforts of mortals pleading for their lives. Their guards, all elves, drove them forward. Tall and lithe, the elves wore armor from ancient times that had long since passed. The black metal gleamed in the moonlight.

"So they are bringing them here," Lore breathed. "For what purpose?"

"To punish them?" Abraxas had a hard time imagining what Margaret's plan was, but he could assume that was part of it. "To enslave them? Who knows? We won't figure it out laying here."

Lore huffed out an angry breath. "And you're not going to let me sneak into the castle, are you?"

"Not until we have an army that can storm it with you." He arched that brow again and met her fiery gaze. "Unless you agree that I can take the castle apart rock by rock to get you back?"

"We don't know what weapons they have that might harm a dragon."

"I'm going to take that as a no."

"It's a no." Lore leaned against the rocks, turning her gaze from the humans, who screamed for help. "We need to keep moving. It's not safe to camp here for the night."

No, it wasn't. He let her sink into her thoughts as she led them away from that cursed castle. So many souls haunted those halls.

Abraxas glanced back at the dark shadow outlined by the moon and wondered how many more ghosts would be added this night.

CHAPTER 5

Lore couldn't sleep. There were people out there who needed her, and she was supposed to curl up on a cozy bed of moss, with the moon over her head. And just... dream? No. She couldn't do it.

Not a single part of her cared that those who were being tortured were human. She'd met a lot of good humans in her life. They'd even helped her out when she was in a bind or hidden her from the eyes of the Umbral Soldiers.

Good people were everywhere. No one could say that all humans were bad, just as no one could say that all elves were powerful. And knowing that those people were the ones who were being hunted? It made her sick to her stomach.

She just wanted to help.

But she couldn't help them because there was a bigger picture to focus on. An entire kingdom waited for her to save it, and yet she wanted to save each individual.

Sighing, she rolled over yet again and stared out into the woods. Could she sneak away for the night? Abraxas was asleep, but he was a light sleeper. If she so much as stood up, she had a feeling he would notice. And he'd know what she was doing. He'd make her lie right back down and scold her for a good amount of time before staying up the rest of the night to ensure she stayed put.

She didn't enjoy feeling trapped. And all of this felt like she had a collar around her neck with a hundred different people tugging her in every which direction.

Sighing again, she rolled over onto her back. Maybe she could save them tomorrow. Maybe, if she was lucky, they would still be alive when she broke down and couldn't take the hollow echo of their screams anymore.

A hand came down over her mouth and she froze. Abraxas loomed over her, crouched in the darkness and nowhere near his bed. "Don't scream."

She furrowed her brows, glowering until he removed his hand from her mouth. "I wasn't going to. You're lucky I didn't pop your skull."

"Well, you weren't sleeping, and that means I wasn't sleeping. So let's go."

"Go?" She sat up, her hair a tangled mess around her head. "What do you mean, go?"

"You want to save the humans, and I want to sleep. So let's get one group freed and then I can rest for the night."

She stared at him while her heart thudded hard in her chest. Sometimes, she was reminded of how much she loved him. How much her heart beat only for him and that he could see inside her head like she was a book he knew how to read.

"Abraxas," she whispered, her throat tight with emotion.

All he did was grin at her and hold out his hand for her to take. "Come on, Lady of Starlight. Do you think I don't know you?"

He gathered her up in his arms, tugging her upright before disappearing between the trees. She'd forgotten this was his home. That he'd had hundreds of years to explore every inch of this forest. No one knew how to get around the castle better than Abraxas.

They snuck through the trees with light footsteps. She hadn't grabbed any of her weapons, and neither had he. Their journey was too swift for such things. And as they crouched just outside of the light cast by fires, she understood why.

Four elven guards stood watch around a group of humans who were all tied with metal chains. They could hardly move away from each other. If anyone needed to lift an arm, at least three others had to do so as well to give them enough slack. It made eating difficult, it seemed, although they had little in their laps for food.

The fires were far away from them, perhaps only lit for the elves themselves. No human huddled around the flames for warmth. Instead, they were curled around each other.

The elves didn't look like they were paying much attention. Maybe they had been nervous in the early days of kidnapping the mortals and bringing them to the castle. Lore couldn't imagine there weren't at least a few people who had wanted to fight back. But now? There was no one left to fight.

Abraxas pointed at the nearest guard. "I can silence him rather quickly, but the other three don't seem to linger close together. They are well spaced."

Or she could create a diversion.

Because what if these guards weren't terrible people? Elves stuck together. They always had. If Margaret had told the elves to fight, then they would do just that. It wasn't a question of why, nor did they need any reasoning. An elf said that mortals were to be rounded up, therefore, they would do exactly that.

Good people, she reminded herself, were hidden all over this kingdom. Killing the good ones to free others meant she was no better than Margaret.

Sighing, she pinched the bridge of her nose. She didn't want anyone to sense the magic, but... Was this worth the risk?

"Don't," Abraxas said, his voice low. "No magic unless necessary."

"Right." Hand to hand it was, then. "Don't kill any of them."

"I won't."

She pointed at the guard she wanted Abraxas to focus on and then burst out of the shadows. Distraction was still the best option, so she ran for the farthest guard. Leaping over the fire, she curved her body toward the man who had already attempted to draw his sword.

A swift kick to the head stopped that, and she landed on the opposite side of him as he fell. Lore crouched, eyes up for the next person who was already running at her. Both of them, actually.

They'd learned well from Margaret, it seemed. If someone attacked, they shouldn't waste any time trying to fight honorably. Mob the person and they were much more likely to make it out alive.

She balled her hands into fists, watching as the men slid their blades out of their sheaths. They'd come at her together, though right now they circled her. Perhaps they hadn't yet recognized who she was. Or they would eventually. Right now, they were focused on staying alive. Good. They would need that focus to fight her.

Lore launched herself at the one on the left, using her momentum to spin him around while she wrapped her legs around his waist. He stumbled at her weight, but didn't fall like she'd hoped he would. Instead, he dropped his sword and reached behind his head for her shirt. He planned to fling her over his head, she realized, and that wasn't something she could let happen.

Hissing in his ear, she wrapped both her arms around his neck and squeezed hard. But then he turned his back to the other man, and she heard the sound of a blade whistling through the air.

Soon, she would feel that sword against her spine. Severing all the nerves there.

The pain never came.

Instead, she heard a snarl that rumbled through the forest and sent a shiver down her spine. That sound reached deep into the part of her brain that told her to run, flee, hide. There was a predator nearby and if she didn't run, then it would devour her as well.

The elf in her grasp sagged. She fell with him onto the forest floor, holding tight to his neck for a few more moments just to make sure he really had passed out.

Then she rolled, crouching in the dirt as she looked up at the elf who had tried to kill her. His eyes bulged, his mouth moving on a cry that would never come out of his mouth. Abraxas had ripped his throat out with one hand and the other was still plunged into the elf's chest, bloody, taloned fingers sticking out the back of the ruined mess of his ribs.

She shook her head in disappointment. "I said no killing, Abraxas."

"He was going to kill you." Her dragon released the man who fell onto the ground, either dead or soon to be dead. Abraxas grimaced at the gore on his fingers. "No one touches what's mine."

And she loved him for that, really she did, but the humans would not love him for his aggression. His actions would only add to their fear.

She shook her head and turned her attention to the mortals that cowered in their chains. No one wanted to look at them. Not a single one.

Then she realized they must fear all magical creatures. Lore no longer hid her ears. They were on full display, with her hair braided on either side of her skull. Abraxas was clearly not human, although most of them would struggle to guess what he was.

None of them wanted trouble. None of them wanted yet another captor who would make them walk miles to an unknown future.

Dropping to her knees next to the nearest guard, the one who was still alive but very much passed out, she rummaged through his pockets. "See if you can find the keys, Abraxas."

"There are no keys."

"There have to be keys. How else would they get them into the chains in the first place?" There was nothing in this man's pockets other than a few vials of unnamed potions and a piece of paper that looked like a child's drawing.

She was suddenly very glad she hadn't killed this one.

"Keys," she muttered, trying hard not to look at the terrified humans. "There has to be..."

"Lore," Abraxas snapped. And then he pointed when she looked up at him. "There are no keys."

She followed the direction of his finger to the humans nearest to her. One man was braver than the others, or perhaps more foolish. He held up his wrists for her to see that there were no locks on any of the chains around their wrists. They were forged onto the humans, melted so that they would never get them off. Not without a saw or something equally as sharp.

Her heart twisted in her chest and she thought she might throw up. Red ringed all of their wrists, burns that she hadn't noticed before. Angry flesh that was likely to get infected if they didn't take care of them.

She sat back on her haunches, staring at the mess in front of her. "Well. Damn."

Abraxas patted her shoulder and approached the man. "If I may?"

Though brave, he still flinched from the intensity of a dragon covered in blood before him. "What are you planning to do to us?"

"We're going to let you go." Abraxas reached for the manacles and took hold of the chain that connected the man to the next. "There is a town not far from here. Get there before the sun rises and find whatever basement you can hide in. There's not many people left, so find a house that's been abandoned. No need for you to go anywhere until it's night again. Keep out of sight. And keep quiet."

The chain link snapped between his powerful hands. The humans all started murmuring, hope in their voices as they stood.

A woman at the end quietly asked, "Just him?"

Did they think Lore and Abraxas were trying to send a message?

Rage simmered underneath her skin and magic bubbled to the surface again. Not a massive amount, just enough to snap the chains with Abraxas. "No. All of you. But I don't suggest you stick together. A large group is much easier to find."

And so they spent the better part of an hour breaking through the chains. There were easily forty people here, although Lore lost count as she freed them. They each wanted to tell her their names, whisper where they came from, and beg her for more information on where they might be safe.

She didn't know. There was nowhere safe left in this kingdom.

"Have you heard of the Stygian Mountains?" She heard Abraxas ask. "They're overrun with spiders, but if you have your wits about you, it's possible to avoid them."

She looked at the woman in front of her, who was frail and thin, but looked quick enough. "The Fields of Somber are safe now. The crypts are not the most comfortable, but most, if not all, of the wights should be gone. Take your time finding a crypt that is empty of bodies and bring food there. Your family can stay."

Over and over again, they advised these people on where to go, how to seek shelter, what area might still have food that they could take with them.

And all the while, she hoped she wasn't sending them to their death.

"Thank you," another woman whispered, reaching out for Lore's hands and holding them tightly. "We don't know what we would do without you. What is your name, miss? So I might speak of you to my grandchildren someday."

Lore looked at Abraxas, wondering just how much he'd heard. Her dragon had stiffened, but he gave her a slow nod. As if to say now was the time for them to spread rumors.

They'd been so afraid of Margaret realizing she was here, but perhaps it would be good to have rumors of a goddess reborn. Perhaps that would give people hope again.

She smiled at the woman and let the moonlight play across her skin. Lore had done this so many times in her life, if only to have light to read by. But she knew what humans saw.

The moon glowed inside her. Its magic glittered like diamonds and lit her entire body up with rays of light that flashed in their eyes.

A gasp echoed from one person, then another.

"Goddess Divine?" someone whispered. "I thought she was only sent for the creatures?"

"No." Lore sought the person who had said that and then smiled at the man. "I was sent for the kingdom, not for the elves or the creatures alone. I never would have left if I knew this was the end of that story."

"But... they claim you were sent to free them from us. That you knew what had happened and you... you..." The man staggered back, fear in his eyes. "That if you ever returned, it would be to destroy us all for good."

"People put words in the mouths of gods. You would be wise to heed only the sights you have seen yourself." Lore shook her head again. "I was sent for everyone. This kingdom is my home as much as it is yours, and I will see no one die or become enslaved. I made a mistake. I trusted the wrong people, and you were the ones to suffer for that. For this, I am sorry. I will repay your pain, but first I have to fix what I broke."

They all staggered away from her, then. Some of them giving her a quick thank you before disappearing into the trees. Others didn't even look at her.

She understood their fear, but she hated that she had become the symbol for it.

"Come," Abraxas said, cupping the back of her neck and pressing a kiss to her forehead. "We need to go as well."

And so they left the fallen elves where they were and disappeared into the shadows.

CHAPTER 6

Lore couldn't get the image of them out of her head. All she saw were hollow eyes and emaciated flesh, bones sticking out of their backs like wings. She remembered their gazes as they stared up at the sky, waiting for someone to help them, but then realizing they were alone.

Was this what it was to be a god? Was she supposed to save them all and somehow set this part of herself aside from what she feared she actually was?

Selfish.

Half-elf.

Not good enough for anyone in the kingdom to see beyond the surface of too short ears and glittering skin.

Her dragon seemed to realize the mood she was in. Abraxas always knew when to let her simmer in her thoughts and when to push her free from them. Their journey after saving the humans was filled with meaningful silences and a man who continually pushed food toward her.

She had moments where she was grateful for him. She couldn't forget all that he did. From making sure she ate, to taking over the directions of where they were going, finding water in the scarce clean sources the closer they got to Tenebrous. All of it fell on Abraxas's shoulders and he shouldered that burden without complaint.

By the time they made it to the marshes, she'd settled a few things in her mind. But then she thought about the humans again and all those thoughts scattered like seeds in the wind.

She was—as ever, she supposed—stuck. And the only person who could help pull her out of that mire was the dragon who had been with her through it all.

Abraxas glanced over his shoulder, his face lit by a hundred will-o'-the-wisps that followed him around their makeshift campsite. Those harsh features never changed, no matter what they went through. He was a solid foundation for her to brace herself against.

"How did I get so lucky?" she asked, her voice carrying through the mist.

"In what way?"

Lore gestured toward the lights, blinking into existence from the meager city of Tenebrous. "I grew up there. I lived in those dirty streets, stealing whatever I could to stay alive. And now I am practically a goddess with the expectations of a kingdom on my shoulders and a dragon who loves me. How did I get so lucky?"

He snorted and shook his head. "You call that luck?"

"I call meeting you luck. Everything else I could do without."

His features softened and Abraxas came to her side. He was never far, but he always seemed to notice when she needed his hands on her.

Cupping the back of her neck, he drew her in close so he could press his lips to her forehead. "You are the best thing to happen in my life, Lore. And I would not trade all this hardship for a second chance at something different. Neither would you, I suppose. Neither would any of the people you're thinking about, most likely."

"Their souls are heavy," she whispered.

"They have been through a trying time."

"No, not the ones who lived." And that was the rub of it all, wasn't it? "I can feel the ones who didn't make it. The anger they carry at not being saved. I can hear them on the other side, whispering that if we had only been a day faster that we might have freed them as well. They blame me, Abraxas, for all that I could not do."

"Then you will stop listening to them." Abraxas gave her neck a little shake, as though that would startle her out of her thoughts. "You will pull yourself from that world, or so help me, I will join them in the darkness. I will hunt them down for you, Lore, to give you better peace in this realm."

As if she would ever let him. But the thought made her smile. She'd been in that realm before herself, and she knew how difficult it was to crawl back out of.

Sighing, she let the lingering tension slip from her shoulders. "I'm sorry. I shouldn't have such morose thoughts when we're here."

Abraxas took a few steps back from her, his eyes still seeing more than she wanted him to see. But he returned to the campsite he was setting up and started their fire. "Here? Of all places? Such a sunny, warm environment for good thoughts, don't you think?"

She shook her head. "Sarcastic dragon."

"Stubborn elf."

Of course, both of them were right. She sat down on a log next to the fire, trying to piece her thoughts together. "I don't want to be happy because of where we are, but because of what we were doing the last time we were here. Do you remember?"

"I remember." His voice warmed with a chuckle. "It was the first time I'd traveled in this form. I was exhausted."

"I almost threw you in the bog."

He grinned, and she swore the marsh lit up with his happiness. "I would have smelled better if you had."

Laughter bubbled up in her chest before she realized what was happening. She let it trickle out of her body in a light rush that lifted some of the heavy spirits from her shoulders.

She missed that time. They had been so frustrated and fighting against what they felt. Their arguments had taken such a long time, and yet they had fallen for each other no matter how hard they'd fought against it.

Abraxas shook his head, that wry grin still on his face. "We should try to get some sleep. There will be time to go over our memories, and for the laughter that we both desperately need. But I, for one, would like to get out of the bog before we reminisce. Shall we?"

He was right. They both needed sleep. But she wanted this bubble of laughter to stay around her, if only for a little while longer.

Lore nodded at the blankets he'd laid out on the ground. "Go ahead. I'll take first watch."

"You need to rest."

"And you need to let me do what I want to do." She tilted her head to the side, biting her lip so she didn't burst into laughter at the frustrated expression on his face. "I'm not tired yet, and I don't need as much sleep as I used to. I'll live in the memories for a little while longer, and you can get the rest you need to get us to Tenebrous tomorrow."

Grumbling under his breath, he settled himself onto the ground and stared up at the sky for a while.

Lore knew her man well, though. He could fight against the exhaustion all he wanted, but he was still exhausted. She would have been as well if she wasn't full of all this power. It fueled her body, pushed her forward to the unknown purpose that still burned in her chest. Soon, she would understand why she'd been given all this magic. Soon, she would fulfill that purpose.

But right now, she wanted to watch her man fall gradually asleep. He was always so peaceful as he did it. Abraxas could fight with the weight of the world on his shoulders, but the moment sleep took him, his face evened out into a quiet calm that she never saw on his features while he was awake.

That handsome face had gotten her through so much more than he would ever realize. She wanted to lie beside him and trace her fingers over the long hawk-like nose, down the thin lips that were usually pressed into a firm line, to his prominent jaw. He had to know that no matter how much time they'd spent apart, not a single part of her loved him less.

In fact, she supposed she loved him even more.

Sighing, she tore her gaze away from the resting dragon and focused instead on the fire he'd built. The flames flickered, moving along with the mist behind it. Pulling her mind away from the moment and into the future.

Or perhaps somewhere else.

She felt the flare of magic rising in her chest before she even realized she was using it. Sometimes the power still did that, as though her mother and the mothers before that were pushing her toward something important that she'd missed.

It was, after all, their power that lived inside her.

Rolling and rumbling through her like a storm just waiting to be unleashed, her gaze soon locked on the flames. They flickered, moving with every breath of the wind. Then she saw it. Images were inside the flames that moved with their own accord.

A summoning spell? No, that wasn't quite right. It was divination in its oldest form.

Divination that let her see through the very veil of the world as though she could transport herself across the entire kingdom. Kneeling in the coals was a young man who was as familiar to her as family.

"Ah," she whispered under her breath, making sure not to rouse Abraxas. "You want me to see him?"

Of course they did. They wanted her to check in on the young man who was very dear to her, and the reason she'd returned to Umbra. They wanted to remind her why she was here.

Lore wasn't supposed to save the humans and disappear. She was here to save her family.

And she'd forgotten that. Rather easily, she was ashamed to admit.

Sighing, she twisted her hair into a knot at the back of her neck and closed her eyes. Careful to not use enough magic to be detected, she let her soul wander from her body.

It was a new talent that one of her ancestors had insisted on teaching her. She wasn't really scrying, so she didn't need an element to look into. No fire or water would show her what her consciousness could.

Lore liked to call it going for a walk. That's what it felt like, albeit much faster than her physical form could move. Her spirit soured over the lands of Umbra, shifting through the very fabric of reality until she was right in front of that horrible place where they were keeping Zephyr.

The shambles of Solis Occasum never failed to make her heart squeeze in her chest. This building had once been great. A reminder of the gifts the sun gave to the people of Umbra and how warm this kingdom could be. That had all changed as many kings tore down the history that had been built here.

Guards stood at every angle she could see. They couldn't see her, though. Not unless she wanted them to.

Lore glided through them, her footsteps light and leaving glowing prints behind her. A guide for her soul to get home when she needed to return to her body.

The images inside the remains of that castle were blurry, even to her. Countless spells wrapped around this place, trying to keep out any and all who would dare come into the kingdom's new dungeon.

Those spells made it hard to guess who many others were in here with Zephyr. It made it hard for her to even walk through the muck of all those tangled spells. Dragging her feet through them felt like someone was trying to toss her back.

But she had all night. And if it took her that long to see him, then that's how long it would take her.

She fought against the spells for a long time. So much so that she could feel her mortal body breaking out into a sweat. Not that it was particularly difficult, just tedious. Lore could almost feel her ancestors feeding her more power because even they were frustrated with all these layers of spells.

She had to weave her way through them. She had to make it seem like no one had ever touched a single thread of those spells, so that no one would ever guess she was here.

But Lore knew the moment she started this journey toward him that she wouldn't leave without Zephyr knowing that she was coming. He would not suffer for much longer, and she had every intent on getting him out very soon.

Finally, the last spell warped around her body like a bubble. It didn't burst, but this one was flimsy and felt as though it would be so easy to tear.

He was right where she'd left him. His arms were strung up too high and his shoulders twisted into an impossible position. Zephyr's knees were bleeding on the ground, the scabs seeming to stick him to the stone floor.

HIs head hung low, as though he had completely given up and she would not see him do that. Not now. Not ever.

Lore knelt in front of him, her heart breaking at the sight. She wanted to heal him, if only a little, but she feared that if they saw he'd healed, then they would beat him again. What if giving him a single night of comfort led to far more days and nights of torture?

It was better to leave him like this, even if it made her entire being revolt at the thought.

Solidifying her corporeal form, she touched her hand to his forehead and smoothed his sticky hair back from his head.

He followed her touch as though it were a cool balm to the pain inside him. And as she watched, she saw the very moment that he realized what he'd done. His eyes snapped open in horror and she wondered if someone had touched him like this, only to force it all to come crumbling down around his ears.

What torment had he gone through to be afraid of a kind touch?

Those wide eyes blinked a few times before he realized it was Lore in front of him. He breathed out a relieved breath, only to stiffen once again. "Are you really here?"

"I am."

"They said you hadn't visited me. That I was mad to even claim it."

"You can't tell them I was here this time." She brushed her hand over his forehead again, knowing that he enjoyed the coldness of her touch. "I'm so close, Zephyr. Abraxas and I are in Umbra. We're coming for you. So I need you to stay alive."

"They won't let me die." His chapped lips pressed together in disappointment. "I've tried."

"You will not try any longer." Her voice was hard, perhaps a little too firm for a man who had gone through so much. "You will stop all that foolishness now. I am coming for you!"

"I'm tired," he whispered, the chains clanking as he tried to draw his arms down around himself. "I'm cold. And I'm so tired of fighting."

Tears pricked her eyes, and Lore did the only thing that she could think of.

She drew him into her arms, wrapping herself tightly around him and holding his head against her shoulder. Though he could not hug her back, she felt a shudder rock through his entire body at the cold but comforting touch. "I'm here now, and I will make sure this never happens to you again. I promise."

He nodded, and she felt him start to drift away. As though his mind couldn't stand the hope that she'd gifted to him.

She'd stay the night. She'd hold him and keep all those monsters at bay for as long as she could. But when the sun came up, she would have to return to her struggle to find him.

And as she felt the sun rise, her heart broke a thousand times over.

CHAPTER 7

Abraxas got them to Tenebrous without issue. He had known that he would, but when he'd woken up the next morning feeling refreshed and energetic, he was horrified to see the dark circles underneath Lore's eyes.

She hadn't slept. She hadn't given him an explanation as to why, either. But he could see it in her eyes. The way her gaze had hardened, and she pushed them to go faster than they had before.

She'd seen Zephyr. Or she'd talked to him. She'd done something with her magic and he was so angry at her for that.

The risk! She always forgot about the risk when it came to herself, and he knew she understood why they were going slow. Margaret would not kill Zephyr. She couldn't chance that. She needed to use him as a puppet for the remaining humans to trust her. Otherwise, she'd have her own rebellion brewing right underneath her nose.

The elf was intelligent. Margaret knew how to keep a kingdom crushed underneath her heel. And Lore knew that as well.

So why was his beautiful, stubborn, annoying, heartbreakingly wonderful mate risking her own life?

Because that's what Lore did.

He'd thought he would have gotten used to it by now, but he had not.

And now he had to figure out how to get them through Tenebrous without anyone realizing who was walking among them. It wouldn't be easy. Lore had grown up here, and there were a lot of magical creatures who would recognize her face. That meant he had to keep her hidden, and of course she wanted to walk through the city at the very peak of daylight.

"Absolutely not," he snarled. "You are going to be recognized the moment we walk through those gates. You are too familiar to these people, Lore! If you are not careful, you'll have Margaret coming down here riding a broom like a witch out of a children's story."

Lore snorted. "Witches don't ride brooms."

"They do if they want to cut the head off their rival, let me make that very clear." Crossing his arms over his chest, he stood in front of her as a physical barrier between her and the people beyond. "We have to be smart about this, Lore. If we aren't, then we'll end up in a very difficult position. Beauty is in there, yes. And that means there are others who could use our help, I'm certain of it. But we do it my way, or I throw you over my shoulder and we go back to the dragon isles."

She glared up at him with so much fire in her eyes, it made him catch his breath. "I could make you do whatever I want you to do, you know. You aren't stronger than me anymore."

"I'm physically stronger than you, and I think even your power would have a hard time controlling a dragon." He hoped, at least. He felt confident she wouldn't use her magic on him without him wanting her to. It just wasn't in Lore to do so.

But considering the look in her eyes, he thought maybe he was wrong.

Sighing, Abraxas uncrossed his arms and tugged her into his heart. "Hush, Lore. A day won't change anything."

"What if Margaret knows we're here, and she's hunting down Beauty?" she muttered into his chest. "We could already be too late."

"You can't save everyone. And Beauty is much more sly than that." He'd always found that the human girl had been able to startle him. And he was a dragon.

He'd never forget the way she had manipulated them all into thinking she was just a goofy potential wife who never should have been sent into the king's bridal event. But she'd stepped in front of an arrow for the king, knowing that it wasn't the right time for him to be killed. She'd secretly been working with the rebellion the entire time, as well. Margaret wouldn't kill such a loyal person.

At least, he hoped she wouldn't.

He felt Lore nod against him. "Fine. We'll wait until nightfall."

"That's what I wanted to hear. And you'll sleep while we wait for the darkness, yes?"

Another small nod. He dragged her off to make sure they had a safe place to rest, which ended up being little more than a discarded pile of hay against the walls of Tenebrous. But they'd slept in worse than moldy hay. And she slept hard.

He held her against his side as he listened to the sound of her breath. Abraxas had taken to counting each inhalation. The sound meant she was alive and well and still with him. Even if he didn't trust that sometimes.

The sun set on the horizon and still he waited. He gave her as much time to sleep as he could before gently shaking her awake.

"Lore," he said, hovering his hand over her mouth in case he needed to keep her quiet. "It's time to go."

She woke in a rush. Her eyes snapped open and her heart raced against his side. But she locked her gaze on him without a single question of what was happening or who he was. She always woke like that these days. As though she'd never been asleep.

Sitting up, he watched as she shook herself out and prepared for their entrance to Tenebrous. At least now he could pull her hood up over her head and the shadows covered almost all of her face. All he could see was the point of her chin and the pretty pink bow of her lips.

He couldn't help himself. Abraxas stole a kiss before he nodded toward the city. "Let's go."

"We'll need an excuse for being there."

"Trade."

"What are we trading?" Her voice sparkled with laughter. "We don't have a cart."

He had no idea, but they'd come up with something. In the end, they didn't have to. The guards took one look at his massive bulk and her flash of a pointed ear and let them straight through.

That had changed.

But many things had changed since they'd first come here. Abraxas could see that. The rickety homes that had once made him wince with their strange architecture were now split into two very different kinds. The ones that were still standing, and the ones that had been torn down.

It took him a while to understand what had happened. After all, he'd seen Tenebrous at its worst. The very foundations of these homes were ready to break apart at the slightest wind. And if there had been any kind of battle here? All the houses would fall at the slightest rumble.

But that didn't appear to be what had happened here. Some houses were fine. Others? They were in complete and utter ruin. The ones right next to each other as well, and that made little sense. If one house had fallen, it should have taken others with it. Not simply shattered, like a spell had been cast to hit it.

Once they stood in front of Beauty's father's manor, the one he'd only seen from afar, he realized what had happened.

"They're all the human houses," he muttered as he scuffed his foot in the ashes left from a fire that had torn through Beauty's childhood home. "Aren't they?"

"Yes," Lore whispered, tears in her eyes as she stared at their only hope. "These were the houses that the mortals used to live in. I think Margaret targeted them first to get them out of hiding. It's much easier to round up humans when they have nowhere else to go."

Perhaps some of the magical creatures had tried to hide their human neighbors, but as he glanced around, he thought it was unlikely. Everyone here still looked the same. Hungry. Tired. Skittering spiders of people who lingered in the shadows, eyeing the pockets of others, hoping they might steal a little comfort for the evening.

The loss of all those people who had once lived here didn't make it easier for the magical creatures. But that hadn't been the purpose of her hunting them down, now had it? Margaret didn't care about the state of Tenebrous. All she cared about was how much easier it would be for her if she didn't have to worry about the humans rebelling.

"Come on," he said, holding out his hand for Lore to take. "We still need to find somewhere to stay."

Lore was staring at the rubble of the once beautiful home with too much intensity. Part of him wondered if she'd bring it back to life. If there was some spell locked away in her head, that would save the home from this terrible end, but he wasn't so certain that he wanted her to do it. Magic was scarce in a place like this.

Someone would notice.

"Lore." He kept his words low, but added a firm snap to the word. "We have to go."

"I have somewhere else to check first," she replied. "Then we can find a place to stay the night."

"Where?"

Her eyes found his, and he already knew he would hate the answer. Abraxas even stepped forward as though to stop her from speaking, as if he could ever do that.

"Do you remember the first time we met?" Her words cast a spell on him.

Abraxas was suddenly catapulted back to that moment when he had known his life was about to change forever. The moment when he'd fallen in love with her at first glance.

"You were beautiful," he said quietly. "Standing in the moonlight like an elf walking out of a storybook legend. I should have known then what you were, but I didn't want you to be in danger, so I told myself you were only mortal. Wild and free like you were, I should have known that the forest was too deeply ingrained in your being for you to be anything but an elf."

"A night full of illusion. Of blue butterflies to catch on the wind for rich people to have a bit of our magic for the first and only times in their lives." Her lips twisted in a smile that was anything but happy. "A creature with great power did all of that. And he lived near here."

He hummed low underneath his breath. "Borovoi."

"Indeed."

"He won't still be here. That monster knows how to flee from trouble at the very first sight. He's a survivor." Abraxas tried very hard not to let his lip curl at the thought of the beast.

"You dislike him?" Lore watched his expression with an amused one of her own.

"I've never liked him." Abraxas didn't have to explain himself, but he did anyway. "He was one of the King's pets. I have no interest in the man, nor do I wish to have any pity for him when he very well could have caused all of this to happen."

"He helped me. He made sure that I was safe and hidden in that party and made sure the King's eyes were on me and no one else. In doing that, he set all of this in motion."

Grumbling under his breath, Abraxas couldn't help but correct, "He was probably the mastermind behind all of it."

"Regardless, I want to see if he's still here. If he can help us."

Borovoi wouldn't. The creature was as monstrous as Zander had been, at least in Abraxas's opinion. Of course, Borovoi had been behind a lot of spells that trapped Abraxas for the King. When the Magician had left, Borovoi was the one to maintain all the old magic.

Not that there were a lot of them. But he very much remembered the man weaving more spells around the box that held his eggs safely at bay from him, and he'd never forgive the creature for that.

Lore was already moving, though. He didn't have any choice other than to follow her.

They picked their way through the city, keeping their eye on a few thieves who trailed them because they didn't recognize the strangers in their midst. And who better to steal from than strangers with cloaks that were a little too fine for a place like this?

One got close and Abraxas bared his teeth at the man.

"Don't," Lore said as the boy raced away. "They'll guess what you are. Those teeth are hard to hide."

His teeth weren't changed. He was just trying to air some of this frustration.

Still, he listened. The last thing he needed was Lore leaving him somewhere in this grimy place that he'd always hated. Tenebrous would never change, it seemed.

Finally, they made it to the damn monster's home. Borovoi had always liked the pretty parts of life. His home was still stunning and standing, and that should have been enough warning for them to leave. But Lore refused.

Instead, she brushed the door open like she owned the place and looked over her shoulder with an arched brow. "Are you coming?"

"Inside?" Abraxas flexed his hands and curled them into fists. "It could very well be a trap, Lore."

"Or he could be waiting for us to find him so he can apologize. You never know."

He doubted Borovoi was in there, regardless of the man's intent, when all of this had happened. Borovoi ran at the first scent of trouble. It was how the man had stayed alive all these years.

Ah, but Lore stood there holding out her hand for him to take and he'd never been able to say no to her. Not when she looked like that.

Setting his hand in hers, he grumbled, "Fine."

Together, they walked into the darkness of the house. His eyes adjusted faster than hers, and he could see how obvious it was that no one had been here for a very long time. Dust had settled on all the tables that were still filled to the brim with magical objects and jars full of beautiful things. The tree in the center was just as lush as before, although its door was no longer open.

He'd only been in here a few times, but he knew that this place hadn't changed since he'd seen it long ago.

"Oh," she whispered in disappointment. "Apparently you were right. He's not here."

"He could still be hiding."

She shook her head. "No, I can't sense him. There's no magical creatures left in this house at all."

Abraxas turned into her, ready to pull her into his arms for yet another disappointment that would surely hurt her, but then he heard the distinct sound of a bolt hitting the hard wooden edge of a crossbow.

"There's still people here, though," a hard voice interrupted them. "I'm afraid I'll need you to get back against that wall and tell me exactly what you're doing here."

CHAPTER 8

Power crackled in her hands at the first hint of danger. The voice was not familiar to her, and unfamiliar meant a threat. Not to mention he'd told them to put their backs against the wall, and Lore had no intention to do that.

If they had to fight their way out of Borovoi's house, then she would gladly do so.

A slight flash of hesitation burned in her mind, though. Why were they having to fight if the magical creatures had taken over Tenebrous? Everyone could see that she was an elf. She wasn't wearing her hood over her head, and Abraxas was anything but human.

She needed to play this right. And they couldn't attack whoever this was like Abraxas intended to. The frame of her dragon's mortal body was already warping with his anger. A shimmering haze changed what he looked like, and she could see red scales rising underneath his skin. They waited to be released, and he would destroy this entire house if he changed inside it.

"Easy," she breathed, her voice measured and low. "Take a breath."

"I will not take a breath," the unknown man snarled. "I'll put an arrow between your eyes before you so much as flinch. Take your time turning toward me and we'll all be fine."

We'll all be fine?

She rolled the words around in her head and wondered if this was the first time he'd held someone hostage. It made her question this situation yet again.

Who was this man?

She turned, knowing that Abraxas had heard her and understood she didn't want him to attack. Not yet, at least. If she had to, she would gladly release her dragon, but right now, she needed to understand what was going on.

Flicking her gaze up toward the grizzled face of the man holding the crossbow, she lifted her hands above her head. "We're not here to hurt anyone."

No ears, scales, tail, or any other quality that would make her think magical creature. His beard covered his entire face, a thin layer of grime caking his forehead. He looked... mortal.

Now that was a problem.

If this man was a mortal, then he was living in a very prominent creature's home. That should make it easy to find him.

But then again, this could be the best place for him to hide. No one would walk into Borovoi's house, assuming they would find mortals here. This might be the best place in the entire kingdom to hide while Margaret's folks meandered around trying to hunt them down.

"We're not here to hurt you," she said, now wishing she had left her hood up. "We just want to talk."

"I'm not talking to an elf."

"I'm not with Margaret and her people, if that's what you're thinking." She inched closer to Abraxas. "Neither of us are. We've been gone for a long time, and we're just now getting home."

"You expect me to believe that? I see those sharp ears and I know exactly what they mean. You can't be here. Because if you are, that means you're here to kill us."

"We're not killing anyone."

He thrust the crossbow at her as though the movement was a threat. But his finger never moved on the trigger. "You think I want to do this? You think I want to hurt anyone?"

"Maybe." Lore lowered her hands, so she looked more like a person to him. Abraxas had never even lifted his, and she placed her hand on his shoulder that was still vibrating with his need to attack. "I wouldn't blame you if it made you feel better. From what I've seen, the elves have done a lot to this kingdom already. And for that, I am sorry."

"Trickery."

"Truth," she corrected. "I do not speak for the rest of them, but I do speak for a small few. I'm certain of that."

She hoped, at least.

Right now, though, he had to put that crossbow down before her dragon lost patience. How could she get him to do that? Lore supposed she could start glowing, but she was the elves' goddess, not those of the mortals. That might startle him even more.

She thought she might survive a crossbow bolt to the chest. Maybe even one to the eye. It felt like her body wouldn't let her die when there was so much left to do, but she didn't want Abraxas to live through yet another attempt on her life.

"Da?" A voice filtered through the door as it opened yet again. "What's taking you so long? You were supposed to help bring everything in."

She knew that voice.

Lore knew that voice as though it were her own.

All worries about that crossbow fled as she staggered to the side to look around the man and fill her gaze with the woman standing in the doorway with her arms wrapped around a large sack.

"Beauty?" she croaked, the word sticking in her throat. "Is that you?"

The sack hit the ground hard. The contents scattered. Maybe a whole bundle of potatoes, she didn't know. Lore's eyes were locked on the young woman, who had lost far too much weight. There were deep hollows in her cheeks and harsh shadows underneath her eyes. Beauty's lovely gold hair was lank around her features, unwashed and clearly not taken care of. But she was alive. She was standing right there when Lore had been so afraid that... that...

"Lore?" Beauty asked, her own voice wavering with immediate tears.

Lore couldn't speak. All she could do was nod as her jaw quivered. She clenched her teeth so hard it hurt, but she refused to start sobbing.

Beauty took a step toward her. Then another. Completely ignoring her father's barked orders to stay where she was. "Damn it, girl, why aren't you listening to me?"

Without a second thought about the dangers of the man with the crossbow, Lore lurched forward and pulled the other woman into her arms. They sank into each other, crying happy tears that they were both alive and finally, finally together after such a long time.

"I was so afraid you were dead," she whispered into Beauty's hair.

"I thought you were never coming back." Beauty tucked her head into Lore's shoulder, tears soaking through the cloak and sticking to her skin.

Lore had forgotten how short Beauty was. Or maybe she had forgotten how fragile the little mortal felt in her arms. So much had changed since they had seen each other, and yet it felt as though she had stepped out of time. Nothing had changed between them, no matter how many years passed. Lore and Beauty were still the best of friends, and nothing would ever change that. Ever.

Leaning back, she ghosted her fingers over Beauty's sunken cheeks and shook her head. "You look awful."

"I feel awful," Beauty replied with a laugh, tears still running down her cheeks. "You look like... like..."

A goddess. The word was there, even though she knew that Beauty wouldn't say it. She knew what she looked like and how incredibly fortunate she was to look like this when all the other people she cared about had suffered so much.

A single instance of death wasn't enough suffering for her to have earned this. Not when so many others had lived and continued onward.

"I'm here now," Lore whispered, brushing aside what was left unsaid between them. "I'm going to fix this."

"How?"

Lore shrugged. "Like I always do, I suppose. I'll figure it out along the way."

Ever the supportive friend, Beauty gave her a nod and firmly agreed. "Of course you will. I never questioned it for a second."

And then Lore realized that Beauty had only looked at her. The tree had likely blocked her companion from Beauty's gaze, and that meant her friend hadn't realized who she'd brought. The shadows in Beauty's eyes said the same thing. She thought Lore had been too late. She thought that by Lore returning here, that meant that she hadn't found Abraxas.

So Lore stood to the side and held out her arm for Beauty to follow her pointed finger.

Abraxas stood with his arms lax at his sides. He didn't even look at Beauty's father, who still held the crossbow trained upon him. Instead, he had eyes only for them. Soft eyes that were currently locked on their dearest friend, who thought he had died.

The air caught in Beauty's throat. She stepped forward once, twice, her eyes wide as though she were seeing a ghost.

"Is it really you?" she asked, her voice heavy with unshed tears. "But you... You said you were going away to die."

And her powerful, stoic, never ending pillar of strength dragon crumbled. Abraxas's features fell as he stared at the woman who had been loyal to them both for such a long time, and then he spread his arms wide. "I'm sorry I made you think that, Beauty."

They came together as only dear friends could. Beauty wrapped her arms around him and held him tight against her. Abraxas looked so large as he folded himself around Beauty, his hands so gentle, as if he was afraid he might hurt her with his claws or his powerful grip.

Even Beauty's father lowered his weapon as he stared at his daughter sobbing in the arms of this man.

"Who are you?" he asked, staring at Lore as she tried her best not to cry again.

She didn't know if she should answer. Beauty's father deserved the truth, of course, but he also didn't need to know everything that his daughter had been up to. What if Beauty hadn't told him about her part in all this? What if Lore was the one who let all the secrets out?

It was Beauty who turned to her father and choked out, "It's them, Da. They came home."

There was no way to know if the old man understood what his daughter was telling him. His eyes widened, though, and then he cleared his throat. "I'll finish up. You bring them down, little one, and I'll get everything we need."

And then he left as though he hadn't just been holding a crossbow to their heads, saying that he was going to kill them at any moment.

"How things have changed," she murmured as she watched him leave the house. "I remember you saying that he was a kindly old man who was afraid to do anything that would change Tenebrous for the better."

"A lot has changed since you've been gone," Beauty agreed. "Him most of all. There's so much I have to tell you, but first, why don't we all get somewhere safer?"

It was left unsaid that Lore and Abraxas would be perfectly safe if they stayed out here. No one cared if magical creatures were investigating an abandoned home. In fact, Lore thought maybe others would be more likely to join if they saw them standing here.

The sad thing was that Beauty herself would be in danger. In the place where she grew up.

Lore had the strangest sense of déjà vu, as though she'd been here before. And she supposed, in a way, she had. This was the very place where she had been in danger for such a long time, with humans hunting her down because she was an elf. Now the mortals were hunted.

She'd thought maybe there would be a small sense of justice in her chest. That it was right for the humans to run and hide when they had been the ones doing this for years. Instead, all it did was make her feel rather sad.

No one needed to experience what she had. No one needed to know what it felt like for their homes to no longer be safe. Knowing more people lived that life now? It made her heart hurt.

"Let's go," she said, her eyes flicking to the door. "Where are we going, exactly? There are very few places here that are safe, it seems."

Beauty nodded. "Borovoi had one last trick up his sleeve, apparently. He took the magic of this house with him when he left, but there was more to this building than he let on."

"You knew Borovoi?" Abraxas asked, a frown on his face.

"Everyone knew Borovoi. But he helped me get ready for the bridal trials. Same as Lore."

"How terrible," Abraxas muttered. "That man had his fingers in more than I ever gave him credit for."

"Which is precisely why I said we needed to come here," Lore said. "I'd like to point out that I was right and that Borovoi didn't just leave everyone to their own devices and then run."

Beauty coughed into her hand. "He sort of did. I mean, he's not here anymore. No one knows where to find him. But I will say he left us a safe place to hide. So I suppose the true answer is a bit in the middle of your opinions?"

Though she and her dragon were still glaring at each other, at least they could let this go. Lore shrugged first, and Abraxas grunted.

"Fine," she said. "I suppose we were both right, then."

The bubble of laughter that erupted from Beauty was music to her ears. She'd thought she might never hear that sound again, and Lore had forgotten how much she loved it.

"I missed you two so much," Beauty said while shaking her head.

"Especially mediating your arguments. The two of you are worse than children, sometimes. Follow me, and try not to argue about who goes through the door first, would you?"

How easily they slipped back into their old ways. Lore had thought maybe someone would be uncomfortable, but they weren't. Not in the slightest.

Shaking her head, she watched as Abraxas held out his arm for her to go first. Clearly indicating that she needed to follow Beauty and he wouldn't take no for an answer.

A childish part of her wanted to stand right where she was, fold her arms over her chest, and make him beg her to go first. After all, that's what they did, apparently. They argued.

Instead, she gave him a bright smile and marched after Beauty, who disappeared into the side of the tree. The same door that had led Lore to the first party where they had met.

She paused only for a moment, luxuriating in the way her heart pinched at the memory. This was where everything had begun, and now she was here again. Starting another impossible journey by walking through a door in a tree.

She took a deep breath and plunged ahead.

CHAPTER 9

Abraxas would follow them to the very ends of the earth if that was what they required of him. He adored both of these women in very different ways. But holding Beauty in his arms after he'd left her in tears? Ah, it soothed the ache in his soul that he had been carrying for far too many months. She didn't deserve to be treated the way he'd treated her at the end.

He was glad she could forgive him. And that's what it felt like. Her tears soaked through his shirt and her words had been muffled against his shoulder, but he knew forgiveness when he felt it.

That little human was important to him. They all were. Each one of them was the family that he'd never gotten to have as a child. Losing them would be like losing a limb.

As it had been.

He rubbed a hand over his heart, wondering what the dwarf would have said to them. Goliath wouldn't have let Lore go to the dragon isles on her own in the first place. He'd have beaten Draven and ended up there adventuring with all the others.

That dwarf hadn't known what fear tasted like. Not even in the end. He'd changed the way their world worked, and he hadn't been alive to even realize it.

As they all walked through the tree and headed down into what he could only assume was Borovoi's basement, he swore he felt Goliath's spirit walking with them.

The dwarf wouldn't be quiet as he clambered down the stairs. His boots would strike hard and his laughter would have filled the dimly lit place.

"Stop looking so serious, dragon," he would have said. "The underground makes you uncomfortable? Good. It should. The ceiling could fall down on your head at any moment, and no one would know what happened."

No one would, and that was why Abraxas hated being underground like this. It always made him feel like he was seconds from being buried alive.

But the women weren't nervous, so he supposed he had no place to be either. As much as he wanted to turn right back around and tell them he'd wait for them outside, he knew he had to be here. Wasn't that his purpose, after all? He was their protector and he would remain their protector until the end of all time.

Sighing, he rubbed the back of his neck and stayed as still as possible while Beauty lit a few candles that lined the walls.

"It takes a lot of light to keep the whole place looking somewhat presentable," she said as she meandered through. "Borovoi forgot to tell us that the whole place was massive. He just offered a safe place to stay, so Da and I quickly said yes. We know what it's like for our people out there, and we were so afraid of what would happen if we didn't..."

Her words trailed off, and no one needed them to be said.

Gruffly, Abraxas added, "You'd think for all the work you did with Margaret, she would have at least given you and your father asylum."

"No one got that." Beauty's lips pressed into a thin line. "No one that helped her was given any kindness at all, in fact. Most of us tried to ask for that, considering that we were all fighters. But no. The few who dared to ask her in person never came back. And eventually, we all stopped trying."

A woman without honor had no place at the head of the table. Abraxas shook his head, then nudged Lore.

She glanced up at him, those lovely starlight eyes all filled with guilt. He'd known this would be hard for her. "Why don't we save their candles?"

She blinked. "I thought we weren't using magic?"

"Knowing Borovoi, he has the whole place shielded. I think, of anywhere in this kingdom, this might be the safest place to use your magic as you wish."

Beauty turned toward them with a bright grin. "You've gotten it under control?"

She'd done more than that. Abraxas felt his chest swell with pride, knowing that Lore was more than just the person everyone thought she would be. The magic inside of her was almost impossible to explain to anyone who hadn't seen it before. She'd come back from the brink of death more times than he could count, and because of that, he thought perhaps she had seen so much more than any of them could imagine.

Lore nodded, her cheeks burning bright red. "I've gotten it under control. Now please, allow me."

She lifted her hands and light glimmered at her fingertips. The glowing orbs pulled off her skin and illuminated the corners of the room, gathering together to hang from the center like a chandelier. Each light solidified as he watched, popping into existence like glass.

"They'll stay that way now," Lore added in explanation. "Whenever it's dark, they'll light up for you. And if you're done with them, just tap on them. They'll go dark again."

Beauty's eyes widened, and she stared at the magical lights with her mouth slightly ajar. "Beautiful."

"They are useful," Lore corrected, though her cheeks were still bright after the compliment. "But I suppose useful things can be beautiful as well."

He glanced around the room and noted the root cellar they all stood inside. Beauty and her father had done their best to make it seem more like a home. There were curtains hanging from the ceilings to mark off different rooms, and furniture that must have come from their house before it had burned to the ground. There were small parts of his friend all around him. Paintings, little drawings that might have been sketches of her father, and so much energy put into making a root cellar a house.

It was a shame their lives had come to this. Abraxas rubbed his chest to banish the ache that grew. Beauty should have been able to live in a home of her own, or stay in the castle with Zephyr. She deserved so much more than this.

"Come on," Beauty said, gesturing with her hand for them to follow her. "When was the last time you ate?"

His stomach growled at the thought.

Both women laughed at him, their eyes sparkling with joy. And though he knew he was the butt of their joke right now, he couldn't help but find it pleasant to see them like this. They were so happy with each other, as if no time had passed at all.

He'd be a joke if they kept smiling like that.

Beauty brought them to a makeshift kitchen. There was no stove, nor were there any ovens, but there was food on the shelves that would keep, potatoes mostly, it seemed. The long table in the middle had six chairs around it, clearly more than she or her father needed.

"Sit," Beauty said as she bustled about. "We don't have anything fresh, nothing to cook it with, but Da has gotten very good at smoking meat."

"As much as I'd love food," Abraxas said while gently sitting down on a chair. "I think it would be wise for you to keep yours. I'll hunt later."

"I can feed you, Abraxas."

He glanced at the meager wall of food and arched a brow. "You have forgotten how much a dragon eats, I see."

"I haven't forgotten a thing about either of you." Beauty turned around, hip pressed against a shelf, her arms crossed over her chest.

And he realized how tired she looked. How the dark bags under her eyes were deeper than ever, and how her clothing hung off her body. She was exhausted, and they didn't need her helping them. They were both well fed, well rested, even though the emotional turmoil of being here wore on them.

They were fine. She was not.

He stood and walked up to her. With brisk hands, he rubbed them up and down her cold arms, and then turned her toward the seat he'd just vacated. "Sit down."

"It's my home, Abraxas. I can welcome you into it."

"But it's not your home, now is it?" He bent his knees so he could look her in the eyes. "Sit down with Lore and let me get you something to eat. You are about to fall over, and you have clearly not been taking care of yourself. We're here now, Beauty. You are not alone anymore."

Tears turned her eyes glassy, but she didn't let them fall. Instead, she sniffed hard and nodded before walking over to sit beside Lore.

Abraxas eyed the shelves, not quite sure what to make of the jars he saw before him. He'd never been a good cook, so at least he wasn't expected to pull everything together so they could eat something tasty. He was much more suited to roasting an animal with flames and calling it good at that.

A jar of peaches would do. And there was cheese there. A memory flashed in his mind, one of Zander's snacks that he'd have the maids bring him. Fruit, cheese, bread, an easy and safe combination.

Gathering up all his ingredients in his arms, he turned toward the ladies to see them both watching him with strange expressions on their faces.

"What?" he asked.

"Nothing," Lore replied with a soft smile. "Just watching you work."

Now it was his turn for his cheeks to burn a bright red as he set everything in front of them. "Come on, you two. Surely you have better things to do."

Beauty pillowed her chin on her fist and shook her head. "Not really. It's nice to see a man working around here again."

He snorted and tried his very best to ignore what she was saying. "Don't you have questions for us? Where we've been? What's been happening? You could tell us everything that happened here as well, you know. Instead of staring at me like that."

"Like what?"

He bared his teeth. "You know exactly what I'm talking about, woman."

Both of them reared back and glared at him. Lore was the first to break saying, "Did you just 'woman' her?"

He rolled his eyes up to the ceiling and took a deep, steadying breath. "Maybe I will join your father outside. He seemed like he was better company."

They both burst into bright laughter, and he tried his best to smile along with them. But the truth was, he felt horribly out of place. Abraxas was more used to being the bodyguard, the protector, not the man who had two women smiling at him and devouring his body with their eyes. Enough was enough.

Grumbling under his breath, he got to work opening the jar and getting plates out for the two incessantly annoying women. "Are you both done yet?"

"We're done," Lore said with a wheeze. "I promise, we're done."

After that, they all settled into a much more companionable silence. He sat down across from them and watched as they ate the food he'd prepared, his hands itching to do more than what he'd already done. He wanted to help them. To do whatever it took to make their lives easier and better. After all, what good was he if he couldn't do that?

But they didn't need him right now. They needed to connect with each other again, through laughter and bubbling noises that filled the root cellar with a happiness these walls had likely not seen in ages.

And for a few moments, it felt like nothing had happened. Like there wasn't a war outside, and nobody hunted them. They were just three friends who hadn't seen each other in a very long time, finally getting to catch up and talk.

He watched them both with a smile that only wilted when Beauty asked about those they'd left behind.

"And Draven?" Beauty sipped at a cup of water. He'd gotten them both when their voices started getting scratchy. "He left with you, didn't he? No one knew where he went, but I was there when Margaret got angry about it. She was certain he'd gone with you."

"I'm sure she thought he was under her thumb, considering he's also an elf." Lore rolled her eyes. "Of course he went with me. I couldn't shake the man."

Abraxas let out a grumble. "I still don't like him."

"Yes, I imagine you have more reason than ever not to like him," Lore replied, waggling her eyebrows. "He's got his sights set on a little one who is very near and dear to your heart."

"She's your daughter, too," he muttered.

Lore shrugged. "And I did foolish things in my youth. I'm not going to tell her what she can and cannot do."

Beauty's eyes watched them both, widening ever further with each word. "But she's just a baby."

They talked over each other immediately.

"That's exactly what I've been trying to tell Lore."

"Dragons age differently. She looks our age."

Silence stretched between them as they both glared at each other while Beauty tried to soak in that knowledge. It wasn't exactly well known, and he didn't want just anyone realizing how easy it was for his children to be taken advantage of. They looked like adults, and that would help protect them in most situations.

Other than Draven's situation, that was. The elf had better be keeping his hands to himself, or so help him—

"Well, that's something else." Beauty sipped her water again, shaking her head. "I wouldn't have guessed that turn of events."

"None of us did," he muttered, leaning back in his chair with his fists curled at his sides. He wanted to punch something at the thought.

If Draven even thought about touching his daughter, who was far younger than was suitable, then he would find a way to kill that elf, bring him back to life, and then kill him again. Maybe a hundred times. Lore could do it.

Lore reached across the table and patted his hand. "I'm sure Draven is being a gentleman. He wouldn't push her if she didn't want it."

"She doesn't know what she wants."

"Yes, well, few of us do at that age."

If she kept smirking at him like that, he was going to bend her over his knee.

Though, they both froze when Beauty cleared her throat and asked the question he'd been afraid she'd ask. "Do either of you know where Zephyr is?"

Her fingers toyed with the condensation on the sides of her cup. She didn't look up, as if she was afraid of what she'd see on their faces.

He glanced at Lore. Would she tell Beauty that they knew where Zephyr was? It might be too much for Beauty to hear that the young man she was in love with was being tortured right now, and that there was nothing any of them could do about it just yet.

Those big pools of starlight stared back at him, and he already knew she'd tell Beauty everything. Their friend had a right to know, even if it hurt.

Lore swallowed hard and replied, "I know where he is. I've seen him.

Talked with him. The power inside me lets me walk through the realm as if a mile is but a small leap. I know where he is, Beauty. And we're going to get him back. I promise you that."

CHAPTER 10

Beauty's father returned and with him came an air of discomfort. Lore knew that the old man had to know who she was and what she could do. Or maybe he didn't. Maybe he wanted some time with his daughter to rest, or at least understand who was staying with them now.

The last thing she needed was to feel like a burden.

Lore excused herself and Abraxas followed her out of the root cellar. Neither of them had to worry too much in Tenebrous. As long as she kept her face hidden, then they were safer than Beauty or her father.

"Do you think you can keep yourself hidden for a while?" Abraxas asked, his stomach still rumbling.

"Go hunting," she said with a laugh. "Everyone for miles around will know that you're starving and wonder why both of us look so well fed if you can't keep your belly quiet."

"Where will you be?"

He stood with the moon outlining his form. His dark hair shifted in the breeze and his broad shoulders nearly blotted out the moon.

Lore smiled. "I'm going to go home for a bit. See if there's anything left in there that might be useful."

His gaze softened, and he tugged her into his arms. "Stay out of trouble," he whispered against her hair. "I won't be long."

"I know you won't."

Lore lingered on their kiss, pressing herself against his body as though this was goodbye. Because neither of them ever knew if it would be goodbye. They still feared losing each other, and she still feared what it would mean if he didn't come back.

Abraxas let their hands clutch each other until the last moment. Her fingers felt empty without his to hold on to.

Sighing, Lore turned away from Borovoi's home and tightened her hood around her head. She could so easily disappear into the depths of Tenebrous. Hadn't she done it a thousand times in her life? Hadn't she walked these streets with Goliath at her side as they ducked away from Umbral Soldiers?

The memories walked beside her as she made her way through the dark streets. There were few people out and about these days. No humans were left to keep the taverns open or the bars bustling at this time of night. Instead, she was faced with a ghost town.

Familiar rungs appeared on the side of a house she'd hoped would still be standing. As she had her entire life, Lore climbed up the side of the building and crouched on the rooftops.

Above her head, far on the horizon, she saw the outline of a dragon. Just as she had years ago. Although now the image filled her with a sense of peace and longing rather than fear and dread.

He knew it was a risk for someone to see him. And yet he still had let his shadow pass in front of the white fluffy clouds and the silver rays of the moon, just in case she needed to see him.

Perhaps he'd already suspected her fears. That she'd have to go through the city and that someone would recognize her. Or that she would find the places she once loved already burned to the ground. He had to know how much it would kill her to see that.

And see it she would.

Lore raced across the rooftops like a woman born of wind. Her feet barely touched the shingles as she moved throughout the city and learned the new patterns and pathways that would lead her to where she wanted to go.

She had to turn back multiple times because the house she'd expected to be there was gone. But eventually she made it to her side of the city. The same place where she'd sat every single night, smoking her elfweed, talking to Goliath on the other side of the street.

As she sank down into her old spot, she shuddered at the sight in front of her. The home where Goliath had painted his rising sun was gone. The ashes still floated in the air when she sat down. They'd gathered on the rooftop like a fine layer of snow and no wind had blown them away yet.

She could still see him. He'd leaned out that window every time she was here, complaining about the smell of her smoke or laughing at the way she'd blown rings at him. He had been perfect. More than that, he'd been the best friend she'd ever had.

And now he was gone.

There was nothing she could do about it, and she knew she couldn't pull him back from that dark place. How would she even find him? Would it be right to even do so? He had no body to return to, no life waiting for him.

And then she'd left. She'd headed out to the dragon isles and left all that they'd fought for and left everyone else under the rule of a woman that neither of them had really trusted. Margaret had betrayed them all, and it felt a little like Goliath had died for nothing.

That warmongering bitch would get what was coming to her. Lore would avenge the memory of her friend if only for this moment, staring at the home where he had rested his head.

Did Margaret even remember? Did she even know that she'd burned down his house? They'd all mourned him together. She'd seen Margaret's face when she realized that her cause had been the catalyst to his death. She knew that Margaret felt guilt after she'd said goodbye to Goliath.

But in the end, had she done anything to make amends for it, or had she simply continued down the same path that had gotten him killed?

Shaking her head, she leaned back on her hands and stared up at the sky instead. "I miss you," she whispered into the wind, hoping that her words would somehow find his spirit. "I've spent far too long looking up at the clouds and wanting to go anywhere but here. Now that I'm older, now that I've seen too much, I have realized that I didn't appreciate what I had with you. Seeing you there in that window used to give me so much peace, and now I don't even have that."

Tears burned in her eyes, but she didn't wipe them away. It felt good for them to drip down her cheeks, even if it meant he was gone. She needed this moment to break.

Sniffling, she eventually stopped herself. There was no use in crying about what had already happened. She had her moment, and now it was time to keep going.

Lore had hidden more than a few spelled items in her old attic room. Some of them would be useless by now. The magic only stuck for a short amount of time before the spells would unravel. But the potions were still good, and a few of the homemade bombs that she'd tried to get to work. They weren't reliable, but they would do something when thrown at another person's head.

Skittering over the roof, she went to the grimy window and pulled it open.

Only to freeze at what she saw inside.

It was supposed to be full of dust and strange creatures in jars. A small cot that was covered in bird droppings, after all this time, would rest against the back wall, where she'd hidden most of her things. The other shelving units were full of whatever nonsense the owner had forgotten about. Mostly creepy and terrifying things.

Except now, the room was clean. It was filled with colorful fabric and hand painted golden stars. A few orbs still danced in the air to give off light that sparkled through the swaths of fabric and made the stars look realistic. Toys littered the floor. Each one very colorful and depicting a different kind of magical creature. Some were dolls, others were puzzles, some even looked like they had to be put back together to be played with.

No bed. No darkness. Only a warm room full of light for children to play in.

So. They'd finally sold the house. Or perhaps the previous owner had died and someone had taken it upon themselves to turn the room into something that breathed again.

Still, it made her heart twist in her chest to realize the last bit of her childhood was gone. Lore and her mother had hidden in this attic for years, and now there was no one left. Her things were gone. Her cot. Not that any of the items left had any significant meaning, but they were still hers.

Now she had nowhere else to go. There was no bed waiting for her if this all failed. There was no hidden attic to hide in or a dwarf across the street who would share his dinner with her.

She was the goddess of this realm, a half elf born to change the very fabric of time. And the woman she had once been was gone.

Stepping away from the window, she let it close so no one inside the residence would question what was happening. She didn't want to harm the safety of the family or make them feel as though this house wasn't perfect for them. It clearly was.

Perhaps it had never been her home. Just the place for her to rest her head.

Staggering away, she stood at the edge of the roof and stared down at the cobblestone streets below. There was a time when those streets were full of Umbral Soldiers. Now, there were only a few magical creatures walking toward their homes. They kept their heads down, not wanting to be seen by anyone else. But they were there. Without shackles.

Her mind raced with the realization that this was what they'd been fighting for all along. A life for magical creatures without humans hunting them. And yes, this was actually a fix for the problem. Margaret wasn't entirely wrong.

The magical creatures were now free. She'd just gone about it in the most bloodthirsty way possible.

Lore didn't know how to fix this just yet. She didn't know how to make it harder for the mortals to wrestle their way into control, but she also didn't know how to get everyone to live side by side peacefully.

It was all... so much.

Pressing a hand to her forehead, she weaved forward. Flirting with the danger of plummeting four stories toward the hard ground. She wouldn't. Her magic would stop her long before she struck the ground, but she was so tired.

Lore wasn't smart enough to fix all this on her own. But she also had no idea who to ask for help.

Now was not the time to spiral. She had so much work to do, and just because a few old memories were gone, didn't mean she could break. Lore needed time, yes, she had to figure out all the nuances of this new kingdom that she'd left behind. But she would do a disservice to those who had come before if she let those thoughts overwhelm her.

The street below her cleared of people, and she let her intrusive thoughts win.

Lore took a step off the roof and fell. The wind whistled in her hair for too short of a time, nothing like riding on the back of her favorite dragon. And when she landed in a crouch on the hard stone, she barely felt the ache in her knees that creaked as she stood back up.

She wasn't the woman she had been before, either. She just had to remind herself of that.

Walking the streets at near dawn was a strange experience. She kept her hood up, fully expecting vendors to be setting out their wares and getting ready for the day. But there were few vendors left.

The only stragglers this early that she saw wore hardened expressions of weariness. They pulled whatever they could out of their homes and set it on the street for people to buy straight out of the pot. As though there wasn't even enough food to sell these days unless it was cooked into a suspicious-looking mush.

A few of them tried to get her to buy something, but she didn't want to risk the food.

Lore met Abraxas at the front of Borovoi's house. He leaned against the worn building, ankles crossed and arms looped around himself. He had his head down, almost as though he were starting to fall asleep. But he heard her quickly enough. His head jolted up, and he frowned at her.

"You're late."

"We didn't set a time to meet," she said wearily. "I had a few things to check over, you know that."

"And I didn't know where you had gone or what you were doing. You can't run off like that, Lore. Not until everyone knows you're back."

"I was careful." She cupped his cheek in her palm, drawing him close so she could smell the brimstone and fire scent that always eased her mind. "I went back to the attic. Someone lives there now. They turned it into a beautiful little playroom for their children."

As always, he heard the tension in her voice. Abraxas scooped the back of her neck and drew her tighter against him. "You should have had that as well. I'm sorry you didn't."

"I'm not. Those children deserve a life regardless of how I led mine. I'm glad they're happy." Her voice thickened. "Goliath's house is gone."

"Ah, Lore." He drew her fully into his arms then, tucking her face against his neck so she didn't have to see the world around them. "I'm sorry for that, too."

"You didn't burn it."

"No, but I set the standard for burning things to the ground, now didn't I?"

She supposed in a way he had, but not like he was thinking. Zander had burned entire cities and the people in them, not just the houses that had once held people.

"It's all right," she whispered against his neck. "I'm all right."

"Are you really?"

She shook her head once. "No. But I will be."

Abraxas drew back and cast a critical glance up and down her body. He squeezed her shoulders, as if that might help ground her. And surprisingly, it did.

He always understood when she wanted to talk, and when she wanted to leave it alone. Abraxas took her hand and led her into the house, then into the depths of the root cellar where Beauty and her father were waiting.

The old man sat at the table, his steepled fingers pressed against his mouth as he stared at them. Finally, when she sat in front of him, he set his hands down on the wood.

"So you're her then?" he asked, his voice a low grumble.

"I'm her."

He paled at her words and seemed to shake a little when she sat down in front of him. "And you're here to help us? Truly? You realize that's going against your kind and everything they stand for."

"I do." She gave him a sad little smile. "Just because they are elves does not mean that they are right. And you forgot, I'm half elf myself. Denying the humans means denying half of who I am."

Beauty's father ground his teeth before nodding again. "Then I'll tell you everything I know."

CHAPTER 11

Abraxas settled at the table with Lore and focused on the elderly man in front of them. Where Beauty's father had looked strong holding the crossbow, now he seemed to have aged years. The old man had been holding a lot of stress, apparently, and had finally let it go.

"There are more people like us, sprinkled around the kingdom. Mostly those of us who had the means to hide when this all first started." He winced. "It should have been more. I wish we had been able to hide others, but we didn't have anywhere else to put them."

Leaning back in his chair, Abraxas crossed his arms over his chest and tried not to glance around them at the large root cellar that had multiple makeshift rooms in it. They didn't have room? They had plenty.

But if the man wanted to pretend they didn't have enough room for all those who had been lost to Margaret's forces, then he would let him pretend. Now was not the time to point out the obvious.

Beauty sat down next to her father and placed a hand on the old man's back. "We couldn't have gotten them to us, anyway. Margaret came in the middle of the night. By the time we realized the houses were burning, it was too late. So many people ran out into the streets, trying to get away from the smoke, and then they were just gone."

"But we have a network," her father interjected. "A network of those who are still here and are trying to get the humans back from her clutches. I hope you might be able to help us with that."

Abraxas glanced at Lore, curious to see what she would say. Obviously, his elf wanted to help. She wanted to bring the humans back home and fill this city with its denizens again. But they had another reason for being here.

Helping the humans wasn't in the plan. They had to get to Zephyr first, and Lore wanted an army. Not another task.

Lore's eyes had narrowed on the old man, her teeth worrying the inside of her cheek. "You know I can't do that."

"You can, and you have no reason not to."

"I have every reason not to, and every reason to help. There is a strange dichotomy in my life, old man. You would do well to remember it."

"All I am asking is a few moments of your time and your power. With that, we could find out where they are and free them. If we do that, then we can move forward with a better plan afterwards." His hands had curled into fists, but he put them underneath the table when he caught Abraxas staring at them. "Surely you can waste a few moments of your time to help us."

"I can't waste much time at all while I'm here." Lore pointed at Beauty. "And I'll need her."

"For what reason?"

Beauty opened her mouth to interject, but Abraxas caught her gaze and shook his head. This wasn't an argument for them. This was between two leaders of Tenebrous and Umbra. They needed to figure it out on their own.

"Why do you need my daughter?" Beauty's father pressed yet again.

"Because I intend to collect the rightful king of this land. She would be the only person he will be interested in being around after what he's gone through, and trust me when I say, he has gone through enough. She needs to be there for him the moment I rescue him or I'm afraid he will have no reason to continue living." Lore leaned across the table and stared directly into his eyes. "I will help whatever humans I come across along the way to save him. You have my word. But we have to look at the bigger picture here."

"Which is?"

Lore sighed and tossed up her arms. She leaned back in her chair like she was arguing with a child, and Abraxas had to cover his mouth with a fist. She was arguing with a child in comparison. Both he and Lore were hundreds of years old compared to this man's sixty years. Though he understood why Beauty's father refused to budge.

He wanted his people back. He wanted them to be alive and well and back in their homes without wondering who was going to attack them next. And could they blame him for it?

"Let me spell it out for you, then. I will bring back the king of your people. The one who should be making deals with the magical creatures and speaking on your behalf. Right now, you are a snake with its head cut off." Lore sliced her hand through the air like a blade. "I want to give you back your mouth. And you will be the first person who talks with him once he is healed. I can promise you that. But I cannot gather your people without doing this first."

Beauty's father leaned back in his chair and mimicked her position. "Understood."

"That is a good enough deal for you?"

"It's the only one I'm getting, I assume."

"It's the only option I can see working. We cannot fight Margaret without an army, and we cannot gather an army without hope. Is there enough of you for that?"

Interesting question. Abraxas watched the man swallow but then nod.

"Most of us are old," Beauty's father said. "Most of us are nobility or those who had money. We are not fighters, but we will fight if necessary. Many of us are not... pleased with the developments and change in this kingdom."

"Then you will not fight." Lore stood and cracked her back. "I need soldiers, not soft handed politicians. But those who have any history in it, then please, let them know they will be needed."

They all stood up as though Lore had dismissed them.

Beauty's father gave her a sharp nod and then blew out a long breath. "All right. When do you want to leave?"

"Now, if possible. I don't have time to wait and neither does Zephyr." She did pause at least and smile at Beauty. "Any chance you could be ready soon?"

With a bright grin, Beauty was already racing away from them. Of course, she'd want to go on an adventure one more time.

Although, Abraxas wasn't so sure this was a good idea.

Drawing Lore away from the others, he muttered underneath his breath, "Do you know what you're doing?"

"I do."

"Are you sure?"

And there it was. The haunted expression that spread across her face and deepened the hollows underneath her eyes. "I have to get out of this place, Abraxas. I can't stay in what used to be my home and what is no longer my city. Zephyr needs us. The kingdom is falling apart. I can't stay here any longer waiting for someone to do something. It's time for us to move."

He didn't want her to feel like this. But mostly, he wanted her to realize that her home was with him. He was her home, just as she was his.

Drawing her closer, he pressed a kiss to her forehead and sighed. "Home isn't a place, remember?"

He'd said that to her once. Home wasn't a place, but a person. They were together in this and always would be. And yet, she seemed to have forgotten that in the shadows and muck of Tenebrous.

Lore pressed closer to him and nodded. "You're right. When we are all together again, I will breathe. But right now, we need Beauty to be our guide."

"Elven stronghold?" he suggested. "That might be the only place where we can rest."

"The elves are the ones doing this, and I cannot help but assume they are aware of all the places that we might hide." She took a steadying breath and then stood on her own, her face a mask that even he could not read. "We will, unfortunately, have to go about this the hard way."

"I never questioned that this would be easy." Though he laughed at the thought, he wasn't exactly excited about it.

Abraxas had forgotten just how difficult it was to trudge through the wilds with little food and heavy packs. He had thought they were past that part of their lives, but apparently, camping it was.

Beauty rushed toward them, dragging three bags that clanked like she'd stuffed them full of metal. "I've been preparing for this, just in case you came back."

"Preparing?" he asked, amused as she struggled to get to them.

"One can never be too prepared, dragon." She flashed him a bright grin. "And in case you forgot, you were the one without a pack during our last journey and sorely regretting your decision."

"I don't need reminding," he growled. Abraxas grabbed the three heavy bags from her before she threw her back out and lifted them for each woman to take. "Where are we heading?"

"To Solis Occasum," Lore said. "And whatever we find along the way will be part of the journey, I suppose."

"To save Zephyr?"

She nodded.

A small whine erupted from Beauty's mouth before she pressed her hands against it to contain the sound. "I'm so sorry. I just... I never thought I'd see him again."

He had nothing to say to that, and neither did Lore. There was too much happening and they couldn't afford to get emotional. Even when Beauty's father tearfully said goodbye to his daughter. They must not have planned to part so soon, and Abraxas knew the old man must be worried about what would happen.

After all, Beauty was no longer herself. None of them were.

He couldn't watch. Abraxas turned away from the women and started toward the tree where he would wait. He couldn't feel like this.

He couldn't get himself all worked up when there was so much left for them to do and fix.

A warm hand landed on his shoulder, and he turned to see Beauty's father had followed him.

"Here," the old man gruffed, handing him a piece of parchment that was worn around the edges. "It's a map. Beauty knows this city well, but she gets turned around sometimes. Best if you have something else to check her with."

"Thank you." Abraxas cleared his throat and rolled the map up in his hand. Should he say something? The old man just awkwardly stared at him. "We know where we're going. It's a start."

Finally, the old man cleared his throat and said, "Take care of her. You hear me? She's the only thing I've got left."

Ah, shit. There was a time when Abraxas would have shrugged that off. But now he thought of Nyx and how he'd left her alone with Tanis, and the guilt that still rode his shoulders that he wasn't there with his children when they needed him to be their father. Sure, they weren't a kingdom that needed saving, but he was supposed to be there for everything with them. And all he'd done was put them aside for the greater good.

Voice raspy and emotions choking him, Abraxas nodded. "I'll look after her as if she were my own."

Perhaps his words confused the old man. Abraxas knew he looked rather young and not at all like someone who had children, especially grown children at that, but Beauty's father quickly regained his composure and nodded. "Good. I'll have to hunt you down if she dies, boy."

Boy.

When was the last time anyone had called him that? Abraxas pressed his lips into a thin line so he didn't laugh, and nodded at the old man. At the very least, he'd make Beauty's father feel like he was involved.

He could do that for the man. He could make him feel like he was the hero of this story.

"Ready?" Lore's voice sliced through their quiet moment.

Beauty trailed along behind her, and even though her eyes were ringed with red from crying, she appeared brighter than she had since they'd arrived. He knew adventure ran through her veins as thoroughly as any other. She was not a young woman who enjoyed staying still.

Abraxas nodded. "Ready. We'll have to get out of Tenebrous during the day. Both of you keep your hoods up, and if everything goes to shit, I'll keep everyone off you while you run."

Lore rolled her eyes. "No one is going to recognize us."

He wouldn't be so certain of that.

They left Borovoi's home behind with only the slightest bit of hesitation. Abraxas had no interest in looking at the cursed place any longer, nor did he want to stay underground. But beyond, Tenebrous was almost more dangerous.

The city had woken, and that meant there were so many opportunities for someone to notice them. The people who wandered the streets wore no hoods, and the three of them stuck out. Eyes were on them, and Abraxas immediately felt every muscle in his body lock up.

It took only three blocks for someone to start following them. Five for the creatures to call out and ask for them to remove their hoods.

Lore glanced back at him and he knew what she wanted. He took his own hood off first, turning toward the men with a wicked grin. "Gentlemen! What can I help you with?"

His size should have been enough to deter them, but it wasn't. This city had become home to the creatures, and though they were kinder than the humans, he wondered if it wasn't by that much.

One of the men who wandered closer had the face of a rat, whiskers and all. He had no idea what kind of creature this man was, but he seemed even less humanoid than the others.

Baring his teeth in a snarl, Abraxas loomed over him. "We're just passing through."

"And we're just making sure you ain't smuggling humans out of Tenebrous. You know how much money those bring in? If anyone's making the profit, it's us." The rat man jabbed a thumb into his chest, then sneered up at Abraxas. "You wouldn't be stealing from Tenebrous, stranger. Would ya?"

"Not stealing anything."

"Then you won't mind if they take off their hoods?" The rat leaned around him to leer at the two women, and clearly they were women. Even cloaks couldn't hide how small they were, nor Beauty's curvy hips.

Abraxas was ready to snap the rat's neck. He had no problem with violence or killing to keep his women safe. But Lore lifted her hand and pulled her hood off. What he stared at was not... Lore. Not quite.

She'd somehow changed her features, just slightly. Her ears were longer, her hair more red than gold, her eyes twisting into a green rather than the blue he loved so dearly. She smiled at the rat, her gaze serene and soft. Not at all like herself.

"We had hoped to keep our journey quiet," she said, her voice light and airy. "I apologize if we've inconvenienced you."

He'd thought the rat man would fall under her spell, but he didn't. Instead, the man crossed his arms and nodded at Beauty. "Then who's that? You expect me to believe two elves are walking through Tenebrous with a lone bodyguard?"

With a deep snarl, Abraxas lunged at him. But Lore whispered a quiet word, and he pulled back at the last second. "They only need one bodyguard," he still growled, making sure the man knew what danger he was in.

Again, the rat only laughed. Did the man have a death wish?

Lore reached for Beauty's cloak and Abraxas could almost smell her magic. It poured out of her skin so easily now that he knew the scent, knew the feel of it as well.

And when she lowered Beauty's hood, his dear friend had tiny pointed ears. She looked right at the rat man without fear and then smiled.

"Is that suitable?" Beauty asked, her voice wavering a bit.

The rat merely tsked and turned on his heel. "Lucky day, strangers!"

CHAPTER 12

Stupid.

Lore was so stupid. Why would she take that risk?

She could have told Abraxas to punch that stupid man's muzzle right into his skull and they could have run. She'd have gotten them out of there long before anyone could find them. Lore still knew Tenebrous like the back of her hand. She could have hidden them. They would have found a place to hide while the entire city looked for them. They would have done anything and everything other than what she'd done.

She ripped the spell off of her face the moment they left the city gates. She didn't care that the marshes stood in front of them or that someone might see her. Now, what was the point? Why would she even try?

The ripples of that spell were enough. Margaret would know they were here. All she had done, everything she'd fought for, and she'd left it in the dirt of Tenebrous, just like the rest of her dignity. Changing her own appearance? That was easy magic. Changing another's? Much, much more difficult.

"Stupid," she muttered. "Moron. Fool. Why would you risk everything for something like that?"

"Lore?" Abraxas called from behind them. "Would you slow down, please?"

No, she would not slow down. They needed to put as much space between them and Tenebrous as possible. If they didn't, then Margaret's men would find them like sitting ducks. She'd put a flashing orb above their head that pointed at them. If Margaret was looking, and she was, then she'd know where to find them now.

Stomping through the muck only made her feel slightly better. She tried to focus on the here and now.

The scent of moss and mud filled her nostrils. The leather straps of her bag dug into her shoulders, but she almost didn't feel the weight at all. Her breath sawed from her lungs, making her ribs go in and out in an exaggerated fashion. She should get her breathing under control because she couldn't hear anything other than that and the thundering of her heart in her ears.

She needed to keep her senses sharp and her wits about her. Margaret would have sent her shadows and her ravens to scope out Tenebrous, and those creatures could see them from above. Which meant she needed to get them out of the marshes faster than she expected. There was only one trail that would take them out of the marsh, and that was the one path she didn't want to go.

Apparently, she would be forced to travel down her memories if she wanted to end all of this. And still, it made her heart twist in her chest.

"Lore!" Abraxas called again, and this time she heard him stomping toward her. The mud sucked at his feet, giving his position away as he did his best to catch up with her. "I said slow down!"

He caught her arm and all that anger and disgust at herself lashed out. A blast of power sent him reeling away. He stumbled a few times and then landed on his ass in the mud.

Her dragon stared up at her in shock. She stared back with wide eyes and a heaving chest that she tried to get under control, but she couldn't no matter how hard she tried.

"Are you—"

"Did you—"

They spoke over each other.

She knew what he was going to ask. Did you mean to hurt me? While she had wanted to know if she'd done just that. It wasn't right. She shouldn't be taking her anger out on him, but what else could she do? She'd put them both in danger, and maybe it would be best if she'd left them both in Tenebrous.

He wouldn't let her do that. And suddenly she felt trapped.

Everyone wanted something from her, and she'd forgotten to steel herself against that. Abraxas wanted her to be herself. Beauty wanted her to save Zephyr. Beauty's father wanted her to save the humans. Everyone wanted her to do something and she couldn't breathe anymore.

She just needed a little time to get her head back on straight. To roll herself up in whatever control she could grasp out of this situation before it was all pulled out from under her again. And she couldn't do that when he was staring at her like she'd lost her mind.

"I need a few minutes," she rasped, stumbling away from him.

"How far are you going?"

"Not far." She didn't think so. She wasn't going to run, if that's what he was asking her. "Are you all right?"

"I've survived worse." He stood, and she watched to make sure he wasn't limping or showed any sign of pain. He didn't, thank goodness. At least he was a dragon and could take a bit of a magical beating. "Are you all right?"

No.

No, she wasn't all right.

She would not be all right until this was all over and done with, and that would not happen any time soon, so if she didn't get a hold of this anxiety, it would ruin her. It would swell up over her head and threaten to drown her in her sorrows until she saw nothing but all the people she'd lost.

Swiping a hand over her mouth, she shook her head and gave him the truth. "No. No, I'm not. That spell... Margaret will know where we are. We need to move."

"I know."

"You know?" She snapped, her words echoing across the marsh. "And you said nothing? You don't care if Margaret hunts us down before we've done anything? You should be yelling at me right now!"

He didn't. Of course he did. Abraxas held his hands up as though she had pointed a weapon at him and quietly said, "You're doing enough yelling for the both of us."

She was. She knew she was and she still couldn't stop. Lore could only hope that he wouldn't be too angry at her when she returned to them, but right now, she had to get some air.

"I'll be back," she said, taking another shambling step away from him.

"Will you?"

His words hung between them, a quiet reminder of the last time she'd said that. And all the times she'd done something stupid in the same state as this.

She swallowed hard before responding. "I will do everything I can to come back to you, Abraxas. I'm not going far. I just need to remind myself why I'm doing this. To plan how to keep us all safe from Margaret. I need... I need to get my confidence back, and I don't think that's something you can help with."

His silence was damning.

Lore knew she'd made him angry with all this. They had promised she wouldn't go running off on her own during this trip, and already she was going to break that promise.

She was a terrible partner. A worse mate, and she knew that would grate on both of them. She had to prove herself to be worthy of his trust or she'd lose him. The painful truth rode on her shoulders so heavily that she stalked toward him with single-minded intent.

Grabbing the back of his neck, Lore tugged him down and kissed him hard. Not a soft kiss or even a reassuring one, but a kiss that bit at his lips and would have drawn blood if he'd let her.

"I'm not going anywhere," she said. "I just can't look at the two of you while knowing that I might have caused all our deaths with a stupid mistake that I never should have made. I need time with my thoughts, and I won't go far. You'll be able to see me the entire time. I just need to be quiet for a bit. That's all. I need to pretend that I didn't just kill my friends."

"You didn't."

"I might have." She stared up at him, eyes wide and heart in her throat. "I might have killed you. And I refuse to let that simmer in my mind while I can see you. I'll just start picturing all the ways they could murder you, Abraxas, and I won't do it any more. I can't."

He smoothed his thumb over her cheekbones. "You'll stay within sight?"

"At all times. Just give me a bit to feel better. That's all I'm asking."

And he let her go.

Lore stomped ahead of them, picking the path of least resistance that would get them far away from her home. From the memories that haunted her every step of dying friends, wars, the screams of people who fought to get their freedom and now had it. The freedom she might very well be taking away from them again.

Shouldn't she feel more guilty about that? Shouldn't she do something to ensure that the magical creatures never returned to the life they had lived before?

Except, she worried they were the problem. Her mind was so twisted up and she couldn't even guess at where to start unraveling all this.

"Mothers," she whispered, her words carrying through the marshes. "If I've ever needed you in my life, I need you now."

But no one responded to her plea.

There was a time when she'd hoped that they would have a more active presence in her life. She'd gotten her birth mother back, and her grandmother, and all the women who had come before her. That's where all this power had entered her body, through the strings and ties of them. But now, they had left her to her own devices. She had to figure this out on her own.

Instead, she reached out with her mind and let her magic spread out. She shouldn't. But Margaret already knew she was here and using magic, so what was a little more power when they already knew she was near Tenebrous?

She needed to talk to someone. And that someone was her daughter.

The thin connection looped around Nyx's thread and then she could feel her.

"Mother?"

She could almost hear Nyx as though she were standing right beside her. As though they walked together through the marsh, even though Lore knew that was impossible.

"I'm here," Lore replied, trying very hard to speak through the thick wave of tears that burned at the sound of her daughter's voice. "How are you?"

"I'm fine." Nyx sounded confused. "I didn't know you could do this."

"I can do a great many things now, and apparently this is only one of them."

How did she explain to her daughter what was happening? Nyx might have absorbed the memories of countless dragons, but she was still just a child. At heart, her daughter shouldn't know about kingdoms filled with turmoil and conflict. She didn't want to tell Nyx that she'd already risked their lives, or about the horrible feeling that still stuck to her skin after being in Tenebrous and seeing the starving people there.

All she wanted was to hear that Nyx was well, and that life had continued on in the dragon isles without them. That they were happy and well and that someone in this family was still a good person at their core.

Nyx cleared her throat, and Lore swore she heard the shuffling of leaves. "Are you all right?"

No. No, she wasn't all right. Would everyone stop asking her that?

She couldn't lie to her daughter, though. And she couldn't tell her the truth. Instead, she asked, "Has Draven been keeping his hands off you?"

"Mother!" Nyx burst into laughter and the sound soothed all the aches in Lore's chest. "You know he has. I don't know why you and Father are so worried about that. He's been a perfect gentleman."

"And why is that?"

"Because he says I'm too young for anything to happen between us, even though I've absorbed the memories of a hundred other dragons that have lived hundreds of years." Lore could practically see the eye roll Nyx ended her rant with.

"That's not entirely why." Lore stepped over a fallen log that was covered with bright green moss. "You know, it's not a mistake to learn more about each other. Even if those memories made you older than you are, which they do not, knowing that he is willing to wait only makes him more serious about you."

"What's so wrong with having a little fun?"

And so the argument continued. Lore defended Abraxas's opinion while her daughter whittled away at any logic in those arguments. It was like she had never left.

Finally, Lore found a spot that seemed safe for the night. The cave had formed out of old mud and billowing moss that must have been pushed up at some point by an air bubble in the swamp. Now it wasn't much, but it would fit the three of them for the night.

Lore leaned over and stared into the shadows, making sure there weren't any hidden creatures within before she sat down inside of it.

"It's so good to hear your voice," she whispered. And it was. It was so good to remember why she was here and what she was fighting for.

With a wave of her hand, Lore projected their images to each other.

To her surprise, they were both in the same position. She sat cross-legged in the dirt in a swamp, while Nyx had settled herself into the crux of a tree with her arms around her legs.

They stared at each other, as though they could reach through the hundreds of miles that separated them and touch.

"Mother?" Nyx whispered. "You look terrible."

"I feel terrible." Lore lifted her arms and grimaced at the sight of them. "I'm already covered in mud and I don't remember ever touching anything."

"Are you in a swamp?"

"We have to go through the swamp to get to the next part of this journey." Lore sighed. "I'm glad you're not here. It's disgusting."

"I could have sent the water away from you. Tanis has been teaching me how to use water to my whim. It's been... Interesting." Nyx made a face that said she wasn't having all that much fun with her teacher. "It was better when you were here. I liked the way you taught us to use magic. Like nature was at our beck and call."

"It is." Lore knew that elves and dragons learned magic in different ways, though. She was grateful for Tanis being there with them. "How are the other little ones?"

"Taking up all the attention."

And there it was. The reason she didn't think Draven should be anywhere near her daughter. For all the memories and magic that she'd built up from those crystals, Nyx was just a little girl. She still got jealous when someone else had more attention than her, and she still wanted all that attention for herself.

Lore shook her head and grinned. "You must learn how to live with them, my darling. It won't always be easy."

"They're not my siblings."

"They aren't. But they are your future." Blowing a kiss to her daughter, she said, "I need to go."

"Can we do this again?" Nyx's spine straightened and her jaw clenched. "It was… It was good to see you, mum."

Mum.

Lore nodded and tried not to let her tears show. "We can, Nyx. Of course we can."

CHAPTER 13

She doesn't seem like herself," Beauty muttered as they wandered through the muck behind Lore. "I remember her being much more..."

"Bright?" he asked with a snort. "Positive? Having an inner light that made everyone else feel rather sunny around her?"

Beauty gave him a look that said she was unimpressed. "Oh hush. She's never been a person with a sunny disposition, I know that. But she's different now, isn't she? I can't be the only one who sees it."

Of course Lore was different. Abraxas didn't know how to explain that without explaining the entire story, though, and he didn't know if it was his to share.

And yet... He looked up ahead of them, where Lore had stayed within eyesight just as she'd promised him, and how angrily she stomped away from them, as though she was having an argument with herself. And he wondered if it really wasn't his story to tell after all. He'd been part of it. He'd been there through all the ups and the downs and the oddities of their story together.

They had more than enough time to tell the story in its entirety. He could see from the set of Lore's shoulders she wasn't going to settle, and that meant they needed to figure things out without her.

Shaking his head, he let the words pour out of him.

"I made it back home with the dragonlings, and that's when I met Tanis." All of the story purged out of him, every single second of it.

How he'd wanted to give up, and how he had known that Beauty was right. He had to keep fighting for his family and his friends, who he'd left behind. How he'd stayed alive, even when he didn't want to.

That evening in the storm. The leviathan that had almost overtaken their ship and how he'd seen a burst of starlight through the water and he'd been certain it was nothing more than the reflection of a falling star.

Beauty's eyes turned glassy when he told her of their reunion, and she laughed at the story of the sailors terrified of their grown children. Together, they relived the moments as though she had been there. As though Zephyr had walked with them as well, because she mentioned how he would have reacted to much of it throughout the entire story.

And when he was finished, he nudged her with his shoulder. "There you have it. That's why Lore is different, why I might seem a little different as well. We've all gone through more than we ever should in a lifetime."

"I should say."

"And you?" He waited for her gaze to find him and then lifted a brow. "What happened while we were gone? I thought you and Zephyr would stick together through all of it. I really thought we'd find the two of you here, together."

He saw her wilt before his eyes. The mere thought of Zephyr made her question everything, and his heart broke at the sight of that. She deserved nothing but the best, and all he'd given her was a nightmare of a memory.

"Sorry," he muttered, holding out his hand for her to take. She needed his help to get around a rather large fallen tree, and he marveled at how quickly she took his hand. Not an ounce of fear in her. "I didn't think when I asked the question."

"No, no really. It's fine." Beauty sighed and shook her head. "It's just that we all thought so highly of Margaret. She promised so much and we were all so certain that we'd be moving toward something better, you know? Zephyr most of all. He'd have followed that woman into battle a hundred times over after what we did."

Abraxas had forgotten the last time they'd all had been together was during that battle, and in the aftermath. He couldn't imagine what Lore had felt waking up six months later, dragging herself out of the dirt only to find that everyone had moved on without her.

Shaking his head to clear his mind of that thought, he heaved in a great breath and let Beauty's hand drop as her boots hit the muck. "I had forgotten..."

"About the battle?" Her eyes went wide as she stared at him.

"No." Abraxas almost laughed at the thought of forgetting that. "No, of course not. I had forgotten the last time we all saw each other was in that state. No wonder none of us made normal decisions."

"Well, and Zephyr least of all." She shook her head again with disappointment and then pointed at Lore. "He was looking for someone like her to follow. And Margaret is an elf, just like Lore. They are two sides of the same coin, he told me. We should listen to what Margaret has to say. She knows how to run a kingdom. He was so full of doubt."

Of course the boy would be. Everyone had looked at him like he was his brother, and he wasn't. Zander had been born and raised to grab a kingdom by the horns and know exactly what to do in every situation that might arise.

Zephyr had lived his life in a crypt while hiding from anyone who might see him. It was ridiculous to expect anything else from him.

Then the thought dawned on him and he snarled, "She used that to her advantage."

"She absolutely did." Beauty lifted a hand for a will-o'-the-wisp to land on, letting the little fairy creature dance in her palm for a few seconds. "Zephyr wanted someone to tell him what to do and how to be the man everyone expected. He didn't want to listen to anyone but the elves, so certain that they would lead us into a new era with Lore gone. For a while, Margaret let him think she was helping him.

"I remember watching them in the corridors, unsure of what they were doing. Margaret would pull him into her office and she always had his ear. He started to twist into a different person. More fearful, always jumping at shadows and I didn't know what to do. I didn't know how to help him, even though..." Beauty swallowed the words. "It doesn't matter. I couldn't stop him from listening to her and now look at where we are."

He supposed that was one way to look at it. But there was another, softer way to view those memories. "You did whatever you could to help him, Beauty. But in times of hardship like that, he was taken advantage of. He'd never been in battle. Never lived in a castle or had people calling him Your Highness. Everything was new to him and she was the predator who took what he could offer and twisted him into something new and ugly."

"She did." Beauty's voice lowered into almost a whisper. "She absolutely did."

They walked on in companionable silence for a few moments, both of them lost in their thoughts. Abraxas couldn't help but feel guilty for leaving them, even though he knew it was the only choice at the time. If he had known Lore would return, would he have left? Probably not. But then he never would have known there were more dragons out there. None of them would have found Tanis, and she wouldn't have hatched more eggs.

No one knew the future, nor could they predict what would unfold. But he wouldn't change how things had happened. Even if that meant his friends had to get hurt.

He glanced over his shoulder to see Beauty had paused for a moment. Her face tilted into the warm swamp breeze, her hair lank around her shoulders with grease and grime from their journey already. But her eyes were closed and her expression was serene.

This was a young woman who had come to terms with what had happened in her life. She was not afraid of the future or her past. She simply lived in the moment because that was where she was. He admired that about her.

"So the kingdom fell," he prompted, one last question burning in his mind. "How did the two of you get separated?"

That serene expression disappeared instantly. "Margaret let us know what she was going to do with the humans. Her plan was, at first, to simply relocate them. She wanted them all out of the spaces where magical creatures lived, and Zephyr agreed to it. I could see that he didn't want to. He just didn't know how to tell her that he didn't. And then... Well, then we started seeing the destruction first hand. I tried my best to get them to see reason, but Margaret wanted me out of the castle."

"Of course she did," he snarled. "You were the only person who could change Zephyr's mind."

"And I almost did." The happiness in her voice and the pride made her shoulders straighten. "But I was too late. Right before they kicked me out of the castle, I saw they were already putting him in shackles."

Then he ended up where Lore had seen him. Abraxas knew he could not bring that up right now.

Beauty didn't need to know exactly what they'd done to him, at least not until after they'd saved him. He knew if Lore was in pain like that, or if he knew she was being tortured by Margaret's people, he would do some very foolish things to save her.

But Abraxas was a dragon. He could afford to do foolish things because very little could hurt him. Beauty? Margaret would flay her alive right in front of Zephyr if she thought it would make him comply easier.

Shaking his head, he let his breath whistle out between his lips. "It's a strange story and an odd life we lead. Don't you think?"

Beauty shook her head as well, a wry grin on her face. "Such a story to tell our children someday when they live side by side with magical creatures, not understanding that there was ever a time when we hated each other."

"It's a future to fight for."

"And one I have fought for my entire life." She straightened and pointed up again. "It looks like she's stopped."

They both froze where they were, undecided if they wanted to join Lore or not. She had made it fairly clear that she needed time for herself, but Abraxas saw that she'd slipped into a cave and seemed to settle. Maybe that was a good sign?

Beauty glanced over at him, unsure herself. "Should I maybe go gather some wood?"

"Might be a good idea. Just let me talk to her for a bit."

"If she's not in a good mood..." Beauty lifted her hand and held up three fingers. "Give me a hand signal and I'll find somewhere else to sleep for the night."

"I'm sure everything is fine."

"I don't want to get in the middle of it." Beauty mock shuddered, but the grin on her face made her seem anything but scared. "You two have a lot to talk about, and I don't need to be a distraction. Like I said, she's not the same person she once was. This version of Lore terrifies me."

As she should. Beauty didn't know that Lore could pop a man's skull with her mind, or that she could slip through the very veil of life and death if she wanted. It was all rather strange to him, as well. Knowing that Lore was this powerful made him feel very weak, and he wasn't so sure how to deal with that.

He'd learn, though. Because he had to.

Beauty wandered off, and he went to see what his mate was up to, and what kind of battle he needed to fight to get her back in the right state of mind.

He stepped into the cave and heaved a sigh of relief to see Lore sitting there, all curled up like she used to. She didn't look all that upset anymore, and at least he wouldn't be blasted back onto his ass again. That was enough reason to sigh in pleasure.

"Better?" he asked, leaning against the open mouth of the cave. "We were both worried about you for a while there."

Lore didn't look at him. Instead, she stared into the darkness surrounding him as though she saw more than just Abraxas's figure. "I'm sorry."

"Apology accepted."

"I shouldn't have reacted the way I did. I know better than to let myself get angry because I'm overwhelmed. The thought that I took it out on you makes me sick. I could have hurt you, Abraxas. I could have really hurt you."

"I know." He shuffled his foot on the ground, still watching her. "And I forgive you."

"I promise I won't ever do that again. I'd rather cut off a finger every time I do it than see your face like that again. You should hate me, Abraxas, or at the very least, be angry with me. Shout! Yell! Tell me I was irresponsible! Say something other than what you're saying right now."

And she still wouldn't look at him. So Abraxas stepped in front of her and crouched, forcing her to look at him. "I'm not angry with you, Lore. You are overwhelmed, and this is a great responsibility on anyone's shoulders. Beauty mentioned that you don't seem like yourself, and I realized something when she said it."

Her wide eyes stared up at him, tears already filling them as though she was terrified of what he might have to say. "What did you realize?"

He hooked a finger underneath her chin, needing to touch her. "You are not the same person. You are not the half-elf scrounging around Tenebrous for a scrap of food, nor the elf who was blackmailed into killing the King. You are not the elf who led her people across all Umbra searching for my eggs, or the woman who led them into battle. You are a new version of yourself. Always and forever changing into someone new."

A single, glistening tear rolled down her cheek. "And what does that mean to you, my dragon?"

Abraxas dragged her forward and pressed a kiss to her lips. Gentle, as always, so she knew he wasn't going anywhere. "It only means that I love you in every season of your life. Every change. Every whisper of difference. I love your mismatched eyes and the power that makes you a little shaky sometimes. I love you even when you do not love yourself. You are part of me, Lore, and how could I hate something so deeply embedded in my soul?"

She swallowed hard, her voice thick as she replied, "I love you too. I just don't want to disappoint you."

"Ah, impossible." Abraxas drew her into his arms and pressed her against his heart. "You could never disappoint me, my beloved, my mate. Never."

CHAPTER 14

Lore forced herself to be more present after her outburst. She focused on Beauty and keeping her little human safe. And the farther they were from Tenebrous, the more that knot in her heart eased.

Margaret might have sent people after them. She might have felt the magic and then burned Tenebrous to the ground.

But she also might be very busy trying to round up all the humans she could, and that would leave her distracted. Perhaps they had gotten away with the simple act of hiding their faces, and that might be enough.

Small threads of magic were hard to pick up on, anyway. And it had been a long time since Lore had been home. Margaret had almost two years of running this kingdom on her own. Perhaps that was enough time to set her at ease.

Lore wasn't so certain that was the case. The Margaret she knew was a woman who didn't know how to put herself at ease. There was no such thing as relaxation to the woman who had created a rebellion and fought her entire life for this moment.

Still, they traveled through the swamps without a single shadow or raven following them. Lore knew what to look for and who to keep an eye out around, and not a single threat had touched them.

Strange.

Still, she shouldn't look too deeply into the situation or she might find there was more trouble ahead. Abraxas had told her to keep her head in this moment. To be aware of everything that was happening to them as though it were merely a ripple in the waters ahead. So she did so. And that had eased a lot of her anxiety.

They left the swamps and skirted around the forest where Draven's family lived. Lore didn't want to talk with any more elves, and though it added a few more days to their travels, no deepmonger stopped them. That was good enough for her.

The Matriarch of that clan was sure to side with Margaret, and Lore had no interest in such a conversation. Draven's mother was very persuasive and Lore found herself enjoying their travels a little too much. She didn't have to hide her face unless travelers seemed like they might recognize her. None of the magical creatures they came across were scared or frightened. They were hungry, yes, but Margaret was ever the warlord and not the farmer.

Still, the land flourished. She noted how tall the trees had grown and how the grass was greener than she remembered. Magic laced throughout and stretched through the veins of every leaf and every blade of grass. The world seemed to breathe easier now that the humans weren't destroying it.

She shouldn't be so pleased with what they had found. She should feel terrible that the world had forgotten the mortals and yet... she couldn't force herself to feel that way at all.

Talking with the Matriarch would only remind her that good things always came from destruction, even if there were others who bled for it. And Lore couldn't afford someone telling her to look a little closer and to see how much good had happened without the humans here.

The cost was too great. There had to be another way, and she refused to believe this was the only option.

Sighing, she brushed a strand of hair out of her face and paused in their journey. Both her companions stopped on either side of her and stared down at what she had led them to.

No one said a word. The ghosts of memories long past overtook all of them.

The field that stretched out before them looked so innocent now. Bright green grass led to a cliff's edge that was not too high and then a wide ocean behind it. The field had bounced back. There were no deep furrows, no ruts where Abraxas had landed. Even the scorch marks were gone.

She glanced over at Abraxas and saw his eyes were trained on a single part of the field where flowers grew in a wide circle. There was still a stone there to mark where she had died. Apparently, people still brought gifts, because there were a few crates of items and plucked petals strewn about. They worshiped her here, and Lore wasn't quite certain how to connect that with herself. She was just a half elf. But they saw her as so much more than that.

Lore's eyes, no matter how hard she tried to keep them trained on her gravesite, always traveled to the right. Toward the edge of the field where she had gathered her own forces and squeezed the King's Umbral Soldiers between herself, Abraxas, and the elves.

The place where she had fallen to her knees with Goliath in her arms. The place where she had said goodbye to her oldest friend.

"Did we have to come here?" Beauty whispered. "This place holds so many painful memories for us all."

"It does," Lore said with a sigh. "But we have to pass this way to get to Solis Occasum. It's the safest route, and the fastest."

Beauty nodded, her eyes filling with tears. "I lost two of my best friends the day we fought here. I thought everything would be fine. I was told the battle wouldn't kill anyone that I loved and so I fought with all of you. And within a year of this battle, I lost everyone."

Lore reached out for her hand and squeezed it tight in her own. "Most of us came back," she replied.

"But not all."

No. Not all of them. No matter how hard they tried to bring him back, Goliath would always end up right where he was. Fate had wanted him to die in this place, and Lore wasn't ready to give him up.

Tears pricking her vision, she sniffed hard before saying, "We'll make camp closer to the beach. I'll want you to turn into a dragon to get us closer to Solis Occasum, Abraxas. Tomorrow."

"They'll see us flying overhead."

"I don't want to fly. I want you to swim, and we will stay on your back." She swiped a quick hand underneath her eyes. "They won't see us coming."

He gave her a look like she was insane, and maybe she was. Crimson dragons weren't meant for the sea, but she had seen him swim in their travels from the dragon isles. And the channel between here and Solis Occasum was not large. It would only take an hour or so of his powerful legs and wings moving through that water for them to reach the shore.

That was all. And then they would finally be within Zephyr's reach.

But first, she had to figure out the plan once they got there.

"Are we going to save him now?" Beauty asked, her voice a little unsteady.

"I want to figure out how we're going to do that before we risk his life." Lore tried to make sure she sounded confident, and not like she was falling apart at the seams. "Just to make sure we all are on the same page and nothing happens to surprise us."

Which meant she would have to walk. She'd have to let go of her physical form and move throughout the world as she had before. Would Margaret be able to catch her? She had no idea.

Abraxas eyed her with a worried expression before he nodded. "If that's what it takes, then we'll figure it out. Perhaps we'll duck into the forest tonight so the deepmongers don't realize we're there."

"They'll know we're here."

"They won't if I keep them busy."

He must be worried. Lore watched him to see the signs of stress on his forehead and how his jaw clenched at the thought of risking their lives again. She knew just how much this wore on him and how little she could do to help. If he wanted to hide in the forest, so perhaps Margaret thought they were seeking the deepmongers' help, then so be it.

Lore nodded. "We can do that. Margaret will think I have fled to the Matriarch."

"And all we can do is hope that they don't already have a deal to give you up if either of them catches wind of where you are," Abraxas growled low under his breath. "This is getting more difficult."

"We knew it wouldn't be easy."

Nothing ever was. It felt strange to think that they were so close to

Zephyr, yet felt as though they were farther away than they'd ever been before.

She needed space to think, and she needed Abraxas with her this time.

"Beauty?" she asked, knowing the other woman would need something to keep her hands busy. "Set up camp for us."

"I can do that. Where are you going?"

Lore wanted to say that she was taking a walk with Abraxas. That the two of them were going to talk strategy and perhaps they would figure out the best way to attack this situation headfirst.

But she knew there was only one thing she wanted to do right now. Her gaze turned back toward the battlefield and to the section of that ground that she would never forget.

"I need to pay my respects," she whispered. "Before we do anything or take another step forward, I need to tell him how far we've gotten. He'd be proud of us, you know. He'd be rushing in with an axe flailing over his head the moment he realized Zephyr had been taken."

"Ah, no he wouldn't," Beauty breathed. "Goliath was too smart for that. He'd have figured out a plan by now, though. He was always so good at making plans."

Sort of. But Lore had seen a different side of him than Beauty. Goliath had been her best friend, but he had worked at Beauty's side with Margaret for years before Lore had ever involved herself. And certainly that meant she knew him better than Beauty, but also... perhaps she didn't.

Sighing, she pressed the heel of her hand to her forehead as though that might press back the headache that had already bloomed. "Either way. He deserves time with me. Just as much as the rest."

Abraxas pressed his hand against the small of her back and steered her toward the field. "Come on, then. Let's go say hello."

Hello? Tears burned in her eyes. Was it hello if she was the reason he was dead? Perhaps it was more of an apology. She had to whisper it into the ground where he'd died because she didn't know where they had buried him. She didn't know if there was even a memorial or a headstone.

Throat closing up, she looked up at Abraxas and begged him to take this weight off her shoulders. "Is there a grave?" she asked.

His gaze turned troubled, and he glanced away from her. "I do not know. We could not find his body in the aftermath. Draven remembered where he was, but there were so many bodies and he was so small. It was hard to find anyone in the chaos, and no one found him after we'd cleaned it up. We assume one of Margaret's people found him and brought him back to the castle. But it's hard to say."

Who would have known who he was? Even to the magical creatures that fought at her side, he was just the dwarf who had arrived with her. Lore had never made it clear how much he meant to her or how integral he had been in getting them to the point of battle.

This was her fault. The fact that he had no resting place was all her fault.

Her stomach twisting and her breakfast rolling up into the back of her throat, she made her way onto the battlefield while memories plagued her. She remembered the shouts and screams of horror. The dark splashes that had painted her body as she'd cut through Umbral Soldiers that bled like people but had no soul inside. She'd done everything possible to stop them, had given her own life, and it still didn't feel like enough.

"You remember it all," Abraxas said as he strode beside her.

"I do."

"I was so far away from you at this point that I didn't see anything happen." He lifted one shoulder uncomfortably. "I don't remember when or how he died, only that you did eventually as well. The rest is a blur after that. I didn't... I didn't take any of this well."

"The memories are hazy for me as well," Lore replied. "So much has happened between then and now and I haven't gotten a single moment to grieve him or think about him at all. I just... I thought I had gotten over this, but now I'm realizing I don't think I ever will."

They reached the spot where he'd died and she felt her heart squeeze in her chest. The uncomfortable feeling didn't go away, not even when she rubbed at it. She'd thought for a moment that she could relieve the symptoms of grief. She knew better.

Lore knelt on the ground, feeling the wet squelch of earth soaking through her pants. She placed her palm on the ground as though she might feel him deep underneath. "He stood between me and a mace. The Umbral Soldier was huge and strong and I just didn't see him. Goliath did."

She squeezed her eyes shut at the memory. It hurt to think about. To remember the life leaving his eyes until his body was just a husk in her arms. It wasn't him. He wasn't left at all after he'd gone. She hated that her last memory of him was like that and not them on some wild adventure together.

Abraxas knelt beside her and sank his fingers through the soft dirt. "He kept you safe when I could not. I will never forget the gift he gave me in doing so. But you have to know, Lore, he wanted you to be safe as well. He wanted you to live, even if he wasn't there to see it."

"He wanted me to save this kingdom."

"Oh, he didn't care about that all too much." Abraxas smiled at her, the expression soft and kind. "The best way you can repay him is to continue living. Don't you think?"

"I do. And I will make sure that he didn't die in vain." Lifting her hands, she pressed a kiss to both of her palms before placing them back on the ground. "He was the best friend I ever had. I'll never forget that."

They both stayed like that, remembering the dwarf who had given so much for them.

Until Lore froze as another voice interrupted their quiet respect.

"You're a long way from home, elf."

CHAPTER 15

Abraxas wanted to say he spun around at the sound of an unfamiliar voice, turning around on his heels with his teeth bared. Ready to protect Lore at all costs because who would dare to speak with them during this quiet moment other than someone who intended harm?

But he'd heard that voice and his mind had disappeared into a time when he'd still had a short friend beside him. A young dwarf who had seen the world in all its shades of good and bad and still wanted to save it.

He'd thought for a few moments that Goliath was right behind them. He knew the gravelly tones and the scent of dwarven magic that filled the air. Abraxas knew it all that so well that it made him hesitate.

Such a mistake could have cost them their lives. Or it could have delivered them somewhere a little better than this.

Sighing, he turned around and straightened his shoulders. The dwarf who stood behind them wore a familiar grin on his face. His ruddy cheeks were wind burnt and bright as a tomato over a long beard that matched the color. His eyebrows were winged and wild above expressive green eyes that sparkled in the sunlight. Riotous curls spilled down his shoulders, equally red and glistening in the sunlight like burnished copper.

This was not Goliath, but it certainly was a dwarf.

Abraxas had thought they were all but gone. And they weren't living in these fields, or at least, that's what he remembered from when Goliath had been here. His old friend had come here seeking the help of the dwarves. As far as Abraxas knew, they were all gone.

Frowning, he glanced at Lore, expecting to see the same shock on her features. But she wasn't surprised at all. She stood slowly, dusted her hands off on her pants, and then nodded at the man who stood before them.

"I am a long way from home." She eyed the dwarf up and down, then lifted a shoulder. "Is there a home any more for the elves, though? You've all made your kingdom far underneath the earth. Lucky you."

The dwarf tilted his head back and burst into laughter. The sound was too loud. Even Abraxas winced and took a step away from the man. Did he really have to shout with mirth?

"I forgot about the humor of elves!" The dwarf shouted before wiping underneath his eyes. "I haven't seen one of your kind in many years, I'll admit. Although some of the others talked about you barging in when that shadow king had us under his thumb. They saw you, you know."

"Saw you?" Abraxas repeated, frowning and looking down at her. "What does he mean by that?"

"No one filled you in on the dwarves we found? They were the ones that made the Umbral armor." She gestured at the other man. "Apparently those suits weren't conjured by magic after all. Beauty said they helped free the dwarves from their chains after everything happened. Where were you?"

Probably still stuck in his madness. They'd likely told him all about the endless wealth they'd found in the dwarven kingdom, the armor and swords which would help them continue to hold Umbra as they desired. But he had been focused on nothing other than the loss of his mate. Of Lore. Of a memory filled with starlight and hope that had sent his world into a downward spiral.

Instead of telling her all that, he shrugged. "I must not have been listening."

A shriek echoed across the battlefield and this time he felt the ripple of a change running over his entire body. What now?

Except when he looked up, smoke already curling out of his nose, all he saw was Beauty charging down the hill with her arms spread wide. She let out another joyful shriek and then gathered the dwarf up in her arms with a giant hug. The man grunted, his cheeks somehow turning even more red.

"Mirin!" Beauty jerked away from him, her hands on his shoulders so he couldn't get far. "I thought you were all gone? You said you were leaving!"

Abraxas crossed his arms over his chest and felt the fires die inside of it. Amusement took its place as the young man in Beauty's arms blubbered like he'd forgotten how to speak.

"Well, uh, yes, uh. We did say that, didn't we? Considering the company you were keeping at that point, we, uh, we couldn't afford anyone finding out what was going on. You see?" Mirin scratched at the back of his neck. "I'm awfully sorry to have lied to you, Miss Beauty."

True to her nature, Beauty rolled her eyes and shrugged. "Oh, you know I don't hold grudges."

That they all did. No one could look at Beauty and assume she was anything other than a kind person. She didn't hold grudges when she should, and she overlooked significant flaws when she should see the red flags waving in front of her.

What Abraxas was more curious about was the bright red cheeks the young man had and the way he shuffled his foot on the ground. The boy had a crush, and a big one if Abraxas was seeing this right.

Mirin caught his gaze, and that expression hardened, as though Abraxas hadn't noticed everything that had just occurred.

The young dwarf cleared his throat and said, "Seeing the company you keep now, I think it's fine to let you know we're still here."

"The company she keeps now?" Lore asked, her eyebrow lifted in surprise. "And what company would that be?"

Mirin nodded at her. "Yourself, miss. The Fallen Star."

Now both of Lore's eyebrows shot up. "That's a new title. I haven't heard that one yet."

"Considering you're here to save the kingdom, I think it's fine to let you know the dwarves have been around for a long time yet. And we're not going anywhere." Mirin puffed out his chest, all bravado and bravery when he likely had no reason to feel that way. "We've been preparing all this time, you see. It's been a long time of waiting for you, though. Even as long lived as we are, dwarves can get real impatient."

Abraxas had never tested his ability not to smile. Now, he realized it was rather hard to keep that emotion in check when something hilarious happened in front of him. He'd always been the man no one could get to smile. And yet, right now? It was taking all he had in him to not laugh at the expression on the young man's face.

The dwarf wanted to impress Lore so badly. He wanted all of them to look at him with shock and awe.

Instead, all he got was three people who were tired, hungry, and dealing with a grief that burned through them. It was a shame. Abraxas could have given him quite the show if they'd been warned that dwarves might still be around.

They all needed rest, a place to lay their heads after such a long journey, and some food in their bellies. If they could get all that while under the protection of the dwarves, even better.

Abraxas kept his arms crossed over his chest and cleared his throat. "You make it seem like you've been waiting for us."

"We have. One of our seers knew that the Fallen Star would return, and that would be a day of reckoning. We've been waiting for when you all might arrive." Mirin could not look more proud if he tried. "That I am the one to find you is a great honor. My family will be so pleased when I return with you."

"What makes you think we'll go anywhere with you?"

The dwarf paused, then looked at Beauty before his eyes found Abraxas again. "Are you not?"

He arched his brow. "There are many people in this kingdom who want to kill us. I don't know you. I don't know your people, and even though you seem excited to see us, that means nothing. I'm not sure if you understand how dangerous it is for us to even be here." The words were all a lie, but he wanted to push the young man. If the dwarf wanted them to see him as anything more than a young man, then he needed to give them a reason to see him as more than that. "So. Why should we go with you?"

Mirin's eyes had gotten larger with every word Abraxas said until the young dwarf huffed and mirrored Abraxas's position. "It seems to me you need a place to stay, dragon. You're out here in the wilds where anyone can find you, and don't think we don't know the risk of it. Margaret and her elves have been hunting down anyone who even says her name."

The dwarf pointed at Lore, who rolled her lips to try to not smile. Abraxas knew that look. That was the cocky look of a woman who thought it was hilarious that everyone was hunting her down, and that she'd like to see them try to harm her.

Damned woman was going to be the death of him.

Pinching the bridge of his nose, he nodded. "Right. So you understand who we're trying to escape from. And the fact that you know her name means you've dealt with her before. So why should we trust you?"

"Because we don't like the shadow elf and none of us want to waste any more time waiting for this kingdom to get back on its feet." Mirin pointed at Lore again, jabbing his finger in the air. "She's the one who's going to set all this to rights."

"Why do you think it has to be her?"

The dwarf threw his hands in the air and started muttering in another language. Considering the violence with which he said all the words, Abraxas thought it very likely that the young man was cursing him.

Beauty eyed them, looking between both men as though she couldn't quite figure out what was happening here. "We should go with him. I know him and his people very well."

Tilting his head to the side, Abraxas sighed. "Have you been in their home before?"

"No one has been in the dwarven kingdom for years," Beauty scoffed. "Of course I haven't."

"Then are you so sure you can trust them when you haven't even been invited to eat with them?"

With a stomp of his boot, Mirin kicked a clod of dirt at him. "How dare you? The dwarves are one of the oldest races in all of Umbra and it is an honor to even be invited within our hallowed halls! I take it back. You can stay out here in the cold with all the dangerous creatures. I hope they skewer you, dragon. The other two can come with me."

Abraxas bared his teeth, knowing they were a little sharper than before. "Please. I'd like to see anything try to skewer me."

They were all interrupted by the bell-like sound of laughter. Lore tilted her head back and shook with the sound as it burst out of her chest. Abraxas first turned to glare at her. She was ruining his act here of intimidating the young man.

But then he found his own lips twitching with humor as well. This was all ridiculous, and they needed somewhere to stay the night. The pissing contest between him and this young man was, frankly, foolish.

Chuckling and shaking his head at her, he returned his attention to Mirin, who stared at them as though they'd both lost their minds.

"Fair enough," Abraxas said. "We'll go with you. But neither of them goes anywhere without me. That's not something we can negotiate."

The dwarf looked at Beauty, then back at them, then back at Beauty. "Have they both lost their minds?"

"A long time ago," Beauty agreed, then slung an arm over the young man's shoulder. "Now, when you say we have a safe place to stay, does that include food as well?"

The two of them started wandering, although Mirin cast a few glances over his shoulder to make sure Lore and Abraxas were following them. His elf was still caught up in her giggles, pressing her hand to her mouth as though that might trap the sounds inside.

With a low growl, he leaned down and whispered in her ear, "If you don't stop, they're going to think we aren't professionals."

"We aren't professionals."

"They think you're a goddess. A fallen star from the sky sent to save them. And I am your fearless protector who has likely ripped open the night so that you could fall. You know how stories like this get started." He straightened with a grin on his face.

He quite liked the idea of people thinking he could tear open the very sky with his claws. As though he had ripped her out of the safety of her home, high in the air, and pulled her down to the kingdom so she could save them all.

"That's quite romantic," Lore said, her voice lighter than it had been for days. "Do you think we could convince them that's the actual story?"

"I think we could convince them of a lot of things." And maybe they should. If they controlled the narrative of the story, then that would make everything a lot easier for them. "Do you think they would believe that one? That I fell in love with a star and I couldn't live without you? And seeing you travel across the sky every night, only to disappear during the day, broke my heart until I went mad with desire."

Lore hummed low in her breath. "So you took to the sky, your wings beating at the north and south winds that tried to force you back to the earth. Instead, you fought and fought until you could claw at the home of the stars and I fell to your feet."

"A vision covered in blush colored flowers," he murmured.

"No," she replied with a laugh. "I believe the dress was blue."

"Pink."

"Yellow?"

"It was pink." Abraxas would never forget the moment he saw her in that forest. "You were covered in cherry blossoms and giant dahlias, with a dress made of spider silk and gossamer. The moment I crossed your path, I knew I would forever be mad for you. My heart stopped in my chest at the sight of you. There will never be a prettier sight than you standing in that clearing, waiting for me."

Lore stared up at him, her heart in her eyes. "I love you so much, Abraxas. More and more every day."

He grinned. "I know you do. Now let's go underground again."

CHAPTER 16

Lore tried to keep the lighthearted nature of their conversation going while they made their way to the mouth of a cave. This one differed greatly from the one she and Goliath had stood at, waiting to go deep into the earth together. She remembered that one was a little muddy and old, surprising that it was even still open.

The opening that Mirin led them to was clean and gleaming with metal that held it open at the top. The brackets made the descent appear much safer than she ever expected.

All around the edges were pretty little embellishments. Runes for safety, a few carved deities that she assumed the dwarves worshiped. All depictions that were pretty and made with an artistic hand.

A small cart waited for them at the mouth of the cave, set up on rail systems that definitely wouldn't carry all of them. Mirin seemed to hesitate when he caught her looking at the cart, but then he shook his head. "We don't use those for travel, if that's what you're thinking."

Oh, thank goodness. She couldn't get in that metal box and plummet into the darkness. Lore remembered what it looked like in those tunnels. She remembered the dark, and the echoes of creatures crawling along the walls.

Just imagining diving into those shadows made her heart race. She couldn't do it, even if that was the only way to get into that home.

"Ah," she replied, trying to hide her embarrassment at thinking they used them to travel. "Very good."

"I can arrange for someone to bring something to help if you're needing transportation." Mirin rubbed the back of his neck, a nervous tick she thought, while looking up and down her body. "I thought you were fine, but I don't know how to tell if an elf is injured."

"I'm not injured," she rushed to interrupt. "I'm fine, really. Thank you."

Abraxas eyed her with a narrowed gaze, watching her for any signs of danger before they all started into the cave. He knew what it was like when she got overwhelmed and these days it was… well. Not safe for anyone else around her.

Lore had expected the cave to be the same as her previous visit. A massive hole with dirt floors and barely held up ceilings. A questionable entrance into a kingdom that was grand and massive. Instead, she was surprised yet again. Metal plates covered every inch of the ceiling. The floor was earth, but quickly turned into polished stone with carefully abraded surfaces where people were meant to walk.

Lights glimmered on the wall, some torches, but most orbs of magic that lit everything almost as bright as daylight. The glow from the polished stone reflected all the lights into a mirror effect that made it difficult to remember they were even underground.

"I'm bringing you right to the king first," Mirin said. "He's been waiting to see you, and I know that he'll be excited to hear you've finally arrived. Hopefully, we can all settle in after that. If you don't mind meeting my mum right off the bat, I think you could stay with us. She likes visitors, you see. She's a bit odd of a woman, but she makes the best honey pies."

Lore stopped listening to him after all that. She hadn't expected to meet a king today, and knowing that she was going to do so while covered in sweat and bog water wasn't exactly reassuring.

But she wanted to know why the dwarves were so interested in her, and why they had been waiting for her arrival for such a long time. They clearly had thought she would come to them first. But that made little sense at all. She'd never been friends with the dwarves, other than Goliath. And he'd been cast out of his family years ago.

So what had changed? Or, she supposed, what was she unaware of?

Her thoughts ran wild in her head until Mirin froze in the center of the tunnel. She could see light at the end of it, the main part of the dwarven home she supposed. Then he turned to look at her and his jaw dropped open.

"I forgot you've been traveling." His eyes widened with horror as he took them all in. "No, this won't do. You can't see the king like this!"

Lore glanced down at her muddy clothing and bog water covered arms. "I was thinking the same thing myself, but then I assumed it was a matter of great importance that your king see me soon."

"It is!" Mirin slapped his hands to his cheeks and groaned. "But if I bring in the Fallen Star looking like that, they'll all question if you are who you say you are! You look terrible, miss. I don't mean that as an insult, but you look like you've been rolling around with the pigs."

The second part was definitely an insult. Crossing her arms, Lore glared down at him. "Then what do you propose, master dwarf?"

His eyes darted around them before he muttered, "Nothing to be done about it. I'll just have to fight the others off. No one is presenting you to himself other than me, that's for certain. Follow me, you three. We've got a bathing house to clear out."

They abruptly changed directions, and Lore had to assume this was a good thing. She could use a good bath, so could her two companions, and... she just wanted to feel clean again. It had been a while, and the salt grit in her hair was still there from a week ago.

Abraxas placed his hand on the small of her back as steam filled the tunnel around them. "I think our guide has lost his head."

"And just a few moments ago, he'd suggested we were the ones to have done so."

"Should we point it out?"

Lore glanced at the young man, who had leaned into an adjoining tunnel and started shouting. "No. Let's let him have his moment."

Amused, she watched as three dwarves exited the tunnel he'd shouted into. A few of the dwarves had robes on, and one of them was wrapped in nothing but a towel. They all glared at Mirin, who seemed all too smug for having kicked them out. Until they turned around and saw her. Then their jaws hung open and their eyes widened in shock, as though they couldn't believe who was right in front of them.

Lore gave them a little wave, after which all three of the young men turned bright red and skittered away. They ran like hounds nipped at their heels, and she could only assume that meant they were racing off to tell whoever they could that they had seen the Fallen Star.

What a name.

She much preferred the others, and that was saying something. Lore didn't like any of the names she'd been given, other than her namesake from her mother. That was it. The more people who called her just Lore, the better.

Mirin bowed low, one arm held out to his side. "For you, Lady of Starlight. The baths are just around the corner. There are plenty of towels and soaps should you wish to use them. Of course, if it is not up to your standards, then please don't hesitate to ask for something else. I can go fetch you whatever you need."

Lore glanced down at her clothes before wryly grinning at him. "If I am to be clean, I'm afraid these will need to be washed as well."

His eyes nearly bugged out of his head. She wondered if that reaction was because he'd forgotten, or because he was imagining her without clothes on. She liked to think it was the latter, only because the young man really did seem rather innocent.

He cleared his throat and nodded. "Right. You all need clothes. I don't think we have anything big enough for him. But you two, I can probably find something that'll work."

She felt Abraxas roll his eyes. Her dragon growled, "I will be fine in the clothes I arrived in."

"Good." Mirin took a step away from them and backed into Beauty. He whirled with an apology already blurting past his lips. "Sorry. Beauty. Right, you need to get clean as well. And then clothing. And I'll try to find some soap that is satisfactory. Perhaps you would like food as well before meeting the king? Shall I—"

Beauty sighed and rolled her eyes up to the ceiling. "I'll go with him. Just leave some water clean for me, will you?"

Lore had to bite her lip, so she didn't burst out laughing yet again. She nodded gravely at Beauty. "I will trust my fashion to you, Beauty.

Make sure I look good for meeting their king."

If she said any more, she was afraid Mirin might faint. The dwarf hustled Beauty away with his hand on her lower back as he muttered about making haste, and if anyone tried to claim the Fallen Star while he was gone, he would have their beard.

Rolling her eyes, Lore turned back to the tunnel that would lead them to the baths and sighed. "Do you think it's really a bath down there? Or are we about to be ambushed by dwarves who have been waiting to meet me for years?"

"Only one way to find out." Abraxas held out his hand for her to take, and Lore didn't hesitate. Anywhere he was, she would go as well.

Together they walked down the tunnel and turned the bend to find themselves surrounded by natural hot springs. There appeared to be four of them. Each one with steam coiling up from the water and filling the air with a wet humidity that made her shirt stick to her chest.

Little glass vials lined the edges of these baths, each one likely filled with some kind of liquid soap that would clean the hair or the body. She could only hope one of them didn't make her want to sneeze. Towels were kept in a glass cabinet wall at the end of the cavern, neatly rolled and stacked in little pyramids.

This was… lovely. She was surprised to find so many creature comforts here. The dwarves really knew how to live.

"Come," Abraxas said, his voice low and appreciative of what they'd been given. "Let's distract ourselves for a few moments. Shall we?"

"We don't know when another dwarf will walk into the room. Do we want to give them an eyeful?"

He arched a dark brow. "I'm sure they'd appreciate seeing everything they could of you, but seeing my bare ass would scar them for the rest of their lives."

"Probably, but we'll never know unless we try." She smiled at him, although the expression felt a little fragile. "I know you aren't suggesting we do anything untoward."

"No, I am not." His fingers ghosted at the edge of her shirt, gently drawing it up and over her head. "I'm suggesting that you let me undress you, and then we will both get into that water where I will make sure you are taken care of. We've come a long way, Lore, and you haven't gotten a moment to breathe. I'd like to give you that moment."

She didn't know what that meant, but it sounded wonderful right about now.

Lore lifted her arms over her head, letting him draw her shirt over her head and then discard it onto the ground. He gave the same treatment to her pants. His hands skimmed down her pale thighs, gently drawing the fabric away until she stood naked before him.

Abraxas pressed a kiss to her belly before he made quick work of his own clothes. And then, like the gentleman he was, he swept her up into his arms. Legs dangling over his forearm, her arm around his neck, Lore had never felt so small.

He waded into the water with her in his grip, a soft smile on his face as he sank them into the heat. And oh, it felt divine.

Humming low, she let him hold her while the rest of her body floated. "When was the last time we had a hot bath?"

She watched his features as he thought about it, but they both already knew the answer. They couldn't remember. She certainly hadn't had one in a very long time, and maybe she'd gotten one when she first came back from the dead? That would seem about right.

"I think my last one might have been after the battle," he mused, walking them a little deeper and moving her in a circle.

Her legs swished in the water, her head pillowed on his shoulder as he carefully held her. "I think mine was after I came back. But then, when would we have had a hot bath?"

"There are hot springs on Dracomaquia."

"Are there?"

"Somewhere." His voice warbled as though he was trying hard not to laugh. "I suppose we could try them out to see what they are like when we return."

If they returned. She didn't want to ruin this moment, though. Instead, she moaned and nodded. "I hope so. This feels far too good to ever give up permanently."

Abraxas released her to float on her own and then made his way to the edge of the pool. He took his time opening bottles, smelling them and making a face when he didn't like the scent. Finally, he picked one and swam back to her side.

"Come here," he said, his hands on her shoulders as he steadied her. "Let me help."

She sank underneath the warm water to wet her hair and then came back up hissing. It was almost too warm for her to stay under the water that long. But then his hands slid into her hair, gently parting any tangles he came across and the lovely smell of lemon surrounded them. He worked the soap into her strands. And he didn't rush.

Abraxas rarely rushed anything, not even this. Lore sank back against him, her head tilted back and the water taking her weight. He massaged her scalp as though they had all the time in the world. Then he drew the bubbles down over her shoulders, lifted her arms out of the water to make sure those were scrubbed, and gently continued through her entire body.

At some point, he settled her on the stones next to the edge, a natural seat that let her recline with her head against the warm rocks. He even paid attention to her feet, which ached from days of walking. He dug his thumbs into the arches until she happily sighed and wanted to kiss him. Just to taste him on her lips for a little while longer.

He glanced up at her and smiled. "How are you feeling, my queen?"

"Like a queen," she replied with a soft smile.

"Good. You should feel like that every day of your life. And I want you to go into this meeting with the dwarven king, remembering that you are just as important as him. Just as powerful and just as influential. You are a queen, my love. To me and to so many others."

Tears burning in her eyes, she pulled close and captured his lips with her own. "You slay me, dragon."

"Isn't someone supposed to do that to me?" He wiped a wet strand of hair from her eyes and tucked it behind her ear. "No fear, Lore. You are so beyond that feeling now."

And kissing him made her feel like he might just be right.

CHAPTER 17

Abraxas surveyed the outfit the dwarf had brought, and he had to admit, he had thought it wouldn't be a good one. The dwarves were so much smaller than the elves, and Lore was already quite tall. He'd expected the dress to be like a skirt and a cropped top on Lore. But they had made it work in a way that turned Lore from a grubby traveler into someone who looked like a royal.

The pale white fabric tumbled off her shoulders in a false robe with gold embellishments at her shoulders. The fabric parted around her legs as she moved, revealing pale skin in only glimpses that tantalized the senses. She looked every inch a woman who should be presented to a king.

Of course, she still had wet hair. But Beauty had slicked that back from her face in a way that seemed intentional. And perhaps in a way that Lore would never have been able to do herself.

Beauty also looked stunning, although a bit more like he'd expected dwarven clothing to fit her. They still complimented her broad shoulders and wider hips. She looked... Well a bit like she belonged down here. No wonder Mirin was absolutely head over heels for the girl. Beauty could walk through these corridors, and none would be the wiser.

Except then they all walked past a group of giggling women, and he realized that Beauty absolutely did stick out. She didn't have a beard.

That image wouldn't get out of his head for a while. Abraxas had thought Goliath exaggerated when he claimed female dwarfs had beards, but they did. Long beards they had braided and twisted around their torsos to somehow intermingle with the clothing they wore. Like the bodice of a dress but made of beard hair.

No, he never would get that image out of his head.

Sighing, Abraxas trailed along behind the rest of them. He stuck out like a sore thumb. He'd tried to wash his travel clothes in the hot springs and had been horrified by the dark brown cloud that had spread around them. Had he been that dirty?

A single wash would not get enough out of these clothes so they could truly be worn in front of a king. But he'd seen his fair share of them in his lifetime, and Abraxas cared very little for their kind. This dwarven king might be better than Zander, or he might not. Either way, Abraxas wanted none of it.

He would be here for moral support. As the shadow behind Lore so she never had to fear what would happen while she stood before a group of people who were ready to judge her.

If it was his choice, they would never have left the dragon isles and their children. But alas, here they were. Saving the kingdom yet again.

Mirin paused in front of a giant opening that led out into a golden room that stretched much higher than Abraxas could see. "The king is just beyond. He's been waiting for your arrival for quite some time, so please be patient with him."

Abraxas narrowed his gaze on the young man and let Lore say what he was thinking.

She straightened her shoulders and asked, "Why should we need to be patient with him?"

"The king is a very exuberant person." Mirin's hands twisted in the bottom of his shirt. "I shouldn't say anything at all, but I wished to warn you in case you were surprised. He has a lot more... energy? Yes, more energy than most kings."

What in the world did that mean?

Abraxas was tired of surprises, and he wanted little more than to rest. Instead, they strode into a gilded room made out of gold that even he was impressed. A dragon, impressed with how much gold someone else had amassed. He stared up at the molten gold ceiling and felt something inside him click into place. The dragon knew how much this was worth. He knew how long it had taken to get every single coin that then melted down under temperatures that rivaled the breath inside him.

Oh, everything in this room eased a torment in his chest. He'd been so busy running around, trying to save the entire world, that he'd forgotten the simple pleasure of a hoard.

Being in this room forced him to remember. He had to feel the joy bursting in his heart at the wealth of it, and battle against the desire to take it.

The dwarves would stand no chance. They could try to beat him off, but they would never move his great bulk as he destroyed every entrance but one. He would take this gold, and it would be his forever.

Oh, it was an old desire. A need that came from being a dragon and living as he had for so many years. His thoughts danced back to when he'd had a hoard. All the gold in the kingdom had rested underneath his belly, and he had been so blissfully happy with that knowledge. Now? His hoard came in the form of people, and they were difficult to control or manipulate.

They did not understand a dragon had to see his hoard regularly. They did not understand his desire to keep them safe.

Blowing out a long breath, he shook his head to clear the thoughts from his mind. They'd already walked past a majority of the golden pillars holding up the massive ceiling and approached a gilded throne that seemed to melt out of the ceiling and land in a thick drop where the dwarven king sat.

The man was young. His dark hair billowed around his shoulders. He wore his beard short, a strange choice for someone with so much power in this kingdom. But his bright blue eyes and hawkish nose gave him an air of aristocracy that commanded attention.

So, the king was young then.

"This is her?" the dwarven king asked. His eyes danced over Lore's form. "Are you certain?"

"She mourned at the grave of the fallen." Mirin dipped into a low bow. "She is who she says she is."

What a strange way to convince themselves that Lore was their "Fallen Star". Just because she had paid respects to Goliath, apparently that was enough? These creatures were far too young.

The king's eyes strayed to Abraxas next, and he lit up like a child who was given a new toy. "So, you are the dragon?"

Abraxas inclined his head. "Indeed. I am."

"Well." With a burst of energy, the king surged from his seat and stalked toward them. His deep blue robes billowed around him, the golden edges flashing in the torchlight as he approached. "I've heard nightmarish stories about dragons from our people. We did not get along for many years."

"That depends on who you ask." Abraxas flashed him a toothy grin. "The dragons always liked the dwarves. You did most of the hard work for us."

Lore gave him a look that was warning him to behave, but he didn't have to be worried about what he'd said. The king tilted his head back and laughed with a gusto that would have made stalactites rain from the ceiling if they'd been in a normal cave.

"I'm sure we did!" he thundered, then clapped a hand hard to Abraxas's bicep. "You may call me Algor, friend. You are welcome in this kingdom for as long as you can keep your hands to yourself. I'd ask you to show me your draconic form, but I fear you'd take the entire cavern down with you! To see a dragon in his true scales, however, that would be quite the sight."

It was. Although he was certain half of the people in this kingdom would claim that he was a menace and a terror that should have been killed a long time ago.

Abraxas lifted a brow. "You are not what I expected."

"You didn't expect a dwarf who has spent his entire life studying the lives of dragons?"

"I did not expect a young man. I certainly did not expect a man who has spent most of his days sitting on a golden throne waiting for people to come to him." The last bit was perhaps more of an insult than he intended.

But Algor took it on the chin and merely shook his head. "When waiting for a goddess, one does not rush." He turned toward Lore and held out his hands for her to take. "My life's purpose was to see you here. To know that a goddess walked these halls and that the dwarves did everything possible to assist. You, Fallen Star, Lady of Starlight, Savior of Umbra, have finally returned to the dwarves."

"Returned?" she asked, her voice echoing in the chamber. "I have never been here before."

"Not in this form," he said with a nod. "But in another? Yes, you have."

Abraxas met Beauty's confused expression, and he shrugged in return. He assumed it had something to do with Lore's powers. She'd been given this magic through generations of women in her family, all gathering their power together through a single person. But he didn't know what else that would mean.

Perhaps one of her ancestors had been here before. Maybe that was how the dwarves had known her, and how they knew she would return.

It made sense. Lore had always drifted toward the dwarves and assisted them with what they needed. She'd taken Goliath as almost family when he gave her but a little attention. Few elves would do that. Even half elves.

Lore hummed and nodded. "So it is that way, then. I did not know that my coming here was foretold, or that your people were familiar with me."

"Few know that history of the dwarves. But it is ancient, and I have spent many years studying all the old texts. Some would say it was a waste of time." Algor shrugged. "I say it was the perfect amount of attention and exactly what we all needed."

A loud clanking filled the room, and a small portion of the gold shifted away. A door, it appeared, although Abraxas had no idea how it had been summoned to open. The dwarves were always working on the next great project.

"Ah, perfect." Algor cast a bright smile upon all of them and then gestured to the door. "Would you be so kind as to follow me? I have a surprise for you all. I'll admit, I wasn't expecting so many of you. But I intended on following through with my ancestors' plans. Part of the surprise is quite ancient."

Ancient? Abraxas felt like he'd been transported into another timeline. This dwarf wasn't worried at all about what was happening above ground.

So much so that Abraxas had to ask, "Are you aware of the current state of the surface?"

"Oh, yes. Margaret has been sniffing around here for ages. Obviously, a partnership with the dwarves would give her a certain advantage over anyone who wanted to oppose her. But the dwarves aren't all that interested in working with elves, you see. Or anyone else after that horrible deal with the Shadow King." He shuddered. "That was a terrible idea. Anyway, this one is much better, I think you'll find. Why don't you follow me?"

And then the dwarf started off as if they had no choice but to follow him.

Abraxas met Lore's surprised gaze, but then she shrugged and started after the dwarf. Did the woman have no self preservation at all? Everything Algor had just said were rather blaring concerns that they needed to clarify before waltzing off into a dark room where they might never get out of.

Dwarves were the only creatures that made dragons nervous. The two species had centuries of fighting between them, and certainly enough bad blood that they would know how to trap him.

It would take a long time for Abraxas to free himself.

"Lore, shouldn't we talk about this?" he asked as she meandered away from him.

"I'm done talking about dangerous things, Abraxas. I think what I want most is to see what the dwarves have made for me." She flashed a devious grin over her shoulder. "Are you coming? The door might close behind us."

The damned woman was going to be the death of him. He needed her to take better care of herself, and she needed to annoy him beyond reckoning.

At least Beauty patted his back. "It'll get easier the more you do it."

"Do what?"

"Watch her risk her life. She won't stop, you know."

Of course, she wouldn't stop. If he had thought she would, then he could have finally relaxed for the first time since meeting her. Grumbling under his breath, he followed behind all of them and stood in the doorway with his feet just over... nothing.

The giant room was dark beyond the doorway, but he could see the cliff that disappeared below his feet. It kept going and going until he could see nothing other than the darkness beyond it. Perhaps it fell all the way through the earth. He knew the dwarves had mines, but he hadn't realized just how dangerous they were.

The others stood on a small ledge that overhung to his right. Just enough for their feet to rest on while they pressed their backs against the stone wall. Algor looked all too happy, and suddenly Abraxas wondered if the dwarves had been feeding something in that pit.

What monstrous being waited for them in the depths?

"Wonderful! You've made it this far," Algor said, his voice echoing in the vast chamber. "Now is the hard part. You have to trust me."

"Trust you?" Abraxas barked. He wasn't afraid of heights, but he feared what waited for them in the shadows. "What is the game here, dwarf?"

"No game at all. It's a trust exercise. I'm certain you've heard of it."

Beauty weaved a little too close to the edge. Abraxas leaned over her and pressed his arm over her shoulders, forcing her back against the wall.

"Dwarf," he snarled.

Lore seemed all too happy to be where she was. With a bright tone, she asked, "What do we have to trust you about?"

Algor slapped a hand to the wall and the sound of rushing water filled the chamber. He could hear it, but couldn't see it. Abraxas looked up, expected a waterfall to open above their head. But no, it was below their feet.

He stared down as the water rose toward them and felt his stomach twist at the shadows that swam through the depths. The dwarves were feeding something in this cavern. Those dark shadows twisted and wove like coiling eels, just too large to be anything natural.

"What have you been feeding down here?" he asked.

"Oh, I'm not sure, really. I've always called them 'the creatures'. My grandfather found them when he was mining this area for the first time. Kept them because they weren't bothering anyone but us." Algor shrugged. "Nasty things, though."

The water was getting closer and closer. Abraxas could almost feel it licking their feet. Surely Algor had an escape plan for himself. Creatures like that weren't picky about who they consumed. Now he just had to find the escape plan.

"Here's the part where you trust me," Algor called out, his voice ringing over the rushing water. "Take a step forward."

"A what?" Abraxas shouted.

And then, to his horror, he saw Lore do just that.

CHAPTER 18

Stepping off into the unknown might not have been her best idea. Lore knew just how dangerous it was to walk over a surface that was clearly water with writhing beasts inside it. Who knows what they even were?

She peered down into the water, seeing red eyes reflecting the light and hungry flashing teeth. And something inside her whispered, "Trust him."

So she did.

Lore didn't even hesitate as she stepped off the ledge and onto the unknown. Maybe she was about to be sacrificed to those creatures. She had no intention of dying today, though, and her powers were great enough to battle them back. But there was also the chance that the dwarven king was truthful and that he had a gift for them. A gift that might help them find Zephyr, who was so close she could almost feel him.

Why wouldn't she take the risk? It was foolish not to. Trusting this dwarf might be the best thing she'd ever done.

And as she stepped off the ledge, her eyes focused on the darkness below her, her foot connected with something solid. Something real that wasn't water at all. Frowning, she scraped her heel against the surface. A loud screech filled the room, and she left a small scuff mark behind.

"Glass?" she asked, her voice filled with wonder. "Is this cave filled with glass?"

The dwarven king clapped loudly behind her, the peals of his laughter overpowering the dwindling sound of running water as he stumbled toward her. His humor was so great that he seemed barely capable of walking.

"Yes!" he finally gasped. "Oh, you should have seen your faces! Terror! It's always terror when people see my grandfather's pet but they never guess that I wouldn't kill them! Oh, oh, oh, that was well worth it. Even the Fallen Star finds fear in the dwarven kingdom!"

She didn't, actually. And if he took one look at her, he would have seen that she wasn't afraid in the slightest. But Lore didn't want to ruin his fun, and she supposed this was a rather ridiculous prank to pull on people.

But then she looked over her shoulder and knew Abraxas was seeing red. Her dragon had been preparing to save them, she was certain. He likely was already feeling the explosive power of his change, and that might actually crack the glass under their feet. Then they would all have a problem, and she was certain the dwarves would not appreciate their disregard for their hospitality.

Sighing, she turned toward him and pressed her hands against his cheeks. "Abraxas," she murmured. "We are all safe."

“This was not a funny joke,” he growled.

“No, it wasn’t. But we are all alive and well.” She thought, at least. They were all in one piece, and that was enough for her. Lore didn’t care if Algor wanted to prank them. It was a funny joke. He got what he wanted out of it, and they were still getting a gift.

“Oh!” Algor’s voice rang out as the last trickles of water died. “I didn’t think about it, but of course, your dragon would be upset.”

Upset? She could feel him burning underneath her palms. So close to a change that she wasn’t all that certain he still wouldn’t turn into the dragon. He could eat the king in one gulp, and clearly was intending to do so if this wasn’t smoothed over soon.

“Considering you threatened our lives,” she muttered. “I’m certain that you can make up for it by reassuring my dragon that you never intended to kill us. Perhaps that would be a good start.”

“Oh, I would never.” Algor pressed his hands to his chest. “I’d never kill the Fallen Star! But really, it was a good test to see what all of you would do. I’m impressed by your bravery. All of you are quite capable of handling stressful situations. The first time I saw them, I think I peed myself.”

That seemed to do the trick. Abraxas eased underneath her hands and she slid her fingers to his shoulders. Giving him a little squeeze, she turned her attention back to the dwarf. “Your grandfather played the same trick on you?”

“Of course he did. Everyone in royalty gets to see them for the first time, and all of us think that we’re brave enough to face death without flinching. Unfortunately, most of us flinch.” Algor shrugged. “You are who you say you are, certainly.”

Lore eyed the strange creatures that followed her every move beneath the glass and shrugged. "I have seen more terrifying things."

"Spiders as big as horses," Abraxas said.

"The undead who move quicker than they should," Beauty added with a shudder.

"Death." Lore's single word quieted everyone in the room. They all appeared much more solemn now that she'd reminded them of what she'd gone through. "A few wyrms in a pit will not terrify me. It would take a great deal more than that."

Algor released a long breath that ended with an impressed whistle. "And here I was, expecting a woman fit for royalty. Instead, I have been given a warrior, as all my ancestors suspected you would be."

"There is no life without war. And there is no need for gods or goddesses if there is nothing to defeat." Lore tried her best to believe the words, but they felt like ash falling from her tongue. "No one has any need of me if there is not something to save them from."

Algor nodded and all the humor fell away from his face. "Indeed, goddess. I suppose you are right about that. Now, come. We've kept this gift for many years in a hidden place within our mines. Even the Shadow King had no knowledge of its existence. And what a mess it would have been if he found it."

Trailing along behind him, she took the time to marvel at how quiet it was in this room. There was no sound other than the amplification of their breath and their footsteps. It added to the eerie knowledge that dark creatures followed just beneath their heels, waiting for the glass to crack.

Illumination poured in from the top of this strange room, and as she looked up, she realized it was moonlight. Somewhere high above them, the moon had come out. Mirrors were affixed to the wall and bounced that light between them until it lit up the entire room like torchlight.

The silver rays played upon her skin, touching her arms and reassuring her that there was always power available if she needed it. And oh, she would have loved to devour more of that power.

It was a curse to always want more. Just when she thought she'd gotten control over the feeling, that was when it came back. It reminded her that her people were in danger, that her friends were suffering, and that she needed to fix all this.

Her power was endless, or so the women in her history had told her. All the mothers that came before whispered in her ear about what she could do, and yet Lore had tried very little of it.

As she walked toward the unknown, following a dwarven king who claimed to have known about her for centuries, Lore wondered if she was just afraid of that power.

It seemed... limitless. And such a gift like that should only be given to the righteous and the few. Was she either of those? No. Lore had come from a hundred people who thought they knew how to control a kingdom like this. She'd been born into a rebellion, and those who whispered in her ears what the world should be. And was she righteous? So far from it, she didn't know what it would take to be so.

Still, here she was. With a power she didn't know how to control, a life that didn't feel like her own, and a destiny that barreled toward her whether she wanted it to or not.

"Now, let's see," Algor muttered as he moved across the glass. "I've always wanted to do this, but I never knew if I'd be the king who got the chance. My father just died, you see. Only a couple months ago."

"My condolences," Lore said.

"No need." The dwarf waved his hand in the air. "He was a terrible man with small dreams. The kingdom is better off without his meddling. We weren't very close. There's seventeen of us, you see. Kings have more important things to do than see their children and I was always the troublemaker."

"Even as the eldest?"

He grinned at her. "Especially as the eldest."

Then he found what he was looking for. Algor stomped hard on the glass, which shattered underneath his feet. A dark splash of water erupted around him, lifting into the air far higher than should have been possible after he barely had touched the surface.

Abraxas bristled at her side again. "Won't that let out those creatures that you keep in the depths?"

"Stop worrying about the creatures," Algor said with a laugh. "They're not going anywhere. None of them would attack the king."

But he still looked at his feet with a nervous glance before then nodding as though he'd confirmed his own suspicions. The creatures were staying away from the crack in the glass, at the very least.

Though Lore hated how thin it was. If it only took a single stomp to break through it, she wasn't so sure they should all be standing so close.

Algor took a deep breath in through his nose and then a low rumble echoed from him. He hummed low and deep, like rocks shifting underneath the earth as the mountains moved and breathed. It was a stunning sound, and one that seemed to slice through her chest and deep into her heart.

Lore pressed a hand to her chest and was shocked to find her ribs vibrating. Abraxas and Beauty had done the same, and they all shared a horrified look before turning their attention back to the dwarf who hummed so low he shook their very bodies.

And then something moved again in the depths. A strange light that glimmered beyond the creatures. She could see them in stark relief. Long, eel-like bodies with feathered edges. No, not feathers, sharp serrated edges that would cut if they merely brushed past their prey. Their heads were small, and filled with sharp teeth that they bared at the light before they swam away from it.

She noted they appeared afraid of the light. If she had to save them all, that was the easiest trick up her sleeve.

But then the glimmer erupted out of the crack that Algor had made. Water splashed around them, surging out of the hole and rolling over their feet as the gift of the dwarves rested before them.

"Here," Algor said, throwing his arms wide for her to survey their masterpiece. "This is the gift that has been centuries in the making. For you, the Fallen Star, only the best that the dwarves have to offer."

A suit of armor stood before them. Not a single ounce of rust or algae upon it. In fact, there wasn't even water dripping down its silver surface.

It was a complete set. Thigh braces that were molded into perfect shape, boots with the tiniest designs of swirling magic that made them seem to almost glimmer with diamonds. The metal skirt would move well with her, and the metal seemed thin enough so that she wouldn't have to worry if it would hinder her movements. But the chest plate caught her attention most.

Flat and sturdy, it was covered in runes. Perhaps only she could see the glowing blue marks, but there were layers upon layers of magic cast upon its surface. Nothing would break through that. Nothing would be able to even touch her. Small links created armor for her arms, and the helm was a stunning, sleek beast. Twin plates of metal would stretch down her face, leaving the middle clear so she could see through it. But the beauty was the way the helm would curve around her skull.

It was both beautiful and deadly. And made far better than she had ever seen before.

"Impressive," she said, her voice ringing out in the cavern. "I have never seen its like."

Algor beamed. "And you never will see another. There is a second gift for the Fallen Star. It is something that I have worked on myself."

With a flourish, he waved his hand, and a sword appeared in it. The blade was longer than he was tall, a perfect length for Lore. It was nearly the length from her hip to her feet, but so thin that it had to be a rapier. Except, when she took it from his grasp, she did not see the safeguard that a rapier should have. This was just a thin, sleek blade. A needle to pierce and tear.

She lifted it, eyeing the metal. "This is not made of anything I have seen before."

"That is because when you were born, a star fell from the sky. My father knew what that meant. He was attuned to omens more than others. That blade is made of that star which fell. It is harder than any metal known to man. So thin it could pierce an eye like a toothpick, but it will not break even if a great sword should lock with it."

Lore swung it in a slow circle, feeling the impeccable weight and how balanced it was. "This is better than elven-make."

She'd thought it impossible for the dwarf to look any more proud, but his chest somehow puffed even wider at her words. "You'll find no better make than these. Even the elves could not compete with what we have created."

She hated to admit it, but he was right. This weapon was impressive and terrifying at the same time. It was one she was lucky to even hold in her hand.

Catching Abraxas's eye, she lifted a brow and gestured at him with the sword. No need to ask him twice. Abraxas took the weapon and swung it, his arm moving much faster than hers. The blade whistled as it swung through the air, but it did not warp in the slightest. It didn't even bend under the great speed that only a dragon could use.

Even more impressive.

Algor grinned at them both. "I'm afraid we were unaware that you would travel with a mortal friend. My apologies, Miss Beauty. But we knew that you would arrive on dragon back and... Well."

He waved a hand, and the waters shifted again. This time, they revealed glimmering gold dragon armor. Larger than she'd ever imagined and beautiful all the same. Gems crusted the edges, a nod toward a creature who desired a hoard. A saddle was on one piece, with a large shield attached, as though they knew she would ride him into battle someday.

Even Abraxas's jaw fell open at the sight. "Armor?" he gruffly asked.

"You're going to need it." Algor shrugged. "At least according to legend. I assume it suits you?"

It did. But, of course, it also made Lore's stomach roll. So they were to battle, then. At least they would be well protected.

CHAPTER 19

Abraxas had made a mistake.

He hadn't known it at the time, of course. He'd thought that Beauty knew about Zephyr's situation, or at the very least, she knew that he was being kept in a dungeon and tortured for information.

The girl knew what Margaret was capable of. She'd worked with the woman for years, so why would she think Margaret wouldn't want to keep Zephyr quiet? Torture wasn't a new tactic, and it certainly wasn't something that Margaret had never used before. Beauty herself had seen people tortured!

Of course, he hadn't thought about the fact that they had been in the dwarven kingdom for days now. Very close to being able to save Zephyr and yet still here. He wasn't even sure why Lore was hesitating. Perhaps it had something to do with talking to the dwarf about an army. She wanted to make sure that the dwarves would be there to fight with them this time.

They would fight if they wanted to, but Algor wasn't interested in risking the lives of his people for nothing. They were going to need some ground rules, and those were rules that Lore had to negotiate.

It left Abraxas and Beauty on their own a lot. And unfortunately, he'd never been able to keep his mouth shut very well with this little human.

She wriggled her way underneath his shell, somehow. Perhaps because she reminded him a bit of Nyx. Or maybe it was just that she was so innocent that it made him nervous.

Whatever the reasoning, she'd gotten the information out of him about Zephyr. And now she was spitting mad.

"Why wouldn't Lore tell me?" she snarled, pacing side to side in the cave room. "She knows how much he means to me. She knows everything that Zephyr and I have been through!"

Actually, she didn't. Abraxas didn't want to point out that Lore had been dead for an enormous part of Beauty and Zephyr's relationship.

Of course, Beauty hadn't even told him if their relationship had gotten very far. He'd been too afraid to ask. Thinking about his two friends even kissing made his stomach turn a bit. Let alone what they had likely gotten into while it was just the two of them and no one else to make fun of them for it.

Making a face at his thoughts, he tried to wrangle his attention back to the present. "She has no idea how close you are. She knew you were closer than the rest of us, but that doesn't mean she knows you two were actually in love!"

"She knew."

"She could guess! It wasn't like you two told anyone. You thought you were being so sneaky gallivanting off with each other." Abraxas crossed his arms over his chest and took a seat while staring at her like a disappointed father. "You should have told us if those feelings were stronger."

Beauty snarled again, baring her teeth at him like she was a dragon as well. "I wasn't aware I needed to disclose my relationship with the two of you. You aren't my parents!"

"No, but we are your friends." He refused to back down in the wake of her anger. Besides, he found it rather adorable that she thought she was terrifying. "How are we supposed to guess when there is a person out there that makes your heart skip a beat? You have to tell people for them to know that, Beauty. I'm not in your head."

"You noticed enough!" She threw her hands up in the air, obviously exhausted from the conversation already. "Now where is Lore? I don't want to yell at you. I want to yell at her."

Neither of them would be yelling at Lore. Abraxas might like the little human, but no one talked to his mate like that. He'd rather Beauty get it all out on him, and then be too tired to actually scream at Lore.

Sighing, he looked up at the ceiling. "Beauty. What are you actually angry about?"

"That you two thought it was appropriate to keep secrets from me when we finally got back together again? That you thought I wouldn't get angry when I found out that you were keeping such secrets that affect my life!"

"Is that why you're upset?" Arms crossed over his chest, eyes filled with disappointment, he watched her with the critical eye of someone who knew when another was lying. "Or are you upset because Zephyr is in pain and there is nothing you can do to help?"

There it was. She exploded again. Lit off like a firework, Beauty launched into an angry rant. "How dare you? You think I can't help him? I would tear this world apart if I could get to him. Not a single one of those soldiers would know what hit them if I knew where he was. And now I do! Now I can go get him because I never thought Margaret would stoop so low that she would actually hurt him to keep him where she wanted him. That bitch. That horrible, stupid, heartless... bitch!"

Ah, yes. The only insult that Beauty could say without hating herself afterward.

She was upset that she couldn't help him. She was upset with Margaret for everything that had happened. And she was even angry at Abraxas and Lore because the two of them had done nothing to help their friend, either. He understood it. He'd have to be dead not to see that she was hurting.

"And how will yelling at Lore about any of that help?"

"It will make me feel better. And maybe it would show her she can't just toss people aside because they aren't useful anymore." Beauty glared down at him, her hands on her hips and her cheeks bright red. "Aren't you mad at her for not telling me?"

"I also did not tell you."

"You do whatever she tells you to do." Beauty waved her hand in the air, as if dismissing the idea of being angry at him. Even though she'd yelled at him just a few minutes before. "This isn't between you and me."

"I resent that you think I'm Lore's puppet."

Beauty's face crumbled as she realized her words were insulting. "Oh, Abraxas, I'm so sorry. I didn't mean it like that! I just mean, I know you would have told me if you could, and that you never would have left me out of the loop like this. You are always thinking about me."

He lifted a hand and interrupted her, forcing her to stop talking for a few seconds. "I very much supported Lore's decision to not tell you, Beauty. In case you are unaware, you're a little impulsive. And you love that boy. If you knew he was in danger, you'd have done something foolish."

Indignation made her shoulders straighten again and that anger flare to life once more. "I wouldn't have done anything foolish. I'd have gotten him back. Which is more than I can say for the two of you."

"We're working on it."

"You're not doing anything! We've been down here for three days, Abraxas. Three days when he's been chained up, beaten, starved. Who knows what they've done to him? I know Margaret well enough to know that if she wants someone to hurt, they will bleed for years before they die."

He saw the worry on her face. And it made his heart twist because he'd been there before. He knew exactly what it was like to have someone he loved in danger and not to know if they were going to come out of it alive. But he also knew that rash decisions wouldn't help.

Beauty was too young to understand. Zephyr would last a few more days. They wouldn't break him because they needed him alive. He'd be well enough when they did get to him.

"Lore has spoken with him," he said. "He knows we are coming for him, and I know Zephyr well enough as well. He won't give up now that we're so close to him. He'll hold out as long as he has to."

Tears thickened Beauty's voice and danced like diamonds in her eyes. "That doesn't mean he should have to wait any longer, Abraxas."

Silence stretched between them. Abraxas saw the shadows shift behind Beauty's shoulder, and he suddenly sensed her. Lore had heard them talking, although he didn't know how long or how much she'd heard.

A blush burned on his cheeks and he was ashamed to feel it. He had nothing to hide from the love of his life. He had no reason to fear what Lore would say. After all, he'd been defending her. And yet, he still felt like a kid who had been caught trying to steal from his parents.

Lore stepped into the room and he saw her face before she cleared it of emotion. The heartbreak. The anguish in knowing that her dearest friend didn't trust her. She had to have known this was coming, though. She had to know that Beauty would be angry to find out that they both had been lying to her.

Still, it hurt. And he was certain that it would be a wound Lore carried with her for a long time.

"So," Lore said as she stepped fully into the light of the room. "You think we've been doing nothing, is that it?"

All the blood drained out of Beauty's face. For all her bravado in front of Abraxas, she didn't actually want to yell at Lore. Abraxas had only a few moments to be relieved about that before it stuck in his gut that Beauty feared what Lore would do now.

He supposed they all had a reason to be. None of them knew the extent of Lore's power, but they had seen what she could do with just a flick of her wrist. Changing people's appearances. Giving light to a dark room. And the way she carried herself now? Beauty was right. Lore was different, with a confidence that she'd never had before.

Now, she looked at the world through a lens of certainty that none of them could ever hold a candle to. She knew she couldn't die unless she wanted to and that... well. That was terrifying.

Clearing his throat, Abraxas moved between the two women. "I'm sure that's not what Beauty meant."

"That's exactly what she meant," Lore said, her voice pitched low and calm. "She thinks I'm wasting time here because I either am too afraid to save Zephyr, or I think Margaret is right in what she's doing. Is that it?"

"It would be easier to keep Zephyr at your side if he was already tired." Beauty tried to remain proud and strong, but her void warbled at the end. "Wouldn't it? I don't know what your end plan is, Lore. None of us do. For all that Abraxas said I should have been more truthful with you two. That goes both ways. You should tell me what your plan is as well."

He glanced over at Lore to see what she was feeling. He had no intent on agreeing with either woman, because they were both right. Neither of them had been truthful, and that was a good way to end in all of them dying.

But he also would not go against what Lore wanted. Not because he was a puppet, as Beauty had so cruelly suggested, but because he believed in her. Lore knew how she wanted this kingdom to grow and change, and he believed it was the right direction. Not because he was blinded with love or because he was only crafted to follow his mate. But because he knew what was in her heart, and he knew how much she wanted this kingdom to flourish.

Lore nodded. "Yes, I should have told you the plan. If I had one. But I will stand by not telling you about Zephyr. You would have disappeared in the middle of the night. I would have had to save you, and then none of us would have gotten Zephyr out. Margaret will move him the moment she realizes we're coming for him. If she hasn't already."

"If she's moved him, it's because you waited too long." Beauty jabbed her finger in the air at Lore. "You. You waited and we've been standing here arguing when we could be saving him. We've been stuck underground for days now, giving Margaret all the time in the world to move him and to hide him again in a place we cannot find him."

Lore tilted her head to the side and for a second, she didn't look human or elf or anything else. She looked like an ancient being who had seen far too much. "We gave Margaret nothing. She likely already got wind that we were here, and that we were in Tenebrous. She's smart. She'll piece together that we wanted to get you and so she will send someone to investigate that. We are here because we're giving her time to check in on Zephyr, to build more guards around that area, just in case. We're lulling her into a sense of security. I want her to think we do not know where he is."

Even Abraxas almost said, "oohh" because he hadn't realized what they were doing either.

Of course that's why they were lingering. Lore wanted to go into hiding, so Margaret did not know where to search for them.

Damn it, that was a fantastic plan. Why hadn't he thought of that? It was so simple and yet exactly what all of them needed.

Beauty let out a huff of breath and rolled her eyes. "Why not just tell us that? And what's next?"

"Because I've been busy. The dwarves would not let us stay unless I put on a show for them. Algor is a good king, despite all of his odd tendencies. He knows that as long as we are here, I am beholden to him. The armor. The gifts. They did not give any of that for free. I have to indulge him and his people while we are safely inside their walls."

Lore tossed her hands up into the air and stalked past them. That confidence leaked a bit out of her, shoulders curving in as she made her way to the beds in the back where most of their things were.

"Now what are you doing?" he asked, amused, as she took a seat on top of the bed and crossed her legs.

Lore gave him a look, one that he knew very well by now, and said, "I'm going on a walk."

Ah. So she was going to scope out the situation. "So soon?"

"Like Beauty said, we've made him wait long enough."

"Wait..." Beauty rushed forward, standing in front of Lore while practically vibrating with emotion. "You're going to look for him? Now?"

Lore met her friend's gaze with a dead-eyed stare. "I'm going to rescue him, Beauty. We were always going to get him back. Now, later, it doesn't matter how long it takes us. But first, I want to make sure we're not walking into a trap. Margaret is smarter than anyone gives her credit for. I want to make sure no one will get in our way."

"Do you think you can?" Abraxas asked, settling down next to her for his long watch as she meandered away from her body.

Lore's haunted expression smoothed into something like glass. "I don't think there's much I cannot do anymore, Abraxas. I'll let him know we're coming."

CHAPTER 20

Lore slipped into the magic like it was a second skin. She floated away from her body and up through the very earth itself. Her mind flickered to another time when she had dragged herself out of the dirt, clawing her way beyond death and into the safety of the realm beyond. It was rather beautiful to remember such a memory and to know that this time, without a doubt, she would make it back.

Walking through the world like this would never be comfortable, though. This manner of travel was eerily close to death. Her body was no longer attached to her soul. She could see through the veil of the world and all those who had died on this battlefield still lingered.

Her heart stuttered. What if Goliath was still here?

What if her dearest friend, her soulmate in another way, had remained just so that he could talk with her one last time?

But she had a job to do. She couldn't give in to the temptation of lingering here when there was another person who needed her. A person who was very much alive.

Still. The tug that pulled deep in her belly was hard to ignore. She wanted to see him one last time, and she hadn't thought being here would be quite so difficult.

It was. It was so hard to know that there were still souls here and that all of them were largely her fault. They shouldn't have died for this. She could have killed the King when she had the chance at the start of all this. If she hadn't missed, if he hadn't healed from her cut the first time, then they would all be alive.

Lore floated over the water that separated them from Solis Occasum. The waves were angry today. They rolled up toward her as though they were trying to catch her so she couldn't reach her destination. Maybe they were.

As she peered deeper through the water, trying her best to see if there was a curse that prevented travel, she saw no lingering threads of magic. Instead, she saw the beasts deep underneath the waves. A leviathan lingered in the depths, its eyes turned toward her as it watched her move. Twin younglings played in the waves, their tentacles slamming against the bottom of the sea as they wrestled and caused the waves to overflow above their heads.

The storm they conjured might linger for days. And that would suit her well.

Lore reached out a hand toward them, her voice whispering through the waves as she urged their mother to move. To bring her children away from this place so that they were not in danger.

And though the creature initially scoffed, she flinched when Lore shared her memories of a much larger leviathan and its death in the waves. Lore didn't want to kill another one of these majestic creatures. They deserved to be alive just as everything else did, but she would not let it stand in her way.

The mother reached out for her children with her long tentacles and tucked them against her side. With her eyes piercing through the waves, the mother glared before it moved on.

Good. The storm they had created would linger, but the creatures would not threaten Abraxas as they swam toward their quest.

Sighing, Lore turned her attention back toward the ruins that were once a symbol of hope for the entire kingdom. Solis Occasum had been made mostly of mirrors back in the days of old. Great circular windows would reflect the sun at all those who traveled anywhere near.

She remembered the stories that her mother used to tell. The capital of Umbra had once been in this place. The sun itself had blessed the building and lived inside it.

Now, it was little more than a wreckage of a hope that was long past destroyed.

The towers had crumbled years ago. Only the short stubs of what they once were remained to even suggest there used to be towers there at all. The main building was largely intact, although it was missing a roof. As Lore grew closer, she could see there were plenty of guards around it.

So Margaret knew that Lore had returned.

But their eyes were all turned toward the horizon. They did not look anywhere other than what was directly in front of them, their eyes trained to seek any movement that might approach the castle.

She floated closer and realized they were all elves. Every single one of them.

Lore hadn't even known there were so many elves still alive. And this must only be a fraction of them if Margaret had stationed them this far away. Where had she found these people? Were they always so close and Lore had just never seen them?

Concerning thoughts danced through her head. What if Margaret had lied to her the entire time? What if Margaret had been hiding them, knowing that they would be available for when she needed them most?

All the possibilities swirled throughout her mind. The elves were the best army she could have, without a doubt. They were fighters who had trained for years.

But they had been beaten before, a voice whispered in her mind. They had fallen to the humans, of all people, and that meant they could be beaten. No matter how many times she'd been told that the elves were the most powerful creatures in all the realm, they were not. They had fallen, just like the rest of them.

Floating past three guards who were clustered together, she discovered the entrance to the dungeons. Apparently most of Solis Occasum had fallen, but not what was underneath the ground.

Torchlight illuminated the stairs that plummeted into the darkness. They were slick with water that dripped down from the ceiling in echoing wet plops. There were three more guards at the entrance, and four stationed all along the stairwell until she reached the bottom.

Then there were even more guards.

Sighing, she shook her head at the over indulgence. Margaret really thought she had protected this place well. And perhaps, to someone who didn't realize how powerful Lore had become, she had. A dragon could not dig through the ground to get to Zephyr. He would have to wait up top or fight down in his mortal form, which they all knew wasn't

Abraxas's strongest form.

The guards were all stationed in a very tight stairwell. It would make it very difficult to fight their way down to him. And so, this would create a rather interesting puzzle to solve.

The first cell she passed by was filled with familiar faces.

She paused in front of that cell, staring at the other women who had participated in the bridal competition for Zander's hand. They were all huddled together with their families, their clothing dirty and their eyes haunted. But they were well fed, and they were alive. It was a start.

She walked past another cell filled with dwarves, more filled with humans she didn't recognize, but from the state of their clothing, they must be nobility. People that Margaret needed to keep alive and to make appearances so the others would remain quiet and calm. It was a barbaric thing to do to the people of this realm, and yet she wasn't surprised.

What did surprise her was the troop of elves trapped in the cell beyond the humans. Elves that should have been guarding the prison not being locked inside with the others.

Peering through the shadows, she tried to see their faces, but quickly lost interest. If Margaret had trapped elves, perhaps they had tried to fight against her. It meant little to her.

There was only one person in this prison she needed to see. And that was Zephyr.

He was at the very end of the dungeon. Far away from the others, so he wouldn't even be able to hear them moving if they called out to him. There wasn't a single sound here, other than the shuffle every now and then of the single guard who stood before his door.

This was a massive elf. The man was almost twice her height and easily twice her weight. He stood with his arms crossed, glaring down the hallway as though he knew she might show up.

Lore waved her hand in front of his face a few times just to make sure he couldn't actually see her. He didn't react, and she considered that to be a good sign. At least he wouldn't try to stop her from what she was about to do.

Walking around him, she slipped through the cage bars and stood in front of Zephyr. The boy was even worse for wear than she'd thought he would be. Apparently Margaret wanted him incapable of walking out of this prison if Lore showed up. His legs were folded underneath his body, forced to be on his knees. And when she peered around him, she could see that his feet had turned a deep, dark purple. How long had he been in this position? Too long, she could only imagine.

She ghosted her icy hand over his features, hoping that a little chill might help him.

"Lore?" he blinked his eyes open, blearily staring into the darkness around him as though he thought he could see her. He couldn't. Not yet, at least. "Are you there?"

"Quiet." The elf turned on his heel and snapped at Zephyr. His teeth were filed into sharp points. "There's no one here to save you, princeling."

She watched as Zephyr wilted in front of her. His head dropped back down to his chest and she heard them whisper under his breath, "I thought I felt her."

"You did," she replied, even knowing that he couldn't hear her. "You did, my boy. I just can't do anything to help you right now or they'll realize that I was here. But we are coming for you."

Even if it took an act of a goddess, she would get him out of this prison. He just had to trust in her a little longer, and then they would be here.

She readied herself to leave, knowing that she'd have to leave him behind, even though it hurt her heart to do so.

The sound of a key in a lock caught her attention. The big guard walked into the cell with a grin on his face that made her want to punch him already. He circled Zephyr, looking at the dark outlines of whip marks on his bare back and his eyes trailing over the shivers that racked Zephyr's body.

"Did you hear me?" the guard asked, running a tongue over his pointed teeth. "No one is coming for you. No one is ever coming for you."

Zephyr didn't respond. He just hung there with his arms over his head, dejectedly looking down at the floor. But she also saw the way his muscles bunched and how his jaw ticked.

The boy still had some fight left in him.

The guard kicked him. Hard. Right in the center of the back so that Zephyr swung forward and his shoulders made a horrible clicking noise. The would-be prince made a noise, then. A wheezing, horrible cry that echoed around him. Neither of his shoulders went back into place. He hung there, his fingers turning blue as the guard came around and crouched in front of him.

"You are a pawn in her plan," the guard said. "Both of them. You think you're important to Margaret? You aren't. And you think your goddess is going to save you? She has forgotten you exist. You are nothing more than a rotten leech that grew up in a graveyard. No one wants you, princeling. You're ours for as long as we see fit, and then I will tear your throat out with my teeth."

Zephyr's eyes locked on the guard's sharpened teeth and Lore could see the fight draining out of him. The hope. All of those emotions that she needed him to keep were slowly leaking out of him.

And she couldn't let that happen.

Magic flooded through her body and into her corporeal form. She felt her hands sharpen, strengthen, become something new. And with one sharp jab, she shoved her hand through the guard's body and wrapped her fingers around his still beating heart.

She could feel it. The warmth and the movement as it thundered against her palm.

She didn't need to see his face. The guard froze as though he knew something was terribly wrong. And then she felt him realize she was behind him. He turned his head slowly, his eyes seeing nothing but knowing she was there.

Lore leaned close to his ear and whispered, "Are you so sure a goddess won't save him?"

Before the guard could croak a response, she squeezed his heart. He let out a gasp and tried to claw at his own chest, but he could not stop her from squeezing the thundering muscle into a still, silent, mush.

He dropped onto the floor in front of Zephyr, dead with blood leaking out of his nose. It was a shame she couldn't do more. She'd like to kick the body away from Zephyr.

But then the power whispered she could. So she did. She kicked his body all the way to the edge of the cell where he would rot for all eternity if she had her way.

"Lore?" Zephyr gasped, his voice hoarse and hopeful. "It is you, isn't it?"

She replied, "Of course it is."

And though her voice rang true and clear in the room, she still wasn't sure if he'd heard her. But perhaps he didn't need to. Because Zephyr still smiled and then bared his own teeth at the body.

His fight was back. His hope had returned, and that was all she could ever ask for from the young man who had trusted her. Believed in her. So few had done that, and she would reward him in every way possible.

She'd overstayed her welcome, and that dead body would raise questions. For now, all she could do was wave a hand and conjure a mimic to stand in front of the cell. It wasn't much of a spell, hopefully not enough to make Margaret wonder why there were spells cast in her dungeon. But the other one? The one that she'd used to kill the man?

Margaret would soon know that all her guards hadn't been so useful to keep them away from her captured prince.

Lore had run out of time. They all had. They needed to get Zephyr out of here as quickly as possible, and then they needed to flee again. Time was no longer on their side.

Bending down, she pressed a kiss to his forehead and promised him they would return quickly. "Just a little longer," she said before fading back into her body. "Tomorrow, Zephyr. Tomorrow we will find you."

And as her soul slammed back into her body, she drew a deep gasping breath and opened her eyes.

Beauty and Abraxas stood before her, staring down at her body with hope in both their eyes as well. "I found him," she said. "We've run out of time. We leave now."

Her two companions eyed each other and then looked back at her. "Are you sure?" Abraxas asked. "You didn't want to rush anything just moments ago."

"I didn't then, I don't now." She leapt upright and raced toward their weapons. "And then I killed a man for touching him. Rash, I know, but it's time to get him. Get ready."

"Now that's the Lore I know!" Beauty crowed before rushing to get her own weapon.

CHAPTER 21

Abraxas wasn't a fan of plans that weren't iron tight. He knew there were a million ways for this to go wrong, namely that they'd already let Margaret know where they were. The elf would anticipate that they were coming for Zephyr, and considering the magical handprint that Lore had left behind inside Solis Occasum?

They would have little time at all to save their friend.

But Lore was adamant that this was their only opportunity. She was frantic as they packed, muttering under her breath about all the weapons they would need. She barely even saw Abraxas and Beauty as she swept past them, her gaze turned inward. As though she had done something wrong and couldn't quite look them in the eye.

He hated it. He didn't know how to fix this, though. They were all very aware that Zephyr's time was limited. And if Lore thought this was the only way to save him, then... he didn't know how to question her about that.

Sighing, Abraxas made his way out of the tunnel, following the two women who were already bickering again.

"I'm going," Beauty said, glaring at Lore as if hoping her eyes might set the elf on fire. "You can't say that I cannot come with you to save him. He will need me."

"He will," Lore agreed, adjusting the strap on her shoulder and ignoring that Beauty was glaring. "But that will not happen right now. He won't even be conscious when we get there if I'm right."

"Why wouldn't he be conscious? What did you do?"

"What I had to do for him to stay alive. They won't kill him outright, but I had to... Look, I don't have time to explain myself to you, Beauty. We have to go. Now."

He moved ahead when Lore glanced back for him. He was not wearing his pack or much at all. The clothing on his form would easily be destroyed, because he already knew what she wanted from him.

Though he hated to be used, Abraxas had already been itching to change. It had been far too long since he'd been in his dragon form. Far too long since he'd heard people scream in fear when they saw his shadow pass overhead.

"So, it is time," he muttered, standing beside her and looking up at the sky. "In daylight?"

"Plan changed." Lore, again, ignored Beauty, who was now waving her hand in front of the elf's face. "We're fighting to get him."

"How many?"

She shrugged. "Not enough. The guards on the outside I can put to sleep, or you can take care of the issue. That's up to you."

Oh, he'd always wanted to be a good man. He'd wanted to be a valuable partner and someone his mate could rely on. There was a time when he thought that man had to be genteel, honorable, stuffy. He'd thought he had to wear nice clothing and sit at a desk, or at the very least smile at strangers as they passed him by.

But now?

His mate had freed him from those terrible thoughts. Lore did not ask him to be anything other than a dragon. He was a man when they mated, and she enjoyed every second of that, but she never wanted him to change who he was or how he reacted.

And the crimson dragon in him longed to scent blood in the air and battle beneath his claws.

Giving her a feral grin, he felt the change rippling through him. "I'll take care of them."

Lore was not the same as she'd been before, either. She did not step away from him in fear of the power blast that would surely knock off her feet. Instead, she stepped closer and placed her hand on his cheek. "My terrifying love," she whispered. "We will take from them as they took from him."

Scales rippled down his body and a blast of air pushed Beauty away from them. But Lore remained. She stayed still with her hand on his snout now, gently petting the warm scales there before she whispered, "Should I get our armor?"

"There is no time." He nudged back against her touch. "We have fought without it before. This is not the battle it was forged for."

Lore's eyes flashed with pleasure, and then she raced up his outstretched wing. They'd done this so many times, but he felt the honor of it every time she settled between his spines.

Though the air rang with Beauty's swears, he still felt the power and the luxury of knowing that he and his partner were ready to take to the skies.

Lore leaned forward and patted the side of his neck. "Let them know we're coming." Her own voice had turned wild and wicked. "Let them know who to fear."

Stretching his neck high toward the sky, Abraxas let out a roar that shook the very clouds. It tore through the air and he knew that all who heard it would tremble in fear. They would know what it meant to be terrified and frozen as they waited for the attack. They would know what Zephyr had felt all these long nights.

His wings beat at the air and they were off. They soared through the air like an arrow loosed from a bow. Two weapons with their sights on the elves, who stood at the ready on the battlements of a castle that once stood for peace.

Though the wind whipped at her words, he still heard Lore as she shouted, "Drop me off in the center! Just get rid of the ones above me."

He would, and gladly.

They were close enough that he could see the white terror in the eyes of the elves, who pointed weapons at him. Acid dripped from the tips of those arrows, so at least Margaret had learned something from all the battles she'd fought before.

It would not help them.

He had also learned from those same battles.

Licking his lips, he gave them all a terrifying, toothy grin while banking low over the courtyard. Though his body was larger than its entirety, Lore had enough space to slip from his shoulders just before the first volley of arrows reached him.

Abraxas banked again, hard. He tilted his body, rolling through the air so that none of the arrows hit him. They would have to anticipate his movements. And considering they had never fought a dragon before, that would be a difficult task, indeed.

He circled the castle and let loose a surge of flames down one side of the parapets. Every elf on that side was soon torched, their bodies flailing as the blast of his flames sizzled the fat on their bones.

Shifting quickly, he avoided another round of arrows before raising up in the air, too high for them to reach. He took his time, watching Lore's fluid body as she fought the elves on the ground. Her fighting style had changed. She trusted her magic, even as she leapt through the air, rolled over the back of a bleeding elf, outstretched her hand to release a pulse of power that sent others staggering back.

Twenty men could not stop her, no matter how hard they struggled to contain her. And ah, it was a lovely sight. His bloodthirsty little mate would stop at nothing to get those she deemed family.

He sank low again, timing the moment when the elves turned their attention back to Lore. This time, he scooped their bodies up with his wide jaws, thrashing some off the edge of the parapets and onto the hard stone below.

The crunch of bone between his teeth was a familiar pleasure, and one he rarely got to enjoy. His eyes rolled back as his hunger abated for a few moments until an acid arrow sank through his wing and tore a hole in the membranes that remembered this pain all too well.

Blinking, he shifted, clinging to the side of the wall like a great bat and glaring at the elf who had dared. There were only two more walls, and one wall was entirely empty where the elves had fled. But the remaining soldiers all started preparing their weapons, their hands shaking in their rush.

Ah, well. Not everyone could be so brave.

Abraxas opened his mouth and a wall of fire dripped out. He burned them all, listening to the sweet sound of their screams. It felt right. It felt wrong. He shouldn't want to be a good man and still be able to do this, but war was war. And he would no longer deny the desires of a dragon.

A sharp whistle pierced through his hunting haze. Peering down at Lore, who stood in the center of the courtyard, surrounded by a ring of bloodied bodies, she pointed at a door that led underground. "We still have to go down there!"

Well, this size would not do then.

His sides heaving with disappointment, he crawled over the edge and then landed as a man at her side. He didn't want to go back to this form. Every ounce of his body wanted to remain as a dragon for just a little while longer.

He'd gotten used to how hard it was to change back into this weaker form.

"Better?" he grunted, teeth gritted against the need to change back again.

"Very." She cupped the back of his neck and drew him in for a long kiss. She tasted metallic and warm and everything that he'd always wanted.

Wrapping an arm around her waist, he tugged her against him. Her hands flattened on his chest and he wanted them on his skin. But he knew now wasn't the time, even if he wished it to be.

Pressing one last lingering kiss to her lovely, soft lips, he whispered, "I had forgotten how wonderful it is to watch you fight."

"I have never forgotten the terror of watching you." Lore leaned back and traced a finger over his bottom lip. "To know that a dragon protects me is a heady dose of power. I adore you, my love. Now let's go get our boy back."

Humming low under his breath, he turned on his heel and stalked toward the door. Throwing it open, he asked, "How many?"

"I have no idea. The last time I was here there were maybe thirty? She might have a lot more now."

A shadow raced toward him from the depths of the darkness. The elf brandished his sword high, clearly thinking he had the high ground, but he had never fought a dragon before.

Abraxas ducked underneath the man's swing and came up with his hand wrapped around the elf's throat. He threw him against the wall, the man's skull making a horrible cracking sound against the stone before he slumped.

"Hm," he grumbled. "I used to think so highly of the elves. Their fighting was renowned throughout the kingdom."

Lore stepped over the man's body and palmed the two knives in her hands. "They were."

Another elf launched at them, smaller than the other. Female, perhaps? Lore parried her sword, catching it in between her knives and twisting them. The woman was unarmed when Lore plunged her blades into either side of her throat.

Tsking, he maneuvered around the woman's body. "Then what happened?"

"Years of servitude? Years of becoming servants and bakers and farmers. Margaret forgot these people are not fighters. They were not born into the life that our ancestors were." Not even breathing hard, she gestured for him to go in front of her. "Your turn."

And so they fought. All the way down the stairs and into a larger room lined with cells. He didn't look at who occupied them. They were not important to him, and Lore knew that. Neither of them would waste time on anyone else. If she wanted to save them, then she would.

Considering Lore also didn't look at them, he could only assume they deserved to be there.

A wall of broad warriors stood between them and a final door at the end of the hall. Abraxas tried to relax his shoulders, but he was getting too old for this. His right shoulder was already stiff.

He should have stretched before they came down here.

Pressing her lips into a thin line, Lore stared the men down. "I will let you leave here alive," she said, her voice ringing in the dungeon. "All you have to do is put down your weapons."

"You think we'll trust you?" The man who spoke was tall and blonde, a lithe looking creature who would likely be difficult to kill. "You forgot your own kind."

"I'm half elf," she snarled at him. "I won't make this offer again. Drop your weapons and leave. Go back to Margaret and beg for her mercy, or flee from this isle and find yourself a new land. I don't care what you do."

Two elves did so. A man and a woman who looked at each other with history in their gazes. They skirted past Abraxas, flinching when he even so much as breathed. But then they raced from the room and up the dark stairwell.

The remaining eleven elves stayed where they were.

Lore handed him one of her knives and rotated her wrist. He heard an awful cracking noise, and then a continuous crunching as she moved it.

Perhaps they both should have prepared better for this. They were far too old for such things.

His mate cleared her throat and then said, "It's a shame you didn't go with your friends. That was a mistake."

She lifted her hand and all the elves froze where they were. Their eyes bulged in their heads and he realized they couldn't breathe. Their mouths dropped open, sucking at the air like fish before they fell to their knees. One by one.

"Lore?" he asked, his voice shaking with the violence of what she'd chosen to do.

This wasn't her. She wasn't the same woman who had urged them to be kind to people or to ignore them entirely. He remembered her not wanting anyone else to die and now...

Reality slammed back into him. The blood thirst drained away as he suddenly worried about what all of this would do to the woman he loved.

She met his gaze and then shook her head. "It's all right."

"Is it?"

A flash of sadness moved through her, and Lore's shoulders rounded in despair. "I gave them a choice. And then I had to make one myself, Abraxas. I will not make the same mistake I did in the first war. I will lose no one else who is dear to me."

He couldn't blame her for that.

Abraxas nodded and moved toward the last room. Wrenching the door open, he saw Zephyr laid out on the floor. Poor boy didn't even move when he heard them. They must have knocked him unconscious.

Without another thought, he ripped the door off its hinges so it wouldn't be in their way as he carried Zephyr out. It was time to gather up their friend and take him somewhere safe.

CHAPTER 22

Her heart hurt.

Every inch of her body felt wrong. She could feel the rage and anger crawling underneath her skin like another person had slipped inside her.

Lore wasn't a monster. She didn't kill everyone and anything who stood in her way. In fact, she'd fought her entire life against doing that.

But then she remembered that elf who had hurt Zephyr all over again. She remembered the man's expression as he'd enjoyed hurting a young man who had done nothing but good in his life. She'd realized in that moment that there was no saving people like that.

Or maybe there was saving them, but she didn't have the patience or the time for their nonsense. All those elves stood between her and the boy who meant something to her. Zephyr, her little brother, a young man who sometimes felt like her son.

They had taken him from her, from his home, from the young woman who loved him. They had turned his life into something horrific and terrifying and she refused to let them continue doing so, even if that meant they had to die.

And so she let them die. She would usher them to that dark place with a smile on her face and a swift flick of her wrist.

The moment she saw Zephyr laying on the ground, she saw red again. Lore wanted to tear the stars from the very sky and rip it to shreds. She wanted to set this entire kingdom on fire because it was full of people just like them.

She saw the madness of this realm inside them. And worse, she saw her own childhood full of pain and hunger and sadness because no one would help a little girl who was left by her mother. No one cared for a half elf who had fought her entire life for scraps of food.

An entire kingdom had avoided her. Looked the other way when she was struggling because no one wanted to be the person with the soft touch who took her in. No one wanted to be the person responsible for her.

Lore recognized them as a group of people who thought maybe, just maybe, they had a choice. A group of people who would stop at nothing for equality and instead went too far, suddenly tearing the kingdom apart again.

Her heart ripped with each memory. It tore and shredded and blew into pieces because there was nothing she could do to stop them. At least, she hadn't been able to back then.

Now? Now she could rip this kingdom apart and do exactly what the prophecy said she would. She would piece it back together after she tore it to shreds.

Abraxas knelt beside Zephyr and put his fingers on his neck. "Alive."

"Good." She hadn't thought there was much of a chance for Margaret to kill the young man. After all, everyone still needed him alive. There were more humans to gather up, more people to prove that she was still a trustworthy person while murdering and stealing from the humans. "Can you carry him?"

"I can." Abraxas gathered Zephyr up easily, arms underneath his knees and shoulders. Though it might not be the most comfortable for Zephyr's wounds, it was the easiest position to get him out of here. "Shall we?"

They had likely already run out of time. Even now, Margaret was likely storming the castle. They were stealing her greatest chess piece, and if they didn't move...

"Let's go." Lore didn't even want to think about what would happen if Margaret caught them. Though she was quite confident she could fight the other elf, she didn't know how well it would go for either of them.

Something deep inside her said that now was not the time to fight. They still had a long way to go. They still had more to this story that they needed to fix.

Striding out of the cell, she led the way with her dagger in her hand and her eyes on the shadows. There were two elves who had fled, and they could easily linger for a better moment to attack.

Except they weren't.

The other cells, however, were lively. All kinds of creatures wrapped their hands around the bars and begged for their release.

"Please!" a dwarf called out. "My family knows where I am. Surely the dwarves told you where we were?"

They did not. But she still waved a hand and released them.

The humans cried out. "I remember you! We were there, together. Don't you remember?"

She did, and she remembered how terrible they were. How most of those women were willing to be cutthroat to get their hands on a throne. But still, she unlocked their doors because she could.

That left the elves.

They stood in their cell, stoic as always. They watched as Lore paused in front of them and she felt something twist hard in her chest. A familiar feeling. A desire to want to be part of their group and their family, even though none of them had ever wanted her.

Because at her very core, Lore still wanted them to acknowledge her. She still needed them to see her and tell her that she was wanted.

She turned only her head toward them. "Do you not have any reason for me to release you?"

The elves all looked at a single elderly man who approached the bars. He wore an outfit that marked him as their leader. But the faded blue cloak with golden edges was moth eaten and worn.

"Would begging really make you release us?" He tilted his head to the side. "You were never part of our family. I will not lie to be released."

"So you still see me as nothing more than a half elf." Her heart stuttered once, twice, then thundered in her chest.

"I see you for what you are. I know the prophecy and I know more about your story that has likely never been told." He reached through the bars, his hand outstretched as though she might touch him. "I call tell you all that you never knew about yourself. I can tell you so much about your story and it would give you more power than you ever dreamed of."

Lore wanted to suck the air from his lungs. She wanted to put her hand through his chest and feel his heart beating against her palm.

"You know nothing of what I dream." Her voice thickened with emotion, her palms sweaty and her words stumbling she spoke so quickly. "I was a little girl who wanted a family. The only people I ever knew were my mother's people. You. I wanted to go home to the elves and have someone read me the same bedtime stories that I was raised on. I wanted to hear the songs of our people and the sound of our language. I wanted to learn how to speak, act, and eat like all of you. And you denied me that."

She drew closer to the cell until her face was nearly pressed to the bars. She wanted him to see her pain. Needed him to realize that he was the one who had done this to her. He and all his people who refused to see a little girl when all they saw was an abomination.

The elder drew back from the bars, not in fear, but in disgust. "You were born this way for a reason. We saw you as the creature who would destroy our home. You wanted us to deny the truth of your existence."

"No," she whispered. "I wanted you to see me. But you could only find it in your heart to be cruel to a child, and that spoke volumes about you and your people. This castle is empty. Find your own way out."

She started to leave, but the old man lunged forward and grabbed onto her arm. His ancient fingers felt like shackles around her bicep.

"Wait!" His voice was filled with desperation. "Don't you want to know more about your prophecy?"

Her spine straightened, stiffened, and her heart hardened into ice. She turned her full attention to him again, and this time, he shrank away from her in fear. "No. I have no interest in learning about the prophecy. Five hundred years ago, elves saw into the future and knew it had changed. Fear spread throughout them because they were not the catalyst of such change, and they knew they could not control me. Perhaps what they saw scared them not because it was bad, but because it was different. I have no use for prophecy. I make my own life, and my own steps forward. You would do well to remember that."

The crowd of elves surrounded him, pulling them into the safety of their arms and their family. But the old man had eyes only for her. "You walk the path of destiny, half elf. Even you cannot step off that path."

She shrugged. "Then the path will bend to my whim."

She turned away from the elves who were meant to be her family, her safety, her people. She left them with only the sight of her back and a dragon who snarled at them as he trailed up the stairs after her.

Everything ached. Her soul whispered that she should return to those people and set them free. It would take them a long time to be freed from that prison, if they were not all left there to rot. Perhaps they could unlock it eventually, or perhaps they would remain as skeletons in that horrible place.

But an equally loud part of her said that they got what they deserved. They would not have taken her in as a child, nor did they care if she survived. They only wanted to control her. To see that she led them into a life only the elves would know and that... was wrong.

All of this was wrong.

She stumbled out of the dungeon and into the sunlight with a gasp. Heat played across her frozen cheeks and thawed the ache in her chest. Even though it smelled like blood and guts and all the other scents that came with death, at least they weren't down there any longer.

Abraxas stopped beside her, staring up at the clouds in the sky as well. "Lore?"

She hummed low under her breath.

"They were never your family."

"I know."

"No, you don't. I never had family either, but at least they told me that. They didn't string me along or give me any kind of hope. I knew my people were dead and that let me move on." He nudged her shoulder with his own, his arms still full with Zephyr. "Letting them go was brave. I hope you see that for what it is."

She didn't.

It took no bravery to walk away from them, not when they had done so much to her that it made her want to scream.

"Someday I might regret what I did," she whispered. "Someday, I might look back on this moment and see only evil in what we have done here."

"Or perhaps you will see this as the first moment you allowed yourself to be free." The sun slanted across his eyes, and he squinted down at her as he tried very hard to understand how she was feeling. "You are known by many names throughout this kingdom, Lore. And the name half-elf is not one of them. Not anymore."

But should she be known that way? Should she deny who she was when there were so many other children like her out there? So many children who just wanted to be accepted and find a family that wouldn't look down on them?

"I am a woman who has lived between worlds," she said. "I have spent a lifetime looking through windows and wishing for the family that lived beyond the glass. But now I have you. I have Beauty and Zephyr and yes, Draven, even though you hate it. I have our children and so much more on the dragon isle waiting for us. Letting those elves go was easy compared to losing any of you."

Her soul settled back in place. It was the truth. She'd never wanted anything more than all the people who were already in her life. Going back in time and getting the elves' approval? It was unnecessary.

She had already found her family and her happiness. Why would she need to work to change anyone's mind about her, when her chosen family already accepted her the way she was?

Turning toward Abraxas, she held out her arms for Zephyr. "Give him here."

"Are you sure you can carry him?"

Lore leveled Abraxas with a look. "How else are we going to get him on your back? I think we both know I have to carry him out of here. Otherwise, I'll try straddling you while you change, but who knows where I'd end up."

Or if she'd end up impaled on one of his spines. Lore didn't want to try that, or test her magic to see how much it would do to keep her alive.

Glowering at Abraxas, she waited until he handed the young man over. And he wasn't that heavy. Not even remotely. The bones of his ribs stuck out and dug into her palms and shoulder where she tucked him. His legs were mere sticks that weighed next to nothing.

Her boy, her poor, sweet boy who had grown up in a crypt and looked to her for guidance, had suffered too much.

She sighed, staring down into his limp face that was already swollen and covered in bruises. "I'm so sorry this had to happen to you."

But really, what had she thought would happen when she left? Of course he would be the easy target. This was all her fault, and she was the only one who could fix it.

A warmth tingled through her body as she started the healing process. Her magic traveled through him, seeking all the hurts and trying to fix what it could. But there was a lot more damage internally than any of them could see. This would take some time to heal, and she couldn't do it on dragon back.

Still, she could make him a little more comfortable and send him to rest with a little more ease.

"Ready?" Abraxas asked, his eyes still on Zephyr. "He looks like he's getting worse."

"I'll hold him in this state for as long as we need." But they couldn't go back to the dwarven kingdom, could they? Margaret would hunt them, and she'd suspect the dwarves. "We need to move."

Abraxas changed, his dragon bursting out of his skin with more speed than she'd seen from him in a while.

And yet, as she carried the young man up Abraxas's wing and sat down with him, Lore couldn't for the life of her see a better way forward than the dwarves. They were officially on the run now.

But at least Zephyr was safe.

CHAPTER 23

He'd never been more proud of her and more worried at the same time.

What Lore had done back there... To her own people? He'd seen nothing like it. And though he agreed with what she'd done—he likely would have left them there to rot as well—it made him afraid to know what would come next.

Her logic was sound. They had never done anything for her. And he'd tried to soothe that ache by reminding her how many people she now who called her family. All of that was true, and it should ease the pain a little.

But she could do that to other elves. He knew Lore understood the implications of leaving them there. Margaret might not even go into the dungeons. The littered mess of dead bodies in the courtyard and the charred corpses on the ramparts were enough for anyone to guess who had been there.

Lore may very well have condemned those elves to death. And

a cruel one at that. They would wither in the darkness, slowly wasting away until they realized no one was coming for them. By then, it would be too late.

He didn't know what was next. They'd gotten Zephyr safe and sound, but there was still a kingdom to save. Part of him, likely the same part that Lore was battling, wanted to continue onward. They could pick Beauty up along the way, and then they would disappear into the sunset.

If Beauty wanted them to bring her father, the more the merrier. Abraxas had carried two dragonlings all the way to the dragon isles. Four humans were nothing at this point.

And no one would know. No one could find his homeland, even if they tried. And if Margaret wanted to make that journey, or had the courage to do so, then she would be greeted by a wall of dragons. Even she wasn't so foolish.

But that would, unfortunately, leave the kingdom at Margaret's beck and call. That would still leave the problem right here when they had fought so hard to fix what was broken.

"I know what you're thinking," Lore said, her voice whispering over his shoulder. "We cannot."

"I know," he growled back. "I know we cannot take them to safety, but that does not make it easier to see him like this. To know that we might have, under better circumstances, saved him."

It was unlikely that they would have saved him, though. Even Abraxas knew that. If they were here, Margaret would have hidden him better. She would have maybe killed him and found some sorcerer who would make a lookalike for Zephyr to still be a walking, talking puppet for the kingdom to see.

There were still humans to save. People who were not the way they should be. And it broke his heart to know that in making an attempt to save them all, they would have to risk their friends again.

Banking hard, he soared over the waters and dipped his wings in the salt spray. It turned to mist at his touch and sprayed back upon his riders. Though Zephyr was likely still freezing cold, Abraxas could feel the boy's heat pressing against his back. Zephyr's wounds had already turned toward a fever, and that meant they were running out of time.

"I don't want to go back to the dwarves for long," Lore said, pausing in the middle of the thought to whisper more healing spells against Zephyr's hair. "They have protected us for too long. The risk for them is too great."

He had thought about the same thing. Abraxas sat with the thought until they reached the familiar clearing. He landed quietly and softly, so as not to disturb the two people on his back. And as Lore clambered off, he knew where they had to go next. Although it was a greater risk than he wanted to take.

He turned back into his mortal form and then spun to gather Zephyr in his own arms. Meeting Lore's gaze, he said the words that he knew she was thinking but didn't want to consider. "The Ashen Deep."

"They could very well have sided with Margaret. They have no love for us." She shifted a strand of hair away from Zephyr's slick forehead. "The chances of them being willing to help are very low. Especially with a wounded mortal."

"A wounded prince," Abraxas corrected. "I have a hard time believing the Matriarch would fall for any of Margaret's lies. Draven came with you, didn't he? That has to count for something."

"I don't think his mother was aware that he was going to travel across the kingdom and come with me," Lore replied, her voice wry and amused. "I imagine the woman will have a lot to say when she sees us all, and a few choice words about stealing her son. But we will discuss this again soon. We need to get him inside."

The unspoken fear was still there. That Margaret perhaps knew where they had fled. That already there were armies marching through the forest just out of their sight, and that they may have brought death to this clearing once again.

He nodded. "She knows the dwarves exist. Didn't Algor say they were working on some kind of treaty before the dwarves denied her?"

"So she has no love for these people and likely no respect left either." Lore's lips pressed into a thin, disgusted line. "If we do not leave, she will know we are here. I fear she will still retaliate against them, even if we have moved on. The dwarves are not prepared for what she will bring with her."

"Actually," the voice of the dwarven king interrupted them. "We are well prepared for that. But I am touched that the Fallen Star herself fears for our wellbeing. Perhaps we have done something right after all."

They both turned toward the voice, and Abraxas was relieved to see the king was alone. At least the man knew enough to not have a large presence waiting for them.

Algor ambled over, his hands clasped behind his back, and peered up at Zephyr. "So, this is the boy?"

"He's the last remaining royal of his bloodline, yes."

"Interesting." Algor's eyebrows moved high on his forehead and his short beard twitched. "At how that girl was going on about him, I thought he'd be more handsome."

Don't laugh, don't laugh, don't laugh, he told himself repeatedly until he could school his expression into one of indifference. "They are very close."

"I understand that, but I'll never understand a woman who puts a man on a pedestal and calls him perfection." Algor shrugged. "Ah well, nothing to be done about the lusts of young women, I suppose. I'm certain there were plenty who did the same to me in my younger days. I've prepared a room for him, and healing."

Lore stepped in, her footsteps quiet as she placed her hand on Algor's shoulder. "I can't ask you for more time in this place. We have already brought enough danger to your doorstep. All I ask is for one evening to piece him together enough to safely travel."

"Nonsense. The dwarves have lived here for ages. I will not have you running to the elves at the first sign of trouble." But even Abraxas could see the shadows in the dwarf's eyes.

He was worried about the same thing. Algor might be flippant about his emotions or even the dangers that they were all facing. But he knew the dangers well, perhaps even better than Lore or Abraxas.

"We leave," Abraxas said. His voice was guttural and offering no argument. "We will not bring about destruction to this esteemed home. The boy will come with us, and we are not running, dwarf. I will have you know that without question. We are going to another safe harbor until we can create a plan that will bring about the end of these times. You will be part of that plan."

Lore met his gaze, and he saw the moment she understood what he was doing. They had to play to this man's honor. They needed the dwarf to understand that even though they were leaving, that did not mean they thought the dwarves were unworthy.

With a slight, grateful quirk of her lips, Lore turned her attention back to Algor. "There is a war coming, dwarf. A war that will end all wars.

I would have the dwarves fight at our side, if you were so willing."

Algor straightened his shoulders and puffed out his chest. "When the Fallen Star calls for us, the dwarves will be ready, my lady."

"And we will all be lucky for it." Lore squeezed his shoulder and then turned her attention to the young man he held against his chest. "Shall we? I want to get started on whatever is happening inside him. There is bleeding I could not pinpoint."

And that was that. He followed her into the depths of the dwarven kingdom and rushed through the tunnels. They needed to get into the room that Algor had provided, and quickly. Though he could still feel a steady breath in the boy's chest, it rattled with fluid. Dangerous fluid. Fluid that could sneak up on them and make all of this infinitely more difficult if they didn't hurry.

Taking a deep breath, Abraxas filled his lungs with the scents that escaped from Zephyr's slightly open lips. Pus wasn't all that helpful. Blood, also not surprising. But there was an acidic scent that came with it that Abraxas thought he was familiar with.

It was a poison that the King had used before. Zander enjoyed playing with things he shouldn't, and sometimes that was giving his servants poison just to see what it would do.

Abraxas couldn't remember the name of it, though. There had been so many poisons and so many opportunities for him to smell all the scents of them that erupted from the servants' mouths.

"Lore," he said as they reached the room. "It's poison."

"Is it?" She gestured for him to set Zephyr on the cot in the center of the room, then folded herself around his head, making sure that her legs were on either side of him.

Abraxas saw the image in front of him and it was overlaid with another in his memory. A moment when Tanis had done the same thing to Lore, keeping Lore alive when she was lost in her own mind. The power inside her had swelled so much that he hadn't been able to... to...

"Abraxas?" Her voice sliced through the terrible memory. "Are you still here with me?"

He pulled himself from that terrible memory, from all those moments that had nearly taken her from him, and forced himself to see reality. Right here. Right in front of him. There were people who needed his help. People he loved.

Swallowing hard, he nodded. "I'm here."

"What makes you think they poisoned him?"

He touched his nose. "I can smell it on his breath. There's something coming out of his lungs. I can't place what it is, though. Zander used to use it on the servants."

"What did it do to them?"

He searched his mind, trying to remember every detail so that he could help. "It made them sleep for a while. A long while. And when they woke, they were quite scattered. As though the world didn't feel very real to them anymore."

Lore nodded. "It's a start. If you can remember the name, then maybe I can send Algor to get us help. Surely, there are some healers here that are familiar with poison. In the meantime, I'll work on getting him to be awake. Lungs are a good start."

He'd done all he could. Every fiber of his body itched to do more, though. Abraxas was starkly reminded of the feeling he'd had when Lore was laid out before him, sick and with no way for him to help her. He had wanted to piece her back together and all he'd managed was to lie at her side and hope that his warmth would make her a little more comfortable.

He hated not being able to do anything. A crimson dragon was meant to tear and rip and protect. Not to stand and wait, helpless, while those he was supposed to protect remained injured and harmed.

A low growl burned in his throat, but then he turned toward the door. And there, standing in the opening with her hands over her mouth, was a person he could protect.

"Beauty," he breathed, reaching for her without another word.

She launched into his arms with a soft sob, burying her face in his chest as though she couldn't stand to look at Zephyr like that. "What did they do to him?"

Tears burned in his eyes and the bridge of his nose ached. He stared up at the ceiling as he said, "They did everything they could to break him. But he is strong, Beauty. He's still here."

"I didn't think..." Her voice broke. "I didn't think she was so cruel. Even after everything that I've seen, I didn't think she could do that to him."

None of them had thought it possible. But he supposed any manner of cruelty could be explained away when saving a kingdom was the end goal. Wasn't that what Lore had just done to the elves in that cell?

As he looked at his elf, working so diligently to save their friend, he wondered just how different she was from Margaret. If their story was told from another perspective, were they the villains?

He already knew the answer was yes. To so many elves in this kingdom, they were the monsters who said the humans had to stay. That magical creatures had to stare their tormentors in the face while smiling and accepting them into their homes and businesses. The kingdom the magical creatures had hoped to build would never become true if the world turned the way Lore was fighting to turn it.

But she was right. He thoroughly and wholeheartedly believed she was right. Two different kinds of people could not continue to rip and tear at each other without ever stopping. The humans would find a way to rebel, just as the creatures had.

He tightened his arms around Beauty and reminded himself that there was good within their ranks. Good people with hearts of gold and souls that shimmered like coins. Just like her.

A soft inhalation from the bed made him stiffen one more time. There Zephyr was, eyes blinking open and staring around the room in disbelief.

"Am I still in prison?" he asked, his voice hoarse as if he'd spent hours screaming.

Lore leaned over him with a bright grin stretched over her face. "No. You're with me."

Beauty struggled out of his arms and raced for the bed. She gathered Zephyr's hands in hers and waited for him to look at her. When his gaze met hers, Abraxas could almost feel the love between them. He could almost see it, bright and powerful and achingly perfect.

"There you are," Beauty whispered as she gently kissed his lips. "We've been looking everywhere for you."

CHAPTER 24

Lore refused to stay any longer. She'd already talked with Algor. He'd understood her need to move and was very kind in providing them with a few enchanted packs to take with them. Lore already had her and Abraxas's new armor packed away in it, and she'd never know the bag wasn't empty.

Handy, having dwarves around. She would miss them quite a bit.

Still, she had to get her head on straight now. The dwarves were easy to bargain with. They were unlikely to be sneaky about what they wanted or what they would do to get that.

In this case, she'd already promised Algor a boon. He hadn't said what he wanted, only that the Fallen Star would help them when they needed it. Whether that was in a few years, or a few centuries. As long as Lore was alive, she would come when the dwarves needed her.

It was an easy promise to make.

She'd have done anything for them, especially considering they were Goliath's relatives. Even being around them reminded her so much of her dear friend, and it soothed some ache in her soul that desperately needed to be soothed.

Their humor, the way they moved, how they laughed in the face of danger, as though living in this place wasn't terrifying at all. Everything made her remember a time when she'd lived across from a dwarf who painted a rising sun on his window because he didn't care if others saw it.

With a soft smile on her face at the memories, she opened the door to their private chambers. They'd added Zephyr now that he was feeling a little better, though not by much.

Two days wasn't enough for him to heal. Two days and he still could barely walk.

Lore couldn't use her power here, at least not in the way she wanted. The strength of the spell she'd have to conjure to heal him would let Margaret know exactly where they were. And they still hadn't figured out the poison that he'd been given, so they couldn't get him up on his feet without fearing that he might fall over.

Pushing his body when there was poison in his veins was sure to speed up the effects of whatever herb or potion he'd been given.

Still, it was good to see him awake. She leaned against the door jamb and watched the three of them talk. Abraxas was telling a story from the dragon isles, his hands animated as he wove his tale. Beauty rested snug against Zephyr's shoulder, holding his hand as she laughed at the dragon's antics. Even Zephyr, pale faced and still slightly shaking, had a smile on his face at the story.

Her dragon was always making sure that everyone was as happy as they could be, she mused. Abraxas would stop at nothing to make sure that his companions were well taken care of. But, oh, it made her heart hurt to see them all like this. As though nothing had happened.

The darkness crept back into her mind. Memories floating in front of her. Zephyr's body limp on the ground. The elf kicking him, threatening him with worse torture and saying no one would ever come for him. Goliath's body laid out on the ground with a heavy mace stuck through his chest. Draven under a siren's spell because she hadn't anticipated that her friend would attack him like that. Beauty, too thin and gaunt with ash on her cheeks and no home to return to.

Abraxas. Poor Abraxas with a pale face, too thin, certain that she had been dead and so he would follow her into that oblivion.

They all relied on her and she had failed them time and time again. No more. She wouldn't fail them ever again, even if that meant she had to crush this kingdom underneath her heel.

"We're leaving," she said, breaking the spell of happiness that Abraxas had woven around them.

The three of her companions froze and then looked at her. None of them seemed to know what to say until Abraxas cleared his throat.

"Now?" he asked.

"Right now."

Beauty struggled to fling her legs over the bed, making sure she didn't touch Zephyr too much in the process. "I'll pack our things up, then. Give me an hour or two?"

Shaking her head, Lore pointed in the corner where three packs already waited for them. "I did that this morning. You were all still asleep."

"Oh." Beauty frowned. "So you knew we were leaving today, and you didn't tell us?"

Maybe she should have told them in the morning, but there was so much for her to do before they could head out. "I didn't want to worry you," she tried to explain. Even Lore knew they were empty words. So she gestured between the three of them as though conjuring back the happiness that had been there only moments before. "I didn't want to stop that from happening. You all need it."

"So do you," Zephyr replied.

It was the first time he'd talked with her since she'd saved him. The first time he'd been able to look her in the eye without getting watery.

Lore held his gaze, forcing him to feel the moment they connected. She needed him to be strong right now, even though he'd had to be strong for far too long.

And now that he'd healed for two days, he could hold her gaze without flinching.

"Good," she said, and the two of them knew it wasn't in response to what he'd said. "Get your packs. Zephyr, you're not walking. Abraxas will carry you."

"I can walk," Zephyr protested, then froze when she leveled him with a glare.

"Either I will carry you, or Abraxas will carry you," she said. "It's your choice."

Grumbling under his breath, Zephyr took his time getting his feet on the floor. Even that little movement made him breathless, though. Finally, he jerked his chin toward Abraxas. "It'll be less humiliating if a dragon carries me."

She'd admit he was right. The prince of these lands had been infected with poison, beaten within an inch of his life, and still wasn't anywhere near the healthy point he should be able. Stubborn arrogance would not be his downfall today. Not on her watch.

After that, it took very little time at all for her three companions to ready themselves and get moving. They stepped out of the dwarven stronghold and into the bright light of the sun. And as Lore paused behind them, the last of their party to leave, she felt her entire body clench at the sight of so few people who stood with her now.

She remembered how chaotic it had been with everyone traveling together. How Goliath had poked at Draven and Abraxas while they bickered like two children. And now? Now their party was quiet as they approached the cold edge of the forest. So fathomless, so dark, it was almost as though she looked into the depths of the sea.

Beyond those trees, the deepmongers waited. The Ashen Deep. The elves who had very much denied her and the last time she'd been in this forest, they'd tried to imprison her.

But then they had fought by her side against the king. The Matriarch had proven herself still worthy of the name as she'd whirled through the Umbral Soldiers, her blades that screamed for souls in her hands. They were the few that could wield those blades.

Lore was not looking forward to their temptation once again. The whispers were terrifying. They called to a part of her soul that wanted power more than it wanted anything else.

A little shiver wracked through her body before she let it go. "Come on," she muttered. "We'll never get there at this pace."

Lore plunged into the waiting darkness and hated the cold, clinging dampness that enveloped her. That magic was likely protecting the forest and letting the deepmongers know when someone had entered their kingdom. Even Margaret wouldn't be so foolish as to stride in here without at least requesting an audience.

The only fools who would do so were Lore and her companions, she had a feeling.

They walked in silence for a few hours, going deeper and deeper into the woods. Lore's feet slid on the mossy ground. Not an inch wasn't covered by some kind of moss or algae. Even the trees were a strange, dark color. They weren't right, or at least the same kind of trees that one would see anywhere else in the kingdom. They moved at the edges of her vision, stretching away from her as though even they were frightened of what had walked into their midst.

"Lore?" Beauty asked, her voice little more than a whisper. "Do you know where we're going?"

"I don't need to." Lore turned her face up to stare at the dark canopy over their head. Not a single ray of light penetrated those leaves, and yet they could somehow see. A silvery light trailed through the forest around them, catching on every glimmering dewdrop on each leaf, petal, or moss.

"You don't need to?" Beauty repeated, her brow furrowing in confusion. "Why?"

"Because they'll find us." She turned her attention toward a particular line of trees whose roots were higher than the rest. And then she pointed up to that line, to a small hill that rose in the distance. "In fact, I think they already have."

At her words, a line of elven warriors appeared from behind trees and hidden in the shadows. Their black armor glimmered in the dim light like slick oil. Their skin had been given a similar treatment, darkening their already deep skin tone into something that was almost difficult to see. But she'd seen the flash of their weapons and heard the familiar whispers of blades that wanted Lore to use them. She could make the world tremble, and they wanted to feel its heart beat, those blades whispered.

Three deepmongers approached them. Their white hair was twisted on top of their heads in intricate braids, appearing almost like crowns. But the woman between the two men wore an actual crown, and Lore knew better than to stare at the obsidian gemstones for too long.

Sinking down onto a knee, she kept her gaze on the ground as she honored the Matriarch before her. "It has been a long time, deepmonger."

"I thought we had seen the last of you." The Matriarch's liquid voice had hardened with hatred. "You are supposed to be dead."

"I did not remain dead for very long. A mere six months to convene with my ancestors, and to learn from the mothers before me." Lore looked up and met the other woman's dead eyed stare. "A feat I have a feeling you are quite familiar with."

If her instincts were correct, the Matriarch's lineage was very similar to Lore's own. While Lore's mothers passed down their magic to her, the Matriarch could convene with those who came before her and use their knowledge as her own. They were not so different, if only in power.

The Matriarch tilted her head to the side and bared her teeth in a snarl. "So that is what the prophecy referred to, then. You are the power of our mothers."

"Generations of women who have lost." Lore stood and dusted off her knees. "And years of heartbreak all rolled into one person. I am here to put an end to that."

A sharp tsk echoed through the clearing. The two young men on either side of the Matriarch reached for the weapons at their hips, but did not draw them when Abraxas gave an answering snarl. Instead, they turned their attention back to their mother, who had not moved other than to make her sound of disgust.

The Matriarch stepped closer, her hand outstretched to cup Lore's jaw. "You are not the generations of pain felt by our people, nor are you worthy of their power." Her hand clenched, long fingernails biting into Lore's skin. "Now, self proclaimed goddess, where is my son?"

Ah. Of course.

Lore had forgotten that the Matriarch likely thought Lore had stolen him away. Or that she'd killed Draven. It was always a possibility in their line of work. Or that her son had died protecting the one creature that the Matriarch did not like.

They might have fought beside each other, but that did not mean the woman in front of her trusted her. Not at all.

Lore sighed and endured the pain on her jaw and cheek. "He is alive and well on the dragon isle."

"Why did he not return?"

Draven had given her a message for his mother, although Lore had forgotten about it until this moment. "He said to tell you he'd found his blade in the shadows, but it must first be tempered. Honestly, he went on a very long time about making a knife and all the stages that he needed to wait for, but apparently that was something you would understand. I don't know what any of it means."

The Matriarch dropped her hand as though Lore had burned her. "Truly? He said all that?"

Lore gave her a wry grin while testing the new holes in her face. "Would I say something so truly random otherwise? I have no idea what any of that means, Matriarch. But you do."

The woman pressed a shaking hand to her lips and stared at her two other sons. They both looked lost, or perhaps shocked. And none of the family had anything to say until the Matriarch nodded.

"Well, if what you speak is true, then that changes things."

Lore glanced behind her with a frown to see Abraxas making a similar expression. "Why does that change things?"

"Who is she?" The Matriarch asked. "Who is this blade that has buried itself in my son's heart?"

Draven was fine. What was his mother going on about? Lore had just told her that he was alive and well and still on the island...

Ah.

Oh.

Lore looked over her shoulder again to see Abraxas's expression had turned furious. His skin flashed back and forth between mortal and scaled, and even Zephyr looked a little frightened to be in his arms.

Her dragon pulled himself together just enough to snarl, "My daughter."

Silence stretched between them all, tenuous and far too brittle until the Matriarch let out a sound that was almost a giggle.

Lore's eyebrows flew up as she turned to see, stunned, that the Matriarch was laughing. The woman even snorted before she looked at her sons, who then lost it as well. All three of the family couldn't stop laughing until their mother wiped a finger underneath her eye, catching the tears that had gathered there.

"Of all the people he could have chosen, of course my son waits for a dragon. Ah, Abraxas, I am sorry for it. First, he tries to steal your mate and now he steals your daughter. That boy of mine has a death wish."

"Indeed he does," Abraxas growled, but there was a lightness to his tone.

Lore assumed that meant all was... well? Enough so that she could breathe, at least. No one would try to kill them, for the time being, and that meant that the deepmongers were not ones she had to worry about.

"Draven has a taste for the dangerous," Lore said, her shoulders relaxing and the knot in the center of her chest loosening. "Although, I will admit, Nyx is one of the most beautiful young women I've ever seen."

"And she is your daughter, as well?" The Matriarch asked.

"I claim her to be."

"Then she will be foolish and heavy-handed, I can only imagine. It sounds as though the two of us will be tied together in more than just duty or honor." The Matriarch waved a hand for them to follow her. "Come. I can see there is one in your company who needs healing."

"And rest," Lore added.

"Such cannot be denied. You all reek of dwarf, half elf. You'll bathe before entering my home."

And so Lore and her companions followed the Ashen Deep back into the earth once more.

CHAPTER 25

Underground. Again.

Abraxas didn't mind so much the Ashen Deep's home, mostly because the depths of where they lived were so deep and tall that he couldn't even see the ceiling. It made him feel more like he was in a dragon's cave. The kind where he could change without fear of hitting his head or causing a cave in.

But he was exhausted by all the time spent underground. He was meant to be on a clifftop, keeping watch over all those who were important. Instead, he was hiding in a hovel with all the others, who were afraid of what might happen to them if they were on the surface.

Sighing, he strode through the dark halls without a light. A few of the Ashen Deep who passed by him seemed surprised that he didn't need a lantern. But then he flashed them a toothy grin, and a gold-eyed stare, and they knew who he was.

Dragons had no need for lights in the darkness. He could see better than they could, even though they had been born in the dark.

Lore was somewhere with the Matriarch and had been for some time now. The two of them had a lot to catch up on, and unfortunately, the Matriarch wanted no one else involved in those conversations.

The memory still sent a shiver down his spine. He didn't like Lore being locked up with that wicked woman who cared very little for his mate. He didn't enjoy knowing Lore was alone, making decisions for the rest of them with no form of input.

Not that he didn't trust her. But she was... different. And that difference could lead to darker places.

"Excuse me," he muttered as he strode through a crowd of deepmongers who had gathered near a door. He pushed through them toward the room, quite certain at what he would find.

And yes, he was correct. Zephyr and another one of the Matriarch's sons, lost in a game of chess that would take hours to finish.

The prince of their land had shown his abilities in chess a few days ago, and everyone had tried to beat him since. Apparently, spending most of his days locked away in a crypt had made him quite good at the game. And the Ashen Deep hated how good he was at it.

Murmurings grew again, their voices rising in the otherwise dead air. Only a few more moves and the Ashen Deep prince would have the mortal one. And then Zephyr made a move that completely thwarted that plan.

Groans of disapproval and money passed between hands all around him. They were betting on the boys now?

Abraxas crossed his arms over his chest with a grin and nudged the deepmonger beside him. "I'm betting on the human."

"What are you willing to bet?"

Flashing a red scale in his palm, he tilted his head to the side and asked the same question. "Now, what are you willing to bet?"

The unfamiliar deepmonger grinned, his teeth flashing brilliant white in the darkness before he held up a bag. "Take a guess."

Abraxas had no idea at all, but he was willing to place a bet for the novelty of it. He enjoyed believing in Zephyr. Namely because he always won. So far, he had two new knives, a very hearty meal that he'd shared with the others, and a pretty necklace he planned to give Lore, eventually. When there was more time for the two of them to linger with each other.

With a quick nod, the two of them continued to watch the game for an hour before Zephyr gave a delighted whoop and money changed hands again. Abraxas took the bag from the deepmonger with a bright smile as he left the small area.

Let the deepmongers be angry with what had happened. They deserved a few nights of frustration wondering how the mortal had managed to beat their centuries of experience.

Grinning, he wandered through the halls back to where he'd been setting up camp. Every day he waited for her to come out of the Matriarch's personal quarters. Every day, she looked troubled and shook her head when he asked her what was going on. She never told him. Never let him in. But at least she knew she wasn't alone.

Sliding down the wall, he opened the bag in his hands and grinned down at the contents. Now, he definitely knew what to do with this. And considering that Lore needed a break as much as he did? It was far pastime that he give her a little gift.

Abraxas leaned his head back against the wall and waited until the door opened. Lore stepped out, quiet and calm. She gently closed it behind herself, as though she didn't want to disturb his rest.

"Are you well?" he asked, his voice a little hoarse as he pulled himself out of the waiting stasis he'd been in.

"Well enough." But she turned toward him with shadowed eyes. "It is simply a lot to take in. There is more at play here than I ever thought and I am... overwhelmed."

"Anything you can tell me?"

She touched her lips and pointed to the door. And he had to wonder just how much the Matriarch was listening to. If they were not safe even in the hallway to talk as they should be able to.

He was her mate. She was supposed to tell him everything without fear or judgment. That was how it worked.

Or at least, how he'd always assumed it would work.

Abraxas stood, his back cracking and his knees aching as he stretched out his long body before her. He followed her gaze, watching as she lingered in staring at his form. And he knew she wanted him. Of course she did. It had been too long for them, and their lives had turned toward duty and honor and a kingdom to save rather than simply loving each other as they were made to do.

"Come with me," he said, stretching a hand out toward her. "Let's have the night to ourselves."

"It's not safe to go above." Lore scratched the back of her neck rather than take his hand. "The Matriarch has told me that Margaret has her ravens, even in the forest."

"Then we will not let them see us." He wiggled his fingers. "Where's your sense of adventure, elf? The woman I knew would never have turned up a moment to shake off her chains and get outside."

"That woman is currently weighed down by the responsibility of a kingdom and a people who need her help."

"Then perhaps I might convince you to come and see the moon."

He had her with that. He saw the desire in her eyes and the wispy expression of hope that crossed her face. "You are not meant to linger in the darkness, Silverfell. The Ashen Deep have their caves, but you have always had your moon."

Lore sighed and rolled her eyes up toward the ceiling neither of them could see. "Ah, Abraxas. You have always known how to get me to do what you want."

Indeed, he did.

But the feeling of her fingers slipping between his, the warm squeeze she gave him in thanks even though she was overwhelmed by her own sense of duty? That was worth any risk that he might have to suffer.

He pulled her through the dark halls, past a group of Ashen Deep who were already plotting their next person to take on Zephyr. Past the room where he stayed with Lore, while Beauty and Zephyr stayed in the other. Beyond the whispering grimdags who remembered her and knew exactly what to say to tempt her.

He brought her to the same exit they had left out of all that time ago. The same exit where they had fled the Ashen Deep for the first time, after traveling away from the castle and toward an unknown that would thrust them onto this path.

"Do you remember where we are?" he asked.

"How could I forget?" Lore shook her head ruefully. "All of you charged in here to save me, certain that I had met some horrible doom at the hands of more elves who hated me."

"You almost did end up dead. You're lucky Draven took a liking to you or the Matriarch would never have given you a chance to live."

"Perhaps." Lore shrugged. "Or maybe she would have seen the power in me, even then. She didn't want to change the prophecy, apparently.

She just didn't want the prophecy to ever come to life. At least not while she was still breathing."

"Has she changed her mind yet?" He started them off at a steady clip, already certain where he was bringing her in this forest of green, growing moss and glittering dewdrops.

"Not really. She doesn't agree with my methods or my plans. But she agrees Margaret has gone too far, so I believe that is progress." Lore stepped over a fallen log and then turned her face into a beam of moonlight.

And she looked so beautiful standing there, with all the stressors easing from her features as she let the moon bathe her fears away. Her hair had grown so long now that she could braid it, but she let it fall loose around her face more often than naught. Those features had aged since he'd first seen her in the forest. Not much, as elves rarely aged at all, but he could see the way she'd changed. Only he would ever notice the featherlight wrinkles around her eyes or the way her jaw had sharpened.

But, ah, she was beautiful. She was his and his alone, and he was the luckiest man in the kingdom for it.

"I brought you a gift," he said, tugging her away from her beam of moonlight to a small mossy patch that he'd remembered. The canopy above it had once been breached, perhaps by a falling dragon who had been desperately searching for his mate. And so the moon illuminated the entire glade.

She gasped at the sight of it, her hands clutching at her chest. "Abraxas. You knew this was here?"

"I had guessed." And hoped, really.

He settled her on top of the moss and watched as she soaked up all that power and her skin turned glittery with it. She looked like she was dusted in diamonds, and his heart stuttered in his chest.

"A gift?" she asked, opening those stunning eyes and staring right through him. "Where would you have gotten a gift? It's not a grimdag, is it? The Matriarch would kill me if I stole another one of those from her."

"No, it's not a grimdag." He rolled his eyes. "It's not anything to do with war, you bloodthirsty elf."

He dropped down beside her on the moss and handed her the bag he'd won from the deepmonger. His winnings were well worth the risk, although he had no idea where the young man had even gotten the contents.

Frowning at him, Lore peered into the bag and then flinched back. A startled laugh burst forth before she looked in again and then back at him.

"Elfweed?" she asked, her voice thin and perhaps a little too high pitched. "You got me elfweed?"

"I remember you saying how much you liked it," he replied. His tone was almost defensive, and that was foolish. Because he knew she would enjoy it, and she wasn't too old to do it again! They just hadn't had the opportunity, and if she was angry at him, then that was stupid.

His thoughts stuttered to a halt as she tilted her head back and laughed. Her joy was so abundant that she even kicked her legs a bit before she stared at him again, her jaw slightly open and her eyes so wide he could see the whites around them. "Do you know how hard it is to find good elfweed? You didn't just find this, did you?"

"Not quite." His shoulders squared a bit with pride. "I won it after a game of Zephyr's. I think the deepmonger was quite certain that his own prince would win the chess game."

She leaned forward, grabbed the back of his neck, and kissed him so hard he tasted blood. "You brilliant, wonderful, ridiculous man. I cannot believe you found me elfweed."

He watched her gleefully pull out a bundle of weed and a small stack of papers. With quick, efficient hands, she'd rolled them both enough to smoke and then handed him one.

"Would you like to do the honors?" she asked, clearly expecting him to provide the flame.

He'd happily do so. Abraxas leaned forward and sparked his fingers together, just enough to light the end of hers and then lit his own. Together, they inhaled deeply of smoke that tasted sweet and savory at the same time.

Blowing out a few smoke rings, he grinned when she made a sound of surprise.

"You know how to smoke!" she said, pointing at the rings that floated up in the moonlight.

"I'm a dragon, Lore. What makes you think I haven't spent years of my life learning smoke tricks?" He raised a brow. "I can make smoke in my lungs without having to inhale it. I spent years learning tricks from my mother and cousins and dragons I cannot even remember."

Not to mention he had the memories of other crimson dragons who had entertained their young in the same way. With a rueful grin, he puffed a few more rings, so they moved through each other.

Shaking her head, Lore added a ring of her own. And for a while, they entertained each other with the tricks they could both do. He hadn't felt this relaxed in a long time.

But then he realized they were completely surrounded by a cloud of smoke and that was just hilarious. He didn't know why or how it had gotten so funny. He saw it billowing around them like a massive skirt and he couldn't stop chuckling.

"What's so funny?" Lore asked, her eyes narrowing on him.

"It's like a dress," he said, barely getting the words out as he gestured at all the smoke surrounding them.

Though she hardly reacted to his words, her lips twitched. A good sign that she saw the same image he did and soon she would also be on the floor laughing.

"Abraxas." The word sounded a little slow. Why was she speaking to him like he wouldn't be able to hear her? "Have you ever smoked elfweed before?"

He tried to control the sounds coming out of his mouth that sounded an awful lot like giggles. "Nope. I have not."

Then she giggled with him, and the sound set him off all over again and he couldn't stop it. No matter how hard he tried to stop laughing, it was just... laughter. Bubbling out of him and coughing more smoke into the air. Was he still smoking? He didn't think he was, but then he found the elfweed back against his lips.

"You're high," she said with another laugh.

"I am not. You're not even close to high and I'm twice your weight."

She shook her head at him. "You're very high, dragon."

And maybe he was. But he was high with the best person he'd ever met. So he handed her the rest of his elfweed, laid back in the moss, and grinned up at her with every ounce of love in his heart.

There was no place he'd rather be than right here. With her.

CHAPTER 26

Lore stared down at the map on the table in front of her. The map that the Matriarch and her boys had been filling out since the time Lore had left. Margaret had been very, very busy.

Pointing to a particular spot high in the mountains, she asked, "So you think that's where they're keeping the humans?"

"I think that's one of the places they're keeping the humans." The Matriarch sighed and leaned back in her chair.

This room was the only place where the woman seemed like a real person. Everywhere else she was this tall, imposing, wise queen who commanded attention. But here in her chambers, she could show Lore just how tired and worried she was.

It made Lore nervous.

Rubbing her chest where there was an ache that wouldn't go away, Lore pointed to another location, near where she had first met Zephyr. "And here?"

"And everywhere, Lore. There are camps full of humans who are starving and weak and want to go home. She's sending them all over our kingdom and keeping them away from everyone they know or love. She's isolated them, but I don't think she knows what she's going to do with them yet."

"Then that is in our favor."

"Precisely. Which is why I think you need to go talk with her."

"Absolutely not." Lore took her own seat again, bracing her elbows on the table. "The last thing Margaret or we need is for her to realize that I am here and messing with her plans."

"She already knows you're back. Who else would be foolish enough to steal Zephyr out from under her nose?"

"Beauty," Lore replied. "Who is now missing from Tenebrous. I'm certain Margaret was keeping watch on her and her father. Considering how helpful they were to the rebellion, they will probably be the last to be sequestered off."

"Margaret needs a conscience."

"Margaret needs to be removed from the throne." Lore sighed and shook her head. "Something neither of us is going to do easily."

"You could." The Matriarch watched her with milky eyes that saw too much. "You could change all of this with a wave of your hand. Why are you not just doing that? Isn't that what the prophecy said you would do?"

Lore pinched the bridge of her nose. "I'm tired of prophecies. I'm tired of people telling me what I am meant to do rather than asking what I want to do. This kingdom will not fall because of the story a group of elves believed. I'm going to make the right choice for everyone."

"And what is the right choice, young one?"

A wry grin stretched across her face. "And here I was, hoping you would tell me that."

The Matriarch rolled her eyes at the insolence. "You are very young for an elf, but old enough to know that there is no right choice. Whatever you do, or choose, or even simply validate, that will make some people angry. And perhaps could lead to their deaths."

Lore shook her head. "I'm tired of death. I have no need for it here, and I will not choose a path where more people die. There has to be another way."

"And you will not find another way unless you speak with Margaret." The Matriarch knew she was right, and Lore knew the same thing as well.

Nothing would change as they stood here grasping at what might be the reasoning behind Margaret's decisions. None of them could assume they knew what was going through the shadow elf's head.

They needed to know what Margaret's plan was. They had to understand the choices, and if Lore was wrong for even wanting to spare the humans.

She knew she wasn't, deep in her gut. Lore knew there was a right thing to do here, and that was save the people who needed saving. But would she always be stuck in this cycle of saving those who needed it?

Shaking her head, Lore dropped her forehead onto the table with a loud thunk. "I don't know if I can talk with her, because I'm so angry I think I might rip her castle down the first moment she opens her mouth."

"Use that anger, then."

"But what if I see her and then she convinces me all of this is right and I have no choice but to come back here with my tail between my legs?" There were certain things about the world that she... liked now. Margaret wasn't entirely wrong about her choices. The magic that flowed through the kingdom felt right.

But what didn't feel right was the lack of humans when she knew they were necessary in this kingdom. And Lore didn't know how to work through these complicated emotions or the complicated path that this realm now had to take.

A chair scraped out from underneath the table and the Matriarch rounded it to pat her hand against Lore's shoulder. "You know the path you must walk."

"If you say one more thing about a prophecy, I will turn you into a toad." Her words were muffled against the wood, though, and that ruined the threat.

"You wouldn't." The Matriarch gave her one more pat and then added, "Now get out of my office, please. I have work to do that does not include you."

"Of course you do." Lore sat up and wearily blinked at the other woman. "You have a kingdom to command, sons to raise, another son to worry about because he's not here, and now you have a goddess on your doorstep sweating all over your table."

"If you left a forehead mark on my table, I will sink a grimdag in between your ribs." The Matriarch leveled her with a glare, her eyes following Lore's attempt to wipe it away with her sleeve. "Now go. Get yourself ready and I will gift you and your dragon two horses. The other two we will keep here, and healing. Your human pet has wounds that even my healers are struggling to piece back together."

"Just the poison?"

"And the curses." The Matriarch shrugged. "Margaret had plans for him, clearly. We are unraveling what she has knotted throughout."

Wonderful. Of course Margaret had cursed the boy as well as beaten him within an inch of his life, poisoned him, and then captured him in a prison with no outside access whatsoever.

Sighing, Lore pressed her hands to the table and stood. "I will prepare myself and Abraxas, then. Thank you for continuing to heal my friends without question. I cannot express my gratitude for that."

The expression on the Matriarch's face softened. "You have no need to thank me, Lorelei. You saved this kingdom, and then you brought my son to the other half of his soul. You have given him leave to court her as she ages and grows. You have given him space and trust. I can only do the same for you."

"If I'd known all I had to do was be nice to Draven to earn your trust, I might have been nicer to him earlier."

Lore made her way to the door and then paused when the Matriarch chuckled.

"I wouldn't have cared if you were nice to him," the Matriarch said. "But the honor and strength it took to not use him or his infatuation? That I respect."

With a firm nod, Lore cleared her throat and escaped out into the hallway. She didn't know what to do with the Matriarch's respect. That was... No. She was a girl from Tenebrous, who had grown up on the streets and had no right to have a woman like that saying she respected Lore.

She refused to think about it because if she did, then she would lose her mind. This was all too surreal. And she wasn't prepared to handle all these emotions.

So instead of going to gather her things, Lore found her feet taking her to the one spot where she knew she would be reminded of why she was doing all this. Not for the fame or the respect or the love of a people. She hadn't started all this to become a goddess.

She stepped into Zephyr and Beauty's room to find him seated alone in a chair before their fireplace. The crackling magic inside was not an actual fire, the smoke was too dangerous this deep, but it gave off heat and looked correct.

He turned at the sound of her approach and a wide grin spread across his face.

"Lore!" He was still pale and thin, but he was alive and that counted for something.

She sat down in the seat across from him and tried her best to smile as well. "How are you feeling?"

"Terrible," he replied with a snort. But then he shook his head. "No different, really. Much better than when you found me, but since getting here, it's a lot slower."

"The Matriarch said they're untangling curses." She ran her hand through her hair and slumped in the chair, staring into the fire. "Not a chance that you remember the words she used to curse you?"

"I wasn't awake when they happened. Or if I was, I wasn't in any state to remember a language I don't speak."

"Right." Her heart twisted in her chest. "Of course you wouldn't."

A quiet silence bubbled between them, broken only by the sound of the crackling fire. But then he shifted, turning toward her in his chair to stare. "You know this isn't your fault, right?"

Lore licked her lips and couldn't look back at him. "I know that if I hadn't left, you wouldn't be in this state."

"And that doesn't mean that it was your fault. If you hadn't left, Abraxas might be dead. Those dragon babies wouldn't even know you existed, and this kingdom might still be in the same state it's currently in. Blaming yourself for all this is foolish, Lore."

Was it? They both knew that perhaps it wasn't fair to her, but it wasn't foolish.

Finally, she let her head flop to the side and met his stare. They both looked at each other, and she wondered if he felt as ragged as she did. Like all her edges were a little torn.

Zephyr frowned at her. "I'm telling you, Lore, this isn't your fault. And if anyone can tell you that, it's me. I'm the one who spent most of the past year locked up in a dungeon while elves tried to tear me down from the outside in. If it was your fault, don't you think I would hate you?"

"I think you are the most forgiving person I've ever met in my life. You look at the evil in someone and you see it as redeemable." Lore swallowed hard, trying to talk over that damned lump in her throat. "You make me so proud to know you, but also terrified to even think for a moment that I let you down."

"You didn't."

"I did. I should have been there, done something more. Even Beauty believes that, and she's like you. So forgiving it's almost a fault."

Zephyr tsked and turned his attention back to the fire. "Beauty can forgive anyone who doesn't cause me pain. But her blame is misguided and I've talked with her about that."

"It will take more than just talk to make her forgive me." Lore had felt the rift between them growing wider.

Beauty was still angry that she hadn't saved Zephyr fast enough. Then she was angry that Lore hadn't healed him immediately and without question. Though it made her heart hurt, it still was the right thing to do. Lore knew that the Ashen Deep were more talented at healing than she was, and knowing that he was cursed? She was very right to have brought him here.

Lore could have made him explode by pulling the wrong thread of a curse. Or killed him if she had tried to heal his wounds without realizing the curses were there.

Movement in the corner of her eye caught her attention. Zephyr reached for her, his hand held out for her to take. And when she slipped her fingers into his, she felt a terrible knot release in her chest.

"I forgive you," he said, his eyes still on the flames. "And I thank you for saving me. That's enough. No more blaming yourself for what happened or trying to say that you will fix what happened to me. Just keep moving forward, Lore."

She squeezed his fingers in hers and took a deep, steadying breath. Then nodded. "All right."

"Good."

"The Matriarch wants me to go speak with Margaret in person."

His fingers spasmed in hers before he controlled his reaction. "Why does she want you to do that?"

"No one knows what Margaret's actual plan is. We're all guessing at what she wants, why she's doing this, what she's going to do next. The Matriarch thinks I might either figure it out myself, or have her admit it to me."

Zephyr let out a long, low whistle. "It's a risk and a half to take. If she knows you're here, then everything changes."

"She already knows."

"Because of me?"

Lore nodded. "The Matriarch thinks that was enough of a reason for Margaret to suspect, not to mention all the charred bodies. Beauty and her father might have planned that to make it look like we're back, but then Margaret was probably already watching them. She might have known I was here since the first moment I hit land."

"Then why hasn't she done anything yet?"

Rolling the question over in her mind, Lore tried to put herself in the other elf's shoes. And the Darkveil elf was one she knew well enough. "Because she's waiting for me to come to her."

"Why would she do that?"

"Margaret doesn't know how strong I've gotten. Or if my magic is capable of what all the prophecies say it is capable of. She wants to see her enemy for herself before she makes any more moves."

Again, the silence between them stretched thin. Then Zephyr said, "Like chess."

"Precisely."

"She's trying to survey the moves you make so she can guess your end game."

Lore nodded and smacked her lips together. "Yup."

"So, how are you going to prevent her from doing that?"

"Fuck, I don't have a plan that goes that far." Rolling her head to look at him again, she grinned. "I'm not a real goddess, you know. I can't see the future and I don't know the right choice here. Abraxas and I escaped to get high on elfweed yesterday. We're not the most responsible people to save an entire kingdom."

His eyes widened, and then his mouth split into a grin as he burst into laughter. "You got high yesterday? And you didn't invite me?"

Laughter filled the room and Lore settled in to tell him what Abraxas had been like while incredibly high for a dragon. She had Zephyr in stitches at the end while describing the moment Abraxas had tried to wear the smoke like a ballgown, and she had the distinct feeling that right now, this was where she was meant to be.

With him. With her family.

But tomorrow she would save them.

CHAPTER 27

Abraxas knew it would be smart to calm Lore down before they approached the castle. But his horse was skittish the moment he swung his giant leg over its side. The forest worked against them, and Lore herself seemed more grumpy than usual.

And if he was being honest with himself, he didn't want her to go into this meeting calm. He wanted her to be angry at Margaret, to force the older elf to see just what her nonsense had wrought.

He also liked the idea of seeing Lore at her worst in a moment like this. She'd been holding herself so honorably the last few days and he knew they should all fear the avenging goddess version of her would kill them all. But the more he thought back to that battle the two of them had fought together, the more he realized she had become justice for this kingdom. He'd make sure it didn't tear her apart.

And so he kept his mouth silent. He kept his words to himself and his thoughts quiet so that Lore could think and prepare herself for this battle of words that would set the pace for the rest of their journey in this kingdom.

Margaret would wait for them. The witch was probably waiting even now, knowing that they were moving toward her castle and placing themselves where Margaret wanted them.

The elf was nothing if not ready for every situation. He remembered how easily she had planned to destroy a king and upend him from his throne. He only hoped that Lore remembered as well. This would not be an easy battle of words.

He could only hope it became a real battle so he could taste blood again.

The castle loomed in front of them, and he had forgotten how sinister it was. Dark stones that ringed the castle were now stained with black watermarks that leaked from the top. The clouds above it loomed heavy and dark, filled with water that would soon rain down upon them. Perhaps thunder rolled in the distance, or that was merely his heart kicking in his chest as he remembered all the terrible things that had been done here. All the suffering he had endured.

"Are you ready?" Lore asked, her voice floating over to him like a salve on a wound.

"No," he replied. "That place is cursed. Only terrible beings live within it and even worse acts are committed there. I am not surprised she was corrupted within those walls."

"Ah, but Margaret was corrupted long before she walked into that castle. She's been planning this for a very long time, Abraxas." Lore leaned forward, the reins loose in her hands as she balanced her elbow on the pommel of her saddle. "She lied to me. To all of us. She made us think we were safe and that our futures would flourish in her hands. Instead, she opened up this world to another war. I am tired of it."

There was that anger he adored so much. The anger that had pushed her to come back here and to see what their people had wrought in the kingdom she had gifted them.

He sat up straighter in his saddle, staring ahead at their goal, and nodded. "Perhaps you should remind her how she won this kingdom in the first place. Make her see who she has to thank for the throne she sits upon."

Lore's gaze turned hard and flinty. "It seems as though she has forgotten that, yes."

"And I believe she has forgotten who lived in that castle for hundreds of years." Abraxas tapped his fingers on his knee, watching the movement of guards along the top peaks of the castle, certain that none of them knew the secrets he did. At least not yet. "Would you like to arrive unannounced?"

"It would leave a lasting impression if it seemed that we appeared out of thin air."

"Could you do that without me, you think?" He was curious now. If she could teleport and bring herself all the way to that throne room without him, it wouldn't be all that surprising.

Lore tilted her head to the side, considering his words. "Perhaps? I'm not sure how I would do it without splitting myself in two."

"Then it's a good thing I'm here," he replied before swinging off his horse. He'd let the beast find its way home on its own. The deepmongers always trained their mounts very well, for the rare moments when they used them.

Lore followed him with ease. And then watched him expectantly, as though she already knew this would turn in a direction that she might find intriguing. "What's your plan, dragon?"

"Ah, nothing all that grand. I merely wish to see what they have done with my hoard." He tilted his head back and took a deep breath in through his nose, already scenting the gold on the air. "Considering most of it was melted, I believe it is very likely that it is still where I left it."

"Your hoard with the hidden entrance into the king's chambers," she whispered. "Zander hid that entrance very well."

"He didn't want anyone but his most trusted to know where it was. Therefore, no one but himself and me remembers where it was. And it would be rather difficult to find, considering the spell that hid it was created by a master magician who the world has never seen the likes of again."

He held out his hand for her to take and then drew her through the edge of the forest. They stayed out of sight, making sure no one could warn Margaret that they were already here.

The waterfall still bubbled merrily, a mockery of what it hid behind it. Though it took them longer to walk up to his hoard in their current forms. But he still smelled gold in the air and gemstones buried beneath. He remembered when this had been the only thing holding him together. That the mere thought of such a hoard had given him peace.

Now, he wondered when he would build another. Or if perhaps he would have the opportunity to take what wealth he had already built.

Guiding Lore up a rather large boulder, he tumbled into the hoard with her, sliding over the molten gold and realizing it didn't matter. He would build another hoard. Perhaps something less metallic and easily melted. Someday he would have a collection of new items to be proud of. A new gathering of objects that brought him peace.

Because this no longer brought him any happiness at all.

Lore stood in the center of it, right where Beauty had tried to hide in her golden gown, and grinned. "It is as beautiful as I remember."

"It is useless," he grumbled, kicking a rather elaborate crown away. "And it will all fade someday. Just like the rest of me."

"But not our legend. Not the elf and the dragon who changed the fate of this kingdom. The goddess and her dragon who tore her from the sky." Lore's lips twisted as she looked at him. "Now, we get to decide what legend the rest will be. Do you want to be the villain? Or the hero?"

His heart thudded in his chest and he knew what she was asking. Would he want anyone to remember this thusly? He didn't know. He didn't care how anyone remembered him as long as they remembered that he was devoted to her.

Abraxas shook his head. "Lady of Starlight, I care not for what anyone thinks of me but you."

"Then let's go meet with a rather evil woman and prove who the real villain is in our story. If they remember her as such, then we have won."

Together, they climbed up the cliff's edge that led to the small platform where Zander used to stand. Where Lore herself had sat after a bridal trial, holding what she wasn't supposed to hold.

All these memories filled this place. This was where he had first met his dearest friends and those who would change the course of his life.

Together they slipped through the cold passageway with wind that whistled down from Zander's personal quarters. And when they stood in front of the door, he pressed a finger to his lips and listened for anyone on the other side.

They were alone. No one stood in Zander's bedroom, and that worked exactly as they had hoped it would.

They slipped through the shadows of the castle like they were born to it. Abraxas remembered all the hidden passageways that the servants still likely used, and he hid her to their advantage. No guards saw them. No one suspected that people were watching them from within the walls and through the eyes of paintings or tapestries.

And when they finally reached the Great Hall, he could hear Margaret's soft voice speaking all too convincingly.

"We need to find them," the Darkveil elf called out. "I know you do not see the value in it, but if Lorelei and her dragon are in this kingdom, then they need to be brought here. I will not tolerate any more of their meddling."

"Understood." The clacking sound that followed made him think the soldier had clicked his heels together. "I will find them."

"You said that last time. Do I need to remind you what the threat is? That I will not tolerate any more failure."

"No, my queen."

Lore looked at him and mouthed, "Queen?"

Much had changed indeed. Wait until Zephyr heard that Margaret was calling herself queen now.

Abraxas gestured for Lore to walk into the room in front of him. He'd make sure no one attacked her from behind. And if they did, he would explode into a dragon and devour them all in an instant.

Not that she needed him to protect her. He did because it helped his ego, and she allowed him to do so because she knew he wanted to.

Lore slammed the doors open so hard they hit the walls and shuddered with the force of her anger. He waltzed into the room behind her, the same massive columns and pillars lining a long walkway all the way to a throne. With an elf draped over it as though she had been born to sit there.

"Margaret," she called out. "I don't think you need to threaten any more of the few elves that remain alive. I'm already here."

He had the distinct pleasure of seeing the Darkveil elf's face go pale before she controlled herself. "Lorelei."

"In the flesh."

"And your dragon has come with you, I see." Margaret's gaze turned to him, and he felt as though she were trying to pull him apart with a single look. "I thought you had gone to the dragon isles to seek your end."

"Clearly, I survived." He swept into a low, mocking bow. "You have set yourself on a cursed throne, I see."

A muscle jumped in her jaw as he watched, and then Margaret dismissed him. She didn't want to talk about what she'd done, but ah, that was what they were here for.

"So the goddess returns to us," Margaret called out. She swung her legs off the arm of the throne and stood, holding her arms wide as though she'd been waiting for Lore this entire time.

"I am what you made me," Lore replied, accepting the term goddess in a way he hadn't expected.

What game was his elf playing?

Arching a brow, he folded his arms over his chest to watch what happened between two old elves who had seen far too much.

"I'm glad you have not forgotten who made you a goddess." Margaret's words sliced through the air. A band of elves moved forward from behind pillars, all standing behind her while wearing ancient regalia. They were clearly from individual clans who had all come to support Margaret's claim to the throne.

They looked like the elves of old. Smooth faced and wearing clothing that Abraxas somehow remembered. Clothing that was equally lovely and terrifying in the runes that were stitched across each of them. He'd forgotten how terrifying the elves could be.

Half of them were soldiers, the other half nobility who were here in the castle. Where they had always wanted to be. Where they thought they were owed an audience with whomever sat upon that throne.

Lore tilted her head back and laughed. "Oh, you did not make me a goddess! You threw me to the wolves. Your plan was never to keep me around for very long, now was it? Margaret, you think I do not know that you would have fed me to death itself, even if you had to cut up my still warm body?"

"I knew who you were, and I made sure you became what you could become."

"You guessed." Lore bared her teeth. "You sacrificed me at an altar of war and then you left me to rot. You thought it was over when I died, but it wasn't. I returned and then you sent me away on an impossible mission to save a dragon on an isle that should not exist. And then you defiled what I won for you. This is not how my kingdom should be led!"

"Your kingdom?" Margaret barked out a laugh. "This is not your kingdom, little girl. We have been here for much longer than you have and we have been fighting for this kingdom before you even drew breath."

"Oh, but this kingdom is my home and I don't think it's ever been your home. Has it?" Lore's entire posture changed. Suddenly she was more aggressive, larger, her whole body tense with the need to fight. "You have forgotten much as well, Darkveil. Though perhaps you put me on this path, you were not the one to give me any of this power."

"Power I have yet to see."

Margaret was baiting her. Margaret wanted to see what they were dealing with and if Lore was actually the half elf from the prophecies. Abraxas almost whispered for Lore to stop moving, to do nothing in response, but he didn't need to.

His starlit beauty merely shook her head in disgust. "You don't get that answer."

"I will have it. Prove that you are who you say you are."

"You will stop what you're doing. You will let the humans go, and they will elect a leader to meet with you. We should work together in building this kingdom to the glory it deserves."

But Margaret had to push. Of course she did. "I will do no such thing. And you will crawl back to your little hovel and keep your nose out of the business of the full-blooded elves."

Right, well. He wouldn't be able to hold her back now if he tried.

Abraxas sighed and looked up at the glass ceiling they'd fixed. Apparently, he'd thought the same direction as Lore, because she lifted her hands and gestured for the elves to look up as well.

And then she pulled the moon in front of the sun.

The light turned red. Her power crackled in the air and every breath fogged as sudden icy rage flowed out between them all. For the first time, they were catching a glimpse of Lore's true power. And it was utterly terrifying.

"You will stop what you're doing." Lore's voice snapped through the air like a whip, and a few of the elves even flinched away from her. "Or I will return and destroy all that you have built."

Margaret tried her best not to look frightened, but even she had gone pale in terror. "You would go against your ancestors? You would go against all who gave you breath?"

Lore shook her head. "My ancestors gave me this power to stop you, Margaret. I am the arrow they created to pierce your wicked heart."

She dropped her hand, and the moon moved back into place, shaking the very earth as it did. And then she turned toward him and Abraxas knew she wanted to make one more display of power.

So he surged forward into a dragon, all the elves tumbling away from him but her. She climbed onto his back, and he shattered the glass ceiling as he launched them into the sky.

CHAPTER 28

Lore gripped onto the spines of Abraxas's back and tried very hard not to cry. The wind whipped at her cheeks, dashing away whatever liquid might fall from her, anyway. It didn't matter. None of this mattered.

It didn't matter that her own people still looked at her as a half elf even though she'd become something out of legend. It didn't matter that Margaret had gathered up the elves and made them think of Lore as lesser even now.

She had her family. She had people she cared about. They were waiting for her, healing after all that she'd done to let them down. And Abraxas had stood there beside her the entire time. With pride and joy on his face because he knew she wouldn't let them walk all over her again.

She'd thought she had gotten over this. That letting the elves go in that cell would have somehow made all this better. But their denial of her, their dismissal of someone they still called a goddess but wouldn't see as anything other than a half elf, it still stung.

It hurt deep inside her soul. So deep that she feared she'd never be able to patch that wound or heal it because they had made it very clear they didn't want her to heal.

After all this time, after all the fighting and surviving and power that coursed through her veins, she was still nothing to them. And she should never have shown them all that she could do.

Now they knew she could move the heavens if she wished. What limit was there to her power if she could do that?

And even knowing that terrified her. Lore shouldn't be able to do that. No one should be able to reach into the sky and move the very moon itself! Yet here she was. Moving the moon. Blocking the sun from the sky until the entire kingdom was bathed in red.

Was she a goddess? Or a demon who had come to destroy them all?

Lore didn't want to be this person anymore. She didn't want the weight of the world on her shoulders and she didn't want people to be frightened of her or even know she existed.

But then, by going back to that life of being nothing and no one, it meant that they had won. They'd reduced her to little more than a bug under their heel again and she couldn't let them win.

Blinking away her tears, she realized they weren't heading for the forest. They weren't returning to the dark caverns that would make her heart turn cold once again. Instead, he'd wheeled them toward the sea.

He said nothing. Only skimmed his wings over the wave as he dipped them low, allowing the water to spray over her face and turn the air into a thousand prisms that cast rainbows all around her. He drifted over the salt air until she realized where he had brought them.

The island where they had first hatched their eggs. The sand was still turned to glass in places where the dragon eggs had burst through so their children could hatch.

And her soul clicked back into place.

Her children. They were waiting for her on the dragon isle and she couldn't return to them until she finished what she had to do here. And in the end, it didn't matter. Because the only people who did matter were those two dragon babes who had sat in her lap on these very sands and watched the waves with her as the moon hit the horizon and turned the water into silver.

How had he known what would ease her torment? Only Abraxas could see through her soul and the pain and know how to make her remember why they were here.

His wings beat at the air as he lowered them down onto the sands and then stretched out his wing for her to slide down.

Lore eased onto the ground, dropping onto her behind and digging her hands into the sand. She thought he would change back into his mortal form, but apparently, he was staying very true to this memory. Abraxas curled his giant body around her, draping his wing all around them until there was only a small sliver for her to see through. Everything was a cocoon of warm ruby.

A giant sigh stirred the sands in front of him as he rested his head beside her. "Do you think they miss us?"

It wasn't the question she'd expected. Lore was so startled by the words that she actually laughed. "I think they do. I am certain that they wish their parents were there, considering how strict Tanis is."

"And Draven," he muttered. "If he's touched her while we were not there, I will swallow him whole."

"Just make sure he doesn't have any knives on him, so he cannot carve himself a way out of you." Lore patted Abraxas's cheek and then leaned her entire body against it. "He would like to crawl out, all bloodied from battle."

Abraxas snorted. "He would like the story, but not the truth of it. It would be much harder than he thinks. My stomach is thick."

"And you have no small amount of ego when it comes to your ability to beat that elf in anything that he or you try." Shaking her head, she marveled at his ability to turn her thoughts away from what just happened.

Abraxas knew how to distract her, but this was not something that would easily go away. Not even with the thoughts of their children. Although, the thoughts were much easier now that she had their souls to guide her.

At her sudden silence, and likely the way her expression fell, Abraxas sighed again. "You know your worth is not weighed by the opinion of elves?"

"I do."

"But I also know that the sting of their rejection will never disappear. You can try to tell yourself that it will, Lore. And it may grow easier with time, but you will always have to deal with the disappointment of them. They are not worth your time, but I also know saying this doesn't help you."

"It doesn't." She hugged her knees into her chest, pressing more firmly against him. "I think there will always be a part of me that wishes they would change their mind. That they would see me for who I am and not for what they believe me to be."

His tail shifted in the sands behind them, lashing for a moment in anger before he forced himself to still. "I wish that as well. But the old ways are hard to break. At least there are the Ashen Deep who have not yet lost their minds to power."

"Because they've always had it." Lore shook her head. "They've always guarded the grimdags and their dark caverns and their Matriarch who leads them. All the other clans barely even have our history, or language, or all that we sought to preserve. Those who fought lost everything. And they think in doing this, they will get it all back."

"They are wrong."

She nodded. "They are."

But they would never see that they were wrong. Why would they even think to admit it? The entire kingdom was exactly as they wanted it. Magical creatures and no one else. It didn't matter that their citizens were hungry, or that they hadn't really fixed any of the problems that were now just passed to their own people.

There was magic in the world again, and that was enough for the elves.

Lore lost herself in thoughts for a few more moments until Abraxas nudged her. "Did you talk with Nyx?"

"What?" She looked into his giant eye before she sighed and nodded. "I did. When we were walking through the bog. I can apparently connect through our daughter's mind, and I think even project an image of her if I wish. It's something to do with the magic."

"Why don't we try to talk with her now?"

Because... She didn't want Abraxas to be disappointed. "I don't know if you can even see her when I do it. Or hear her."

He shrugged. "I'll follow along on your end, if I must. You can tell me what she says, or perhaps I will just listen. I enjoy hearing you speak with our children, Lore. Even if I am not involved, it still makes me happy."

She wondered how much he missed their dragon babes. He had been the one to guard them for centuries, after all. And she had only known them for a few moments.

Cheeks flaming with embarrassment that she hadn't tried this with him already, Lore used her magic to tug on the thread that connected her and Nyx.

An answering tug almost immediately reached out for her, and then she could feel her daughter's presence in her mind. And with one last push of power, she could see Nyx in the rolling waves before them. There were sprays of water that lapped up at her face, as though she was in the sea as well.

"Mother?" Nyx said, her voice filled with excitement. Her wings spread wide in surprise as her eyes got even bigger. "Father?"

Abraxas sat up, his eyes filled with love and the scales on his back rising in surprise. "You can see me?"

"I can see you as if you were standing before me! Can you see me?" Nyx splashed a bit and Lore swore she could feel the spray of water on her face.

"I can see you, child." Abraxas looked down at Lore as though she were a gift given to him by the heavens. "Your mother's magic is impressive, is it not?"

"Mother is impressive," Nyx corrected.

Oh, she needed to hear that. She'd needed those words so much just to know that her children at least thought she was worthy of something. And Abraxas must have known.

He glanced down at her with a prideful grin and a wide-eyed stare that said he had known Nyx would say that. "Indeed, she is. Probably the most impressive woman I've ever met."

"And if you said anything else, I would have to fly all the way out to wherever you are to bite some sense into you." Nyx bristled, but then rolled her eyes. "Should I call for Hyperion? He'd like to see you, although it would be fun to hold this over his head again."

"Please don't start a fight with your brother already," Abraxas grumbled. "Yell for the boy."

Lore covered her ears. She even had to use a bit of her power to dampen the sound of her daughter screaming for her brother. The roar would have shaken the ground if she was here, and almost did even though it was just magic amplifying her voice.

But then Hyperion tumbled into their few, his giant body splashing into the water before he wrestled himself upright and draped himself over his sister. "Is that them?"

"I told you I wasn't making it up!"

"You tell stories all the time. How was I supposed to know that Mother could project herself like this?" He loomed far too close to them, his giant mouth gaping open and his beard longer than she remembered. "Hello!"

"Hyperion," she sighed. "You do not need to get so close to us. We can see you just fine."

"I'm looking to see how tired you are and if Father has let you run yourself ragged again." He peered even closer and then snorted. "Yes, he has. Father, didn't we talk about this before you left?"

Abraxas rolled his eyes up toward the sky. "I remember telling you to take care of your sister, and to keep an eye out for that ridiculous elf that's been sniffing around her."

Of course, they were already on this, but before Nyx could argue with her father, a very familiar voice interrupted them. "I take offense to that. I know how old she is, curmudgeon."

Draven appeared in front of Nyx, then Tanis and Rowan, who were both in mortal forms and dragging three dragonlings behind them.

Tears pricked at her vision.

This was her family. Her people who waited for her back home. And oh, how she loved them. Their wild antics and their laughter as they all told stories about what she and Abraxas had missed. They all flailed their arms about and made the stories seem all the more wild and messy. But she knew what they were doing.

Because Nyx's eyes never left her. Her daughter saw too much, just as Lore had seen too much in her own mother. Perhaps when she died, Nyx would get this power and she would become a dragon goddess who razed the kingdom to the ground as her mother had not been able to do. But that was not Lore's path. Not yet.

Hyperion and Draven were performing a small battle that apparently they had learned together, as Draven wished to fight dragons now. For whatever reason. Abraxas leaned low and muttered in her ear, "Isn't it better when they're all involved?"

"It is."

"Don't you think it would be better if they were here with us?"

Her heart fluttered in her chest, but then she shook her head. "Ah, I do not know. I need them safe, and safety is not in this kingdom. Not for anyone in our family."

"Look at them, Lore. You have a young elf who can fight dragons now. Two full grown dragons who may not be adults yet, but who are capable of fighting. Another full grown dragon, an ancient elf with knowledge of fighting that neither of us could dream of."

"And three children who need their parents."

He hummed low under his breath. "Perhaps we can lose the guidance of one elf, then. Let the dragons come to Umbra, Lore. It is time that we let them grow up."

And as she watched them all, Lore thought maybe he was right. As much as she wanted to shelter them, they were larger than before. Grown up while she wasn't even there to see them. And did she want to miss more time with her children, even though that meant spending time with them in the middle of a war?

"Tanis," she interrupted, speaking for the first time in a while. Everyone froze and looked at her. "Are my children ready to fly?"

Tanis gazed back at her with what looked like respect in her eyes. "They are, goddess."

"Then I would like you to send them to me. Abraxas will guide them, and he'll meet you halfway in case they need to rest. I find I want my family around me now, more than ever."

And though they all stared back at her in silence, Lore could feel in her heart this was the right choice. It was time to bring her family back together. To show them her home.

CHAPTER 29

He hated saying goodbyes. Abraxas could handle almost anything, but goodbyes had never gotten easier over the years. Especially saying goodbye to these people, these companions, who he had only seen for a short amount of time.

He wanted more time to hear what they had to say about their lives. Abraxas had so enjoyed listening to their laughter and their stories and watching them together. Beauty and Zephyr had built a relationship that he respected. That he actually liked.

They were sweet and kind to each other. They cared if the other was well, and how many relationships had he seen like that?

Even the deepmongers made him nervous to say goodbye to. After all, they were now going to be the sole people taking care of the most precious thing in his life.

Lore let him gather her up in his arms and hold her close to his heart. She snuggled her face into the base of his neck, her arms wrapped around him just as tightly.

It wasn't goodbye forever; he told himself. He would find her again, even though they had only just gotten to be with each other after the worst experience of their lives.

"I love you," he whispered into her hair. "I will love you for the rest of our days. This is not goodbye."

"I'll see you very soon," she replied, then leaned back to press her tear slick lips to his. "You will be safe, dragon. You will come back to me and you will keep our children out of that damned ocean."

"No leviathan will touch them." Abraxas trailed his clawed hands down her cheeks and blew out a long breath. "You will not take any unnecessary risks. You will stay alive for me."

Her eyes filled with more tears. And likely everyone watching thought them ridiculous, but he refused to even think about that when his woman was in his arms and needed him.

Lore nodded. She looked fierce and determined, as though what he had asked of her was an impossible task. "You will come back and you will not find a single scratch on me, my love. I will stay alive for you."

"Good." He pressed a kiss to her forehead and then forced himself to take a step back. He'd already said his goodbyes to the others. Tearful, heartfelt goodbyes that had made his stomach twist in his chest.

None of them could ever promise that they would forever be well. Not in a kingdom like this, while they were all being hunted by the best of the elves. But they were all so used to this kind of goodbye now.

If he had his way, this would be the last time they ever had to say goodbye like this again.

Stepping away from all the others, he let the change flow through his body. Red scales dusted over him, covering him from head to toe as wings burst out of his back and talons ripped from his hands. He surged forward into the world as a crimson dragon, the protector of all those he loved. And he refused to be anything but that. He would keep his family safe, from now until the bitter end.

Lore approached him, her bag in her hands in her heart in her eyes. From the depths of that dwarven magic, she pulled out the armor he had been gifted. The armor that would keep him safe.

Though it would be difficult and heavy to wear, he would bear such discomfort to know she didn't worry as much about him as she might have before.

Docile and still, he froze as she placed the armored plate on his chest, pressing against the rune that made it widen and thicken and stretch over his form like a second skin. It spread up his neck, the links clacking into place up and around the sensitive flesh of his spines and all the way over his shoulders.

The saddle she kept, though. She did not want anyone to see him as anything other than an avenging dragon fleeing from this realm once more.

"You will bring them back to me." Her voice rang out through the small clearing in the forest where all the Ashen Deep stood to watch. "You will bring the dragons back to Umbra, as they should have been for years. We will show everyone and everything in this kingdom that the dragons are alive and well. We will strike fear into the hearts of those who defy us and hope into the hearts of all those who are still kind."

The Ashen Deep cheered as one. And for the first time, Abraxas thought he could see a future where dragons like him were accepted. Where they were not seen as weapons to be used, but as a people to be bartered with.

Perhaps the future that Lore fought to bring into existence was possible after all.

Swallowing hard, his eyes trailed along the ranks of elves to Beauty and Zephyr, who sat side by side on a stone just outside the Ashen Deep home. They both watched him with the same hope that Lore spoke of. They saw more than a beast in him, and for that, he would fight. He would prove to them that they were right. He was worthy of that hope.

Shaking out his neck, he readied himself for a long flight and a hard battle to get his children here. Tanis knew what island to meet him at, the same one with the oasis in the center where he'd stopped with his children for the very first time. He'd reach it before them, and then he had to wait until they arrived.

Tanis would bring them and then return to her own children. They could not risk having more dragonlings here when their focus needed to be on the war itself. A last war. The final one until they could reach the end.

Lore stepped in front of his face and ran her hands down his muzzle, her touch soft and loving. "I love you," she whispered against his scales. "I don't know what I'd do without you, dragon, so you have to come back in one piece."

"I'm risking very little on this journey. But you are risking much." He had heard her talking with the Matriarch in the darkness. He knew they were going to use this time to gather as many people into an army as they could.

Soon, they would make their final stand against Margaret, who would never back down. No matter how foolish it was to fight against a goddess.

Oh, by the gods, it was time for him to go. He didn't want to. He had to.

Abraxas spread his wings wide, and because they were no longer hiding, he let the flames build in his throat and then let out a roar that shook the very forest. It would spread across the kingdom, and those who feared the dragon would know he was here.

But then they would also see him leave, and he wondered how that would leave his friends. What danger would follow them to this forest where they no longer had a crimson dragon to watch over them?

His goddess grinned up at him and as he watched, she called a storm over their heads. Black clouds blanketed the sky so no one would see him leave, no one would even know that there was a dragon flying over their head.

And he felt better knowing that he left his dear friends in the hands of a goddess.

Bursting into the air, he fought through thunder and lightning. Flashes pulsed around him, but none ever touched his scales until he burst out of the storm and into the bright, clear sky above.

Alone.

But not for long.

Opening his wings wide, he soared over Umbra, but could not see when he passed the castle or any of the other familiar landmarks. The only one that remained was the high peak of the mountains far beyond, where the spiders now lived and a magician's tower had once stood.

And then he passed the storm to find himself over the sea once more. The sea where they had found themselves and their future all laid out before them. With it came a sense of peace. Of understanding that he was headed in the right direction. Toward his children, his family, and to gather them up where they all belonged for the first time in a very long time.

Abraxas let his mind settle and his thoughts fade away as he flew. He was nothing but the wind that flowed underneath his wings, the water that sprayed up against his scales, and the clouds that meandered above his head. This was where he was meant to be. He was going to gather up the pieces of his heart so they could all finally be together.

The island appeared on the horizon. A storm had hit it recently and most of the trees he remembered had fallen after the wake of the wind. But the rest of it was the same as he remembered. Abraxas landed hard on the ground beside the open pool of impossibly fresh water.

Dipping his head to take a drink, he remembered how many days it had taken him to get here last time. How he had struggled with the weight of two half grown dragons and the heartache that had dogged his every step.

Now, he had made it in only a day of travel and had to wait for the others longer than he'd anticipated. Or perhaps he was stronger this time. All the flying he'd done over long distances, learning how to use his body not as a weapon for others but as a dragon really should.

Curling into a ball near the lake, he settled in to rest and wait. There was no telling how long it would take for his family to get there.

It took them three more days. He knew exactly how long because he watched the sun rise and fall, and he stared into the moon as though Lore herself could feel him watching. He wanted to be there for her, even if he wasn't physically beside her.

And then he saw them. On the horizon, there were three dots and two of them moved ahead of the last. One speared itself in a blinding flash of blue into the water and, like her mother, Nyx became a glittering glow beneath the waves that raced toward him.

Spreading his wings wide, he launched himself into the air. A green streak had already darted toward him, and he'd been so worried about his son, who had smaller wings and wasn't made to fly long distances like Nyx. His daughter could swim for the greater part of the journey, at least. Even though he'd promised her mother that he wouldn't let her.

He got closer to them and a sapphire spiral rotated out of the ocean. She spun in a giant circle as water flowed off her form and then snapped her wings out wide. With a bright grin, his daughter joined his son and together they flew toward him, then circled as he beat his wings to remain still in the air.

They were here.

They were flying, and he'd missed it.

But they were alive, and they were well and they looked more like dragons than he'd ever imagined. Tilting his head back with a roar of delight, he swooped low underneath them. Nyx was much more agile. She spiraled around him in the air so he could get a good look at all the colors that flashed on her bright underbelly. Hyperion flew beneath him, tilted onto his back so he could stare up at his father with a teasing expression.

And oh. They were here.

If he was a mortal man, he would have cried tears of joy. Instead, all he did was let out another trumpet of triumph that his children were flying. They were dragons, through and through, and he'd never been more proud of them.

Together, they all flew back toward the familiar island and landed in a heap of scales, wings, and claws. He dragged them closer to him, holding them out with his wing like it was an arm, forcing them to stay still.

"Stop wiggling," he snarled as he looked them over. He nudged Nyx hard with his big head, making her stand up straighter as he circled his children. Hyperion wouldn't stop bouncing. The boy never could control his energy, but by all the gods in the sky, they were perfect.

"My goodness, look at you," he said as he leaned back and stretched his body out as large as it could get."You are stunning, the both of you. Exactly the dragons I always hoped you two would be."

They preened under his praise, just as he knew they would. And before he knew it, another heavy thud landed on the isle. Tanis, with all her glittering amethyst scales, made quite the presence here. He hadn't thought to ever see her out of their homeland, and it made something in his heart twist to know that another full grown dragon had joined them.

A dark elf slid off her back, wearing a large pack that squirmed with something inside it. And to his surprise, a second elf slid off as well. Wearing yet another squirming bag.

He frowned. "Rowan? I thought you were staying behind with the children."

"Ah, well." Rowan shrugged the bag off and opened it to reveal a small, purple dragon that tumbled out into the dirt. The little one snorted hard to get the dust out of its nose before catching a scent and snuffling off.

He was... shocked. Why would they bring their baby dragons here, and why were they still so small? Was Tanis not feeding them?

Draven took his own pack off and let out the other two. The crimson one was much larger, as expected, but the little gold dragon was almost smaller than his claw and it made his chest flush with flames in fear of what might happen to the three of them.

"The dragonlings," he muttered, meeting Tanis's gaze with a shocked expression. "Why would you bring them?"

"This is a war, I know. But you need your family with you, Abraxas, and that includes all of us. If we cannot save Umbra, they will come for the dragons as well." She grinned and shook off the weight of the elves and the flight and suddenly seemed larger. Stronger. More capable than he'd given her credit for. "Besides, I have plans for Umbra. And if you are going to fight against an elf who has an entire elven army at her disposal, then you will need both of these men to advise you."

When Abraxas slid his gaze to the deepmonger, Draven puffed out his chest in pride. "I have been learning much in the months since you've been gone. Rowan and I have spent countless weeks learning the history of our people, and what Margaret might do. Battle tactics. Weapons. Spells. Armor. I have studied, Abraxas. I will be of use, if you'll have me."

"That's the first time you've asked to be of use to me."

"And the only time I'll likely mean it."

It wasn't Draven's words that convinced him. It was the ease with which he bent down and scooped up the golden dragon. Draven held the child like a natural, and he gently stroked underneath its chin on a hidden spot that made the small dragon go limp in his arms with pleasure.

A man like that, who could hold a baby dragon without fear, was a worthy advisor indeed.

Spreading his wings wide around all the people he loved, even Draven, he let out a low growl of pleasure. "Good," he said. "I am so happy to see you all, even if now we must fight."

CHAPTER 30

The Ashen Deep's forest was closest to Margaret, but Lore and the Matriarch knew it was the safest place for everyone. As much as she hated to admit it.

Lore didn't want to be any more indebted to the Ashen Deep. Already the Matriarch had sunk her claws into Lore and even a goddess had to pay her debts. Lore had no idea what the Matriarch would eventually ask for, but that debt grew larger by the day.

She'd thought it would take weeks to find the leaders of every group that might help them, but the reality was there were very few people willing to help.

There were the humans, and those were limited in numbers. Scared, nervous. Their only leaders had hidden in Tenebrous for a while, and some were on the outskirts of other towns, but none of them were quite interested in helping. Beauty's father had come to the forest, of course, and a few other nobles who hadn't lost as much family as the others.

The dwarves were waiting for her the moment she called upon them.

Lore had smiled at Algor and promised to keep his people safe as best she could, and he'd waved her off, saying that he had always known it would come to this. And as a dwarf, he'd always wanted to see what the Ashen Deep had built in comparison to his own home.

And that was... it.

Not an army. Just a band of people who had no idea what they wanted or how they were going to take their kingdom back. Just a handful of nobility and those who thought they might be able to help.

It wasn't what she'd hoped for, that much she knew. Algor and his people were at least useful. The dwarves could fight well, and the Ashen Deep were powerful allies. She'd seen them fight and had fought beside them. Their grimdags made a significant difference, along with their ability to fight like the best of the elves.

But it still wasn't enough. It wasn't nearly enough.

Standing at the table with the few leaders surrounding it, she eyed the four humans, two dwarves, and three elves who stood around it with her.

"I want to fight for this kingdom," she started, trying very hard to not look behind her at Zephyr and Beauty. "I want to take back what is ours. I know some of you do not trust me or any of us because we are magical creatures. Because we once stood by Margaret, but I need you to understand. This is not how it was supposed to go."

"How was it supposed to go?" The tall gentleman who stood behind Beauty's father was a general in his day. The others looked at him with a significant amount of awe, so she knew she had to get his trust first.

"The rebellion was never meant to harm the mortals in exchange for them harming us. We only wanted equality. That was the reason for starting all of it." She met his gaze and did not flinch at the hatred in his eyes. "What shall I call you?"

"Baron Edgerton," he replied.

"Baron. I understand you have good reason not to trust me. But we all have good reason to not trust each other here. Do we want to pull out all those bad memories and feelings, or do we set them aside for the good of our kingdom?" She arched her brow. "I, for one, would rather fight and get back all that we have lost, then let it fall between our fingers because we yet again cannot work together."

She'd put him in his place, certainly. But it hadn't won her any friendships on the mortals side.

Algor cleared his throat and said, "The dwarves are more than happy to fight. Margaret's behavior toward us has become disturbing. I fear it is likely that she sees anyone who is not an elf to be lesser, and that is of great concern to my people."

Lore nodded. "I'm certain that you are right, my friend. The elves have always held themselves in higher regard than the rest of the creatures in Umbra. I fear the same fate as you if we continue along this path."

And what a dark path that would be. Margaret would ensure that no other magical creatures had as much as the elves. For no matter what they had given the world, the elves were always the same. Prideful, boastful creatures who wanted to control all that they could.

The Matriarch stepped in, her milky eyes seeming to follow the movements of every person in the room. "The Ashen Deep will fight at your side. We have ties to you that we cannot break now. And if the dragon wishes us to fight, then we will do so."

Ah, of course. Because the Ashen Deep would have done nothing without their ties to Lore's family. That was not reassuring, and it made her fear that if Abraxas could not bring back the dragons, or if Nyx or Draven had not come with them, that the Ashen Deep would pull away. Such a situation would result in not only the loss of the war, but a significant amount of lives.

Shaking her head, she pressed her fists into the table. "We need the humans to stand at our side on this. If you do not fight with us, then we are fighting for you, yet again."

"We have given you enough, have we not? Thousands of humans all disappearing," Beauty's father snarled.

Lore peered through her hair at Beauty's father, who glared down the table at her. "Do you think I'm not aware of that? I saved a band myself. Who knows where they ended up? But I gave them a few more days. I am fighting for them. Besides, we know where your humans are kept, or perhaps where they might be kept. But I need your leaders to stand beside me or I am doing all of this for you."

"Are you not a goddess?" he asked. "Were you not sent here to do just this? Why do you need us to risk our lives when you could snap your fingers and be done with all this?"

Rage moved through her whole body until she couldn't think or breathe through it. These people. They wanted her to do everything for them, gift them a kingdom on a golden platter and then whisper in their ear what is the right thing to do.

She was not just a goddess, she was a woman who had lived in these streets and who had begged them for any amount of attention or care, and they still were not willing to see that.

Lore kept her head down, speaking to the table as she chose her words carefully.

"If you wish me to win this kingdom back, Lords of Men, I will do so. I will slay all those who stand in opposition to me. I will stack their bodies in a pyre that will burn so brightly everyone in Umbra will see its flames. But if I do this, I will not do it for you. And you will have a woman sitting on that throne who has no weakness. This kingdom will be mine and mine alone. I will do what I wish with it. You will have no say, no power, no ability to change anything for your families. And trust me when I say this, if you think to betray me at any point, I will take over your minds and you will lick my boots clean."

She looked up at the horrified expressions on their faces. Because they could hear the truth in her voice. That she wasn't lying. Lore would never lie to them about the darkness that laid within her and the truth that she could destroy whatever she wanted.

"Or," she lightened her tone, "you could take back your kingdom on your own. Together. With the creatures who do not enjoy what has been done. This is your choice. Whose kingdom is this, Lords of Men? Talented Dwarves. Deadly Elves. You are the people who must choose, right now, whose kingdom this is."

They all stared back at her, silent with their tongues tied and incapable of understanding what she was suggesting.

Lore prodded them and added, "Because if this kingdom is mine, then I will take it. I will lay waste to everything that stands before me and I will sit on that dark throne. But I cannot promise you that you will like what I do with that power."

Finally, she heard a scrape of a chair behind her. Zephyr had stood, limping over to her side because he was still too weak to stand on his own. He placed his hand on her shoulder, both for balance and in solidarity as he stood before the Lords of Men who glared at them both.

"I am Prince Zephyr. It is my bloodline that has sat on the throne of this kingdom for hundreds of years. I stand beside Lorelei of Silverfell, of Tenebrous, the Lady of Starlight who gave her life for our kingdom. If she wishes to take this for her own, I will still stand by her. But I believe this kingdom is ours. All of ours. And so I will fight as a mortal beside her. If I am the only one of our kind brave enough to do so, then so be it."

Oh, but she had so much pride in this young man. He had never once disappointed her and she could hear how disappointed he was in the other mortals like himself. They were letting him down in this moment.

But the Baron, one of the few men to actually speak, cleared his throat. "I will say, the humans would follow you, my lord. You are the leader we have been looking for, not an elf who considers herself a goddess."

Ah, there it was. All the people in her life wanted to leave the elves in the dust. "I am not an elf," she snarled. "I'm half elf. Half your people, half theirs. Don't you understand that means I have been denied my entire life by both men and elves? All I want to do is help you people and instead, you squander that help by claiming I am lesser because I am not like you."

The last words were shouted, and she felt the entire earth tremble with her anger.

She needed to get better control of herself. And she couldn't do that in this room with so many people looking at her with fear, disgust, or disappointment.

Patting Zephyr's hand on her shoulder, she gently moved it away. "Talk with your people, my friend. Guide them to see reason or I will take this kingdom for myself and lead all the fools who refused to save it."

Zephyr met her gaze and seemed to straighten, as if the poison in his veins and the curses that had taken their toll had never happened. "I promise you, Lore. I will fix this."

And perhaps for the first time, she looked at him and saw a king.

Thoughts boiling in her head, she stalked out of the Ashen Deep's home. They had not gone far, as the Matriarch did not want anyone knowing how deep these tunnels went or in what splendor her people lived.

Still, it took longer than she wanted to get outside and drag the fresh air into her lungs. And she was so tired of living underground. So tired of being far from the moon and without the only person who had always spoken reason into her heart and struggling mind.

Had her dragon made it to the island safely? Were her own children with him already? Safe and sound and whole? If only she knew that they were fine.

She could use her magic again, but she didn't want to hover around any of them for too long. They were all adults now. All capable of taking care of themselves and she couldn't be that mother that never let them grow up, or the partner who did not trust her mate.

"It's a rather hard life, isn't it?" The voice was strangely familiar and yet not. Turning away from the opening of the Ashen Deep's realm, she saw a shadow in the forest. One with a light beard and hair that floated around him like snow. A brightly colored bird sat on his shoulder, watching her with human eyes.

"Lindon?" she asked, shocked to see a magician in the middle of the Ashen Deep's forest.

The old man had no magic left. How had he gotten past the wards and all the magic that the deepmongers had laced through the trees?

He stepped toward her with a small smile on his face. He finally looked older, though nowhere near his much advanced age. "I heard tell there was a goddess who returned with a dragon at her side. And I thought, perhaps, I might be of use."

"You have no magic left." She eyed him with no small amount of distrust. "Unless you lied."

"Oh, I have no magic." He tucked his hands behind his back and approached her, the sylph on his shoulder ruffling its feathers at her nearness. "But I still have use even without it. It occurred to me that you would need someone to fight by your side, and while you do not have a lot of someones to fight with you, there is knowledge that I have which may be useful yet."

She tilted her head to the side. On one hand, Abraxas would be furious that she was even talking to this man who erred toward evil. On the other hand, this was the first time she'd even thought the magician might stick his neck out for people like her.

"Why?" she asked.

"Because I do truly wish to make amends, and I am tired of seeing my home in constant turmoil. I started all this, Lorelei. I was the one who urged people forward onto a path of destruction and hate." He spread his hands wide. "I thought, perhaps, I might be able to help end what I began. And I thought that was perhaps with you, but then another took your place on the throne."

Lore tilted her head to the side. "And just how are you suggesting to help?"

"The spell that was given to Zander long ago, the one that created the Umbral Soldiers, can be edited by someone with a power equal or greater than my own." He eyed her with a meaningful gaze and an intent in his eyes. "You could alter it, my dear. If you would like to. I can gift you an army that the dwarves can build."

And, oh, that was tempting. That was useful.

"What do you want in return?"

He grinned, and that's when she knew, of course, there would be a bargain. "A safe place to rest. I'm tired of sleeping on the sands by the sea. After spending time with you and Abraxas, I realized I am still better suited to court."

"You want a position as an advisor." It was not a question.

"Indeed."

"Of who?"

He tilted his head. "Whoever is on the throne, my dear. Whether that is you or someone else."

Lore needed time to think about that. She needed time, but... Damn, it was tempting.

Finally, she nodded and swept her arm toward the entrance. "Why don't you join us at our table, magician? Though you may have lost your magic, that does not mean you have lost your use just yet."

CHAPTER 31

Abraxas allowed his children and companions a few days of rest. They'd traveled farther than any of them ever had before, and though his children's boundless energy was beautiful to behold, he also knew that Tanis must be tired.

The amethyst dragon had carried both Rowan and Draven far longer than she should have. All while keeping an eye on Abraxas's children and her own. The female dragon had proven herself on this journey, and now it was time for him to make sure that she was taken care of as well.

And so their children explored the island together. His heart melted in his chest as he watched Nyx and Hyperion with the other little ones. Though his children were much larger and significantly older than the others, they were still soft and kind with them. They played with them in the water, watched them with keen eyes, and seemed to not mind in the slightest that this task had been given to them while the adults rested and hunted.

Lumbering toward the sea cliff where he knew Tanis was resting, he laid his giant bulk down next to her and huffed out a long breath. "I have not been in this form for this long since I left the dragon isles."

"And why should you be confined in such a large form?" Tanis laughed at him, her throat vibrating with the sound. "The mortals would quake with fear every time the ground shook as you walked. You know they are far too sensitive."

"They fear what they do not know."

"As they always have." Her eyes saw far across the distance, and he realized where she was looking.

Umbra.

The island was out there, somewhere. Just beyond their sight, and it held all unknowns for them. The dragonlings couldn't change, so Tanis and Rowan would have to keep them hidden. They'd have to keep them safe.

Sighing, he shook his massive head and lifted it to stare out past the sea smoke. "Tanis, I thought you would stay. I didn't think that all of you would come, and that was never my intent. You have to know the dragonlings, your little ones, are..."

He let the words trail off, because she knew what he was going to say. Of course she knew. They were more important than anything else in this world to him and the thought that he might be the cause of their death?

His fear overwhelmed him. If he was the reason the dragons died out this time, he would never forgive himself. They had a chance right now. As they always should have. They had a chance to rebuild and if they were wasting it to save this kingdom that couldn't care less if they lived or died? It would be the greatest waste.

"You thought I would send your children to battle without coming with them?" Tanis asked, though there was more mirth in her tones than his. "Abraxas, I look at them as though they are my own. All the dragon children are and will be. Do you not look at mine and feel the same?"

Of course he did. All dragons looked at their small ones and thought they were their own. It would be impossible for him to see that crimson dragon and not see a piece of himself in the little boy. And it would be impossible not to see their future in all the others.

Sighing, he nodded. "I see them as my own as well, Tanis. And thus I want to risk their safety even less. The things I did to keep my own eggs alive, when they were not even..."

"I know," she whispered. "I have seen much in my years and I know exactly the lengths a dragon will go to in keeping their own well and healthy. I trust that both of us know the truth in this matter. I am not risking my children without knowing the potential cost. But I am here because I remember what you said about Lore and her dreams for this kingdom. The dragons will no longer turn their back on their neighbors and not expect that to return to us tenfold. The downfall of the dragons was that we ignored this the last time it happened."

Ah, she was right. But it burned through his chest to know that he was going to bring them all back to Umbra. He needed a safe place for them, a place where no one would find them.

An invisible place no one but the elves could find, and even then, they would have a hard time when one of their ancient elves perhaps fiddled with the spells.

Abraxas sat straight up, his long neck craning to find Rowan, who had just sat down next to Draven at the fire. "Elf," he barked.

Both of them looked over at him.

He shook his head in exasperation. "Not you. Rowan, come here for a moment."

The old man groaned and got to his feet slowly, his hand pressed against the small of his back as though he was in pain. "What is it? I just sat down, Abraxas, and I've been running after those little ones all day. They keep insisting on being thrown into the air, but you know I can't do that endlessly. I'm not one of you."

He had to try very hard to control the eye roll that threatened to have him seeing the back of his skull. "How familiar are you with the old magic? The spells that elves used to cast on their citadels?"

"Well enough." Rowan's back straightened immediately, his hands clenched at his sides in excitement as though the pain was all for show. "Do you know of such a place? I was under the impression they were all torn down or destroyed years ago."

"I do, actually."

Draven meandered over to them, his hands tucked behind his back as he nodded. "Ah, the one up in the mountains? Cold for the little ones, but a good place to hide them."

"Hide them?" Tanis sat up as well, joining the conversation with a gracefully stretched wing. "And this place is safe enough? You think the elves cannot sense the old magic?"

"There had been no elves visiting it for years by the time we had gotten there." Still, it wasn't enough. Abraxas looked at Rowan and nodded. "That's where you come in. If you can change the spells, make them more your own than the old elves. I think it would be very difficult to find."

"It sounds like it was already well hidden," Rowan replied. He tapped a finger on his chin, as he always did when thinking. "Perhaps it is doable."

"You must have cast such magic before?"

The older elf shook his head. "I was no enchanter. I was a scout at best, and it has been a very long time since I've touched elven magic. But, I suppose it should be easy enough to figure out, as long as the person who created it had wished for elves to manipulate the original spell."

Likely, the original elf had not. But Abraxas still had hope. "The spells are very old. Most of the castle is no longer there, but from what I could see, there is a mural in the old courtyard that depicts Lore. I think, perhaps, the old elves wanted her to be there. And if you can use that to your advantage, it may be best for all of us."

"Ah." Rowan nodded again. This time the spark in his eyes looked a little more hopeful. "Then there is certainly reason to try. And if I cannot change the spells, then I will set wards around the place. Elven scouts are very good at those, and they will let me know the moment someone comes near us. I can run with them, if I must."

Abraxas felt a little better knowing that the children would be safe at least. Or Tanis's children would be. He needed his own children to fight with them.

Sighing, he looked at Tanis, and he knew the other dragon had seen what was in his mind.

She tilted her head to the side, eyeing him and the armor that covered his body. "I know you wish us to fight with you."

"There is to be another battle, and I believe it will be the one to end the war."

Draven shuffled his feet on the ground, drawing everyone's attention to him as he took a deep, steadying breath. "Why is Lore not ending this? She has the power to do so, does she not? She could wave a hand

and crumble the entire castle to the ground if she wanted."

"Then it would be hers." Abraxas remembered the conversation they'd had in the darkness, where she'd bared her soul to him the night before he left.

He had known the deep fears inside her. He'd seen the darkness that lived within her heart as she sent all the elves in that prison to their doom. As she'd enjoyed the feeling of blood and the splatter of death that surrounded her. His Lore had changed with the powers that came from inside her. It had made her more wild, more feral, more a goddess than an elf. And he knew that was a dangerous place for her mind to be.

"She has changed," he said quietly, trying his best not to sound as though he were judging her for it. "Lore's mind is not at the place it needs to be to run a kingdom. And if she wins this battle, she wins the throne. I do not believe she would give it up, and neither does she."

"Would that really be so bad?"

"Yes," he growled. "She would lose herself in this power. Lore battles for this kingdom and also to remain herself. We are going to be there for her, fight for her, with her, let her know that there is still a place for who she was before this power was gifted to her."

It wasn't that Abraxas was all that worried. Lore would be fine. She would be his no matter how many times she changed and turned into a newer, better version of herself. He'd be there for all of it and love her all the same through every step of the way.

But he refused to see her hate herself. He refused to watch her turn down a dark path that she never wanted to step down in the first place. Not for this kingdom, for their children, for anyone.

And so they would all do their best to ensure her safety and her life were well preserved.

Grinding his teeth, he eyed Draven, who stared up at him with sadness in his eyes. "So the prophecy," the elf started, clearing his throat. "It could be true?"

"There is no prophecy about Lore. Only about a half elf who changes things. The elves saw a future they did not like and so they spread fear throughout their ranks." He lowered his head, so he was on eye level with Draven. "And I need you to hear this now, deepmonger. She is not a monster. She will not become a monster. The kingdom she leaves behind will be better than it was before."

Draven nodded. But he still swallowed hard and looked around himself as though hoping someone would agree with him. "If the prophecies are correct, though, she might need..."

"They are not," Abraxas growled. "Prophecies are what we allow them to be. We can all stand here, fearing what Lore would do and then abandoning her because we no longer trust her. Or we can all say fuck the prophecies, she is ours. Our mate. Our friend. Our mother."

He looked over Draven's head and met Nyx's gaze, who had paused in her play to listen. To show him the shadows in her own eyes because she had known.

Of course she had known.

He straightened, his wings flaring wide behind him. "She is ours," he repeated, and the words felt like a new kind of prophecy. "And we will not let her go."

And all he saw were his family and friends nodding along with him. They were here. They were going to stay and fight and love Lore through all of it. Just like he did.

His heart thudded hard in his chest as hope filled him up near to bursting. They would fight with her and she would not leave again. She wouldn't dare leave when there were so many people arriving at her side to love her. As they all should have from the first day they met her.

"Abraxas," Tanis said as the elves returned to their fire. "I did not come only to fight with you. I am not the kind of dragon who fights, but there is something I think would be best to do before we arrive back with Lore."

He would have lifted a brow if he had them. "You wish to delay our return? Even more than it will add to get to the mountains?"

"I do." Tanis's tail lashed in the air behind her, then dipped over the edge of the cliff. "Your children do not know how to fight. And neither do I. If a battle is what awaits us, then it would be foolish to throw them into the mix without trying to teach them and me how best to use our abilities. A dragon is formidable until it is grounded. Do you understand me?"

His first thought was that he would protect them. He'd turn the world into a blazing inferno before the humans would ever ground one of his children. But he also knew that was a foolish response when her fears were warranted.

"Indeed. But there is very little we can do about that," he replied.

"There are still crystals left in Umbra. Ones that are not connected to my own." She swallowed hard and then eyed him as though her plan was bound to anger the dragon before her. "I suspect you've had the same thoughts and have banished them. But perhaps it is time that we sacrifice a few memories to keep the few dragons alive."

She wished his children to absorb more memories. Memories of war and bloodshed and battle.

He shook his head. "The greens and blues have never fought alongside my kind. They cannot take the memories of crimson crystals, can they?"

"Perhaps, and if those memories are not of battle, then you can. You can find more memories and take the knowledge of a thousand dragons inside you. You can lead them, while they can learn what it is they do best. Then you will listen to your children, and we will all decide how best to fight in this battle. Do you hear me?"

He shook his head. "They still stay beside me."

"And they will likely die." Tanis's eyes welled with tears, those violet eyes staring directly into his soul. "We must protect them, Abraxas. And this is the only way."

By all the dragon gods, he hated this. But he knew she was right.

"How can we even find them?"

"I am the last Memory Keeper," Tanis said, her wings tucked tight against her sides as she lowered her head to the ground. "I will find them. And we will teach your children to battle."

CHAPTER 32

She would never forget the words when they came.

"Lore?" Zephyr had said, poking his head into her room. "They've agreed to fight."

She had no idea what had brought about that swift change in opinion. Perhaps Zephyr had done an amazing job of convincing them. He was their rightful heir to the throne, and perhaps they thought there was some bit of control they could grasp. Or maybe it was the magician, famed and powerful, who had once ruled the kingdom at the side of Zander and Zander's father. The man who now sat with Lore while watching all the mortals with disapproving eyes.

A magician who had been surprisingly kind throughout his stay here. He'd not even flinched when the Ashen Deep pressed grimdags to his throat and threatened him for the truth of why he was here.

Shockingly, he told them everything.

Lindon had never been a liar, he claimed. He'd told the king all that he wanted, and all that he planned on doing. Both of the kings he'd served under enjoyed his ideas and wanted to see him put this kingdom on its knees.

And when he'd explained why he'd done it, how the power had consumed the good man he once was and he was all too comfortable to bend to it, his eyes had watched Lore. As though he knew what the power could do to her. What she could feel underneath her skin every time she used it.

But Lore was not Lindon. She could feel the compulsion to take. How the frustration rolled in her belly and up into her heart because she knew she could end this at any time if she so wished. But this was not entirely her battle. It wasn't a war meant to be fought by a goddess, who then took what she was owed.

And Lore would. She had no interest in giving up what she'd won for herself. Thus, the fight had to be battled by human and creature alike. They needed to work through their issues with each other, or this would never stop without the hard hand of a powerful goddess guiding them.

She did not want to remain here for long. They would not trap her in this position when she did not desire it.

Now, they needed a place to put everyone. At first, it had only been a few dwarves who showed up because Algor had requested their assistance. The Ashen Deep had very quickly told Lore that this was unacceptable. There would be no dwarves in their hallowed halls.

Then a handful of humans approached, also told to stay out in the cold forest because the deepmongers refused to provide any other suitable housing for them. This issue quickly grew out of hand.

Now, there were people pouring in from all areas of the kingdom. Zephyr and his people had attempted to build temporary housing, but the Ashen Deep refused to allow any tree to be cut. This meant they could only build with materials that the Ashen Deep had on hand, which were few and far between. Most materials were made of metal and stone.

Thankfully, the dwarves had some experience with this material. But the human builders wanted nothing to do with the dwarves, and now the arguing was giving Lore a headache.

Lindon stood next to her, his hands on the knotted pommel of a staff he'd brought with him and used like a cane. "How long are you going to let them struggle with this?"

"As long as I need to. They have made it very clear my intervention is not welcome." Lore pointed at the gathering of humans, one of whom was the Baron with the loud voice and mistrustful eyes. "In fact, I believe I was told that dark magic has no place in human dwellings."

"Dark magic," he snorted. "Is that what they think your power is?"

"That is what they believe all magic to be. It is why there has been so much struggle for so many years now." Lore shrugged. "If they want to waste their time and energy building tiny shacks for their people, which will certainly not be welcomed with smiles and thanks, then they can waste that time."

"Or, you could stop this foolishness now and provide them with a safe place to hide." Lindon arched his brow and met her surprised stare. "You don't have to make everything difficult for them simply because they do not worship at your altar."

"And they do not have to deny me as though I do not exist." Lore wanted to argue more with him, but she also knew he was right. She could make this easier on all of them. She could keep them safe in the night and keep their family warm.

The worst part was that a man like this was telling her to do so. Lindon had committed worse crimes than her standing here and making them work before her. She hated that he was the one who called her to task for such a thing.

Huffing out an angry breath, she glared at him. "You are supposed to be evil."

"Yes, I'm certain your dragon still thinks that, and he has good reason to." Lindon squinted off into the distance as though he could see the sky from their shadowy position. "But not everyone with dark magic is evil, just as not everyone with light magic is good. Besides, aren't we all old enough now to realize evil and good are just a matter of perspective?"

"Gah. Old man, go away from me."

"Only if you agree to help those poor sods who are breaking their backs while dwarves laugh at them." He pointed in the direction of the newest house, currently surrounded by swearing humans and snickering magical creatures. "You'll lose your army before you even build it."

"I don't like it when you're right," she muttered. "It's downright disheartening."

"Helpful, you mean."

"Disturbing." She winked at him. "The last person I want to get advice from is a man who quite possibly destroyed an entire kingdom with magic he should not have had."

"Magic that you now understand," he murmured. A shadow crossed in front of his eyes. "And should you need to speak of it..."

His words trailed off, but she knew what he offered, and she was grateful. "I will find you, Lindon. Should it come to that."

It wouldn't. It couldn't. She would never let this power corrupt her, even though it was a great amount of it. She could always feel it, whispering in her mind about how much she could do and change. But that wasn't her place. She wasn't actually a goddess of old, or if she had become one, then she was so new at all this. Lore didn't know what was acceptable or fair or what was even right. This was not the first time she would make decisions for the whole of a kingdom.

Still, Lindon was correct that she needed to intervene. Her people, her soldiers, were taxing themselves with undo cause and damn the Baron, who already sneered at her as she drew closer.

"The goddess approaches," he said, his voice little more than a rasp of hatred. "Are we too loud for you, m'lady?"

She'd had just about enough of him. "Silence, Baron, or I will weave your lips together permanently so that I no longer need to listen to your childish prattling."

"I'd like to see you try."

She lifted a hand and grinned as he flinched. So he was not entirely foolish. At least he thought she had the power to do it, even if he laughed in the face of that fear.

Looking around, she caught the eye of the Matriarch and called out, "Do you mind if I borrow a bit of your forest for a time? I'll make certain that it's returned to its previous state once we all leave."

"Please." The Matriarch's hand went to her temple, a subtle nod that even she was growing tired of the sounds of hammering and men arguing.

Good.

Lore lifted her hands and drew them together in complicated patterns that lifted the stones and metal all together. They rolled toward her, shaping into a new form, squishing and stretching until a small stone hut stood before her with a metal roof. Moss grew on the top and twigs poked out from the single window, looking very much like a completely and utterly abandoned building.

The Baron snorted. "This is what you provide us? The great Lady of Starlight, the Fallen Star the dwarves keep prattling on about? A hut?"

She gave him an unimpressed look before Algor suddenly popped up beside her.

"It ought to be fine enough for the likes of you," the dwarf grumbled. "I've seen your human homes before and the states of them. This is better than what some of you live in."

"I live in a manor, you little—"

Lore stepped in between them, her hand raised in something like a claw. "What did I say about your words, Baron? If I need to pluck out your tongue on top of sewing your mouth shut, I will."

He silenced himself, though his ugly face turned red with the effort.

Turning around on her heel, she tried to split her face into a believing smile as she gestured at the hut for Algor. "Would you like to inspect it first, honored guest and king of the dwarves?"

Algor inclined his head, though there was a question in his eyes as he straightened. "Is it safe?"

"Safe?" The Baron choked, but then he ground his teeth so hard Lore could hear them.

At least he was still quiet.

"Yes," Lore replied. "It's quite safe, and I believe there will be enough for everyone."

"Everyone?"

She grinned at the curiosity that burned in his eyes. He hadn't seen much of her magic just yet, and Lore had enjoyed using it freely as of late. "Everyone. The dwarves. The humans. All the creatures that will surely come and join us because the guilt will gnaw at them and they will miss their neighbors. Even the mortals that we will save from Margaret's camps. They will all come here until we are ready to fight."

With a bushy, red brow lifted, Algor walked through the thin leather curtain that served as a front door and then... silence. Nothing.

Lore waited with her arms crossed over her chest, amused as the whispers started up among the dwarves. Where had he gone? What had the Fallen Star created? Surely it did not take such a long time to inspect a little hut?

Even the humans started to get a little nervous, their whispers floating through the air. Had she killed him? Did she think there wasn't any more use for the dwarves? Was this a warning for them all to work harder, quicker, better?

And then Algor burst out of the door. His loud voice rose into laughter as he wheezed. Sweat streaked his brow and true joy filled his being near to bursting.

"My king?" A dwarf stepped forward and allowed Algor to lean against him. "Are you well?"

"Well?" Algor clapped his hands hard on the other dwarf's shoulders and shook him. "Well? How could I not be? You must see what she has done! I've never seen the likes of it before, brother. This is... is... remarkable!"

The dwarves were quick to move then. They all darted toward the hut as one, their trust in her intertwining with a curiosity that always lived in their kind. And she saw Goliath in them. She saw her dearest friend who always leapt head first into adventure, no matter how dangerous it was.

As expected, the humans still eyed her with suspicion. Until she gestured for them to walk through as well, and that was enough.

Beauty's father was the first to walk through the doors, then the Baron, who straightened his shoulders as though going to battle. More and more people until the clearing was no one but her, Beauty, Zephyr, and Lindon. Standing and staring at the hut.

Lore kept her arms crossed over her chest, a pleased expression on her face as her friends tried to figure out what she'd done.

"Is it..." Beauty cleared her throat. "A portal?"

"No."

Zephyr leaned against her, his breathing rapid just from standing. "Is it larger on the inside? Like a magic tent?"

"No," she said with a smile.

It was Lindon who hissed out an impressed breath. "You created a new world, didn't you?"

"Hm." She lifted a hand and pinched her fingers together. "Not quite a world. Just a bubble, if you will. It's enough space for us all to hide while Margaret tries to figure out what happened to her humans and all the rest of the people who will come to fight with us."

"What makes you so certain they will come?" Zephyr asked.

Lore wrapped an arm around him and tugged him even closer to her side. "Because the people of Umbra are good, at their very core. And they will know to come to us because it is what is right."

She did not look back at Lindon, who trailed along behind them, fear radiating through his entire form. She knew what she had done was not usually accepted in magic. Creating a new world, even the smallest one, was a dangerous practice indeed. If she could create one, then she could create many hidden pockets all over the realm where she could hide forever.

Such dangerous games were bound to make anyone nervous. Anyone who knew what that power could do.

Keeping her eyes away from even the Matriarch, she walked through the door and into the sunlight.

Beyond the hut was a giant beach. With cliffs on the right side, hidden caverns there perfect for the dwarves. She'd built their homes into the sides of the cliff, making sure there were all the amenities and comforts she remembered from her time there. The humans had small cabins to the left that rose on emerald hills, stretching on for as long as the eye could see.

Some people had already started to explore, but Algor, Beauty's father, and the Baron stood waiting for her. They all watched her with no small amount of awe as she released her hold on Zephyr's shoulders and approached them.

"Well?" she asked. "Will this suffice?"

The Baron grumbled under his breath, but it was Algor who bowed low and deep. "We are lucky to have a goddess on our side, Fallen Star. Thank you for our new and temporary homes while we prepare to save the humans who have been enslaved by the dark and dangerous woman who sits on the Umbral Throne."

Lore grinned at him, and then nodded. "Shall we plan for that, then? I believe there's enough room for everyone now. And I would like to steal back what Margaret has taken."

CHAPTER 33

Abraxas soared through the clouds with his son at his side. And even though it felt strange to fly with his boy, knowing that he soon would be stripping away even more of Hyperion's childhood, Abraxas took the time to enjoy this for what it was. What no one could take away from either of them.

This was the first time they'd flown together. The first time that they'd gotten an adventure alone. Without Nyx. Without Tanis. Without even Lore.

Hyperion wheeled through the sky in front of him. His wings spread wide and the sun glittering upon his emerald scales. The long tendrils of his beard and mustache floated behind him as though the wind had untangled them almost straight. And his long, serpentine body flowed like the undulating waves of the sea.

Abraxas had never seen a green dragon up close like this. He'd never even thought it would be possible until he saw the color of Hyperion's egg. And now? He counted his blessings for what they were. His son was the first of his kind again, and soon, there would be ever more dragons awaiting them back home.

"We're getting close," he rumbled, his voice slicing through the wind toward his son's ears. "We'll have to be more careful that we are not seen."

"And why don't we want to be seen?" Hyperion slowed in his wild careening through the sky until he was next to Abraxas. Almost as though the fear had gotten to him. "Don't we want the people of Umbra to know that we're back?"

"We want them to know we've returned when we want them to know. The last thing we need is mass hysteria befalling the entire kingdom because a handful of mortals saw dragons that they no longer thought existed."

And that was exactly what would happen. The humans would spread the word, or perhaps the magical creatures. And he didn't know if that would be a good thing, or a bad thing.

Lore would know where the rumors came from, of course. None of that would be a surprise to her or the people helping her.

Margaret, on the other hand, would know something was up. She'd get a whiff of that and wonder about Lore and Abraxas's plan. Perhaps she would even realize that they'd brought their children over and that could only mean one thing.

He didn't fear the other magical creatures so much. They would be pleased to see that there was more of his kind, perhaps. There had to still be some of them who saw the dragons in the sky and remembered a time when they had been the guardians of Umbra. But there was still the very real possibility that no one remembered such a thing, and all they remembered was Abraxas melting the skin off their family.

Sighing, he shook his head again. "It's too great a risk right now, my son. Soon they will know that we have returned. Soon, they will know that our family is here to stay. But right now, we have to focus on getting the memories into you so that you know how best to attack this new stage of your life."

"Attack." Hyperion snorted and his wings spread wide as he plummeted from the sky, wheeled in a circle, and then appeared over Abraxas's head. "I know how to fight already. A few measly humans won't take me down."

Abraxas had a flash of memory, as though he could see the future. Giant green balls of acid that melted through wings and wriggled underneath scales to burn against skin. Burning such as he'd never experienced, and he was a dragon. He was meant to burn.

Abraxas tilted in the air until his wing was before his son's face. A wing that was ragged and tattered, with holes all through it and many scars scratched permanently on the surface of his scales. "Battle is not fun, my boy. It's not a battle of wits where you might win. No one wins when there is a war, and we all leave with scars just like this. Even dragons."

As his son stared at the wounds, he mellowed. The bravado that Abraxas was proud of melted out of Hyperion until they reached the shore. And when they did move through the clouds, jumping from each one as the sun allowed them, Hyperion stayed very close to his father.

If he was a better man, he might have tried to ease the tension in Hyperion's wings or reassure his son. Instead, he only felt his chest puff with pride that even now, with Hyperion half the size of Abraxas, his child sought him out for protection.

They glided in as much cover as they could until they reached the small forest near Lux Brumalis. Abraxas remembered this place well. The Hall of Heroes where monks lived who had given themselves no leave for happiness for virtue. And, of course, how could he forget their proximity to the most evil magician alive? Or perhaps the most unfortunate.

He landed hard outside the forest, his gaze already sweeping for anyone who might have tracked them. Abraxas lifted his head, scenting the air and drawing it deep into his lungs.

To his immense pleasure, Hyperion did the same. His boy lifted his head and muttered under his breath as he picked out each individual scent. "Deer. Boar. A mating pair of foxes. Why isn't there more in this forest? Certainly that's not all the animals here?"

"The forests have been dying in Umbra for a long time." Abraxas settled, certain there was no one close to them that might bother them on their journey. "I told you that."

"You didn't tell me they were so... sad." Hyperion stepped between the trees, his form already loose and limber as he maneuvered between the thin trunks. "They are hurting."

"Many people cut them down." Abraxas shifted back into his mortal form, otherwise he'd never be able to follow his son. "Most of these trees are younger than the ones you've seen."

He could almost feel the discomfort rolling off Hyperion in waves. His son was so connected to the forests and the trees, apparently it was almost like a physical pain to him. As though the trees themselves were whispering to Hyperion of all the dark deeds that had been committed here.

Hyperion shook his head and moved deeper into the young, meager forest. "This place used to have trees taller than you can stand. There were hundreds of them, all stretching as far as the eye could see. The elves came and cut down some, but not all of them. Then the humans came, and they destroyed the entire forest for their homes."

"I was alive for it."

"These trees are so young and they have endured so much." Hyperion paused and gently wrapped his tail around a tree that was larger than the rest, and maybe the only one in the forest that could hold up Hyperion's weight. "This one has been here longer. It remembers the pain. The screaming as all the trees were sliced down. Not with magic, but with axes. They bit, they struck, and the trees bled."

"Ah, my son." Abraxas walked up to him and gave a little tug on his beard. "We cannot stop what has already happened. All we can do is continue to move forward. Do the trees know where the dragons have hidden the crystals here? We flirt with danger if we stay too long."

Hyperion nodded, but the frown was still on his face. He still lingered in that hatred that could easily spread like poison.

Abraxas knew that Hyperion would have fought against the humans at that time. He would have guarded the forest with a ferocity that only the emerald dragons had over such places, and he would have lost. The humans had been deadly and certain that they were doing the right thing. As all creatures were when they saw their future threatened and made a choice.

But he had known, even then, that nothing would stop the rising wave of mortals that would soon overthrow everything. And he had known as well to not interfere any more than he had to.

Time would come for the humans, and it had. Now they suffered as well.

Hyperion drew them deep into the heart of the forest. And there, the trees began to pull up their roots. These young trees were not meant to move yet. Some of the saplings would lose their lives to show them the crystals hidden in their roots.

He remained silent as his son moaned with the trees that pulled themselves out of the earth for him. They gave their lives willingly for the dragons of old, the dragons who would soon come and change the realm. But it did not make their sacrifice any more terrible or heart-rending.

The last of the roots snapped out of the ground, the sound echoing through the forest like the breaking of a neck. It fell to the side, pulling out the last remnants of the earth with it and revealing the long emerald crystals that grew jagged beneath them.

They were not for Abraxas. He knew that. Their whispers were tempting, though, even though the memories would be of no use to him.

But his son? Ah, his boy's bright green eyes flashed with a certainty that he'd never seen before. Deep inside Hyperion's heart, he knew his boy had heard the calls of his ancestors. Of all the emerald dragons who had come before him and now whispered that they could help.

Hyperion glanced over at him. "So I just..."

"Touch them," Abraxas said quietly. "Tanis said it'll all happen rather quickly after that, but if you feel any discomfort, you make a noise and I'll pull you away from them."

"And it won't hurt?"

There was his boy. His young man who hadn't been given the time to develop the strength and courage that he would need. And here Abraxas was, shoving him into being an adult before he was ready.

Before he knew what he was doing, he lurched forward and pressed both his hands to Hyperion's snout. "If you don't want to do this, we will find another way. You do not need to grow old so quickly, my son. You can be as you are, whole and untouched and unchanged, and I will love you no less. Your bravery is not being tested by whether or not you do this. You know that?"

Hyperion nodded, then nudged him back. "But I want to help. I want to make a difference and I don't want to see what happened to these trees happen again. Father, I will do this for the kingdom and for you."

His heart broke. No child should have to make a decision like this. It was wrong. He'd pushed Hyperion into growing too quickly, and he'd made them into little adults far too soon. He was pulling out of this plan, and Tanis could be angry all she wanted. He refused to make his son suffer through a single more moment of his.

But his boy had already moved forward and dropped his head on top of the crystals. And those emerald eyes that were always so bright and filled with mischief closed as he sank into the memories that the emerald dragons had to share with him.

In the end, this wasn't Abraxas's choice. Because he was blessed with a child who had the heart of a hero and no matter what he did, he couldn't change that.

Rubbing at the sudden moisture in his eyes, Abraxas settled onto the ground and waited for the crystals to share whatever they had to share. No matter how long it took, he would be right here when Hyperion woke.

It took until the next morning. Abraxas almost interrupted the exchange multiple times. Hyperion's eyes fluttered beneath his closed lids, and a few times he'd moaned. Abraxas wanted to shred the world every time it sounded like his son was in pain, but he hadn't... couldn't... Ah, the world had shattered around them and no matter what he did, he'd never be able to piece it back together for his boy. Not any longer.

Finally, Hyperion pulled himself out of the memories and sat up straight. His head weaved a bit like he was drunk, his eyes not quite seeing Abraxas until they focused on him.

"It is done," Hyperion said, his voice rough and gravely as though he'd been screaming. "We can go."

But he tried to take a step and almost immediately fell on his face. Abraxas stepped out of the way, watching his boy try hard to stand up straight. "You cannot fly like this."

"I can."

"You cannot." Abraxas stepped forward, placing his hand on Hyperion's cheek and forcing his son to look at him. "I will carry you. You will fly on my back, as your mother does. Now change."

"I don't..." Hyperion winced. "I don't know if I can."

"You are stronger than this, son. Discomfort is bound to happen, remember? That's what Tanis said. So you are going to change and I will take care of you."

"Shouldn't I..." A loud click echoed as Hyperion swallowed. "Tell you?"

Oh, Abraxas didn't know if he would survive it. He could already see the shadows in Hyperion's eyes and the horror that lingered there. He'd seen darkness in those memories, likely more than he'd seen light.

"When you are ready," Abraxas replied, smoothing his hand down Hyperion's scales. "You will tell me. But no sooner."

Hyperion's dragon form melted away, leaving his son standing before him with glittering eyes and moisture already on his cheeks. This form was even more exhausted than the dragon, but Abraxas had no problem swinging the young man into his arms and walking out of the forest with him.

He set Hyperion down on the sands beyond and changed, before picking up his boy in his claws when Hyperion couldn't manage to struggle onto his back. And along the flight to where they had said they would meet, a small island just off the coast of Umbra, he felt rage burning in his chest. He wanted to protect, to destroy, to maim. And he could do none of that.

Tanis and Nyx already waited for them. His daughter sat at Draven's side, her troubled gaze locked on the flames they'd built. And he wanted to shatter everything again. His daughter should never look like that. Not once in his life did he ever expect to see her so... broken.

Tanis approached him, already in her mortal form as well. She gestured for Rowan to help Hyperion before she muttered under her breath, "I have them. They are well enough, and I will guide them through the memories. This is my purpose. Remember?"

"I do."

"Your rage will be your undoing, Abraxas. But I fear there is more for me to ask."

More? What more could she want?

Tanis swallowed hard. "I found crimson crystals here as well. And I think... I think you should seek them out."

Ah, of course. Why would he be unscathed in all this? Abraxas nodded, though, because she was right. Because war took from them all. Even him.

"Where?"

CHAPTER 34

We've brought a third group in," Beauty said, her eyes scanning over the paperwork in her hands as she read through all the names and occupations. "A better group than the last time. We've even got a few people with a medical background, four farmers, and three soldiers who will be quite helpful. The rest are the same old peasantry, but they will learn quickly. Just like the others."

Lore leaned back on the log, turning her attention up toward the dark canopy above their head. She'd seen Lindon's sylph up there yesterday, wheeling around and getting some exercise while its colors had cast rainbows above it. "That's good."

"And of course, the Baron and his people were quite pleased that we've gotten so many people out of Margaret's clutches. He's actually coming around to the idea of an elf leading us, you know. Had a compliment for you yesterday."

"What was it?"

"That you look quite pretty when you bathe." Lore could almost hear the wince in Beauty's voice. "It's not a delicate thing to say, but I suppose it is still a compliment and we should be glad that he's not outwardly mocking you anymore."

"I should have sewed his mouth shut when I had the chance."

"I don't think that would have won you any favors from the rest of them." The sound of shuffling papers echoed through the clearing before Beauty slumped onto the log beside Lore. "It's all a lot to keep track of, but I think we're doing remarkably well."

Rolling her head to the side, she watched Beauty's profile as the young woman stared into the forest. The awkwardness between them was still there. Stretching as it did, pulling and tugging at both of their hearts until Lore finally sighed.

"Have you forgiven me yet?" Lore asked. "I did all I could, you know."

"You didn't have to be so cold about it."

"I did. If I went in angry, then I would have done so much worse." Lore shook her head. "I already left a mound of bodies for Margaret to find, and a cell full of elves that I left there to rot. They could still be there, you know. Starving. No one deserves that. But every time I think about them and the choice I made, I don't feel like going back to save them. I'm all right with their end and knowing that those deaths are on my shoulders because Zephyr is here. Safe and sound."

Beauty nodded, her breath catching in her throat. "I know that. I do. I just don't know how you can be so calm about all of it."

Because if she wasn't calm, then Lore would set the entire Gloaming on fire. She'd turn this world into a mess of darkness and death and she would laugh as it happened because that was what they all deserved. She would ruin this entire kingdom with a glut of power and control.

Lore couldn't tell Beauty any of that, though. She didn't want her friends to be afraid of what happened and she certainly didn't want them to believe, for an instant, that she was evil or just as bad as Margaret. She was... Just herself. Just Lore, their friend, the woman who had helped them for years now.

Sighing, she shook her head and resumed staring up at the canopy above them. "There was nothing I could do, Beauty. My hands were tied just as much as yours were, and I would not go back and change how I addressed it. Zephyr is safe and alive right now because we waited. He's with us because we waited and I know how difficult that was for all of us to do, but it was still the right choice."

"You aren't getting it." Beauty finally looked at her, leaning down to stare into Lore's eyes. "I know why you did it, Lore. I understand that there was no other choice. I'm angry at you because you did it so coldly. Nothing that you did affected you. You weren't angry or sad or even confident! You were just cold and numb, and that scared me."

Ah.

Well.

She supposed that made sense. Lore had to be a little different right now because otherwise she would lose control. She'd lose herself.

Slowly sitting up, she laced her fingers together in her lap. Her spine curved in on herself, as though making herself smaller might somehow make her feel better. She knew it wouldn't.

"It's..." Lore struggled to find the words. "I have to be cold about it, Beauty. I cannot make these decisions with my heart or anything else. I have to do the right thing and I have to do it without emotions leading me in one way or another."

"But why?"

Because she'd end the world. Because she'd tear it apart and laugh as it bled into her mouth.

"Because it's the right thing to do." She stared into Beauty's eyes, willing her friend to see her. "Umbra deserves someone who isn't making decisions for themselves. It deserves a ruler who can see the good and the bad and somehow bring it all together with a positive attitude and hope."

"I don't think that person is you," Beauty whispered.

"Neither do I." And for once, they saw eye to eye on something. "But here I am. The most powerful person in the kingdom with a prophecy over my head saying I have to fix this. And I'm doing it whatever way possible because I don't think I'm the right person for this."

Beauty bit her lip and nodded. She clapped her hands onto her knees and stood, her troubled gaze on something in the forest. "All right. I'll take that answer and we can talk more about it later."

"Is this done between us?" Lore asked, because she damn well hoped it was. "I don't want to be at odds with you, Beauty. Not because your father is helpful in this or because I need more mortal friends. You mean something to me. You always have."

Beauty sighed. "Of course this is over. I don't enjoy fighting with you, Lore."

"Good. Then maybe we won't have to fight again for a while, yet."

The way Beauty's lips twisted to the side made Lore feel rather silly for even saying it. But then Beauty added, "I'm not the only one who wishes to talk with you today, Lore. Unfortunately, I think you might be in for another argument."

Lore's eyes trailed over to where Beauty had been looking, only to see Zephyr standing there. His tall form almost blurred in her memory, turning into that of a shadowy king who had haunted her dreams for far too long now. He looked so much like his brother, it hurt sometimes.

"It's a talking day, I see," she muttered before standing. "Apparently, I cannot get away from the lot of you."

"Unlikely to get away from us now that you've saved so many humans." Beauty did at least clap her on the back, though. A sign that perhaps their argument was well and truly over. "He'll be nicer than me, though."

"He always is."

And wasn't that the beauty of Zephyr? The reason why so many people loved him and looked up to him even when they did not know him?

Zephyr even had a smile for her as she walked toward him. A smile for the woman who had made his life a nightmare after yanking him out of relative safety where his mother had hidden him. Lore was the reason he'd been tortured for months when she could have come home and saved him earlier. And he'd never once held that over her head.

She didn't deserve the amount of kindness and love he had in his heart. But then again, who did? Who was good enough to deserve all that?

"Lore," he said quietly, his bright beaming smile dimming into one of softness. "Do you mind if we talk?"

"Not at all." She gestured back toward her log, only to pause when he shook his head.

"Not here. I'd rather... I'd rather no one overheard what I have to say, if you don't mind."

So it was a very serious conversation then, and one that she wasn't certain she wanted to have. Lore ducked her head though, tilting it low and nodding for him to walk ahead of her. Mostly because she wanted to see if he could do so. The Ashen Deep had been working hard on the curses, and he was finally making significant progress.

He strode ahead of her like a man who had never been cursed or tortured. His shoulders straight, his spine stiff, his legs strong and powerful once again. Perhaps a little shaky when he had to go over stones, but certainly not enough to make her grab for his arm and help him.

He looked better. A lot better, and very quickly at that.

"You seem more like yourself," she said as she stepped over another fallen log and into a clearing with him. The moss underneath their feet was less squishy here, and there were more beams of sunlight than she'd expected. It turned the entire area into one of bright emerald colors, with yellow pollen and dust motes floating all around them, catching in the light.

"The Ashen Deep said there's only one more curse to undo, and that you could have the honors if you'd like." He swallowed hard. "They said to tell you it's just one hard tug and that will be the end of it."

Really? How curious.

Lore frowned at him and extended her power, prodding around his body until she found it. The last one wasn't tangled like the others had been. The curse wasn't wrapped around his heart or lungs or even anything important. It was wrapped around his neck, though, and must have been uncomfortable.

She gave it the hard tug they'd wanted from her and watched as it slithered off his form. The spell landed on the ground and left a small black smudge in the moss, a terrible reminder of what elves could do if they wished.

Zephyr sighed in relief, rubbing his hand over the skin there. "That's much better. Thank you."

"I did very little of the work. Don't thank me, but I can help you find something that the Ashen Deep will enjoy." Perhaps a little more elfweed. Certainly that deepmonger had found it nearby, or someone was a growing stash that she had yet to sniff out.

He chuckled, "Yes, well, you would know more of what they like than I do. I'll admit, it's been a relief to be around so many humans of late. Being surrounded by elves makes me a bit... twitchy these days."

"Understandably so. At least the Ashen Deep are nothing like the rest of us." In more ways than one. She narrowed her gaze on him as Zephyr started kicking his foot at the moss and looking anywhere but at her. "What did you want to talk to me about?"

"Uh, the... The humans have been... Well, you see, they've been talking. And it's nothing against you. They just aren't comfortable with elves either, or any magical creature, and I know the dragons are coming as well." He'd started babbling like he always did when he was uncomfortable. "They think that... Well, it's easier for them to talk with me, you understand? I know that's strange to think, but they tell me more than they should. And they keep talking to me like I'm making decisions, and I'm not. You are. You're the only person who I want to make decisions, too. I trust you, you know—"

Lore held up her hand for silence, and Zephyr nearly bit his tongue in his haste to shut up. "You're rambling, Zeph. Just tell me what you came out here to say. You will not insult me."

He took a deep breath, and she felt all the tension leak out of him as he blurted out, "The humans want me to take the throne when all of this is done, and the Baron has been rather vocal that they will not accept anyone but a mortal on that throne. And I would like you to take the throne instead."

Sucking in a deep breath, she repeated to be sure, "You want me to take the throne when all of this is done?"

He nodded firmly. "It makes the most sense. You are the most qualified for the position and I think you would make a very good queen. I trust you and Abraxas."

Oh. All the breath wheezed out of her lungs and Lore wished they had stayed next to her log because she would very much like to sit down. "No," she finally said.

"What?"

"No," she repeated, although the temptation lingered. "I will not take the throne."

"But you have earned it. You came back from the dead, Lore! You have saved all of us countless times, and this throne was made for you." He threw his hands up in the air. "There's a prophecy and everything! You're supposed to be on that throne, and I will not stand in your way. Neither will I ever align myself with people who do not see you for who you are."

"Oh, you sweet young man." Lore felt all the power in her vibrating, and she knew she had to share with him the struggles she faced. Lore let it out, showing him the glimmer of moon magic that had always turned her skin to diamonds and how it had changed. How her skin no longer glowed with moonlight but with a darkness that had an edge, a rippling power that was black and red like poison. "If I took the throne, you would have an avenging goddess ruling this kingdom. I wasn't lying when I said it. I am undying and so powerful that I could wipe all of Umbra clean. I would rule over a vast and barren world, for power always corrupts."

"Not you," he denied her words. "You would never be corrupted."

"I already have been," she whispered, and the power flowed out of her again. "My path is not goddess or queen. What Umbra needs is a kind and giving ruler who sees the good in everyone that they meet. Someone with patience, who hasn't had hope stamped out of their very soul. They need someone who will give them the time to grow, and will nourish them with happiness and light. This kingdom does not need a goddess, Zephyr." She stepped close to him and put her hand on his shoulder. "This kingdom needs you."

He gaped at her, his mouth moving like he was trying to speak, but couldn't get the words out. Until he wheezed, "I am not fit to be king."

"Because you believe that, Zephyr, I am certain that you are very much fit to be king."

And it felt right. It all clicked into place so perfectly and she knew what to do after all this was said and done.

She squeezed his shoulder. "You will rule Umbra as you should have after the death of your brother. You will have advisors from all walks of life, and you will listen to them as no one else ever has. You will prove to the magical creatures that you care about their wellbeing and you will work to make their lives better. And the mortals will see you do that, a king that they stand by, and they will follow in your footsteps."

He swallowed hard. "I am afraid."

"We all are. But you will never be alone, Zephyr. I will always be here with you, but I cannot and will not take that throne. I give it to you, Zephyr. So you can lead this kingdom into the light."

And though she knew it terrified him, he looked up at her and she saw the change. She saw the hope build in his chest and when he nodded, she knew this was the right step.

The right way forward for them all.

CHAPTER 35

He skirted around a cloud, tilting his wings so he could maneuver through it without being seen. This felt… strange. He remembered the path that Tanis had detailed to him. He remembered this journey as though he'd done it before, but he couldn't have gone this way before. Abraxas stayed away from this side of the kingdom.

Solis Occasum had already fallen, but there were cave systems beyond it. Tanis had felt them as she made her journey here, and she had been certain that was where the crimson dragons had spoken with her.

It was the final resting place for many of his kind; she had said. She'd warned of what he might find within those caverns. If there were any other hidden crystals, she would have sent him there. But this? This was the journey he had to make.

And so he landed outside of the cave system and tucked his wings tight against his body. These caves were made by dragons. He should journey into them with the bravery and body of a protector who had seen his family through much hardship. He should hold his head high and proud.

But, as he stared into that darkness, he found himself wavering. Hesitating. Fearful that in this moment, he was about to find something equally terrifying and heartbreaking.

His first step into the caves was into darkness. His eyes took a moment to adjust to the dim light, and then to the blackness that surrounded him.

Then his foot crunched on something that felt like bone.

Abraxas tilted his head to the side, eyes closed in horror that threatened to eat him up inside. He'd known this was where a massacre had taken place, but he hadn't... He'd never expected the mortals to leave them here. He'd thought this place would be raided by those who knew dragon bones and scales would come at a heavy price.

Surely the magician himself had come here. Lindon would have sensed the strange pools of magic that had come from crimson dragons spilling their lifeblood on the ground. Surely one such as that would have thought that desecrating such a burial ground was worth it if the magic he gained was much more powerful than ever before? Or had even Lindon realized that was too far?

And he still hadn't opened his eyes.

Abraxas took a deep, calming breath and blinked his eyes open to see the horrors that surrounded him. Dragon skeletons littered the floor. Too many for him to count, considering they were scattered about in pieces where animals had come to feast. Many of their giant heads had glittering scales decorating the stone around them. Glittering scales that looked like droplets of fresh blood.

His heart lurched and his stomach rebelled. These were the last of his people. The last of the crimson dragons who should have protected their own kind, and instead, they had died in a cave. Terrified and trapped because the humans had forced them into this position.

He wanted to tilt his head back and roar with the injustice of it. He wanted to tear apart any human who stepped in his path for the next hundred years.

But his heart whispered this was not the way. He could not destroy an entire kingdom because of the pain in his chest. He had to find a new way forward so this would never happen again. And if he fell into the same trap that his people had fallen into before, then his end would surely look the same as this.

Slithering through the remains of the fallen, he picked through their bodies as the skulls stared back at him. They watched his movements with judgment, with hope, with the terrifying realization that they were still here. They were alive and well because they were inside of him.

And he felt so young.

Abraxas had lived for hundreds of years. He'd seen kingdoms rise and fall, and yet, in the weight of their dark eye sockets, he realized he was still so young. Still a child who needed the help of his ancestors and wanted nothing more than to hear the sound of his mother's voice one last time.

And how small was he? He had thought he was a massive dragon, huge in comparison to all others, but he stood beside a skull of a dragon who had died with his head in a hole on the ground—perhaps what had once been a pool of water—and he was scarcely more than half of its size.

Would he continue to grow? There was no one to ask the questions he wanted answered. Would he only get larger as the years passed? Was it truly all right for him to mate with an elf, and not have to worry about the other generations because he'd already hatched two other eggs? He was replaced by two creatures who would make at least two more. Surely he'd done enough and now he could just rest with his beloved?

Abraxas continued moving through the massive cave system until he found them. The crystals. Glowing red and gleaming in the back of the caves, their light casting the entire space in an ominous and terrifying glow. This was where his people had died, protecting their memories with their bodies and their lives.

Shaking his head, he made his way closer to the tallest crystal, as Tanis had told him to do. She said all he needed was to touch it, just like his children, and the memories would come. It was less about maintaining them, protecting them, ensuring that the memories were exactly as they were meant to be. Instead, this was about consuming them so no one else would see them ever again.

And so he rested his giant weight next to the crystals, feeling the rocks biting against his scales and scratching his sides. Then he reached out and touched the tip of his nose to the crystal and let his eyes flutter shut.

At first, he felt nothing. Just the sensation of magic flowing over his body. Until it wriggled underneath a loose scale and his mind fractured.

He was himself and not. He was a dragon and two dragons and more, suddenly filled with a rush of souls that shouted for his attention.

They flooded through him, a sudden spiking headache splintering through his head as so many memories threatened to overwhelm him. They all wanted to show him what they thought he needed to know. What he needed to see. How he needed to act, to be, to move forward in his life as a dragon. And it was too much. It was all so much.

Until it cleared, and all the memories and souls moved aside for a vision of a much larger soul. The soul of the dragon who had died in the water. Abraxas suddenly knew he'd done so to leave a message. A message for Tanis, it seemed, as he filtered through the massive dragon's memories.

Attor.

The dragon's name was Attor, and he had been the greatest crimson dragon that this world had ever seen. He'd led the battle here, drawn all the dragons he could toward Umbra where the boats had come from. Where they had started a battle that would end the very lives of all the dragons in their homeland. He'd tried to fight for them, to bring an end to the madness, and he had failed.

But where he had failed, Abraxas would not.

Attor's soul remained in this place, waiting for the perfect moment, the perfect dragon, to finish his work. Not to destroy or maim or ruin an entire kingdom. But to build back the hope and connection that dragons had once brought.

If another battle was the only way to bring about that new age, then Attor would share with him all that he knew.

Abraxas lived through the memories of training that Attor had given. To sapphire dragons who had only known how to fight in the water, but they could bring the water with them. To the emerald dragons who had only been wise and kind, and how he'd used their quick wit and intelligence to make them fierce warriors. Gold, red, shimmering purple. They'd all fought alongside this massive dragon who had led them toward what he had been certain would be a victory.

He watched them arrive with hope and determination in his chest. He'd known that all the colors of dragons arriving in one place was risky. That he could leave his homeland completely unprotected, but no human had ever made the journey to the dragon isles.

All those dragons had come together, and they had fought. At first, it was with success. They had rejoiced and the happiness that had flowed through his veins made everything all right. He could feel the pride that Attor had felt. He knew the sensation of relief and the hope that maybe this was over. Maybe it could be over and that he'd done the right thing.

And then Abraxas watched them all die. He watched as they bled and they screamed and they cried out for the crimson dragons to save them. He knew the struggle as the dragons fought their way through hordes of humans and elves and other creatures who had tried to imprison them.

And he knew the moment that Attor did. The dragons would fail. They were the monsters in everyone else's story. None of the creatures wanted them to be here, because then there was nothing that could stop them. Until they realized even swarms of ants could destroy a rat, and that was the end of it.

They had realized, if they wished, they could all kill dragons. They could destroy them and hunt them and turn them into little pieces of what they once were to use in magical spells and to make themselves feel more powerful.

Just like the dragons were.

Abraxas nearly wrenched himself out of the memories. He wanted no part in this, because his heart was near breaking and all he could think about was how cruel and unjust this had been.

The dragons had suffered protecting themselves. They had suffered because everyone had wanted them to suffer.

All the memories flattened then. They smoothed out of heartbreak and blood into nothing more than a dragon staring down at himself in a pool of water. And Abraxas saw so much of himself in that massive head. The scars, the haunted eyes, the way the weight of the world seemed to weigh upon his shoulders.

Attor spoke, and his voice was like thunder. "This memory is for you, and you alone. I do not know who you will be, or what madness has brought you here." A burst of fire flared behind him, and shouts erupted in the middle of the message. "But I need you to listen to me. War only brings more war and hatred. Our people failed to realize this, and once we did, it was far too late. Bring about a new age. An age of dragons who listen and learn and make time for the others that live in this realm. A place where dragons can... be. Without having to fight. Without having to hold to the old ways."

Abraxas winced as another blast of flames erupted behind the dragon's head and he knew, he knew, this was the moment Attor had died. The moment that the crystals had barely stored and perhaps it was his blood that had drawn the memories to their sharp edges.

"We hid them," Attor added, his eyes slanting behind him before he stared down into the water one last time. "We hid the eggs. In the mountains. The Stygian Peaks the mortals call them. They are all throughout the lands, tens of them. Enough to restart everything should this... should this..."

The memory ended there. It snapped to a finality that made him flinch back so hard that Abraxas jerked himself away from the crystals.

There was more, he knew. More he could see and learn because the crystals were still glowing bright, bloody red.

If he wanted, he could dive back into those memories after he got his bearings, but... Damn, he wasn't sure that's what he wanted. Abraxas wasn't sure he could handle more.

And the longer he was away from the thrall of the memories, the less he thought he wanted to see. He knew his people had suffered. He'd seen that suffering firsthand now, and perhaps... Perhaps part of learning these new ways and acknowledging that the old ways were dead, was taking care of himself first.

He knew where the crystals were. Attor had given him all the knowledge he could need, while understanding that there needed to be space for Abraxas to digest what had been given to him.

He knew, without a doubt, this was the right way. Someday he would return. Someday, he would come back and learn more from his ancestors and take their memories into himself.

But right now, he needed to heal.

He needed to give his mind time and understanding to grow and learn and...

Gods, there were more eggs.

There were more dragonlings to find, and he knew that was important. More important than this war, but he couldn't split himself into two people.

He already had a family to protect. He had a dragon and an elf and dragonlings who still needed to be looked after, and he was a fool if he risked their mother's life. Tanis needed to know this. She needed to know that there were more eggs for them to find and gather and that they needed to...

He was moving out of the cave before he even realized it. Until he stood beside Attor's skull and stared into the dark spots where the dragon's eyes should be. And then he bowed, low and long, even though the dragon was no longer here with him.

"I will return." His voice boomed through the cavern. "I will come back to honor your memories and your bodies. I will not leave them here, but first, I must save this kingdom as you all wished to do. I must piece it back together with honor and life. And then I will ensure that your bodies are remembered and your final memories are safe."

Then he fled that cave of darkness. He flew through the skies without care if anyone saw him, because this was the moment he needed. This was the time when the entirety of Umbra needed to see a crimson dragon once again.

Landing hard on their island, he didn't stop until he stood but a few breaths from Tanis. "There are more," he said, breathing hard and his eyes wild. "There are more eggs."

Only silence was his response as Tanis paled even through her scales. She swallowed hard and then said, "What did he tell you?"

Tears pooled in her eyes and he thought perhaps she might faint. He twined their necks, holding hers up with his as she tried to catch her breath. "More... of us? There are more of us?"

"In the mountains."

"I cannot... I can't..."

"You will go with Rowan," he ordered, already knowing that she'd agree. "You will search the mountains for these eggs and you will bring them home with you, Tanis. You will."

And though her eyes were as haunted as his, she nodded. "I will find them, Abraxas. I will bring them home."

He glanced at his children, who stood with their spines straight and their heads raised high. "And we will fight to keep you all safe."

CHAPTER 36

Lore knew when her family was coming. She'd woken up that day with a pit in her stomach that was both hope and dread. Hope that she would see them, finally after all this time, and dread that she was dragging them toward their doom.

Everything here was going to plan. Zephyr continually told her that all the mortals who could fight were ready. Magical creatures from all over the kingdom had arrived, sheepishly offering their help in whatever they could do. The dwarves were already wearing full battle regalia whenever they came out of their homes.

And of course, the Ashen Deep were prepared. Their grimdags already whispered for the souls of elves who had gone back on their ways and who needed to taste what it felt like for their souls to whimper and scream.

Lore tried not to listen to the grimdags that much, because she agreed with them. And she would greatly enjoy listening to all those elves cry out for help that would not come to them.

She was not their goddess. She wasn't even their kind.

Lore was the half elf they had denied and now they would understand just how far that wound would slice.

Now she stood on the original battlefield with her arms loose at her sides. She didn't know why she'd come out here with Zephyr and Beauty in tow, but she knew that it was an important day to stand out here. With the dwarves. They'd made the entire battlefield into an armory of sorts. And apparently they weren't worried about Margaret finding out because they continued to tell her over and over again that no elf would ever find them.

What that meant? She had no idea. But Lore had long ago learned to trust the dwarves when they were adamant about something.

Instead, she kept her eyes on the skies.

"Why are we out here?" Zephyr asked, his hands twitching by his sides where she knew he had a small knife that he always kept with him these days. "Isn't this risky for you?"

"Margaret already knows I'm here," she replied.

"Then she could send out her armies here. The only reason she hasn't attacked the Gloaming already is because of the Ashen Deep. Her ravens will find you. Those shadow creatures are always watching." Zephyr turned his gaze to the sky as well, his eyes narrowing. "Or is that what you're watching for?"

"I am not." Lore was waiting for familiar shadows, not those of Margaret's magic. "Today feels like a good day, doesn't it?"

Beauty laughed at her side, crossing her arms over her chest as she joined them staring up at the sky. "A good day? I haven't seen you like this in a while, Lore. If you aren't careful, someone might say you were happy."

"I am," she replied. And then she pointed toward the clouds that had shifted just beyond the sun.

And there, silhouetted in the sunlight with colors gleaming through the thin membranes of their wings, were three dragons. Red, green, and blue. They cast multiple colors all over the ground as they slowly glided toward them.

Her heart caught with the sight of her children flying. She had known it would be glorious and wondrous and overwhelmingly beautiful. She had known that it would feel like her soul had ripped out of her chest as she watched them glide toward her.

But she hadn't realized how much she would feel her love for them. She hadn't realized that her soul would fly off to be with them as well, when she damn well knew she couldn't, or shouldn't, fly.

And still, she felt every bit of anger and fear inside of her settle into a resounding silence that she hadn't experienced for ages. Just peace in her heart, mind, and soul.

They were here.

They were all finally here.

A few dwarves looked up and let out a round of pealing laughter. They pointed up toward the sky, ripped off their hats, waving up at the dragons who made their way down as though giving everyone a chance to get used to the sight.

But ah, they'd all been waiting for what felt like years to see dragons like this. Three massive dragons that filled up all the spaces of the very sky. And those dragons didn't inspire fear. No one was running from the sight of them.

Tears pricked Lore's eyes as the three of them landed and a dark figure leapt off Abraxas's back.

Beauty choked. "Was Draven just... riding Abraxas?"

Oh, how the times had changed. Lore ground her teeth together, so she didn't burst into laughter and then she was moving. Running. Racing across the grass toward her mate and her children and her future, all wrapped into one.

Abraxas was the first to change out of his dragon form, and maybe that was because he knew these people. None of the dwarves threatened him, but no, it wasn't that. Of course it wasn't.

He met her with a hard thud of their bodies striking against each other. He gathered her up into his arms, both of them breathless as all the fear of the past few weeks melted out of them. They were together again. They were both alive, and they'd both done what they said they would.

"You are well?" he asked into her hair, his lips pressed tight against her head.

"I am well." She held him harder, her fingers digging into the muscles of his back. "Everything happened as expected?"

"Nothing happened as expected, but we will have time for me to tell you about it all." He drew back to stare down at her, his eyes missing nothing as they narrowed. "You haven't been sleeping."

"I've been gathering an army."

"Or eating." He pinched her thin arm.

Lore rolled her eyes. "I've been eating when I can. Do you think it's easy to gather everyone up in two weeks?"

"I think you can do anything you set your mind to." He dropped his face to where her shoulder and neck met, inhaling her scent deeply before sighing. His voice was low, only for her ears, as he growled, "As much as I'd like my time alone with you, your children have been clamoring in my ear for hours now about how excited they are to see you."

"Our children," she corrected with a snort, but he shook his head with a wry grin.

"When they annoy me, they are your children, elf." And obviously they had annoyed him far too much because she could see the anger still simmering, cold and quiet underneath his usually calm demeanor.

"Ah, well. Then I better gather them up." Flashing him a bright grin, she strode around him and opened her arms wide.

And just as they had when she'd first arrived on the dragon isle, her children swarmed her. They were much larger than they'd been back then, and all she could see was a flash of scales and thin wings, their bodies coiled and tangling around each other as they both tried to get closer to her.

But they were never so close that they might hurt her. They never miss-stepped or tromped on her foot or even so much as nudged her off balance. Instead, they were aware of their mouths as they shouted at each other about who would tell her what they'd learned in the crystals first.

Lore tilted her head back and laughed. The sound ripped out of her form, joy and happiness and utter bliss that they were here and they hadn't changed even though she'd had asked the impossible of them. Her children were still just as ridiculous and wonderful as they'd always been and, oh, she had missed them.

"Enough!" she said, clapping her hands loud to get their attention. "You are both far too large for such antics! Change, now. So I can hug you and then hit you both over the head for annoying your father."

"That wasn't me!" Nyx insisted, pulling away from the tangle of dragons to glare at her brother. "You know Hyperion doesn't ever shut up! It was him the entire time. All he wanted to talk about was trees and forests and saplings that leak syrup in the spring."

"It wasn't me!" Hyperion reared up, his beard twitching with anger before he snorted a ball of fire out at her. "Father likes to hear my stories about the forest and he was the one who came with me to get my new memories! Of course, he wants to hear about what I found and what good that will do all of us."

"He wanted to hear about battle tactics and what you learned from your ancestors, not how to grow more trees!" Nyx stomped her foot on the ground, and then flared her wing wide and knocked her brother over.

Ah, so it wasn't that their children had been annoying Abraxas, but that he was tired of getting in between their squabbles. Clearly, even though they had found more crystals and absorbed those memories, her children were still very much... children.

A deep sigh echoed beside her, and she felt Draven step up beside her. His arms crossed over his chest, his eyes ruefully watching the two siblings lunge at each other so hard that the ground shook with their anger.

"They've been like this the entire journey," he said, shaking his head with amusement. "They knocked each other out of the sky twice and Abraxas had to help them out of the sea. The man has an impressive amount of patience."

"You knew that." She nudged him with her shoulder, a grin on her face. "He had more than enough patience with you."

Draven tsked. "He had to have patience with me. He knew someday

I'd end up marrying his daughter and if he wasn't nice, I wouldn't let him see his grandbabies."

"Babies?" Lore arched a brow. "I'm not sure it works like that."

"Eh, adopted children are still children." Draven shrugged and his eyes turned back toward Nyx who currently had her brother pinned to the ground by the throat while she still somehow snarled more insults. "She has to grow a lot more before then, though."

"You'll be waiting a long time."

He nodded. "It'll be worth the wait."

And her heart cracked right in two. This elf had done so much for her family. He'd trusted her, traveled with her, kept her safe, fought by her side, and now he was willing to wait years for her daughter to grow.

Damn it. Those tears were back, and she didn't know what to do with them now.

Wiping a hand underneath her eyes, she wrapped an arm around Draven's waist and tugged him close. "It's good to have you back. To see you alive and well. I told your mother what you asked me to, and I thought she was about ready to snap. What in the world is a knife in the shadows?"

"A forever kind of mate," he replied, tossing an arm over her shoulder. "The other half of my soul, I suppose you might say. Was she surprised?"

"She didn't know whether to kill me or kiss me."

"Sounds like her." Draven gave her one more squeeze before laughing and releasing her. He held his hands up, backing away carefully. "I should go see my mother, anyway. Give the old bird what she's been waiting for, I suppose. Thanks for the ride, Abraxas!"

Ah, of course. Lore's confused expression cleared as she looked back toward Abraxas to see him glaring after the elf. "You let him ride you. I assumed that meant you had fixed things between the two of you."

"He couldn't ride either of them unless I wanted to see him dunked into the ocean."

"Not too long ago, you would have enjoyed that."

Abraxas snorted, but there was a softness in his eyes that she'd come to expect. Even though Draven would never be his best friend, or even close to a person that he favored, Abraxas saw the use in the elf now. And perhaps he'd seen how gentle Draven was with their daughter, and how precious he thought she was.

Her dragon shrugged. "He gets testy when wet. I have no interest in listening to all three of them complain for the entire trip, and why would I?"

Hyperion let out a squeal that made even his sister stop and step back. Nyx's eyes had turned dark with worry. "Did I hurt you?"

Her brother sat up slowly and his dragon form melted away. Instead, he was just a handsome young man sitting there, glaring at his sister with a bruised eye. "What do you think, Nyx?"

"Oh, it's just a black eye." Her daughter melted into her human form as well, her lovely dark hair a waterfall at her back. She shook out her hair with a huff. "Don't get in a fight with a lady if you're going to complain about it."

"A lady?" Hyperion shouted, hopping up to his feet with his fists already raised. "You are so far from a lady—"

"Enough, you two," Lore called out the words before she could stop herself. Obviously, they should fight out whatever disagreement they might have, but the two of them had a lot of people to meet. "Introductions must be made, and I'd rather you not meet everyone with dirt all over you and twigs in your hair. Yes?"

Like the good children they were, the two teens walked over to her with chagrined expressions and eyes that didn't quite meet hers. "Yes, Mother."

"Good." Lore released Abraxas to insert herself in between her children and wheel them toward the wall of dwarves that were waiting. "The dwarves are making all our armor and our weapons. They are very good fighters on their own and look at me like a goddess. Let's be nice to them, yes?"

She pointed to where Zephyr and Beauty still stood at the edge of the forest, their eyes alight with glee. "Those two met you when you were just baby dragons. Hopefully you remember them. If not, their names are Zephyr and Beauty. He's the brother of the previous king, but the good version of him."

And then she moved her hand just to the trees beyond. "We'll eventually end up in that forest right there to meet Draven's family and the rest of the humans. I'll need you both to be on your best behavior and impress everyone with how much you know. Got it?"

Though they both swallowed and nodded, it was Nyx who seemed to have more nerves than her brother.

Lore released the both of them, but held Nyx's hand in her own and squeezed. "They're all going to love you," she added. "How could they not?"

Both her children meandered off with all the confidence Lore had never had. They strode up to the dwarves, introducing themselves, laughing and smiling at the antics of the dwarves and...

Oh.

Lore leaned back against Abraxas's chest and pressed her hand to her heart. She felt full. Happy. This was everything she'd wanted and even though they were on the brink of yet another battle that would decide the fate of this kingdom...

It didn't matter. None of it mattered right now while she watched her two worlds collide, meld, and then bloom.

CHAPTER 37

"Are you sure about this?" he asked, making sure his lips were close to Lore's ear.

They stood outside the Gloaming, staring together at the castle on the horizon. Lore had made it very clear that she wanted only her and Abraxas to go first. She refused to risk anyone else this close to the battle.

And perhaps, because his Lady of Starlight wanted to give the other elf one last chance. It was an unusual show of pity from her when she so rarely offered it these days. He needed to keep an eye on that behavior.

If she was going to get nervous, or perhaps even lose the ability to see reason at this moment, then he would have to make the choice for her. Margaret knew what she was doing, and what she had done. Margaret was a terrifying beast who had laid waste to this kingdom and needed retribution. They all knew this to be true.

Still, Lore wanted to give her that one last chance. And he wasn't so sure he agreed with her that anyone deserved this. Not after what

Margaret had done.

"Yes, I'm sure." She kept her eyes on the horizon, not on him. "I don't want her to feel threatened until the last moment. If I can save us all a battle, then that is even better. Wouldn't you agree?"

"I don't think it's likely any of that will happen. I think she will rain arrows down upon us and laugh as we run."

"Then we won't run," she replied.

Abraxas saw it. The darkness in her eyes that had never really gone away since she'd come back to him. The darkness that he'd come to realize was the power welling up inside her until she couldn't think or breathe through it.

It was... Horrifying.

Wonderful.

A nightmarish twist of the women he knew and a woman he now knew to fear.

But it was still Lore underneath all of that. Still his elf who had come to him in a forest with starlight twinkling on her skin. She was still the woman who wanted to save this kingdom and would stop at nothing to see it returned to its former glory. Or better.

And that meant he had to trust her in this. He would keep her safe. He would become the shield she needed so that she could continue forward and save everyone from this cursed throne.

Nodding, he turned his attention back to the castle, where he could already see soldiers lining up. They'd been spotted, but then again, that's what Lore was hoping for.

Her dwarven armor gleamed in the morning light. The metal molded to her skin like it had been made perfectly for her. The runes glittered, protective spells ready to beat back any blade that even got close to touching her. She held the helm on her hip, and had promised she'd put it on, eventually. If it came to that.

She rolled her shoulders back, teeth bared in a grimace. "Stay alive for me."

"It would be impossible to do anything else." He reached for her hand and brought it to his lips. "You lead us all, my love, my life. Your taloned heart will bring us into a new world. Not because of any prophecy or elf that predicted it. But because you have fought tooth and nail to get us here."

Her fingers flexed against his, and he felt the little breath that came out of her mouth brush his knuckles. When had she gotten so close? It didn't matter, though, because now she was here and he could smell her and feel her. Their lips touched, clung to each other, with hope and love bursting in between them like a bubble of magic.

"Thank you," she whispered. "I will remember that through all this."

"We will fight if we must."

"And we will win."

She pulled away and Abraxas saw that darkness slide over her eyes. He saw her turn into the goddess before him, the woman who would turn this entire kingdom to ash if she desired, but never would, because she loved the land she walked on with all of her heart.

Together, they strode out of the Gloaming and into the dangerously open fields toward the castle. He could feel their armies behind them. Countless humans who were ready to fight, dwarves in all their armor, magical creatures who had arrived out of the fog to say they didn't agree with the way their neighbors had been treated. Even the Ashen Deep, waiting in the shadows where they would eventually appear like wraiths in the night.

Their people were ready to fight if they needed to. They all expected this to be a battle. Today they would take back their throne in a single, bloody fight.

Margaret likely thought that was impossible. She thought this battle would rage for months on end as they slowly picked each other off. But that was not Lore's plan.

It was the only time he'd seen Beauty's father and the Baron look at her with respect. They knew she could uphold what she was saying. They knew she would make her promise come true.

Even if that meant sacrificing the last pieces of herself that remained.

The guards on the towers and walls all turned their weapons toward Abraxas and Lore. He stiffened, his chest already filling with flames as the dragon in him readied to burst out.

"Not yet," Lore muttered. "I'll tell you when."

He hated waiting. He hated this.

But when he saw Margaret step up onto the wall nearest to them, he knew that settling was the best choice of action. If only to hear what this Darkveil elf had to say for herself.

"You've returned," Margaret said, her voice wringing out in the clearing. "Alone."

"I am never alone," Lore replied. And somehow, her voice was even louder than Margaret's. "But your numbers are few, Darkveil."

"Not so few when there are trained warriors who have spent hundreds of years learning their craft."

He watched Lore's expression, seeing it shift with anger as she stared up at the wall. "Aren't you missing a few humans, Margaret? I have found them in places all over the realm. You've been hiding them away from me."

"And I had plans for them. But if you want to fight with a few starving humans, then I will let you watch them die."

A flash of anger turned Lore's cheeks red. "So you knew they were starving? You knew you had sent them to places where they could find no food. You sent them there to die."

"I sent them to where they deserved to go." Margaret thudded a fist over her heart. "I did what you were supposed to do! I became what our people had prophesied when I saw that you would not become that person. I remade Umbra into a better place for our children and our children's children. Our people were dying out, forced to work as slaves and viewed as little better than animals. Umbra now bows to us, as our ancestors foretold!"

Oh.

Oh.

That was what Margaret had been working for all this time. She thought herself the elf in the prophecy. She thought that she was meant to save this kingdom, because Lore had failed to do so.

Or perhaps she had been working to get Lore on her side simply because she knew that Lore had the power to be the person in that prophecy. And then Lore had gone off on her own. Lore had thought her own thoughts, and as such, that had turned her path away from what Margaret thought was the right direction for this kingdom to go.

Abraxas felt his heart squeeze in his chest at the realization. This was almost... sad. He almost wanted to look at Margaret with pity.

This poor, misguided woman had led all her people into ruin.

She'd led them straight into a lion's den because she truly believed that the gods or their ancestors would forsake Lore at the last moment. That they would see Margaret was right, and the power would transfer over to her.

He stepped up beside Lore, glaring with his mate up in the Tower. "The ancestors and your seers have always seen the future clear and bright. That was the saying, wasn't it? The elves see the future as we see the sun."

"You stay out of this, dragon."

"I will not," he replied. "If you believe that your seers knew the future, and that there had to be an elf to save us, then you know they were not wrong in choosing Lore. You know the future she has selected is the one that they saw and wanted."

"It is the one they warned us about." Again Margaret thudded herself on the chest, and a few elves beside her did the same motion. "The elves warned us of a half elf who would deny her lineage and her people. They warned us she would come to destroy our kingdom and that we must do all that we can to fight her."

"Twisted words," he snarled, his lips curling in disgust. "You seek to manipulate the prophecy to fit what you desire, that is all."

Lore placed her hand on his back and drew him away. Abraxas knew he could not battle this woman for her, but he hated that Lore felt as though she needed to do this on her own. She should not have to prove herself. She should not have to fight so much, but she had and would for the rest of her life.

"Margaret of Clan Darkveil," she shouted. Lore's voice thundered through the open field like the bellow of a goddess. "I call upon you to stop this madness now, at the source. You will vow to no longer hunt humans. You will vow that the castle remains open for all those who desire to improve this kingdom. And once that is complete, I will leave this place alone. There will be no bloodshed in either of our hands."

Only laughter rang out after Lore's declaration. Margaret's laughter spread until it was a wall of elves, laughing down at the half elf who dared threaten them.

And when they all finally controlled their mirth, Margaret grasped the edge of the castle with her hands and leaned over the edge. "You seek to threaten us, but we do not fear one such as you. My hands are already dripping with blood, little girl. And so are yours. What is one more battle? We look at a half elf and a dragon, neither of whom scares us. Parlor tricks and a beast we've already beaten? You wish us to run from our own fears."

So that was what she'd told the elves. That Abraxas was easy to beat because they already knew the acid balls would wound him. And that Lore had moved the moon in the sky, but it was only an illusion. That her magic was limited to just illusion meant to scare or that she couldn't actually do all the things that she threatened she could do.

And as he watched all the elves, their eyes still filled with mirth and their faces wearing wide grins, he realized he was afraid for them. All of these people were going to die because Margaret had lied to them. Because they had trusted that Lore wasn't a goddess reborn or that a dragon was easily defeated.

"They're all going to die," he said quietly. "All the elves."

"Not all of them." Lore shook her head and glanced back at him. "There's an entire clan behind us who listened. An entire clan who heard the truth of what was, and they stuck to that truth no matter how difficult it was to hear."

"But what of the other clans? Are they so worthy of death if they do not know how to listen?" He shook his head. "These are the last of the elves, Lore. Your people."

"Then they should have been better." Little lines appeared between her eyes. A frown, perhaps, or worry that bubbled out of her chest. "They can still run."

"They have no reason to run."

She swallowed hard and turned her attention back to the Umbral Castle, where so many wrongs had been committed. She took a deep breath, her shoulders moving with the force of her inhalation, before she tilted up her chin and spoke once more. Her voice thunderous and strong.

"I do not ask you to run from your fears, but from a very real threat that stands on your doorstep. I never wanted to be the reason that there were even fewer elves here. I call upon you all to realize that if we do this, there will be no more elves left. We will wipe ourselves from Umbra until only whispers and legends remain."

A few of the elves shifted on their feet, looking at each other with nerves before they steeled themselves.

Margaret, as always, wore her bravado like the dark armor she never took off. "It's just you, Lore. Just you and a dragon and a few mortals who have never fought in their life. You wish me to lay down my weapons at your feet for a threat that does not exist?"

Lore nodded, then lifted her hand into the air.

Abraxas felt the earth rumble as their army stepped out of the trees. Hundreds of dwarves, hundreds of humans, hundreds of elves. All walking as one. Intermixed were so many magical creatures he couldn't name them all. Satyrs, giants, domovoy, ents, and more. All of them walking as one as they strode across the field toward the castle.

He spun just in time to see Margaret's face pale. He wondered if this was the first time she'd taken this seriously. Perhaps she'd looked at Lore as an annoying fly that buzzed around her head. Now she realized there was a very real army standing in front of her. An army that would be difficult to defeat.

Except then Margaret bared her teeth at Lore, shadows whirling around her. "You forget the elves have magic. We have fought and trained for years. This castle is ours, and the future is for the elves. You will not take this from our people."

"My people stand behind me," Lore called out. "They are here to fight for our home, and we will drag you out of this castle if we must."

"We will rain arrows down upon you."

Lore looked up at the sky, and Abraxas knew this was his moment. A blast of power rolled out of him, the loud bang startling many of the elves on the wall as they realized a dragon of his size stood before them. He rose on his back legs, his roar shaking the very stones they stood upon. His head reached up to the same height they stood at, and then he turned his attention to the sky where his children blotted out the sun.

Someone screamed.

"Dragons!" they shouted, and a few elves tumbled down the steps toward the castle. Fleeing the sight.

He roared again and his children echoed his call. Three dragons who had come to take back the dark memories that haunted them. Three dragons who would change this kingdom forever.

CHAPTER 38

Lore had known everything would fall apart after that. She'd threatened Margaret with the reality of what she'd been faced with, but also with the truth that her elves now knew her lies.

Lore was not a weak little half elf who was playing at taking a kingdom. She was a goddess, a warrior, a woman who had fought countless enemies to get to this point, and nothing was stopping her from taking what she wanted.

It was a hard truth. Perhaps a bit unfair to those who had believed Margaret's nonsense. But their reality was now a battle.

And Lore hadn't lied when she said they could run. She hoped they did. A world without elves in it would be sad indeed. And she had no intention of hunting them down afterwards. They could live their own lives. They could hide in the ancient elven ruins if they wished, but they would not be hunted like the mortals had been.

They put their trust in someone who did not care for them. That level of trust would be honored, but they would need to learn just how important it was for that trust to be in someone better. Someone worthy.

She already knew who that person would be. She'd seen how Zephyr worked with the humans, those who had been beaten and starved. The kindness in his soft hands, the smile on his face that tore at her very soul? All of that would make him a good king.

Glaring up at Margaret, she marveled at the similarities between herself and the Darkveil. Neither of them would have been good for that throne. Neither of them knew what it took to run a kingdom with a softer hand and guidance that would bring them toward better years. And yet, Margaret fought against that truth. She raged against it, clawing tooth and nail to get herself more power rather than realizing there was no stopping this. Lore had learned long ago to let it go.

She was not what this kingdom needed. She would never be the kind queen they wanted or deserved. But she would be its sword and shield when she was needed.

Perhaps forever. She hadn't gotten that far yet.

Margaret hissed out a long breath and spun from the wall. "Release the arrows!"

Of course.

Lore had thought they might fight these battles with honor, but no. Margaret wanted this to end quickly because she feared what the outcome might be if she fought fairly.

Lore could play that game as well.

She'd promised that she would let these people take their kingdom back on their own. A goddess should not interfere in a battle that required them all to prove themselves worthy of the land they walked on. And she knew, deep in her chest, that this was important. They had to fight this battle on their own.

But she would damn well give them the chance to fight. Throwing up her arm, a spell flashed out of her hand and settled upon her army like a blanket. All the arrows that rained down upon them shattered into a fine powder. Like ash, it coated her people with a soft gray, but that was all. No arrows touched them. No wounds, no screams, nothing.

A few startled gazes flicked over to her. And she knew how strange she must look. A woman standing in the middle of a battlefield, one hand raised, her helm not even on her head. A giant crimson dragon looming over her with his teeth bared and a snarl warning away all those who might touch her.

She would not actively partake in the battle, she realized. Lore stood there, watching as her people poured toward the castle and started hammering at the front gate.

The first battle she'd fought with them, Lore had been in the thick of it. She'd lifted her blade above her head and screamed to the heavens with her wrath. But now, she was merely a spirit who stood on the sidelines and watched them. Casting blessings as she saw fit.

It was... strange. It was the first time she'd felt like the goddess they had all named her. Because she knew if she waded into the battle with her dwarven sword, that no one would come out alive.

"Should I even fight?" she asked, the question meant for Abraxas. "Should we get involved?"

"How many deaths do you wish for?" He peered down at her and nodded toward where Hyperion had already latched himself to the wall.

Their son was fierce in his anger. He could sense those who had caused his forests pain, and in that, his anger was great. He was no longer the young man who had made them laugh, but an avenging dragon who devoured all those who had wronged him. Nyx banked low over the castle and opened her mouth wide. Rivers flowed out of her, pouring down the steps of the castle towers and sweeping elves down into the courtyard below.

It would be a slaughter. There would be so many dead on both sides. Though her people had wished for such a thing. They had wanted this to be over with quickly. They had desired to see an end to all this.

But... Did Lore want that many people to die?

She sighed and pulled her helm over her head. Her hair disappeared into the smooth metal and she could feel it molding to her features, the spells in it forcing the metal to fit better.

It did not obscure her vision, but it made all of this so much more real.

She was going to wade into that battle, and she was going to end this quickly.

Abraxas spread his wing wide around her, creating a cocoon for the both of them. He leaned down and nudged her with his nose. "You will stay well, my mate. You will stay alive for me and I will never be far from your side."

"I won't leave you this time." She grinned up at him. "But I've already died, my dragon. It is you I worry about now."

"Worrying about a dragon? You're losing your edge, elf." He winked at her before taking off. His massive form soared over her head with so much ease, it was like he was part of the wind.

She watched him join his children in clearing out the walls of the castle. They'd all planned this, knowing that arrows from the walls would be their greatest threats. And the dragons were the best way to keep those safe. If they could trap Margaret and her people inside the castle, then they could hunt them down. Control the battle.

This would not be like the last time. They would not fight with just magic, they were going to fight with skill.

Lore strode toward the forest's edge, where an elderly figure waited for her. Lindon and his bird would stay out of the fight until she called upon them.

"Are you ready?" he asked, his eyebrows raised. "I thought you'd give them a little more time before you wanted to cast this spell."

"I remember how to cast it," she hissed. "And now is not the time. We'll let them prove themselves for a bit longer before we call in the reinforcements."

"That was an impressive speech," he called after her as she stalked past. "Almost spoken like a real goddess."

She flipped him a crude sign with her fingers before she drew her sword. The long, thin metal gleamed in the sunlight. No one would stand in her way. She wanted all of her people to be... What? She didn't know. Lore wanted them happy and alive and well and living their lives without her.

The first elf that lunged at her wore full armor. It was easy to dodge their attack and slip her blade between their ribs. Bright red blood splashed out over the dark metal before the elf stumbled and then fell.

Again and again she fought until her silver armor was coated with splashes of blood. She never attacked someone unless they attacked her first. She never killed any elf who did not beg for their end on her blade.

And then the first elf without a helmet attacked her. She watched the man's face as he tried his best, but there wasn't rage or hate on his features. It was fear.

He was afraid to attack her, and he was still doing it. Why? Why would he fight her when he knew he wouldn't win?

Linking their swords, she dragged him closer to her and forced him to look her in her eyes. "Why?" she hissed. "Why are you fighting?"

"For the elves," he snarled back.

But his eyes were wrong. His face was wrong. He was terrified of her and he was still fighting and why was he still fighting?

She threw him off her. Their swords screamed against each other as he stumbled back before catching himself. His hair was light for an elf, not quite like a Silverfell, but perhaps another clan that had come from the forests. The elf put his hand on the ground, breathing hard and shaking his head as he slowly stood back up and raised his sword. Ready for battle. Ready to fight.

Lore shook her head and frowned. "You don't have to do this."

"I will protect our people."

"You don't have to fight me. I don't want the elves to die, but I don't want anyone else to suffer."

He bared his teeth in anger. "They enslaved us. They tortured us. They will know the same pain."

And that was the problem, wasn't it? Everyone wanted everyone else to feel the same pain they had gone through. And she could make them feel that, if that's really what they wanted.

The thought echoed through her head over and over again. A shadow passed over the sun, and she heard Abraxas's angry roar as the gates opened and trebuchets were shoved outside. She turned her attention toward those, knowing already that there were the balls covered in acid that would hurt her children. They'd hurt Abraxas.

Her perfect, sweet dragonlings would wear scars for the rest of their lives if the elves let those acid covered balls fly. And she refused to see that happen.

The elf she'd previously been fighting flew at her. She dodged, turning on her heel and ducking underneath his blade until she was suddenly behind him with her arm wrapped around his chest. She dragged his back to her heart, pressed her lips against his ear and whispered, "You wanted them to feel your pain, but first you should feel theirs."

Magic pulsed at his back and he fell onto his knees, clutching his head as he screamed. All those memories. All thrust into his mind so he could see what the elves had done to the humans. How many hundreds of years had been wasted as they tormented each other over and over again.

Lore did not look at him again. She raced through the courtyard, leaping over fallen soldiers and rolling over bent backs. She shoved her way past countless enemies who raised their swords but were stopped by her own people.

They'd seen where she was going. The humans knew what she was trying to stop, and many of the magical creatures knew exactly what would happen if those acid balls flew.

And then she was trapped. Trapped and stuck between walls of people fighting and she couldn't...

She could.

Lore was a goddess reborn, and she'd be damned if those acid balls would fly. Words slipped from her tongue, ancient spells from her mother and mothers before. And in those words was power that lit those acid balls on fire long before they reached the slings that would let them fly. Burning acid sparked off them and flung onto the elves nearby. Their armor sizzled, and then they screamed, tearing at the molten metal that dripped onto their pristine flesh.

It was... not what she wanted to do. None of this was. Her first real battle had felt so right. She'd wanted to destroy the Umbral Soldiers and everyone that ever came near the people she loved.

But standing in the middle of this battlefield, she realized these people were part of her as well. These were two sides of her soul, fighting and tearing and killing. Two sides that could never get along, no matter how hard she had tried to be part of them.

Algor's laughing shout echoed nearby, and she turned to see the dwarven king wielding double axes. He fought with a fluid grace she wouldn't have thought possible from a man like him. He leapt through the air and those axes flew out of his hands, hitting heads and chests and anything else that stood in his way. And then when he opened his hand, they flew right back into his palm. There were gloves on his hands and she wondered...

He did it again, the axe flying through the air and then back. Magnets? Had the dwarves figured out how to battle with high-powered magnets?

But then another cry echoed, and she turned to see Beauty and Zephyr fighting together. The damned young man was supposed to stay back with Lindon, but she had known he wouldn't stay there. Not when his people were fighting.

She kept him safe, though. Beauty moved with the natural grace of a woman who had learned how to fight her entire life. She'd built back the muscle and bulk that she'd lost after Margaret had taken over Tenebrous, and now she moved with a power that few could fight against. Certainly not any elf.

And behind her, Zephyr was swift and efficient. His sword bit out at anyone who came near them, his hand on Beauty's back as she whirled around him with her great sword flashing.

The dragons thundered over their heads, keeping everyone safe from overhead attacks, and it was... working. All of this was right. This was exactly how it was supposed to go and still her stomach twisted. Because her gut said this would not end well. It would not end at all if she didn't hurry and do... something.

But what?

Then she noticed movement on one of the farthest walls. It was a small haven between the three dragons that flashed from wall to wall. A haven where a Darkveil elf slipped into a secret entrance to the castle.

Margaret wasn't getting away that easily. She would not run and leave all her elves to the slaughter like the coward she was.

Anger flashed heavy and hot in her chest, and Lore thought for a moment that maybe she'd taken on some of Abraxas's qualities, because she sure felt like she could breathe fire right now.

Her people would take care of this army without her. Lore had to hunt an elf.

CHAPTER 39

Abraxas watched Lore slip away into the castle and his gut churned. He knew this was a trap. Why couldn't she see this? It was so clear to him that Margaret was going to use whatever cards she could pull to get them apart.

The last time it had worked. Lore had died and everything had fallen apart. Sure, they'd all won the war, but everything else had shattered in the wake of his darling, wonderful mate. And if Margaret thought she was going to make a repeat of that damned moment, then he would make sure that she was stopped.

Abraxas landed hard on the edge of the castle, scrabbling with his claws to haul at least half of his body up onto the top of it.

"Hyperion," he barked out, his eyes catching on his sons. "Keep the elves off the wall. I'm going after your mother."

His son nodded, and he saw the rage blooming again in his emerald eyes. Hyperion was enjoying himself, just like a true dragon should. His son was ready to beat at the world and rage with his flames until it was all ash at his feet. And then he knew without a doubt that Hyperion would take his time to make sure that green things grew upon the graves of those who fought against him.

Turning in the other direction, he locked eyes with Nyx. "Make sure the others stay alive," he snarled, glancing down into the courtyard where their people were fighting for their lives.

He'd hoped...

Well, it made little sense to hope right now. Lore had done what she could, and in doing so, she'd saved him and his children from the wounds that the acid balls would have left. But their people were still fighting. Just as she'd promised they would.

She was no goddess to walk into a battlefield and end the fight there. They needed to prove themselves to her, and they would.

"Father!" Nyx shouted, sweeping elves off the castle ramparts near her. Their screams echoed for a few moments before she snarled for their silence. "Bring her back to us."

"I will."

And then he let the change ripple through him. He was still half on the wall, even in his human form, so he had to drag himself upright. Already breathing hard, he rolled onto his feet and balled his hands into fists.

Three elves stood between him and the door that Lore and Margaret had slipped through. Three elves who would now meet their end.

He stalked toward them, shaking out the tense muscles in his shoulders. "Have you heard what happens when a dragon kills you?"

They looked at each other, then back at him. The elves gripped their swords a little more tightly, bringing them closer to their bodies as they walked toward him as one.

Perhaps they thought it would be easier to attack him because he was no longer massive. They must look at him now and think that even though he was a significantly large man, that he must be less of a threat.

They were wrong.

He didn't have a sword or a weapon, but he had his body and that was all he needed. These elves had no clue what they were about to fight, but he would at least warn them. Like the good man Lore had taught him to be.

"The old legends say if your body is burned by dragon flame, that your soul is consumed." He flashed the three elves a grin. "Are you willing to risk your soul?"

Again, they all looked at each other, as though they could bolster courage just by looking at other elves. It wouldn't help. One of them dropped his blade, lifted his hands, and backed away. The other two remained where they were and only gripped their sword hilts with even firmer grasps.

Abraxas tilted his head to the side. "Your friend is smarter than you two."

"You are not a dragon at this moment," one of the elves snarled, her voice revealing that she was a woman. "If only you had your scales and your flames to intimidate us."

Ah, so Margaret had lied to them about his abilities as well, or perhaps they were merely too young to remember that a dragon was to be feared in whatever form they chose.

He gave them both another sharp toothed smile and then held out his hand. With a flex of his stomach, he expelled a bright flame that turned into a fire sprite in his palm.

They had frozen where they were, suddenly realizing that they were in more trouble than they had realized. And when he smiled, their hands trembled and shook their swords.

"Burn," he said, his voice guttural in his order to the sprite that suddenly looked so pleased to do as he asked.

It would burn whatever stood in front of it, and right now, that was the two elves who now would know what true terror felt like. The sprite hopped off his palm, struggled to stand on the ramparts, and then sprinted toward them with all the speed of lightning.

One elf shouted, the only remaining man. The sprite went right for him. It grabbed onto his leg and tunneled underneath the armor. Though it would not melt the metal, it could melt whatever was underneath.

The elf's screams echoed across the castle as he desperately tried to yank his armor off, but whoever had put it on him had done so very efficiently. He was having a hard time removing it, and that left Abraxas staring at the female elf, who glared even harder at him.

"I will end you, once and for all," she snarled.

"You will not," he replied, and cracked his knuckles. "Now, fight."

She sprinted toward him, all lithe body and smooth movements. Abraxas recognized her attack form. It was one that Lore used to use. He'd battled with Lore before, and his elf would not confuse him with her liquid moves. He dodged and ducked, moving away from the blade step by step until he had her where he wanted her.

And with a snap of his arm, he grabbed her around the throat. She thrust her blade up between them and it caught on wood. She stared down, realizing that he'd placed his body behind a rack that held their arrows, and she was on the other side of it. Now her blade was stuck, and he had her by the throat.

"You should never fight a dragon," he said, his voice tired and disappointed. "What have they taught you?"

Then he threw her off the edge of the castle. She let out a little shriek before her body hit the ground, and he could not find it in himself to feel any pity.

There should be more elves. He wanted the world to see them more and to experience all that the elves had done. He wanted them to fall in love with the world, just as he had. But these elves... They were a poison to this world and did a disservice to their kind.

The elves he knew of, the ones in the old legends, were more interested in growth and expansion and adventure than war. These sad little ploys to drag more power toward them made them seem more like dwarves, wishing to find treasure like they could bury themselves in it.

It was a sad day when he realized the elves had fallen so far from what they once were.

As he strode past the elf, who was still struggling to get the fire sprite out of his armor, Abraxas shook his head in disappointment. He'd thought to call the creature off. Perhaps it would be more useful in the battle below, but... Now he just wanted the other elf to suffer. This man had stood between Abraxas and Lore and all that honor and respect for their kind disappeared.

He hated how he felt this way. But the dispassionate view of this elf could not be shaken, no matter how hard he tried.

And so he left the man there. Boiling alive in his own suit of armor as he moved away toward the door where Lore and Margaret had slipped through.

Their scents were still strong in the air. Lore's like a sea breeze and a warm summer day. Margaret's reeked of fear. The bitter tang of her scent had always bothered him, but now it almost smelled acidic. Like she was leaking the very substance they used to harm Abraxas all those years ago.

He wanted his retribution.

He wanted to take her neck in his hands and squeeze until she could no longer breathe. He wanted her to look him in the eye as she felt her life draining out of her body, so she knew even in death who had killed her. He wanted that satisfaction to know without a doubt that she was wrong, she had died, and that he could be certain she would not come back.

The halls seemed different as he stalked through them. He was used to more silence in a castle like this. But he could hear the tiny scrapings of little creatures moving through the stones. As though the hidden passageways hadn't been used for months on end. The rats were already taking this place back.

And though the areas where he and Lore had walked before had been pretty and clean, this area of the castle was falling apart. No tapestries remained on the walls, dust had settled in the corners, even smudges of dirt and growing moss on the ceiling. It concerned him. The elves were always so clean.

They surrounded themselves with beauty. That was their greatest vice. They'd always loved things that were made carefully and that proved how much they adored their talents. Margaret and her people should not have been living in squalor.

None of this made sense.

None of it.

Margaret should have at least given her people somewhere clean to rest. Or were there not that many elves here left? He knew that wasn't true. He could smell them. The hours of time that had passed were not enough to hide the scents of hundreds of people who had walked this very corridor. So why were they subjected to living like this? Why had they agreed to live like this?

Fear reeked. He could smell it, coating his skin like a thick slime. They had all been afraid in these walls for such a long time that the emotion had bred a monster. It was now a living creature within all the elves.

He tracked them through the castle and saw a splash of blood leading to one of the servants' corridors. Bursting through it, he ran as soon as he scented it. Elf blood. That's all he could tell, but the metallic scent sent him surging through the halls in fear of what he would find. Lore was stronger. Lore was faster. She had more power than Margaret had, and surely that meant something.

One door had a bloody handprint on it, and so he burst out into the sun in human form to see two elves locked in battle. Lore's blade flashed in the air, and another arc of blood splattered upon the grass.

There was no one here but them. No one but Margaret, who eventually ended up on her back with Lore crouched above her. The sword flashed again, but this time it was interrupted by the bitter sound of laughter erupting from the Darkveil elf.

Even Lore paused. She held her blade over the other woman's throat, hovering there.

Lore spat, "Why are you laughing? You are defeated!"

"Am I?" Margaret asked. "Or have you fallen into my trap? Did you think I was so much a fool, so doddering and old, that I would sacrifice my entire army in a courtyard full of weaklings? You have led them to a slaughter, goddess."

Margaret spat the last word as though it was a curse, and Abraxas's mind tried to catch up. What did she mean she hadn't sacrificed her army? That was all they had expected. Surely they would know...

Except, he'd smelled hundreds of elves in that castle and they had been there just hours before. Where were they now?

Shit.

His eyes met Lore's as she glanced over her shoulder as though she'd felt him there. They stared at each other, both of them realizing the danger they were in and how much more they were going to fight.

Their people were far behind them in the castle. He had to...

"Go," Lore shouted, and he knew what she meant.

The change rippled through him again. He was too close to the castle and bumped up against it until the stones rocked against the blast of his change. He was fine, but he needed to lumber forward so he could take flight. Hyperion and Nyx would shield their humans while he doused the courtyard in flames.

But Margaret swung her legs, knocking Lore off and standing. She pointed at Abraxas and he saw the rage in her eyes. The rage that threatened him and sent his blood running cold.

"First, I will take your dragon!" the Darkveil elf screamed. "And then I will take all the rest!"

He smelled it first. The bitter scent of acid that had seemed to surround Margaret. It swelled in the air like a wave that threatened to overtake him. Then he saw it. The flames that scattered sparks of green and blue. They launched up from the ground behind Margaret, where he realized they'd dug trenches. Deep into the earth where countless elves waited.

Those green acid balls flashed in his vision and he remembered the pain of them. Just three that had shattered through the ceiling of the great hall and sizzled through his wings.

This time, there were twenty. The first round was that many and Lore quickly threw up her hands, holding them at bay. But then another volley launched at the same time Margaret struck. She had twin blades in her hands, wicked and black, and were those grimdags. It wasn't possible that a Darkveil elf had those.

Lore had no choice.

She could not allow her soul to be sucked up in those knives or they were all lost. She had to turn her attention to saving herself and, in doing so, her spell slipped.

The acid struck him hard. Countless strikes that rained down upon his head, his wings, his chest, his back. They sizzled and sparked and sank underneath his scales, that melted beneath the weight of them. At first, he did not feel the pain. He only felt the shock that they'd touched him, and his eyes widened as he met Lore's stare.

"No!" she screamed and threw Margaret off herself as a wave of elves erupted from the ground and sprinted toward the castle. Elves. More magical creatures. So many powerful beings, so many he couldn't count their number.

His breath rattled in his lungs that were dissolving as acid poured through him. He staggered, falling onto his belly on the ground.

He couldn't get up.

Why couldn't he get up?

Abraxas had always fought through the pain, no matter how bad it was. But he tried to lift a wing and shove himself upright, but there was no more wing there. Only bone and ragged flesh hanging from it.

He could feel himself dying. The darkness that seeped through his eyes and hovered there, waiting for him to let out one long breath and just let go.

Until it stopped. Death waited as though it were ordered to do so and he... waited. He waited, and he did not know why or how.

Abraxas only knew that he existed in pain and torment, with no relief.

CHAPTER 40

Lore watched everything happen as if it was in slow motion. The elves appeared beyond her sight. She should have seen them. She should have expected that Margaret would have another plan if something had gone wrong.

And Lore was very wrong.

Margaret had expected her to be weak and essentially useless. She hadn't expected Lore's power to not only have strengthened through magic but also through the very people of Umbra. She'd clearly shown up with an army that Margaret did not want to fight. Or at the very least, was larger than expected.

And then she saw the flames. She saw the acid.

How could Lore forget what had happened the last time that acid had rained down upon them? It was the first time that Abraxas had attempted to save her. The first time that he'd looked down at her with eyes filled with a promise. A promise that she knew he would never break.

One she knew he wouldn't break even now, when the threat of his death was upon them.

Her magic could hold the acid. She caught it in midair, twisting her hands as she tried to figure out where the largest grouping of elves were set. If she could put the acid right back on them, then she would take care of two problems at once. The anger in her burned. She wanted them to feel what they would cast upon another so carelessly. She wanted the elves to hurt, as they wanted to hurt others.

How dare they? How dare they even think to harm the people that were hers? She would destroy them, bit by bit, until they knew what it felt like for their flesh to rot from their bones.

Until she heard the sound.

The whispering.

The desire to take the blades from another and to use it upon the previous owner. Whispers that spoke of how powerful she would be if she would only take them and use them and run their sharp edges along soft flesh. It would be so easy now, they whispered, if only she would take them.

Grimdags. She swallowed hard and looked down to see that Margaret held two in her hands. Where had she gotten them? How had she gotten grimdags?

A flash of cold nerves poured over her body. Had the Ashen Deep betrayed them? Surely not. Draven wanted to be with her daughter, and no elf would go against blood like that. The Matriarch wouldn't... couldn't...

It was enough of a distraction. Lore flinched back, curving her body away from Margaret's first strike. And her spell... slipped. It just fell out of her hands as though she had been holding onto the tiniest of threads and once it was gone, she couldn't lunge forward for it.

Screaming out her anger, knowing that she had just cost Abraxas more pain and torment, she instead twisted for Margaret. She let her anger take control. Lore moved like a being made of light. She twisted and curved, grabbing at flesh and uncaring of what danger lay in the blades that Margaret wielded with deft hands. It didn't matter.

The woman would die. She would weep upon Lore's blades and then Lore would laugh as her blood ran out.

The power inside her turned into something dark. It ached inside her and screamed with a thousand years of women being beaten back and told they were not good enough. it didn't matter that her grandmothers had been elves; they had still suffered at the hands of everyone who touched them. Centuries and centuries of labor and torment and fighting tooth and nail to be something.

No more.

She would be the end of this cycle and that started with proving to Margaret that she was more than just a half elf. More than a goddess. She was Lorelei of Silverfell, and all would fall before her blade.

The rage screamed out of her and suddenly her hands were locked around Margaret's wrists. The grimdags whispered for her to use them, but she couldn't risk touching them when she knew just how dangerous that was. How much she wanted them in her hands and how she would fly through the battlefield letting them feast.

"Yes," they whispered in her mind. "Feast."

And if they were hungry, then she knew one who should not be able to return to the elves' sacred hunting grounds. Margaret would not go to see her ancestors. She would stay here for the rest of eternity.

Lore snapped Margaret's wrists and drew the woman closer. Whispering in her ear, "Thank you for giving me all this power, Margaret. I will take it, and I will use it, to make sure that this kingdom becomes exactly what you fear. Humans and magical creatures, all living in harmony. And no one, I mean no one, will remember who you were."

"All the elves will remember," Margaret wheezed. "The creatures who fight with me now they will remember. They will know the message that I have spread. I have made myself immortal, no matter what you do now."

"You don't understand." Lore drew back to stare into the elf's dark eyes. "You made me a goddess, Margaret. And I will wipe all memory of you from their minds. They will not even know you existed."

Horror blossomed on Margaret's face, and Lore felt only the slightest twinge of guilt as she buried both the grimdags in the other elf's heart. The daggers shrieked with pleasure at being used to kill the one who wielded them.

Margaret's eyes turned pale and colorless, her body withering before Lore's sight. And she let the body sag, then kicked it away from her with a heave that threw her into the ranks of elves that ran toward her.

But Lore didn't care about them. They wouldn't touch her if she didn't want them to. Until she turned and saw Abraxas.

Her heart. Her soul. Her reason for being.

All the acid dripping off his body slid onto the ground below and turned the grass black. His breathing was labored, massive sides heaving as his wings flexed over his head, struggling to get himself upright so that he could crawl to her side. Even now, even with holes ripped in his sides and acid steaming out of his wounds, he still wanted to save her. He wanted to be with her.

Tears pricked in her eyes and that anger boiled. She would kill them all for this. Damn the world, needing more elves. Damn all the creatures who dared to stand against her. She would not see him like this.

Lore could feel his soul parting from his body. She felt the moment when it tore away from his physical form and started off toward whatever end dragons had. She screamed out her rage in a single word.

"No!"

And then she reached out her hand and stopped it.

Horror had no place in an action like this. She twisted her fingers and then slammed the soul back into his body. She forced it to remain trapped in that prison of flesh and pain.

His ribs stood out with each breath, the white bone gleaming in the sunlight that suddenly illuminated them.

The power inside her flexed, stretched, and it spread darkness through her veins. It let her know that vengeance could be hers. She could destroy and maim and murder if she wished. But she didn't wish, because she knew this man right here would be saddened to know what she had done.

But this was not the right end to their story. This was not the end she would ever suffer again, and she refused to let him die. Not like this.

So she touched her hand to his nose, pressed her lips against his warm scales that shuddered now with pain.

"I will heal you," she whispered. "I will put you back together and you will be perfect again. In every way. Neither of us will have to suffer like this ever again. We're going home, Abraxas, and I'm sorry, but I can't let you go anywhere else without me."

She'd killed the woman who had started all this, and yet it was not enough. It would never be enough to know that Margaret was rotting in the ground somewhere with her soul in twin grimdags that would sink into the earth with her. It wasn't enough to know that her torture would forever be stuck in the dirt with her.

Lore wanted more. She wanted screams and blood on her hands and as she raced back to the battlefield, she gave herself permission to seek out that terrible end for all those who dared attack her.

And there were many.

She ran her dwarven blade through anyone who tried to stop her in the castle. The first two she split in half, right down the centers of their body and they parted to allow her to step right through the remains of what they once were.

Four elves ran toward her with twin witches that stood behind them, whispering spells that were supposed to hurt her. Lore merely laughed, the sound dark and disappointed as she drove them into the wall and then ripped out their hearts.

The witches were more of an annoyance, but she would fight them in the same way they wanted to fight her. Lore used her magic and fused them to the stone wall, allowing them to feel their bodies being crushed by the castle they so staunchly defended. The women screamed, but Lore did not stop to free them for pity. They would not have freed her.

She walked out onto the courtyard to see that Margaret had not been lying about the size of her army. They had twice the amount of elves than expected. And now Lore's army was split in two. Fighting those who were still in the courtyard and those who were outside the castle walls. They were pinned down, just as Margaret likely wanted them to be.

Algor fought like a whirlwind. He never stopped moving, those hammers flying all around him so quickly they had turned into a blur. But the newer elves were more fresh. One of them fired an arrow, and she didn't see it in time. It struck the dwarven king directly in the eye and Lore felt that anger surge again.

She grabbed his soul too, slamming it back into his body and making him stay like that. It was wrong, but it didn't matter. Not right now.

Snarling, she turned to see Hyperion fighting with a group of elves who fired arrows through his wings. The pain rocked through her just at the same moment that Nyx screamed. The acid balls had found her children.

Draven's answering scream was one of complete and utter anguish. She knew that pain. It rained down upon her and Lore couldn't think, she couldn't fight, she couldn't get through it.

And all the while, her power bubbled through her.

Zephyr hissed out a breath as a sword ran through his belly and an elf snarled, "Now they will have no king."

Beauty laid out on the ground, her eyes staring up at the sky as she prayed for death. It would not be swift, with her guts hanging out of her belly like that.

They were losing. All the elves, all the people she loved, everyone was dying and Lore stood above them on the castle walls like an avenging goddess who had wanted them all to die.

But she did not want them to die.

And Lore realized at that moment, they didn't have to. It wouldn't be difficult to hold them all in their bodies while she worked, and that was the moment she realized how infinite her power really was.

She wasn't just able to move the moon in the sky or call upon the land to help her. She could stop death itself. The power surged inside her, whispering of a dark throne and a dark goddess who would rule this land with the iron fist it needed. These people were corrupt. She could not trust them to run this kingdom on their own. If she even tried, they would fail and she would be here again, watching those she loved die and die and...

Die.

Pulling herself out of the darkness, Lore reached her arms over her head and she called out for the moon. "Goddess, guide me."

And she felt it. The moon whispering to her of a thousand years of knowledge, of goddesses who had walked this earth and knew that their power came not only from the moon. Didn't she remember?

She was not the Lady of Moonlight.

She was the Lady of Starlight.

Lore felt her chest expand as she started down the stairs to the courtyard. Her voice deepened in a low hum as she called upon all the empty soldiers they had created. Animating them with the dark magic that Lindon had whispered in her ear. These toy soldiers would fight for her. They would destroy all those who stood against her people, not just Lore, but those who fought on her side. They would leave those who ran, but they would follow them until Lore knew what to do with their insidious ranks.

And as she walked, she pulled off her armor. Her warriors froze all around her, staring at the goddess who dropped metal armor on the ground as she strode past them. First her boots so her feet could sink into the earth. Then her leg guards so she could move easier. Her chest plate thudded onto the ground so she could summon with her heart.

Lore removed her helm last, shaking out her sweaty long hair and licking her lips. A few of her own people had rushed toward her, their swords raised as if to protect their goddess, but they did not need to do that any longer.

Lore touched them and their entire bodies shivered. "You have fought long enough," she said. "You have proven yourselves brave and worthy. Now, I will end this."

Those who fought in Margaret's army ran from her. She had no idea what they saw, only that she was glowing. She paused by Algor's head and ripped the arrow out of his eye. "Thank you, my friend."

And so she strode out onto the battlefield, barefoot and weaponless, other than the bloodied arrow she held in her hand. Margaret's forces fought against her people who had streamed outside with Lore, renewed by the sight of their goddess and those who had dug themselves out of the ground.

Lore glared up at the sky, and then to the battlefield. "This is your last chance." Her voice snaked through the air, whispering in the ears of all those who were still alive. "Run now."

A few did. But not enough.

The elves would be few indeed, but they would know suffering when she was done.

Lore lifted her arms and pulled the moon in front of the sun. Her goddess would watch as she ripped down the very stars from the sky and used them to defeat those who fought against her.

Balls of fire and flame, bright white and burning, rained down from the sky. She kept shields over those who fought with her, ensuring there were still some people alive to talk of what their goddess had summoned. And they all stood, watching in awe as Margaret's armies burned.

Her stars rained down. They blasted the earth into great hollows, cooling into molten glass as they pooled and sucked in any elf or creature that tried to run from them.

Screams filled the air. Cries for mercy, but Lore had none of that left.

She had given them so many chances, and now they would find nothing less than vengeance in her eyes.

"Death," she whispered. "For all those who stood against me."

And Lore stood there, unmoving, as she watched the world burn.

CHAPTER 40

Lore stood on the broken, bloodied remains of the battlefield and stared at the tangled mess around her. Yet again. Another mess that she'd caused and more blood and pain than she'd ever thought possible.

This was wrong. She shouldn't have done this and yet, how could she have done anything else?

They needed saving. She needed this kingdom to be on its own feet, so she could leave it and not be eaten alive by the guilt.

She lifted a hand and waved it in the air. The remaining metal soldiers she'd summoned fell to pieces where they stood. The dwarves would pick their mess up at some point. She'd send someone to help them bring all the parts back to their forges, where fire and embers would melt them into liquid.

What would become of them? Would they be turned into necklaces that eventually noble women would wear around their necks? Never aware for even a moment of what that meant? Of what that metal had once done?

Running a hand over the back of her neck, she wondered if her fear was really how people would remember her. Would they remember a goddess who saved them in the middle of a battlefield? Or would they forget she ever existed?

"This was well done." Lindon's voice interrupted her thoughts, and his sylph fluttered in front of her face before landing on the back of a dead elf. "You made the right choice."

"I used the power you warned me about."

"You used it to help others."

"I used it and became the monster I feared I would become." She'd felt that power running through her veins and whispering in her ear. It had wanted more than what she'd done. It had wanted to tear the entire castle down. "I'm afraid I will never be able to stop listening to it now."

Lindon clapped his hand on her shoulder, then gave her a little shake. "You have to stop thinking of it as something that lives inside you, Lorelei of Silverfell. You are the magic and the magic is you. You are the one who wanted destruction. You are the one who wanted to tear this entire world apart and set it ablaze. Only then will you reach the peace that you seek."

And he was right.

She knew he was right and that he'd been right this entire time. It wasn't the magic that whispered with dark intent in her mind. It was her. She had been the one desiring and wanting and needing to feel blood on her hands and a sky darkened by clouds.

Broken, afraid, she looked to Lindon and tried not to let the tears fall. "What do I do with it now?"

"You choose." He bent down and picked up his lovely bird, letting it settle on his shoulder before he turned his attention back to the forest. "You choose how you want to be remembered. Me? I will always be remembered as a tyrant and a villain. But you don't have to walk that path, if you do not wish it."

Taking a deep breath, Lore felt that desire shudder through her. She wanted to be remembered as a good woman who had helped this kingdom back on its feet and then let it stand on its own. That was what she truly wanted, no matter the temptation of a dark queen seated upon a cursed throne.

So she turned away from Lindon and started back into the castle.

The few humans and magical creatures who were still well enough to stand on their own seemed to stare off into the distance as she passed. Their gazes saw something she couldn't, perhaps, or their minds only remembered the terror of battle.

Lore first stopped next to Beauty. The little human was still alive, somehow, and she made a gurgling sound around the blood that filled her mouth.

"Shh," Lore soothed as she started placing Beauty's guts back into her body. "I'm here now."

A flutter of magic stirred in her chest and then poured down her hands. She smoothed them down Beauty's stomach, gentle, oh so gentle, as pristine, soft flesh was revealed in the pass of her palms. Lore knew nothing about human bodies, but her magic did. It healed, it mended, it stitched, and Beauty was bruised and bloodied and battered when she was done, but the little human could stand.

Beauty's eyes were wide with shock, and she pressed her hands against her belly through the tattered remains of her shirt. "How... How is this..."

Possible? Lore had no idea. She wasn't about to look at the magic inside her and beg for an explanation, though. Instead, she hooked her hand behind Beauty's neck and drew her in close.

Breathing in, together they stood in the middle of the battlefield as Lore let out a pulse of healing magic that spilled out of her and onto the soldiers who weren't hurt quite as badly as who stood around them.

She could feel their wounds healing. The skin that knit together and blood that rushed back into their bodies. She could feel them all, even the ones who had died. The souls she hadn't locked inside their bodies to save.

Lore released Beauty's neck and strode toward a small gathering of humans around Zephyr's body. He should be dead. His heart had stopped beating a long time ago, but his eyes still roved toward her. His chest didn't move. He didn't breathe. But she knew he saw her.

"Absolutely not," the Baron hissed. He stood and jabbed a finger toward her. "You will back away, witch. You will not touch him."

She pushed him aside, and every time he tried to grab her, he struck a shield of power around her.

Lore ignored the man's shouts and threats. She tilted her head and met Zephyr's gaze. Beauty's father also crouched beside the young man, his hand over Zephyr's heart that should have been beating.

"What did you do to him?" Beauty's father asked.

She stroked a strand of hair off of Zephyr's forehead. "I kept him."

And then she slammed both her hands down on the center of his chest, magic and healing energy pouring into him, slicing through his body just as sure as the blade that had cut through him. Zephyr seized, his eyes widening as his heart suddenly thundered in his chest again. He breathed in, sucking in a hissing gasp of pain and then... Then he relaxed.

He settled down against the ground, breathing hard and staring up at her as though she really was the goddess they called her.

Beauty staggered to their sides, falling onto her knees with a keening cry. Then Zephyr sat up, gathering her into his arms and pressing her against his suddenly beating heart as he stared at Lore over Beauty's shoulder. Shock and maybe... horror were in those eyes.

What had she done? His gaze seemed to ask. What madness was this that she could deny death itself?

Lore nodded at him and then jerked her chin toward Beauty. He had more pressing issues right now than asking questions he didn't want answers to.

The dwarves were suddenly there with her. They shouldered aside the humans who tried to stop them, cursing back at the mortals who dared yell at them, while they all grabbed at Lore's arms. Making her stand and drawing her to their king, who somehow was still alive.

Unlike the humans, the dwarves didn't hesitate. They pulled her to Algor's side with whispered praises and pleas for her to save him. To bestow upon them the gift they had given the humans, for surely they were worthy of such praise after the battle they had fought.

And this was the difference, she realized. The humans saw her as a nightmare, a villain in their story that she would surely become. The dwarves saw her as a goddess, as someone who had come to save them all.

As she knelt beside Algor, passed her hand over his eye and pressed down into the empty socket, she realized she wanted to be neither of these people. She'd never wanted to be a goddess or a villain. They had needed her to be those things and now her story would forever be told by two kinds of people whose mouths would be impossible to control.

Staring down at Algor, though, she thought she'd prefer to be the goddess.

"Honored dwarf," she said. "Your kind has given me more gifts than I have ever received in my life. You were my friends, my family, and now my soldiers in a war you did not need to fight in."

His other eye opened under her palm, widening as he realized who hovered over him and that it was not death who was ready to greet him.

"I give you what gift I can," she whispered, pulling him upright and keeping her hand over his eye. "You, dwarven king, are more than this world deserves. You and your people will continue to be that because the dwarves have always been special." Tears pricked her vision, turning him blurry. "The last thing I can do is give you this back."

And then she moved her hand. The dwarves around her gasped, and Algor stared at her with two eyes. One normal, brown eye, and another that looked like glass containing the very stars inside it.

"I cannot regrow what you have lost," she whispered. "But I can let you see."

"My goddess." Algor's hands shook as he reached up and held her hand in his. "You saved my life."

"You saved mine." She drew his hands to her lips and pressed a kiss to his knuckles. "See to your people, greatest king that the dwarves have ever seen."

He swallowed hard and nodded. She saw the determination blooming in his eyes as he stood and flexed his hands before thrusting them above his head. The dwarves shouted out their victory, and Algor directed them to return to the battlefield to seek any friends who still needed help. If there were elves who had fought with Margaret, bring them to the castle. Do not harm them.

Lore had never been more proud to stand beside a king than she did at this moment. She patted his shoulder and leaned down to say, "There are a few more people I need to save."

"Go get your dragons."

She'd kept them alive for too long. Far too long. They were suffering, and they needed her, and she was tired of choosing the kingdom over her family.

Lore could feel them. They'd all gathered together around Abraxas. Her children, wounded and battered, but alive well enough. They'd somehow survived the acid and the fires and the arrows. Though they would hold those scars for the rest of their lives. She had not spared them that.

Draven was with them. She launched herself over the wall and landed on the dirt behind the castle and saw her friend standing at attention in front of them. He was dropped low, in a position that said he was ready to fight anyone who dared come near those he cared about. The last remaining dragons were under the protection of the Ashen Deep.

And then she saw a ring of more elves. Ashen Deep, who had surrounded her family with grimdags bared and eyes watching for any movement that might approach.

They had protected her family.

Her people. Elves who saw her for what she was. They had protected her family.

Draven noticed her first and immediately snapped to attention. He put his grimdag away and strode toward her, his face lined with worry. "We've done all we can, but he's..."

"I know."

She didn't tell him she was here when Abraxas had been injured. She didn't even look at the hole where she'd thrown Margaret. The elf was dead. Lore had made sure of that. Her body meant nothing when Lore's family was right here.

Nyx and Hyperion looked up, their massive heads swaying back and forth over Abraxas's body.

The acid still steamed where it had slowed, but still burned through his flesh. The white bones of his ribs stood up out of his body, gleaming in the dim sunlight, and she could see that he wasn't moving at all. Like the others. Like all the others she'd forced to stay here in unmeasurable pain.

Dropping to her hands and knees in front of him, she pressed her palms to his nose and kissed the scales that were slowly cooling.

She could feel him in there. The pain and the heartbreak and the worry. Even now, locked in the prison of his own body, he feared for his family, not himself.

"My love," she whispered. "I'm so sorry. But I cannot let you go."

Magic flowed over him, pulsing in visible rays of light that rocked over his body and surged through his wounds. She healed him from the inside out, using all her magic and power and concentration to rebuild a massive body that was even stronger than before. Lore felt the limits of her abilities stretch and grow and the pain of it rocked through her because this was her fault. All of it. Every injury, wound, and moment of pain was her fault. She could have done more. She should have done more.

And then Abraxas took a deep breath.

His ribs expanded, now covered with a thin stretch of flesh and the fine glimmer of ruby scales that would grow bigger and stronger as he healed. A wing spread over her, protecting her from the gazes of all those who surrounded them and from anyone who might hurt her.

Even now, her dragon sought to protect her.

The bump of a cool blue nose pressed against her side, then a flicker of green tucked against Abraxas's healed belly showed her that he hadn't just protected her. He'd gathered up his family underneath those massive wings and held them close to his sides.

His eyes opened, those golden orbs staring straight into her soul. A low murmur echoed through him, and Lore patted her hand to his muzzle one more time.

"I'm not done yet," she said quietly. "Keep your strength for now, my love."

"I didn't leave you," he replied. "I didn't want to."

"Oh, you think I would let you leave us that easily?" The darkness flared inside her again, but then she banished it with a soft smile. Lore leaned her head against Nyx's side. "I'm sorry, Abraxas, you'll have to try a lot harder than that if you want to get away from us."

His soft snort pushed her back in the dirt, her knees sliding away from him until Nyx shoved her back against his now warm scales. "I would never want to leave you."

She smiled at him and looked at Hyperion and Nyx, who stared back at her. They were all covered and tucked in by the strength and power of a crimson wing, and she knew deep in her heart that this was all that mattered now.

She'd saved the kingdom again. She'd set up a court and a way for all the magical creatures and humans to talk. That was it. She was done. They could figure out the rest of this on their own if they actually wanted it to work. And if it didn't, then they would deal with the consequences on their own. She was tired of being a goddess, and she'd never meant to be one, anyway.

Tears pooling in her eyes, she struggled not to blink, so they didn't fall down her cheeks. "Do you want to go home?" she whispered. "Just say the word, my love. I will take us all out of here and we will leave this moment."

Abraxas shifted his head in the dirt and drew them all closer with his massive wing. "Ah, but my home is right here. My home is in you, in our children, in our family. I'm already home, Lore. Always have been."

And the shattered pieces of her heart knit back together as her little family breathed each other in.

Alive.

Full of hope for what their future might be.

EPILOGUE

3 months later

Abraxas tugged at the uncomfortable neckline of his shirt. Zephyr had insisted that he dress in royal clothing, even though Abraxas hated the stiff fabric. His neck was too thick for clothing like this. It made him feel trapped, and a dragon feeling trapped was a dangerous thing indeed.

An angry hiss from behind him suggested his son was feeling the same.

Abraxas turned, grinning at Hyperion as he wrestled with the neckcloth that was supposed to be folded delicately around their throats. Another angry hiss was then followed by a belch of fire that incinerated the fabric.

"Hyperion," he groaned. "That was the last one we had. I don't think the servants will bring you another."

"Then I won't wear one." With a sly grin, his son turned toward him and pointed. "And neither will you. We'll match, Father, and then no one will think anything is wrong at all."

Sighing, he tossed his up into the air and sent a blast of flames at it. "Fine, but you're telling your mother why."

"That you didn't like the necktie and made a decision? I couldn't let an old man wander out into the crowd looking like he'd finally succumbed to his age, so I also decided not to wear the necktie?"

The gleam in Hyperion's eyes suggested he would absolutely throw his own father to the wolves.

If his timing had been better, that is.

Lore leaned against the door jamb with a sparkle of laughter in her eyes. "Yes, Hyperion, that would work if your mother wasn't a goddess and couldn't see through walls."

She wore a lovely pale blue dress that synched in at her waist. He knew it was supposed to have a corset, but she hadn't worn it. Instead, she looked like a woman who had just left her home on a bright summer day. So lovely it made his heart twist in his chest. Her hair was supposed to be up in a complicated coil, but instead, it was loose around her face. A bright mane of hair that was now slightly curled. He'd forgotten what it was like to see her so clean, so often.

Hyperion leaned his head back and groaned. "Mother! You are not supposed to be spying on us all the time!"

"Sorry, love." She strode into the room and messed with his hair. "You know I can't help myself. You two are always getting into trouble."

Though it was clear, his son wanted to argue, Hyperion tossed his head and shrugged. "I can't help it if this kingdom needs a little lighter heart. Zephyr hasn't minded at all."

"Zephyr wouldn't mind. You two saved this kingdom and gave him a throne." Lore tsked. "He would let you fly over the castle upside down while raining seaweed down upon their heads and he would laugh and shrug like you earned your moment."

"Seaweed?" Hyperion grimaced. "Speaking of, I better go find Nyx. She's been hiding in her room all morning."

"I wonder why," Abraxas growled as his son raced from the room.

Both of his children had been at each other's throats for weeks now. If Hyperion wasn't telling his sister that no one wanted her around, Nyx was telling her brother that all his projects were a waste of time and energy. The two of them were going to be the death of him, and it didn't help that they both looked like adults.

Sighing, he pinched the bridge of his nose and waved for Lore to come over. "If anyone thinks that the dragons are uncultured because of that boy, I swear—"

Lore tucked herself underneath his arm and hugged him tight around the chest. "No one will think that. They will all be wonderfully honored that any dragon at all was at the coronation. And we are going to be late, so there's no time for anything else."

"But Nyx—"

"Hyperion will find her room empty and a deepmonger waiting for him to bring him to the Great Hall. We'll be meeting all of them there."

He felt some of the tension in his shoulders ease. "I am lucky to have you."

"Yes, you are."

Lore pressed a kiss to his cheek before drawing him out of their rooms and down the halls.

The castle was completely new. Tapestries of colorful threads covered the entire room. The floors and ceilings sparkled, they were so clean, with plants in pots rather than growing out of the stones themselves. The floors were covered with blush navy carpets and servants rushed from room to room, readying the bedrooms for the guests that would be staying.

It all suddenly felt... real. They'd done it. They'd saved the kingdom, and this right here was their proof.

And proof stood next to him, her hand held in his and squeezing his fingers as they reached the Great Hall. A man at the front was already placing a crown on top of Zephyr's head, but Abraxas could barely keep his eyes away from the crowd itself.

Elves, dwarves, giants, ents, creatures from all shapes and sizes. They stood intermingled with humans, who looked decidedly nervous, but they were there. Standing with the rest of them. And they all watched their new king with a mixture of fear and hope. He knew that feeling. Better than he should.

Abraxas looked down at Lore, attached to his arm, hugging his bicep close as she watched with wide eyes. And he knew that the only feeling any of them should have was hope.

She'd made it so.

He pressed a kiss to the top of her head as Zephyr turned to address the crowd. He held a small staff in his hands, a symbol of his status, and his crown was slightly tilted to one side.

Zephyr looked more like himself than he ever had. Standing right there, nervous and uncomfortable but ready.

"This kingdom has seen its fair share of kings." His quiet voice rang through the sudden silence of the crowd. "I don't know if I'm the right one. I'll be honest. I know nothing about running a kingdom, nor was I trained in politics or much other than what my mother thought I'd need to know. But a good friend told me that these are the reasons I am a good choice for your kingdom. Because I don't think I deserve to be here, but I want to be. And I will do everything in my power to earn your trust, and to learn from all of you who know more about this than I do."

Abraxas found his breath catching in his throat as Zephyr looked up, and he could see the determination on the young man's face. He wanted this. He wanted the kingdom, and all who came with it, and he wanted to do it right.

"Now," Zephyr continued. "I would be remiss not to thank the dwarves for what they did to get us here. I must also thank my peers and all the magical creatures who fought beside us during the war. I must thank the elves, especially the Ashen Deep, who went against their brethren to fight at our side. And, of course, the dragons who came to our rescue when all hope was lost. We are lucky to have such symbols of hope in our lives again."

Abraxas felt his chest swell with pride. He peered through the crowd and found Tanis and Rowan standing with their arms full of baby dragons. Tanis had found the eggs, although she was waiting to hatch them until they were all safely back on the island. A whole mess of dragon eggs, and a wealth of possibility for their kind. Draven stood beside them, holding the little gold dragon in his arms. All three nodded at him, their prizes clutched close to their hearts.

Zephyr held out his arm and gestured toward Abraxas and Lore. "If it were up to me, I would have crowned the Goddess Divine. But she did not want this throne, nor did she want to take her place amongst my advisors. Instead, she will return to her home with her family. It is my hope that she will visit as often as possible."

Lore inclined her head with a proud smile. "Make no trouble, my king! And you won't see me."

He pretended to clutch at his chest, his head shaking with laughter.

"Ah, no, Goddess. I have no plans to make trouble for you. As we all agreed, you have earned your rest and your happiness."

Then Zephyr did something that Abraxas had not expected. He turned toward the back of the stage and held out his arm for Beauty to join him. She wore a molten gold gown and a crown atop her head, a soft smile on her face that was eased by the blush on her cheeks.

"It is my honor to present to you now, your queen!"

The cheers from the crowd rose and Lore pressed tighter against him. "I love you," she whispered into his ear. "Thank you for giving me such a wonderful family."

Abraxas swept her up into his arms and kissed her with all the passion and love and hope that he felt. "Thank you for loving me," he replied. "And thank you, Lorelei of Silverfell, for becoming my home."

Thank you so much for going on this WILD journey with me! It's been so surreal to write through this entire series and fully follow Lore and Abraxas as they totally changed their world for the better.

Thank you for joining me.

Thank you for reading.

And most of all, thank you for being you and enjoying fantasy books like this one. You're all amazing.
If you enjoyed this story (or series!) please don't forget to review. They really help a lot.

ABOUT THE AUTHOR

Emma Hamm is a small town girl on a blueberry field in Maine. She writes stories that remind her of home, of fairytales, and of myths and legends that make her mind wander.

She can be found by the fireplace with a cup of tea and her two Maine Coon cats dipping their paws into the water without her knowing.

For more updates, join my newsletter!

www.emmahamm.com

Made in the USA
Columbia, SC
26 October 2023

25003629R00246